S0-AVS-645

The Murder Artist

Also by John Case in Large Print:

The Genesis Code
The First Horseman
The Eighth Day

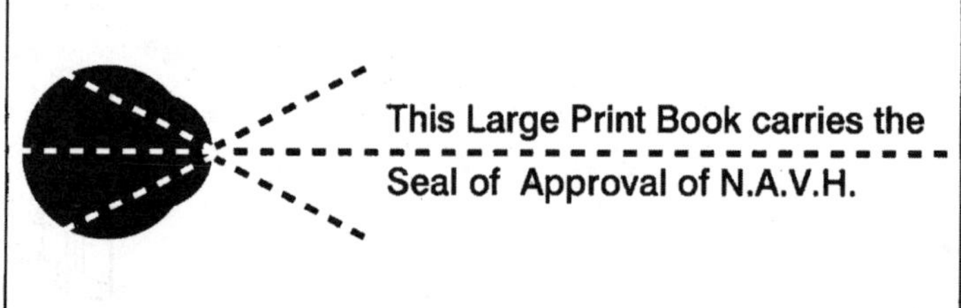

The Murder Artist

John Case

Thorndike Press • Waterville, Maine

The Murder Artist is a work of fiction. Names, characters, places, and incidents are the products of the author's imagination or are used fictitiously. Any resemblance to actual events, locales, or persons, living or dead, is entirely coincidental.

Published in 2005 by arrangement with The Ballantine Publishing Group, a division of Random House, Inc.

Thorndike Press® Large Print Basic.

The text of this Large Print edition is unabridged. Other aspects of the book may vary from the original edition.

Set in 16 pt. Plantin by Minnie B. Raven.

Printed in the United States on permanent paper.

Library of Congress Cataloging-in-Publication Data

Case, John.
The murder artist : a novel / John Case.
p. cm.
ISBN 0-7862-7168-X (lg. print : hc : alk. paper)
1. Television journalists — Fiction. 2. Separated people — Fiction. 3. Fathers and sons — Fiction. 4. Kidnapping — Fiction. 5. Twins — Fiction. 6. Large type books.
I. Title.
PS3553.A7914M87 2005
813′.54—dc22 2004059940

To Sam Johnson
Shooting star.
We miss your light.

National Association for Visually Handicapped
serving the partially seeing

As the Founder/CEO of NAVH, the only national health agency solely devoted to those who, although not totally blind, have an eye disease which could lead to serious visual impairment, I am pleased to recognize Thorndike Press* as one of the leading publishers in the large print field.

Founded in 1954 in San Francisco to prepare large print textbooks for partially seeing children, NAVH became the pioneer and standard setting agency in the preparation of large type.

Today, those publishers who meet our standards carry the prestigious "Seal of Approval" indicating high quality large print. We are delighted that Thorndike Press is one of the publishers whose titles meet these standards. We are also pleased to recognize the significant contribution Thorndike Press is making in this important and growing field.

Lorraine H. Marchi, L.H.D.
Founder/CEO
NAVH

* Thorndike Press encompasses the following imprints: Thorndike, Wheeler, Walker and Large Print Press.

chapter 1

Five hours of sleep. I rub my eyes, head out front, and bend down to extract my rolled-up copy of *The Washington Post* from beneath an azalea bush. I never know where I'm going to find the thing; whoever pitches it never got past T-ball.

"Good morning! Beautiful day in the neighborhood." It's Yasmin Siegel, my eightysomething neighbor from across the street, with her black Lab, Cookie.

"I guess." I slide the paper out from its transparent plastic sleeve.

"Seriously, Alex, a day like *this* in Washington, D.C." She shakes her head in disbelief. "It's a gift. End of May? You can get some real stinkers." She points her finger at me. "You enjoy it, you and those boys."

"I was hoping for rain," I tell her, looking up at the cloudless blue sky.

"Ri-ight," Yasmin chuckles. "O-*kay,* Cookie. I get the message." She gives me a jaunty wave and heads toward the park.

Actually, I *was* hoping for rain. I check the weather map on the back of the Metro section, just in case.

No. No rapidly moving front, no storm pelting toward D.C. from Canada or the Outer Banks.

A beautiful day.

Back in the house, I set up the coffeemaker. While I wait for it to do its thing, I put out bowls and spoons for the boys, pour two glasses of orange juice, tear off a couple of bananas from the bunch, toss them onto the table, get the giant box of Cheerios down from the cabinet.

The problem with the beautiful day is that I've got work to do, last-minute cuts on a piece scheduled to air tonight. But cuts or no cuts, I promised the boys — my six-year-old twins — that every Saturday they could pick out some kind of excursion. And they're dead set on this Renaissance festival, which naturally enough is all the way to hell and gone, way out past Annapolis. The drive alone will take more than an hour each way. It's going to kill the whole day.

And since this is the boys' first visit since Christmas — and only their second visit since Liz and I separated — this is the first of these excursions. No way I can bail.

I tell myself there's nothing for it. Get on with it. I need to make the cuts in time to drop off the file at the station on our way out of town.

The boys and I are doing great so far — although after only six days, I'm already wiped out and playing catch-up at the station. This would make Liz happy, both the sleep deprivation and the fact that after less than a week, I'm already falling behind at work. She built in the time crunch when she set up the conditions for the visit. She wouldn't let me take the boys on a trip, for instance, not even for part of the month. "How can I compete," she said, "if every time they're with you, it's a vacation?" (I took the kids skiing in Utah during my allotted four days at Christmas.)

What Liz wants is a month of "regular life," as she puts it. She works full-time at the Children's Museum in Portland. She wants me to experience the reality, 24/7, of having kids and a job, wants me to hassle with car pools, laundry, bedtimes, picky eating habits, friends, the parents of friends. If there's any chance for a reconciliation, I have to see that I can't just phone it in — having a wife and kids. Being a single parent for a month will force me to put family first.

Instead of work. In the station's official bio, I'm the guy who "goes after the toughest stories in the hardest places." This has won me several awards, but it's beginning to look as if it might cost me my marriage. And my family. I was in Moscow when the twins took their first steps, in Kosovo when Kev broke his arm, in Mazar-al-Sharif on their first day of kindergarten.

"Minute for minute," Liz said, "you'll probably see more of the boys this month than you have for the past two years. Maybe you'll even like it."

Coffee's ready. I splash some milk into it and I'm about to leave the plastic bottle on the table for the boys, when I remember that Kev won't touch milk if it's the slightest bit warm. I put it back into the fridge.

The thing is I *do* like it, having the guys around, even with the hassles. Liz was right about that. I guess it was always easier to let her do most of the "parenting," or whatever you want to call it. Turns out, that routine stuff is when you really get to know your kids. I forgot how much fun they are, their bursts of insight, the earnest concentration they bring to certain tasks. How much I missed them.

This Renaissance thing, though — I'm *not* looking forward to that. After a long and traffic-choked drive, I'm guessing it will be a hokey and overpriced tour through what amounts to a faux Elizabethan amusement park. Costumed knights and ladies. Jousts and faked swordplay. Jugglers and magicians. Not my kind of thing. Not at all.

I tried to promote an O's game, a trip to the zoo, a movie and pizza — but the boys wouldn't budge. They've been relentless about the festival ever since they caught the ad on TV.

By now, I've seen it too because the kids taped it and forced me to watch. A knight in shining armor gallops into the foreground. Behind him, a half-timbered facade bristles with wind-whipped pennants. Huge lance in hand, the knight reins in his horse, lifts his faceplate, and in hearty Elizabethan English invites one and all to "Get thyselves to the Maryland Renaissance Faire!"

It all seemed kind of lame to me, and I made the mistake of saying that to Liz last night on the phone — looking for a little good-natured mutual grumbling about parenthood.

What I got instead was a chilly lecture from my wife. Didn't I get it that what parents enjoy is their *kids'* enjoyment? What did I think — that Liz was crazy about Barney? Teletubbies? *Return of the Clones*? "And here I was going to compliment you on finding something that fit in so well with their after-school enrichment program," Liz said. "I should have known."

I didn't have a clue about any after-school program and that, unfortunately, became crystal clear. She explained: the boys have been up to their ears in Arthurian lore.

This had gone right by me; although once Liz mentioned it, I realized the kids had been rattling on about the Round Table and Merlin. And they'd spent hours out in the backyard, dueling with plastic swords. Plastic swords that, yes, they brought in their suitcases.

Okay, so I demonstrated a lack of curiosity about the plastic swords — is that so bad? Or — is Liz right and I'm the most self-absorbed parent on the planet? Unlike their tuned-in mother up in Maine.

Maine. I drop down into the chair in front of the iMac in my study. *Could she have moved any farther away? Without expatriating?* The answer, of course, is yes: she could have gone to Alaska. Hawaii. L.A. She could have gone lots of places. But . . .

I tap a key and wait for the screen to

shimmer out of sleep mode. My segment — "Afghan Wedding" — was all wrapped and ready until nine last night, when I got the word that the addition of some promotional clips meant I had to cut another two minutes. I made the logical cuts last night, but I still need to lose forty-four seconds. The segment's only seven minutes long now, so cutting is harder. Whatever goes at this point will be something I don't want to give up.

Originally "Afghan Wedding" was part of an hour-long special about Afghanistan, pegged around a Donald Rumsfeld we-haven't-forgotten-you visit to that beleaguered country. I got a nice long interview with the secretary of defense about the state of the postwar recovery. I interviewed Karzai. We got some excellent tape of the crew working on the reconstruction of the Kandahar-Kabul road. And then there was a pastiche of feel-good stuff about life in liberated Kabul and Kandahar. Girls going to school. The opening of a health clinic for women. Exhilarated Afghanis listening to music. Dancing. Capped off with the wedding: Afghan couple celebrates long-postponed nuptials.

The wedding was to take place in a village near Kandahar. A safe zone, or so we were told. The crew and I got there with our equipment, no problem. Even with the cameras, the wedding got started on time. And then the happy occasion turned into a nightmare when the crew of an off-course U.S. F-16 seeking a rumored Taliban conclave misread the wedding tableau on the ground.

Four killed, fifteen wounded.

The segment was removed from the hour-long progress report about Afghanistan. Now the wedding footage was going to be part of an ambitious show about collateral damage: Gulf I (Saddam and the Kurds), Mostar (the bridge), Gaza and Jerusalem (noncombatants killed by both sides), Afghanistan (my wedding piece), Liberia (chopped-off hands and feet), Gulf II (friendly-fire fatalities). The show — Big Dave was angling for an Emmy — would finish with a segment about the mother of all collateral-damage stories: September 11.

I cue up my segment on the iMac. On the monitor, the nightmare has not yet begun. The camera cuts between the glowing faces of the bride and groom, then moves in for a close-up of the tiny American flags pinned to their nuptial finery.

"Dad, can we eat breakfast in the TV

room and watch cartoons?"

I jump. Liz took off with the kids more than six months ago and one week into their visit, I'm still not used to the way they just *materialize*. "Jeez, I gotta put bells on you guys."

Kevin laughs.

Sean says, "Can we?"

"What?"

"Eat breakfast in the TV room? *Please?*"

I shrug. "Why not?"

"Great! C'mon, Kev."

But Kevin doesn't budge. "When are we going to the Renaissance Fair?"

I'm wondering what I can get away with. "I'm thinking . . . noon."

"No way!" Kev complains. "We'll miss the whole thing."

"Kevin," his brother tells him, "it doesn't even *start* till eleven. And it goes till seven." Then, because he's just learned to tell time, Sean adds: "P.M."

Kevin gives his brother a look. "No kidding, P.M." He turns to me. "You promise? Noon?"

I pretend to think about it. "Nahhhh, I can't *promise*."

Sean gives a little gulp of a laugh and then the two of them moan in chorus: *"Daaaaad."*

At least they know, after a week, when I'm kidding. The first couple of days, worried looks flashed from one to the other. To say they'd forgotten my sense of humor understates it: they'd forgotten *what I'm like* — a depressing reminder that five months had been just about long enough to turn me into a stranger to my sons.

When the kids are gone, I cue up the bits of footage I picked out last night for possible cuts. I mute the audio and lean back to watch. I take some time checking out how various cuts will affect the transitions.

And I decide that maybe the dark-man sequence has to go. It's thirty-eight seconds long and if I can live without it, I'm just about home free.

One last look.

The dark man is one of the bride's brothers. The ceremony is over and he's holding his weapon — it's an AK — in one outstretched hand. With a loopy grin on his face, he squeezes off a few rounds in sheer jubilation. I like this, the irony of gunfire as celebration in a country where the sounds of war never seem to stop. Just as the camera closes on the man's gleeful face, the whole screen jumps.

That jolt was, in fact, the impact of the first bomb from the F-16.

The dark man's grin collapses into slack-jawed astonishment, then turns into a puzzled contemplation of his weapon, as if it might somehow be responsible for what's happening. He's still connecting the dots when the second bomb detonates, this one so close the screen instantly fills with dust and debris. Visible only in silhouette, the dark man goes airborne, body hurtling through the air. Then he's propped up against a rock, powdered in dust, eyes dazed, blood seeping from an ear.

The camera shifts to me. I'm coated in dust, too, standing in front of a rocky outcrop and talking into a microphone. Then we see a group of women, wailing and pointing toward the sky. Me again. Then the bewildered bride staring at the face of her fatally wounded groom.

I roll it back, check the frame counter. The sequence is good, but it's peripheral. I tap a few keys and it's . . . gone.

I tinker with a cut I made last night and shave off the remaining few seconds I need, then roll it through. I stop when I hit the image of the dark man — somehow a few frames survived my edit. I delete them and roll forward, just to make sure the transitions are clean. I freeze it when the kids come in — for what must be the tenth time now — to remind me that it's time to go. "*Past* time to go," Kev says. "Almost twelve-thirty."

"Let's go-ohhhh!"

"Let's be off," Kevin says in a funny, stilted voice — a *knightly* voice, I realize.

"Yes! Your loyal servants Sean and Kevin beg thee!"

Suddenly, I'm engulfed by the two of them: the towheaded Lord Kevin and his mirror image, Sir Sean. They tug at my sleeves and rock from foot to foot, as if they have to pee.

"Just let me —"

"Pleee-eeeeeeze!"

With a sigh, I reach for the mouse. "Okay."

"Who's that?" Sean asks, pointing at the monitor.

I paused on a frame that shows the groom's face, his eyes wild, his face obscured by a skein of blood.

"Just a guy," I tell him.

"What's the matter with him?" Kevin asks as the haunted and battered face of the wounded groom disappears from the screen. What the boys couldn't see was that his legs had been blown off. What they did see was the terror on his face.

I click through the shutdown procedure to close out the application, then pop out the disk. "He was scared," I say.

"Why?"

"Because he was in a war, and he was hurt and that's . . . that's scary."

"I want to see it," Sean insists.

"No."

"Why not?"

"Because we have to *go*," I tell them, pushing back from the desk.

Sean bursts for the door, but Kevin stays where he is, big blue eyes locked on me. "Is that man going to die?"

I hesitate. Finally, I say, "Yeah."

I put my arm on Kevin's shoulder and try to steer my son toward the door, but Kev doesn't budge. "Dad?"

"What?"

"Were you there . . . with that man?"

"Yes."

"Couldn't you help him?"

I take a breath. "No. No one could help him."

While this is true — the man died less than three minutes after the footage was shot — Kev's question makes me uncomfortable. The groom was beyond assistance, yes. And I was able to help some of the others. Still, we kept filming.

Kevin nods, but after a moment, he says, "Daddy?"

"Yeah."

"I don't think the man wanted someone to take his picture."

I get down on my haunches, so I'm at my son's level. "Sometimes if you show a terrible thing — like war — then people all over the world can see how terrible it is and that can help stop it. I think the man —"

"What are you guys doin', anyway?" Sean blasts into the room with an impatient look, then shoots back through the doorway. "Come on!"

"Yeah," Kevin says, hurling himself into his brother's wake. "Let's go!"

I'm grateful for the interruption, not at all sure I buy my own rap. It's a fine line. What's hard-hitting, unblinking coverage? And what's exploitation?

In Kandahar, the camera crew freaked. I was the one that kept the film rolling. It still gets to me. Sometimes I can't help feeling guilty. The deal is that I make a living from suffering and death; hell, I even win awards for it.

"Daaaaaad!" the boys yell from the front room as I slide the disk into a plastic sleeve. "Let's go!"

"Tears are good," Jerry Tumolo, the first producer I ever worked for used to say. "Tears are good, but blood is better. A little blood really gets their attention."

chapter 2

Kevin and Sean are on their best behavior at the station, where I turn over the segment to Kathy Straight, one of the techs.

Back in the car, they point out the monuments as we head out of town.

Taking the curve off the parkway, they shout, "Lincoln Memorial."

A few minutes later, they yell, "Big french-fry!" This bit of enshrined toddler wit celebrates Sean's keen observation, at age two, of the similarity between the shape of the fast food staple and the Washington Monument. It never fails to trigger a cascade of cackles.

Then there's the one whose name they've forgotten until I tell them: the Jefferson Memorial. "Jefferson, Jefferson, Jefferson," they chant, as the Jeep passes the Tidal Basin.

"Can we go on those sometime?" Kevin asks, pointing to the flotilla of blue-and-white paddleboats.

"How about right now? We could skip the festival."

"Daaaaaaad."

They don't mind my lack of excitement. I used to fake it, revving up bogus enthusiasm on those occasions Liz guilt-tripped me into going along on some kid-centric outing. It didn't fly, so it's a relief to realize that they don't actually care if Dad is having a good time. They're kids; it's about them.

The stop at the station means we end up taking the long way out of town, looping down along the river before heading out the Southwest Freeway to New York Avenue. Volleyball games on the Mall give way to the Mint. Five minutes later, we're heading east through a canyon of crumbling town houses and burnt-out stores.

"Is this the hood?" Sean asks.

"Yeah."

"Cool."

Soon, the zoning changes from gang-related residential to light-industrial. Abandoned warehouses with punched-out windowpanes, fast-food restaurants and welfare motels with drawn curtains. Sean can't get enough of it.

But Kevin couldn't care less. "Are we almost there?" he asks. And laughs. "It's *a joke* — get it? Becuz: *we just left!*"

An hour-and-a-half later, we *are* there. I

park the Jeep amid thousands of other cars baking in an open field in tiny Cromwell, Maryland. The boys are excited, running ahead toward a pair of crenellated towers (don't look close, they're made of plywood). Banners flutter from the ramparts on either side of a lowered drawbridge across a "moat" that seems newly enlarged. A muddy backhoe sits outside a shop where costumes can be rented for the day. "Slow down," I tell the boys as the three of us join a stream of families ready to cross the bridge into another world.

"One lord, two squires, is it?" the costumed woman at the gate asks, taking my credit card. "On Her Majesty's royal Visa." And then we're in.

Suddenly, it's four hundred years ago. Wood-chip paths wind through a forested Elizabethan settlement of shops and food stalls, open-air amphitheaters and "living chess" games. The dividing line between imagination and reality is blurry, at best, with many of the fairgoers also in costume, some simple and homemade, some as elaborate as those of the actors — and probably rented from the shop near the entrance. It's like one of those Civil War reenactments, I decide, thinking that it might be interesting to make a film about people who have given their hearts to another age.

Meanwhile, the boys dash this way and that, tracing in the air a sort of five-pointed star that connects a falconer to a shop selling armor, a magician doing card tricks to a jester, a group singing madrigals to a man making candles. And everyone, even the foodmongers and shop clerks are in costume, holding forth in a semblance of Elizabethan English, with lots of *ye*s and *thee*s and *thine*s.

The boys' excitement is contagious and before long, I realize that I'm actually having a good time. The place is interesting and impressive, half amusement park, half time machine. And educational, too. Liz would approve. And she's right: it's great to be with the kids when they're having such a ball.

Liz, sweet Liz. She should be here; she'd love it. For a moment, my longing for her nags at me. She left only after a series of failed promises about how I was going to change my workaholic ways, but I still felt blindsided by her departure. I knew she was right, that's the thing . . . but I just never quite got around to making the changes I promised to make. News can become all-consuming. You can always do more, edit a little better, write better, check out one more source — but you always have to do it *now* because you're always on a deadline.

So yes, Liz was right, I concede that. I'm a workaholic. I neglected my family. I admitted all that to the marriage counselor. I just thought we had time; I thought we were making progress. I guess I never thought she'd actually *leave*. And then she and the boys were gone, leaving a hole in my life the size of the Grand Canyon.

The campaign to get them back is not going so well, either. This summer is kind of a last shot.

In the meantime, I'm worried she'll find someone else, some new age guy. Attentive, sensitive, one of those guys who wears a T-shirt that proclaims I'M THE DADDY. One of those guys willing to carry a baby around in some marsupial pouch. This is a repulsive thought — Liz and some other guy with their *baby* — and I cast it out of my mind. "Let's go get some food," I say.

"Yeah!"

We line up at a stall selling hot dogs. "Would the young squires like a widgeroon of the King's mustard on thy flaming mongrels?"

The boys look stunned, then collapse

into paroxysms of laughter. *Get it? Mongrels? Dogs? Hot dogs? Flaming mongrels!?*

Me — I'm surprised they know what *mongrel* means.

The three of us spend the afternoon wandering from surprise to delight. Kevin and Sean gasp at the sword swallower, a handsome sweaty man in a leather vest who leans back and gulps down the blade of an outrageously big scimitar. Along with all the other kids, they can't decide whether they're impressed or grossed out. A street magician tears up a card picked by an onlooker, does some elaborate shuffling and fanning of the deck, then plucks the magically restored card out of a woman's hair. Kevin gapes at Sean. ("How did he *do* that?") They watch wide-eyed as mud wrestlers dump one another in the muck, and stare at the bulb of glowing glass expanding at the end of the glassblower's tube.

The three of us watch as fairgoers, kids and adults, try their luck at climbing the Jacob's ladder. No one makes it more than two rungs up the wobbly affair before a failure of balance causes the whole contraption to pivot with a savage twist. Dumped hard, challengers land on a big pile of soft hay, most of them laughing in surprise. Some keep at it two or three times before moving on. It's a buck a pop, and even though the twins are strong and athletic for their age, it's pretty clear they don't have a prayer. Still, they want to try it and I give in. Wiping out is obviously half the fun.

They both get to the third rung before they lose it and they both beg me to let them go again. I think about it, because at a dollar for thirty seconds, it's pretty expensive entertainment. "One more time," I say, and they get back in line. Kevin wipes out immediately, but Sean actually negotiates the swaying rope loops and makes it to the top. The crowd, which has seen every contestant defeated, goes crazy. Kevin is a little jealous, but happy for his brother and proud, too. "Way to go, way to go, way to go!" The guy running the concession makes a big deal of giving Sean his prize, a huge "silver" medallion embossed with a fleur-de-lis. I adjust the leather thong, shortening it so that the medallion rests on Sean's chest. Sean's success has encouraged the crowd and several onlookers join the growing line.

We watch for a while, but then we move on. All three of us try our hand at juggling and archery (without much success), and we make messy brass-rubbings of knights in chain mail. The boys are wired. They're bored. They're excited again. They really go crazy when a raggedy man who identifies himself as the Groveler hurls himself at my feet, beseeching "milord" for "a bit of silver." Seizing an ankle, the mad actor sends the boys into a delirium of grossed-out laughter when he actually *licks* one of my dusty Tevas. Then smacks his lips, as if savoring the grit.

So it's a blast — or at least it is until I reach for my wallet to pay for snow cones and find that it's not there. My mood goes into free fall as the coming hassles stack up in my head. I'll have to replace all my IDs, my credit cards, my driver's license. Is there enough gas in the car to get us home? I keep an emergency twenty in the glove compartment, but I spent it a couple of days ago at a pizza place that didn't take plastic. I don't even have any change — I gave it all to the Groveler.

We retrace our steps — and then Kev, walking behind me, finds my wallet. "It's in your *pocket,* Dad," Kevin says. When I reach back for the wallet, Kevin says, "Nuhuh, the other one."

And he's right. There it is. I pull it out. "Duh," I say, "in my pocket. Why didn't I think of that?"

The boys respond with a nervous laugh. I'm left shaking my head. "I *always* keep my wallet back here." I slap the back pocket, left side.

"Not this time, I guess," Sean says.

"I guess not."

It seems strange to me that I would change the habit of a lifetime, so strange that I open the wallet to check. "Looks like everything's here," I tell the boys. "And you know what — feeling stupid is a big step up from the way I felt when I thought I'd lost it."

"So let's *gooooooo*," Sean bellows.

"To the joust, good sir!" adds Sean.

And so we're off to the pièce de résistance of the waning afternoon. The boys have been hectoring me for the last hour about this, Kevin checking the time every ten minutes. The jousting match is scheduled for four-thirty. As we turn down a lane and enter the amphitheater, I can see that it's good we came when we did. There's already a big crowd gathered; we have to sit quite a way back from the action. The seats consist of bales of hay, arrayed on the shallow concentric tiers surrounding the central arena.

The joust involves four knights, decked out in full armor. As they prance around the ring on their beautiful horses, presenters dressed as squires work up pockets of support for the different contestants. Each part of the arena sports flags and pennants of a different color — red, green, white, black — and these match the colors worn by the knights and their respective mounts.

We're sitting in the green zone. Each squire rouses support in his section by cuing the crowd for cheers and leading it in taunts. "The Black Knight is a clumsy oaf. Together now . . ." As part of the buildup, young well-wishers for each knight are summoned forward to the fence surrounding the ring.

The boys clamor to join "the Green Machine," a band of children assembled to cheer the Green Knight. I hesitate.

Liz would never let them. She knows she's overprotective — she even worries about it. "I know it might make them feel insecure," she admits. "I'm sending the message that the world is full of danger." But she can't help herself. Even I have been the focus of this kind of worry. I used to love rock climbing, for instance, but Liz just hated it. After the boys were born, she begged me to give it up. I didn't put up much of a fight. I saw her point, for one thing, and for another, I was so busy at work by then I didn't really have time for it.

As for the boys, it's worse. She can hardly bring herself to let them get into another mother's car for the car pool without checking the seat belts, the car seats, the car's safety record, the driver's apparent skill.

"*Daaaaad,* please." Down in front, the green squire is handing out emerald pennants and green balloons. The "Green Machine" kids wave the pennants, jump up and down. I tell myself this is exactly the kind of thing they *should* be allowed to do. I'm right here, after all; I'll be able to see them. What could happen?

I give in and enjoy their exuberant delight.

"Okay! Let's go!"

"Yesss!"

I watch their blond heads bob down the aisle as they make their way toward the fence to join the cheering throng of children. The squire hands each of them a green pennant. Then the joust begins and, to my surprise, the horses are as spirited as they are large. You can sense their power. The ground seems to tremble as the red and white knights charge, leaning over their lances, eyes locked on each other's hearts. When the riders come together, the clash is loud and violent. A roar goes up from across the arena as the Red Knight tumbles from his mount and goes sprawling. The White Knight plants a kiss on his lance and raises it into the air. The white cheering section goes crazy. I check for the kids and spot them toward the right of the cheering section. Along with some other children, they're petting a little dog. Even the dog is in costume, wearing an Elizabethan thing — a ruff — around its neck.

All eyes return to the arena as a trumpet heralds the next match. Green and black charge toward each other. After a tremendous collision, the Black Knight crashes to the turf. Even I have to admit it's exciting. These are real jousts, and I'd be surprised if the riders didn't keep track of winners and losers. When the Black Knight gets to his feet and slinks away, rubbing his backside, it's impossible not to applaud.

This is great, I'm thinking, and turn to see how the boys are liking it. My eyes go to the fence where the Green Machine is gathered, but I can't find Kev and Sean in the crowd. Not at first, anyway.

And then: I really can't see them.

Getting to my feet, I crane for a better view. People behind me start yelling "down in front." I ignore them and continue to look. But the boys — they just aren't there. A sizzle of panic surges through my chest. I suppress it.

In the arena, the victorious knights prepare for the final joust, their horses at either end of the arena, pawing the ground and shaking their massive heads. The green squire leads his kids in a chant. "Green! Green! Green! Green!"

"Kev?"

I tell myself they're right there, right in front of me somewhere, but hidden behind some older, taller children.

"Sean!"

The squire is leading a new cheer — "Gooooooooo Green" — as I work my way through the crowd, down to the fence. *"Kevin?"* I raise my voice, so that I'm shouting louder than the cheering.

Arriving at the fence as the Green Knight charges toward his opponent, I realize that I'm more terrified than I've ever been in a war zone. *"Sean?"*

I'm shouting at the top of my lungs now, and looking wildly around. And I see: other kids. Lots of them. The Green Knight goes down and a disconsolate moan ripples through the section while a roar erupts across the arena. At the bidding of the squires, balloons are released en masse. I push my way to the fence and scan the mob, searching frantically for blond hair, a yellow T-shirt. I can't see them. Kids begin to disperse, skipping back toward their parents.

After a minute, I return to the approximate hay bale where we were sitting. I fasten my eyes on the dissolving crowd, willing it to reveal my sons, but after a few minutes, except for a woman a few rows down soothing her screaming toddler, I'm alone.

It's five-twenty-two in the afternoon, and the twins are gone. *Gone*. I sit there hoping the boys have gone to the restroom and will soon be back, but I have a terrible feeling in my chest. I know they didn't go to the john. Not without telling me. Not in the middle of the joust.

So where *are* they?

It's not entirely rational, but for a few minutes I can't bring myself to leave the jousting area. It's where I last saw them, where they would come back to — if they just wandered off. I shake that phrase out of my mind, an expression I associate with news stories about kids who go missing, who are never seen again, who end up with their faces on milk cartons.

I sit on the hay bale for longer than I should because, as I eventually figure out, the moment I leave and walk away from the jousting arena, I'll be admitting that my sons are really *gone,* that something terrible is happening, something that requires the police. It's dumb fear wrapped in desperate hope, but several minutes tick by while I'm paralyzed in this fog of superstition.

What bubbles up through me as I break my inaction and rise to my feet is an electric rush of sheer terror. Within ten seconds, I'm running full out, so recklessly that the meandering crowd parts for me in alarm and voices rise in complaint and irritation.

"What's *his* problem."

"Hey!"

"There's little kids here, man!"

"Hey, buddy, watch it!"

It takes a while to find someone from the fair's security staff.

"Prithee, stranger —"

"I can't find my kids." The edge in my voice dissolves the centuries. Suddenly, it's 2003 again.

"Happens all the time," the guy tells me.

"People get distracted. A juggler comes along — we got a dozen jugglers, y'know? So it's easy to lose track."

"I didn't lose track," I insist. "We were watching the joust . . ."

Everyone's sympathetic. Announcements go out over the P.A. system, informing "Prince Kevin and Lord Sean" that their father is lost. Would the lads be good enough to make their presence known at any of the booths?

I wait, telling myself the boys will be along any minute. But even as I try to reassure myself, I don't really believe it.

chapter 3

I sit marooned on a bench outside the small rustic building that houses Her Majesty's Headquarters. There's nothing medieval about the interior. Half a dozen fair employees work in a large modern space. The section devoted to security is crowded with desks, computers, an elaborate communication system. The building also houses First Aid and the Lost and Found.

A gray-haired man pokes his head out the door. "Offer you a beverage?" he asks. "Coffee? Soft drink?"

I shake my head, keep my eyes on the crowd. Any minute, I tell myself, the boys will come around that corner.

"Suit yourself."

The gray-haired man is Gary Prebble, chief of security for the fair. He wears a basic uniform, pale blue with gold stripes down the legs, badge on the chest pocket, equipment belt with polished billy club, aerosol cylinder of mace, walkie-talkie. A rent-a-cop, in other words, who works weekends at the fair.

The word *beverage* marks Prebble as a man who's spent his life in a certain kind of job, a job where generic terms foreign to ordinary life hold sway: beverage, occupation, vehicle, firearm.

When I arrived and told Prebble I couldn't find my kids, he directed a heavyset woman in braids to read out a plea over the P.A. system. Then he methodically took down the details on what he called an "incident form."

"When kids go AWOL," he told me, "which they do all the time, every single day, what we do is basically we put out the word, and then wait for 'em to turn up. They *always* turn up, sooner or later." He advised me to "stay put." "I been at this some time now." He placed a consoling hand on my shoulder. "When folks get separated, it's best if one party remains in a fixed location, you know what I mean?"

That was ten minutes ago. Now Prebble joins me on the bench, drinking coffee from a Styrofoam cup. I can't say a word. My mouth is as dry as sand.

Prebble's a talker. "I do miss my weapon," he says, patting the belt. "I was thirty years with the Prince William force — over in Virginia. Retired five years ago. Moved down here to be close to my grandkids." He gives me a buck-up smile. "Don't worry too hard about those boys. They'll turn up. I guarantee it."

There's warmth in his eyes, a demeanor of reassurance garnered from a long life of being a man people turn to in a time of trouble. I'm heartened by his anecdotal confidence, but it only goes so far.

Where can the boys be?

People wander in and out of the building. One couple leads a screaming toddler with a gash on his knee. A nervous pair of teenagers escort a hopping girl who's been stung by a yellow-jacket. A weary man explains that he's lost his car keys. A woman complains that she was shortchanged ten bucks at one of the food stalls.

I do my best to believe that the boys getting lost is just another one of these pedestrian events, that any second, some helpful adult will come around the corner with Kev and Sean in tow. But after a while, there's no way I can just sit there any longer.

"Look," I tell Prebble, "if they show up —"

"They will, Mr. Callahan. You want to go looking for them? You go right ahead. When they show up, we'll call you over the P.A. system and we'll keep them here. I can promise you that."

It's a relief to be in motion. Doing something, *anything*, is better than just waiting. First I head out to the Jeep figuring that maybe when we got separated, the boys thought of going to the car. Is this what they'd do? It seems logical to me, but I've spent so little time with them in the past half year, I'm not sure how they'd act. Anyway, I can get my cell phone. They know the number. Before the trip down from Maine, Liz made them memorize all my telephone numbers. Maybe they called.

"Thou dost seem in a hurry," a heavily made-up woman says in a flirtatious voice. She places a restraining hand on my arm. "Prithee, why not tarry —"

I'm not quite rude enough to just brush by her. "I'm looking for my kids."

She drops the accent. "Let me stamp your hand," she says. "Otherwise they'll make you pay to come back in — even if it's only for ten minutes."

Before I can answer, she's stamped the back of my hand with a fluorescent pink rose.

I lope through the acres of gleaming cars — noticing quite a few empty spaces close to the entrance now. The vast parking lot is surrounded by a dense and lush forest, and from it comes the fervid din of cicadas, a rising and falling crush of sound that for a moment almost makes me dizzy. A bright green John Deere Gator rumbles by, its small truck bed full of Day-Glo vests and the bright orange wands used to direct traffic. They're getting ready for the mass exodus.

It takes me a while to find the Jeep and when I finally locate it, the boys are not there. I didn't expect them to be, not really, but I'm still disappointed. I hit the button on the key to open the door — and grab my cell phone — with a brief surge of hope that I'll find a message.

But there's nothing. I shove the phone into my pocket, then pull it out again and call the machine at home. Nothing there either, only a message from Kathy at the station, "Is there a chyron for the opening shot?"

I trot back toward the gate and reenter the fairgrounds — flashing the pink rose at the attendant, who clicks me through a turnstile. I grab a map of the fair, and with this in hand, begin my search.

I plan to be methodical, to check every stall and concession, every amphitheater, large and small, the phalanx of Porta-Johns, every single shop. As I go around, I call out the boys' names. I'm doing my best not to panic, but every once in a while my voice gets away from me, and the tone of desperation startles those around me. I can see it in their eyes; they look wary and alarmed.

"Kevin! Sean!"

After a while, I start to stop people at random: "I'm looking for twins?!" . . . "Twin boys, have you seen them? Six-year-old boys, blond hair." . . . "Have you seen two boys? Twins."

The layout of the fairgrounds is complex, set up in the manner of big retail stores to encourage meandering. Searching for someone in the chaotic, people-jammed sprawl is not easy. Several times I realize I'm in familiar territory, that I've doubled back over an area already visited. Every few minutes I run over to the jousting arena, just in case the boys returned there. Then I check in with Gary Prebble in case someone's brought the boys to Faire Headquarters.

After about forty-five minutes, I've covered most of the fairgrounds. Some people remember seeing the boys, but when pressed, many of these recollections are from much earlier in the day and others are so vague as to be useless. Some people seem to produce memories of the boys for my benefit. My impression is that I look so distraught they want to help. ("I *think* I saw a pair of twins during the falconry exhibition.")

Then comes the P.A. announcement informing the crowd that the fair is scheduled to close in thirty minutes, that visitors should make their purchases and leave enough time to return any rented costumes. Almost immediately, people begin streaming toward the exits. I head for the fair's headquarters.

What I want is for Gary Prebble to throw a wall around the place.

"We can't do that," Prebble says.

"Why not?"

"Can you imagine the panic if we try to pen all these people in? I can't do that! Besides, the fair *is* enclosed, except to staff. Everybody has to go in and out through the one entrance — that's how we make sure everybody pays on the way in, you understand? In fact, why don't you and I go on over to the exit? Maybe the boys will head for your car."

"I already checked."

"Still, now the fair is closing. They will have heard the announcement. Everybody heads for their cars." Prebble disappears into his office for a moment, and I hear him call out to his assistant: "Jackie, you touch base with the crew. Tell them don't anybody go home, a'right?"

The two of us stand on the bridge that crosses the moat, scanning the exiting crowd. "One way in, one way out," Prebble tells me. "On the way in everybody pays, and on the way out, visitors are funneled straight to the parking lot so they can't intrude on the privacy of the performers and artisans who live on the premises."

"They live here?"

"Oh, some of 'em, sure. Out back, behind the mud-wrestlin' pit. They got Winnies and campers and the like. There's fairs like this all around the country, all round the *world*, matter of fact. Some of these folk, they just travel from one to the other. And that's their life, you know, just like the circus."

I focus on the approaching crowd, my heart picking up a hopeful beat every time my eyes catch on a couple of blond kids — or even one. But each time, the hope lasts only a few seconds, fading as the fair-haired children approach, their features clarified by proximity.

Not Kevin. Not Sean.

Some fairgoers stop at the costume shop before exiting, exchanging their Elizabethan finery for blue jeans and T-shirts, tank tops and shorts. Weary parents shepherd tired children with rainbows painted on their cheeks. Toddlers scream to be picked up and carried. Two giggling teenagers in Goth makeup walk past, leading a little girl with a garland of flowers in her hair.

The crowd is noticeably thinner when Prebble's walkie-talkie crackles. As the gray-haired man steps a few paces aside, a torrent of hope floods through me. It doesn't last. I can see from Prebble's face that it isn't news about the boys. "Before we left headquarters," he tells me with a somewhat pained look, "I had Mike call Anne Arundel County to alert them we might have a situation here. They'll be here any time now."

Five minutes later, the exodus is down to just a few stragglers. Inside the fairgrounds, cleanup crews begin to collect trash and litter, lifting off the crenellated trash can covers and extracting big clear plastic bags of junk. A gangly youth in a jester's hat drives by in a fat-wheeled John Deere Gator and tosses the bags into its small bed. People in shops near the entrance stow wares for the night — pewter mugs, hammock chairs, candles, framed woodcuts of knights. At the costume shop, a woman totes up earnings on a calculator. Behind me, at a shop selling candles, a man slides a painted plywood panel into place over his storefront.

Prebble checks in with the security crew by walkie-talkie, but no one has seen the boys. "Well," he says, "maybe they fell asleep somewhere. The fairground is full of nooks and crannies." His voice isn't so reassuring anymore.

In the vast parking lot, hundreds of engines rumble and rev, drowning out the occasional wails of tired children. Handlers in Day-Glo orange vests, wielding orange flags, direct the streams of departing traffic.

A brown-and-beige squad car, blue and red lights flashing, threads its way through the streams of exiting cars and pulls up outside the entrance gate.

Detective Shoffler is a big guy, ruddy-faced, with dirty blond hair. He's fifty or maybe a little older and forty pounds overweight. Despite his rumpled khakis and a blue blazer that's seen better days, he gives the immediate impression of authority.

And heavy or not, he carries himself like an athlete.

Officer Christiansen is a skinny guy with a buzz-cut, buckteeth, and a high-pitched voice. He wears a brown uniform that's more or less the same color as the squad car.

Shoffler's hand is big, the skin rough, and he does not release my hand immediately, covering it instead with his other one. "Mr. Callahan," he says, and fixes me with a gaze so piercing that it feels to me as if I'm being scanned by a biometric device.

Then Shoffler releases the hand, and points an accusing finger at Prebble. "Gary, you shoulda called me sooner. Damn it, you know better." He shakes his head in a disapproving way.

Prebble shrugs. "I figured —"

"How long these boys been missing? More than two hours now?" Shoffler heaves a sigh. "All right. What you got in the way of a crew today?"

"Me plus four," Prebble says, and then, when it seems clear Shoffler is waiting for more, lists them by name. "Apart from Jack here" — he nods toward the pale man seated at the desk — "there's Gomez, Arrington, and, oh yeah, Abigail Dixon."

Shoffler makes a face. "Get 'em down here."

Prebble nods, then lifts the phone away from his ear as if he's going to say something, but Shoffler stops him, holding up his hand like a traffic cop. "I'm gonna get K-9," he says, snapping a cell phone off his belt. He turns to Christiansen. "In the meantime," he says, "we're gonna seal this place up."

chapter 4

You'd think this burst of purposeful activity would make me feel better, but instead I'm paralyzed by fear. If I wasn't quite buying Gary Prebble's schmoozy air of reassurance, Shoffler's serious and industrious manner is infinitely worse. I think of the Ramirez boys, California twins murdered a few years back. I think of Etan Patz and Adam Walsh, of Polly Klaas, Samantha Runnion, of all the less famous missing children whose faces haunt the world from milk cartons and post office walls.

The fear must show on my face because Shoffler reaches out and grips my upper arm with one of his big hands. "Kids hide," he says, and now he *is* reassuring. "That's the thing. They get lost, they get scared, and usually, what they do is they hide. They might even think you're gonna be mad at them, you know? Because you couldn't find them? So we're going to look for them, we're going to take a long hard look at the fairgrounds. The dogs might help, that's why I summoned K-9. Okay?"

"Right," I say. "I understand."

He frowns. "You look familiar. You a lawyer or something?"

"Reporter. Fox."

"Right," Shoffler says in an automatic way, but then he actually remembers. "*Right*. Okay." He pulls a small spiral-bound notebook out of his blazer pocket and opens it. "Now," he says. "Your boys. They're what? — six years old, Gary tells me."

"Kevin and Sean Callahan," I tell him.

"Birth date?"

"January 4, 1997."

"Describe them."

"They're, I don't know, up to here." I hold my hand out at their approximate height. "Blue eyes, blond hair —"

"What kinda blond?" the detective wants to know. "Dirty blond like yours or more like platinum?"

"Almost white."

"Any distinguishing characteristics, scars, anything like that?"

"Well, their front teeth are only halfway in."

"Good," the detective says, nodding as he writes this down, as if the state of the boys' dentition is a really useful bit of information. This strikes me as nuts, given the one truly unusual fact about Kevin and Sean.

"They're twins, you know," I say. My nerves have notched up the volume and this comes out much too loud. I'm shouting. I take a breath. "You know that, right? They're identical twins."

"Right," Shoffler says, "but see — they might get separated. So . . ." He shrugs.

"No," I insist. "They'd stay together." I hate the idea of Kevin and Sean not being together.

"They dress alike?"

"No."

"So tell me what they were wearing. Kevin first."

"Yellow T-shirt with a whale on it, jeans, white Nikes."

"And Sean?"

"Cargo pants, blue T-shirt, black shoes with white stripes."

Shoffler takes it down then turns to Gary Prebble. "Gar — I'm assuming you got a list of fair employees, who's working where and what hours? I'm going to need that. Now let's talk about how best to search the grounds."

The two men walk over toward the large wall map mounted behind the Lost and Found, discussing how to deploy the available manpower. "When you search the residential area," Shoffler says, "which I would like you to do personally, Gary, ask permission to look inside campers and Winnies. But don't push it. Just keep track of the hesitant ones because that might mean coming back with a warrant."

"Do you think?" I blurt out, "I mean —"

Shoffler gives me a look. "I don't think anything, Mr. Callahan. I really don't. It's just — we have procedures, you understand?"

I nod, but I'm losing my mind. *Warrants.*

Shoffler turns back to Prebble. "Take down everybody's name, note whether you took a look inside or not. Ask about folks who work for them, who might not be on the fair's official list of employees. If this turns out to be an abduction, we need to ID potential witnesses."

Although I've thought of this — of course I've thought of it — I'm still hanging on to the idea that the boys are lost. The word *abduction* crashes through my head like a dum-dum bullet.

Once Shoffler dispatches the search crew — the security personnel, Christiansen, and the newly arrived K-9 team, with their jumpy German shepherd Duchess — the detective lowers himself onto the bench outside fair headquarters. He pats the seat next to him. "Now you tell me about it," he says to me, "your whole time here at the fair. Where you went with your boys, everything you can remember." He pulls a small tape recorder out of his pocket. "Myself, I'm partial to handwritten notes," the detective says, "but if you don't mind, I'll record what you say, too."

"Why would I mind?"

Shoffler shrugs, turns on the machine, then speaks into it. "Saturday evening, May thirty-one, two thousand three." A glance at his watch. "The time is seven-thirty-two p.m. I am detective Ray Shoffler, responding to a two-four-two called in by Mr. Gary Prebble, who runs security at the Renaissance Faire in Cromwell, Maryland. I am speaking to Alexander Callahan, the father of the missing boys, Sean and Kevin Callahan, who are six-year-old identical twins."

He holds the small silver recorder between us. Its red diode glows.

"By the way, Mr. Callahan, where's your wife? She at home? She know about this yet?"

Jesus. Liz. "She's in Maine," I tell him. "We're separated."

The detective hitches his head to the side with a little frown, as if this is not what he wanted to hear. "Uh," he says.

"The boys are with me for their summer visit."

"And where do you live? You local?"

"D.C."

"Address?"

I give it to him.

"So you came to fair headquarters at, let's see, five thirty-six. How long would you say the boys were miss—"

"What about an Amber Alert?" I ask him. "Isn't that something you should be doing?"

Someone at the station did a segment about this a few months back. I don't remember all the details, but the system, named for a murdered child, raises the alarm about missing children, triggering an elaborate network to inform the public — bulletins on TV and radio stations, crawls at the base of the screen on all the major channels. It even flashes information on those big electronic highway signs that usually warn of fog or accidents.

I feel a rush of guilt, remembering an argument at the station. I was opposed to screen clutter, the weather, the breaking-news crawls, which, in my opinion, distracted the viewer. The Amber Alert seemed like more of the same.

"Afraid we can't put Amber in play," Shoffler says. "Not yet, anyway. An Amber requires specific, time-sensitive information: a description of the perpetrator, a vehicle make and model, a license plate." His hands float up into the air and settle back down on his thighs. "Something. Amber — it's strictly for abductions. At the moment, far as we know, your boys are lost."

"Right."

"We're not sitting on our hands, Mr. Callahan. Soon as Gary called me — before I even got here — and I realized these boys had already been missing almost two hours, I went ahead and issued B.O.L.'s to the surrounding jurisdictions."

"B.O.L.'s?"

"Be On the Lookout."

I nod but say nothing.

"Okay," Shoffler says, smacking his lips together, "so start with where you were when you last saw your boys, and then let's go from the top through the day, what you did this morning, how you got here, when you got here, and everything you did within the fairgrounds proper. Let's get this down while it's fresh in your mind."

"We were at the joust," I say. "The boys

went up to cheer for the Green Knight . . ."

Once I've recounted this part, we start at the beginning. I attempt to reconstruct the day. The red diode glows, I talk, Shoffler listens.

The fair is for the most part deserted now, the booths shuttered and padlocked. Shoffler and I head toward the jousting arena. The detective stops everyone we meet, noting name and position at the fair in his careful handwriting, telling them they'll have to check out with Jack at headquarters before they leave the grounds. He asks each of them if they remember seeing a set of twins. No? What about me? No.

We've been through about a dozen such encounters when Shoffler stops walking, cocks his head, and looks at me. "Hunh," he says with a look on his face that I can't read.

"What?"

Shoffler shakes his head. "I'm just surprised nobody remembers them, that's all. I mean — identical twins."

The remark skitters past me like a mouse in the walls.

At the arena, Shoffler follows me as I walk through the hay bales.

"About here," I tell him, coming to a stop. "We were sitting just about here."

"And you were here the last time you saw them?"

"More or less."

"And where were they?"

I gesture toward the ringside, where "the Green Machine" once stood cheering. I describe — for what must be the fourth or fifth time now, exactly what happened. Shoffler pages back through his notebook and checks something. "So the last time you saw them, they were down there, cheering for the Green Knight."

I close my eyes, concentrate. "No," I say. "That's not right."

"No?"

"Last time I saw them was right before the final joust. They were in a crowd of other kids, petting a dog."

"A dog? What kind of dog?"

"Skinny dog — what do they call it? Like a greyhound, but smaller."

"Whippet?" Shoffler asks.

"Right. It had a thing around its neck — you know, a collar. A ruffled white collar."

"You mean — like out of Shakespeare? A . . . what do they call that? A ruff?"

"That's right. A ruff. In fact" — the

image jumps into my mind — "the guy was wearing one too."

"What guy?"

"There was a tall guy with the dog."

"And they were both in ruffs. In costume."

"Right."

"Huh," Shoffler says. "So you took your eyes off the kids to watch the joust and then the next time you looked, they're gone."

"Right," I say, with a trapdoor feeling in my chest, as if I'm on a plane that's suddenly dropped twenty thousand feet. "They were gone."

As we approach the ring, I see that someone's inside the arena: a skinny guy in a faded red Adidas T-shirt. He's raking up horse manure.

He answers Shoffler's questions politely. "Allen Babcock," he says in a British accent. "A, double L, E, N. I'm the head groom, take care of the horses and all that." He gestures to the manure. "Take my turn doing the scut work, too. Mind if I ask what's this about?"

"We've got a couple of young boys missing. Twins."

Babcock's eyes dart over to me. "Your lads, then?"

I nod. “Six-year-old boys. Blond hair. You see them?”

Babcock shakes his head. “Sorry. No one’s about now, and if you mean earlier — I’m not out front much. A few fans find their way back to the entrance chutes, but not many. No twins. Not today. I’d remember.”

“Entrance chutes? So where exactly are you during these events?” Shoffler asks.

“Have a look?”

We follow Babcock through the arena and out a gate at the opposite side to what amounts to a staging area. Two metal chutes, consisting of lengths of tubular metal fence chained together, lead to two wooden corrals. “In one chute,” Babcock says, “out the other. The horses can be a bit headstrong — they don’t like all that fancy tack they have to wear for competition. So I’m back here, helping with the horseflesh, and getting the knights on and off their mounts — a right trick with all that armor.”

“What happens afterwards? You trailer the horses away until the next day or the next weekend?”

“No, no. We stay right out back here.”

“Where’s that?” Shoffler asks.

We follow Babcock toward a six-foot-high perimeter fence. "This fence enclose the entire fairgrounds?" Shoffler asks.

"Right," the groom says, unlocking a padlock and pulling open the gate.

As soon as we walk through the gate into the area outside the fence, into the wide-open world, I feel panicked. There's a whole wide world out here. If Kevin and Sean are not inside the fairgrounds, they could be anywhere.

"Horses and tack in there," Babock says, nodding toward a white clapboard barn. "Humanfolk in the caravan." He gestures toward a large Winnebago. "The knights — well, they're actors really, aren't they? As well as riders. They live in the compound with the others. It's just me and Jimmy here where we can look after the animals."

Beyond the barn, a field enclosed with white four-board fencing leads back toward the dense woodland. The cicadas roar.

A huge black horse stands next to the barn, tied on either side to a framework. A short, dark-complected man holds one of the beast's massive hooves and pries out dirt with a metal pick. Babcock introduces the man as Jimmy Gutierrez. After a few words with him, Shoffler writes down his name and telephone number in his notebook.

"Mind if we take a look in the barn . . . and in your Winnebago?" Shoffler asks.

"Bit untidy in the caravan," Babcock says. "But go ahead."

We're through the perimeter fence and on our way back into the jousting arena when I see it, near one of the metal chutes: a small white Nike shoe with a blue swoosh on it.

The sight of it stops me cold. Shoffler and Babcock are through the gate and into the arena before the detective notices I'm no longer with them.

"Mr. Callahan?"

I beckon, unable to speak. I stare at the shoe. It's just sitting there, in the dirt, perfectly upright, as if someone just stepped out of it — although, I see that the laces are still tied.

"That looks just like one of Kevin's shoes," I say.

"What?"

"Right there. That shoe." I point to it, a small white shoe with a smear of mud on its laces. "My son Kevin has shoes like that."

The sight of the shoe there in the dirt, its laces still tied, reminds me of all the times

— the surprisingly numerous times — when I've caught sight of shoes separated from their owners. Tied together and dangling over a wire. Stranded solo on a roadside shoulder. Dumped in a trash bin. There's something about abandoned shoes — even shoes outside hotel rooms, even tagged shoes in a shoe repair shop — that's always struck me as sad, even ominous.

And this shoe — *is it Kevin's?* — seems to me a terrible sign, proof of haste and violence. I lean forward, as if to pick it up, but Shoffler stops me, extending a stiff arm across my chest.

"Wait a minute," the detective says, his voice suddenly sharp. "Don't touch it."

Ten minutes later, Christiansen arrives and the shoe ends up with its own little fence of traffic cones and yellow police tape. Christiansen will stay to await the arrival of the evidence technician. The word *evidence* worries me almost as much as the shoe itself. Allen Babcock claims he never noticed "the trainer" (as he calls it). Jimmy Gutierrez never saw it, either.

"How do you know it belongs to Kevin?" Shoffler asks, as we walk back toward the entrance gate. "I thought they're identical twins?"

"They don't dress the same," I tell him.

"Right," Shoffler says. "I forgot."

"Now, let's take it from the top, from when you got here," Shoffler says. "What time was that, by the way? What'd the clerk look like?"

I pull my wallet out of my back pocket. "I should have the receipt." Pulling out the wallet makes me remember how I thought I'd lost it earlier in the day. Something about that incident worries me, but I let it go when I find the receipt.

"Two-eighteen," I tell Shoffler, reading the time stamp.

The detective has his notebook out again. "And the person who sold it to you?" he says, without looking up.

The question bothers me. My kids are missing and it's like the detective is checking on me. I answer the question. "Thirtysomething, eyebrows plucked almost to oblivion." The woman's voice comes back to me: "One lord, two squires, is it? On Her Majesty's royal Visa."

Two squires . . .

Shoffler eyes the wallet. "You happen to have a photograph of your boys in there?"

"Yeah. I do."

Shoffler taps a finger against one eyebrow. "I might send one of the detectives back to the station with a photo. Put us a step ahead. We can prepare to distribute to the surrounding jurisdictions. And to the media."

I knew that the police would want a picture of the boys, but somehow the official request depresses me. "This is almost a year old," I tell Shoffler, sliding the studio snapshot out of its transparent plastic compartment. I look at it for a moment, before handing it over.

In the photo, my sons are wearing matching blue-striped T-shirts, which is unusual for them. Liz must have talked them into it, because they balk at wearing identical clothing and have only a few such outfits, gifts from Liz's mom. Liz and I always let the boys pick out what they want to wear (within reason), and they almost never choose clothes that would make them seem interchangeable. Except when they want to mess with people and play what they call "the twin game." They can't fool their parents — but anybody else is easy game.

Despite the matching clothes, there's no question who's who in the photograph. Placed in front of a camera, Sean does not comprehend *smile* — or any of the expressions photographers use in its place. No matter how many times Liz explains to Sean that the way he contorts his face is *not* a smile, no matter how many times he's shown the evidence, it doesn't matter. Every posed photograph of him taken from the age of three — and counting — features Sean's *idea* of a smile. This exaggerated and mirthless grimace, lips stretched away from each other as far as possible in every direction — is something like what an orangutan does, drawing its lips apart to bare its teeth.

The photograph is almost too much. It feels as if my chest is full of broken glass. I hand it to Shoffler with a strange reluctance, as if by turning it over to the detective, I'm somehow relinquishing possession of my sons.

"I thought you said they don't dress identical," Shoffler says.

"They don't," I tell him. "Most of the time."

"Huh."

Half an hour later, after a tour through the fairgrounds — refining my account of the day — Shoffler's satisfied. He switches off the tape recorder and sticks it in a pocket. He pulls out his cell phone, takes a few steps away, and turns from me. I can still hear what he says. He's summoning everybody to headquarters.

I'm in a fog, shuttling back and forth between disbelief and panic. One moment, I can't believe this is happening. Then I *know* it's happening — Sean and Kevin are missing, they're *missing* — by the cold fist squeezing my heart.

"I think while we've still got some light," Shoffler is saying into his phone, "we'd better expand the search into the woods."

chapter 5

I don't notice exactly when the rose-and-peach sunset drains away beneath the horizon, but suddenly it's night. A crescent moon, startling in its clarity, hangs kitty-corner in the inky, star-strewn sky. I pull my cell phone out and call voice mail at home — for about the tenth time.

Nothing's changed, no messages.

Shoffler wouldn't let me go out with the initial search teams. Everyone offers the same advice: the best thing I can do is wait. It's my sons who are missing, yet I'm supposed to sit and watch, a spectator at my own disaster.

And yet it's oddly familiar, this sense of being in the audience while the well-oiled machinery of catastrophe rolls into action. Between the news and TV crime shows, disaster flicks and reality TV, we're prepped for every kind of nightmare. No matter what it is, it's already happened in some form to someone else — filmed in gritty detail and with a musical score to punch it up. I should know.

From my bench, I can hear Shoffler from inside headquarters, voice at volume: "Start at the intersection of 301 and Shade Valley Road. Then the bird should deploy at point 19, first sweep the fairground . . ."

At first the words make no sense. And then *bird* and *deploy* and *sweep* drop into the proper linguistic slots in my brain and I understand the detective is talking about a search helicopter.

Christiansen says: "If the kids're in the woods, you won't see them from a copter."

When yet another squad car arrives with a trunkful of powerful flashlights and four more uniformed men from Carroll County (with more on the way), Shoffler organizes new teams.

Food has appeared from somewhere. Papa John's Pizzas, Gatorade, cans of Pepsi, big aluminum thermos dispensers of coffee, inverted towers of white foam cups. Someone's pinned a topographical map to the wall and marked it into a grid. The first search party departs in a welter of raspy walkie-talkie communication, and then the second. When the third, consisting of four men and two women, assembles to watch Shoffler delineate their area on the topo map, I find myself on my feet.

"I'm going."

Shoffler hesitates. "If we find them," he starts, "it's possible . . ."

His voice trails away, but I can read his mind: *It's possible they won't be alive*. I nod to show I understand.

Shoffler opens his mouth, as if he's about to launch into his tired spiel about the best way to help being to stay put. But then he changes his mind, nods his assent. "What the hell," he says.

We walk through a densely wooded area in a ragged line, each person separated from the next by the prescribed double arm's length distance of six feet, a span that shrinks and expands wildly depending on the terrain and its obstacles. Flashlights burrow into the darkness, probing and tunneling in well-defined cylinders of light until the beams fray off at the outer reaches of their scope and then dissolve into incandescent mist. The beams of the flashlights pry into hidden corners of the dense underbrush, illuminating tangles of multiflora roses, the crevices of big moss-covered rocks, the rough bark of tree trunks, leaves and branches, patches of glittery streams, the bright startled eyes of animals. Beams skid wildly through the sky as the searchers clamber over rocks and fallen logs. Every once in a while, the jaunty tune of a cell phone makes its anomalous intrusion and someone conducts an awkward conversation with spouse or friend.

The search party, a segmented monster, makes a huge amount of noise as it crashes along, each man or woman yelling, "Sean! Kevin!" Above, the helicopter contributes even more noise, the thudding of its rotors as it makes methodical sweeps over the fairgrounds throwing up such a din that we can hardly shout over it at times. The voices calling for Sean and Kevin sound thin and puny, hopeless cries into the wilderness.

We trudge and grope and clamber our way through terrain that's not only rugged and full of unexpected and hidden ravines, but choked with brambles and vines, this underbrush often head high. It's very tough going, as Shoffler warned us all, and it takes its toll. Every few minutes, there's a yelp of pain, a curse. Within ten minutes, my legs and arms are torn up from the thorns, and my face is bleeding.

An occasional raspy bulletin from

Shoffler crackles out from the leader's walkie-talkie. We halt until it's clear that the communication is routine and involves no news of the boys. Each time this happens, my heart bangs against my rib cage and there's an electric surge of adrenaline. I'm suspended, teetering between hope and dread.

The search group also pauses when the helicopter hovers, as it does every few minutes, hesitating in one of its sweeps to cast a brilliant cone of light beneath it, so powerful it turns night into day. Then someone says, "Let's go," and we continue, clawing through the dense foliage, shouting until we're hoarse.

I sink into a kind of trance, focused only as far as the end of my beam of light, which I swing from side to side, methodical as an automaton, making certain to cover every inch of my patch of terrain. Many times, the light falls on a branch or a clump of leaves and tricks me into the momentary belief that I've seen a pant leg, an arm, a shoe, the curve of a head.

They're so small, really. When I check on them, asleep in their beds, when they're quiet and inert, I'm shocked sometimes by how small they are — considering the space they take up in my life. If they were covered with leaves, even some halfhearted effort to hide them . . . It would be so easy to miss them.

I blink my eyes, sharpen my focus, close my mind to the thought: *covered with leaves.* But I can't keep from my mind the terrible notions that float into it. I can't stop thinking of that shoe, for instance, Kevin's shoe, derelict against the metal of that chute. The way it sat, inside its barrier of police tape, waiting for the evidence technician.

These are words I don't want in my vocabulary: *evidence technician, K-9 team, search grid.*

When Shoffler orders the team to return "to base," not a single member of the unit wants to do it. Everyone grumbles, pleads for more time. "We don't want to give up," a man named Rusty, who is the leader, barks into his handset, "we're *rollin'*, Shoff."

But Rusty surrenders grudgingly to Shoffler's insistence. Replacements are standing by. Exhaustion causes mistakes. Fresh eyes are better. "And besides," Shoffler says, his voice ragged with static, "I need to discuss something with Mr. Callahan."

The room is a mess, the area devoted to a kind of makeshift canteen already overflowing with foam cups, doughnut and pizza boxes, water bottles. Untidy mounds of clothing and shoes obscure the counter of the Lost and Found desk. Heaped on the floor are piles of communication equipment, stacks of orange traffic cones, vests shiny with reflective tape, a small mountain of olive-green fleece blankets still encased in plastic bags.

I wait for the promised discussion, so tapped out that for the moment I lack the energy to imagine its subject or purpose. It's not about the boys being found (or a replacement team would not be heading out into the dark), and that's the only item of interest to me.

Shoffler slings a big arm around my shoulder and tells me it's time to go home. I sputter my objection, but Shoffler gently reminds me of two matters.

"We've got no evidence of abduction," he starts. "There's the shoe, but" — he shrugs — "you couldn't positively identify it."

"I'm sure it's Kevin's shoe."

"You're sure it's his shoe because he's got a shoe kinda like it and he's missing."

"And he was there, at that jousting ring."

Shoffler shakes his head. "You know how many kids come through this place every weekend? Who knows how long that shoe's been there? It's a pretty common type of shoe." He shifts from foot to foot. "If this *is* an abduction, and there's a call, they're not going to leave a message on your voice mail. They're gonna want to talk to you."

I nod.

"We'd like to install a trap and trace on your phone, and that's gonna go much faster if you're there — otherwise, we got to get a form signed, get it to these guys, get 'em some keys, it's a whole rigmarole. If you're there, it's done inside a coupla hours."

"Okay."

He purses his lips for a moment, cocks his head. "Second thing is," Shoffler goes on, "you can't have all these people, helicopters" — he makes a sweeping gesture with his arm — "and keep it secret. Point is, this is gonna make the early news in some bulletin kind of form, and then, by the regular morning news . . ." He shakes his head. "Well, you would know. . . ."

"Right," I say. And of course Shoffler *is* right. I should have thought about this, but didn't. Not until this moment.

Parents all over the country are already on edge, thanks to a recent series of highly publicized child abductions and disappearances. There's a trial going on right now in California, in the abduction-murder of a five-year-old girl. It's an atmosphere in which any new missing child is instantly big news, a national story.

And from the media's standpoint, the disappearance of Kevin and Sean will be pure gold: photogenic twins vanish in the midst of jousting knights, Elizabethan ladies, men in waistcoats and doublets. It's not just going to be a news story; it's going to be a monster.

"And that's good, that's all to the good," Shoffler is saying. "It's time to enlist the public's help. And the media, they will do that for you, they will get the word out."

He stops talking and waits for me to say something. I can tell I'm supposed to be connecting some dots here, but I don't see what the detective is after. "You probably got people," the detective finally says in a patient voice, "shouldn't hear about this on the TV, or because they get a phone call from a reporter."

Christ! Liz! I'm going to have to tell Liz.

"I think you should go home."

I stare at my feet. *Liz.*

"Chris here," Shoffler continues, with a nod toward Officer Christiansen, "he'll go with you."

"I'll be all right," I say. Shoffler obviously thinks I shouldn't be alone, but the last thing I want is Officer Christiansen for company.

Shoffler ignores me and nods at Christiansen, then walks us toward the entrance gate. "You got juice in your cell phone?" he asks Christiansen, who lifts the phone from its holster and flips the top open.

"I'm all set."

Outside, it's quiet. A faint murmur of traffic. The rhythmic rise and fall of chatter from cicadas. The helicopter is gone for now, having returned to refuel. For a moment, I think I can hear the faint cries of the search team, but then a breeze rustles through the trees and swallows the sound.

We walk through the small cluster of cars and squad cars parked near the entrance gate. "Well," Shoffler says, stifling a yawn. "We'll do our best here." He offers his hand and I shake it. Then he gives Christiansen a little tap on the shoulder and heads back into the fairgrounds.

In front of us looms the vast empty space of the parking lot. Near its far perimeter sits the small squarish shape of the Jeep, alone in the huge field. Christiansen walks beside me, talking in nervous little bursts about "a kidnap case I worked on couple of years back." "They found the kid in Florida," Christiansen says. "Boyfriend's backyard."

On the long walk to the car, the notion that Shoffler sent the officer with me out of some kind of compassion, because he didn't want the bereft father to be alone in his distraught state, dissolves into a darker truth. I realize this as I fumble in my pocket for the keys and press the button on the remote. The door locks pop. The headlights tunnel out into the darkness. "That's what they say, y'know," Christiansen rambles on. "Nine times out of ten, it's someone who knows the kid. Nine times outta ten, it's a parent."

Here's the truth: Christiansen isn't babysitting. I'm a suspect.

I stand with my hand on the door handle. I can't bring myself to get into the car. Going home without the boys is . . . *wrong.* It feels like a signal of defeat and surrender, as if I'm giving up on them.

"Hey, you want I should drive?" Christiansen asks.

Then a sudden effervescence of hope bubbles up in my brain and I can't get into the car fast enough.

"I guess that's a no," Christiansen says, sliding into the passenger's seat. "Suit yourself."

By the time I flip on the brights and make it from the grass parking lot to the gravel drive, an entire hopeful scenario has constructed itself in my head. Maybe the boys got disoriented, tried to come back to their hay bale and took a wrong turn. When the joust was over, everybody was leaving; it was chaotic.

I turn from the gravel drive onto a paved road. When they couldn't find me, maybe the boys met someone — someone from the neighborhood, someone they hadn't seen since Liz took them to Maine. And these people, they drove the boys *home*.

Or maybe Liz . . . Liz followed the boys down from Maine. She wanted to prove some point, so she waited until Alex and the boys were separated . . . Or not Liz herself, but she hired someone . . .

I'm filled with maybes, filled with fear and hope. On one level, I know these notions don't hold up, not if I give them a minute's hard thought.

Now that I'm on the road, I have an irrational need to get back to the house. As if that will make things right somehow.

Tagging home base. I'll be safe. The kids will be safe. Somehow it's in my head that the kids will be there, waiting for me.

"You better slow it down," Christiansen whines.

I glance at the speedometer. I'm doing eighty.

"Come on, man. This road —" The policeman's voice sounds like a mosquito.

I slow to seventy-five, and then my cell phone rings and I hit the brakes, fishtailing onto the shoulder in a spray of gravel.

"Jesus Christ!" Christiansen squeaks, as I fumble for the phone.

Finally, I've got the thing pressed to my ear. "Hello? Hello!?"

"Who is it?" Christiansen asks, but I hardly hear him.

"Hello? *Hello!*" I'm yelling. It isn't that the connection is bad, it's crystal clear, there's no static at all. But no one's there, just the silence.

"Sir? Who is it?" Christiansen bleats, but I shove my hand toward the cop to shut him up. I don't hang up because I realize it's not quite silence I'm hearing. It's breathing. Someone breathing.

"Who is this?" I ask, trying to control my voice. "Who *is* it?"

Nothing.

And then a Roman candle of relief explodes in my chest as Kevin's voice flutters into my ear, tremulous and tentative: "Daddy?"

chapter 6

Then a *click,* and the candle goes out as suddenly as it flared.

"Kevin? *Kevin?!*"

I punch on the Jeep's overhead light and stare at the tiny glowing rectangle of the phone's LCD screen. Like most cell phones, mine displays the numbers of incoming calls. But only, I remember, until you press the key to answer. The screen tells me: CURRENT CALL: 18 SECONDS.

"Sir?" Christiansen says. "Who was that? Who called you?"

"Hang on just a minute." I stay with the telephone, tapping through the menu selections until I get to RECEIVED CALLS. The list keys up. I tap RECEIVED 1, and read: 202-555-0199.

This can't be right. It's the number at the house, my own home phone number. Does this mean — my heart does a somersault in my chest — that the boys are at home?

I don't see how it's possible, how the boys could be home, and yet no one — not the boys or whoever took them there —

ever bothered to call on my cell phone during the eleven hours they've been missing.

It makes no sense, but still, I go nova with happiness.

My cell phone must have cut out on Kevin's call. I drove through a black zone; it happens all the time. The signal is strong now, though, so I press the 2 key, which automatically calls the house. I'm impatient for the sound of my son's voice, and the explanation.

The phone rings four times, and then I hear my own voice. "Hi, you've reached Alex Callahan. I can't come to the phone right now, but . . ."

I hang up. The phone has call waiting, so if you're on the line and you don't cut over to the new call, the machine picks up. The boys must be calling at the same time I'm calling the house. Our calls are blocking each other. I wait, try again, get the machine again. Repeat the process, in the meantime explaining to Christiansen what I'm doing — and that it was Kevin who called.

After the fourth try, I give up. Maybe I jumped the gun, maybe it took a minute or two for calls to post up. I click back to RECEIVED CALLS, but the number displayed for RECEIVED 1 is still the same, my home number. I press the tab for *time of call.* The time tag pops up: 4:42 a.m. A glance at the dashboard tells me it's 4:48. So that means the call from Kevin *did* come from the house in Cleveland Park.

In which case — why doesn't anyone answer?

"Mr. Callahan," Christiansen says, "you sure that was one of your kids?"

"Yes, I'm sure," I say, voice shaky with emotion. "It was Kevin."

"How could you tell — them being twins and all?"

"Because it sounded like Kevin," I snap. I don't bother to explain that most of the time Kevin still calls me Daddy while Sean calls me Dad — and is quite militant about it.

"No kiddin'," Christiansen says in a dubious voice.

Suddenly, I'm not so sure. Maybe it was Sean. The lack of certainty bothers me.

"So what did he say?" Christiansen asks. "What happened to them? Where are they?"

I'm pulling back onto the road, accelerating into the traffic. I don't answer Christiansen, but what I'm thinking is: *What did he say?* He said, *Daddy.* I can't get

Kevin's voice out of my head, the sweetest elixir, the hoped-for sound:

Daddy.

I flick on the phone's light and try home again, impatiently waiting for the end of the message and the beep. "Whoever is there with the boys," I beg, "please pick up the telephone. *Please.*"

Shortly after the kids were born, Liz and I got so busy, we developed the habit of letting the machine answer the phone most of the time — leaving the speakerphone on so we could hear whoever called and pick up if we could . . . or wanted to. Friends and family knew this, as did half a dozen people at the station. Messages often started, "Alex . . . if you're there, pick up. . . ." Or "Liz — it's Mom. Don't bother picking up, I just wanted to let you know . . ."

There are several telephones in the house, but I focus on the phone in the kitchen. It sits on the little red table Liz bought at a yard sale. The phone is an old one, beige, its black curly cord extra long and usually bunched into a messy tangle. Next to it is the square, white answering machine, red button flashing to indicate it holds messages. It is from the tiny grid of this machine's microphone, that I imagine my amplified voice speaking into the kitchen.

"Kev? Sean? If you're somehow there by yourselves, pick up the phone, okay, guys. It's Dad. Just pick up the phone."

Nothing.

Above the telephone table is the bulletin board, its wooden frame stained with green ink in one corner, where Sean colored it as a toddler. In Liz's absence the cork rectangle has become the permanent home of a haphazard collection of cleaning tickets, news clips, take-out menus, Post-its with scribbled names and numbers, the carpool schedule, photographs, kid art, old lottery tickets.

"Pick up," I plead, "come *on*."

The machine picks up and I hear my own robot voice again: "Hi, you've reached . . ." I try to imagine Kevin or Sean with the same detail in which I saw the bulletin board, but for some reason I can't do it.

"What are you doing?" Christiansen asks.

I ignore him, punch 411. I ask for Yasmin Siegel's number but then change my mind and instead call my next-door neighbor, Fred Billingsley. Yasmin is in her eighties. It will take her too long to get out the door. Fred, whose wife Nancy died two years ago, lives with his adult daughter. He's efficient and reliable if not friendly.

"Sir," Christiansen says, "I need to report to Detective Shoffler. Can you tell me —"

Fred is more than surprised to hear from me at this hour. "Alex? What time is it?" His voice is alarmed. "Is there a problem?"

"Can you do me a huge favor?" I ask him.

I explain the situation, tell Fred where to find the key for the front door. Fred promises to go right over; he'll call me back on my cell phone in a few minutes.

Christiansen leans over, peering past his shoulder toward the dashboard. "Whoa!" he squeals. "Sir! Sir! Slow down! You've got to slow down."

I'm on the Beltway by the time Fred gets back to me. "No one here," he tells me. "I don't see anything unusual or peculiar or out of place. You sure they called from here?"

I tell him my cell phone listed the call as originating from home, but maybe there's some mistake. I thank him profusely.

"Your boys are really . . . *missing?*" Fred

says. "Good Lord, is there anything else I can do?"

I have it in my mind that the kids are in the house, hiding from Fred. For no particular reason besides the man's stiff formality, they've always been afraid of "Mr. B."

"Thanks for checking, Fred. I owe you one," I say. "I don't think there's anything else you can do. I'll be there in half an hour. You should just go back to bed. I'm really sorry I woke you up."

"Not at all," Fred says, in a remote voice. "Glad to be of assistance."

Christiansen finally gets through to Shoffler just before I turn off Connecticut onto Ordway. They're still talking when I pull into the driveway. And then I'm out of the car, running toward the house.

I yank open the screen door, turn the dead bolt, and then I'm inside, charging from room to room at warp speed, yelling the boys' names, throwing open doors, flipping on lights, my eyes practically strip-searching the rooms. I check their bedroom last. Some demented optimist inside me continues to hold out hope that somehow I'll find them here, asleep in their beds.

But their room is deserted. A void.

With Christiansen trailing behind, I check the attic, then the basement, then make another round of the rooms, this time opening closet doors, looking under the beds, behind furniture, anywhere, everywhere that might conceal a little boy. Again I finish in their bedroom, drifting toward the front window.

Yasmin Siegel is not just a night owl; she claims to sleep only two or three hours a night. She's also one of those women who seems to know everything that happens in a neighborhood. Maybe she saw something — a car, the boys, whoever brought them to the house — something. She's awake, too. I can see the bluish glow of the television through the windows of the Siegels' family room.

I'm on my way out of the bedroom, heading for the phone in my study to call Yasmin, when my eyes catch on something I never noticed before.

It's some kind of little rabbit, perched on the double dresser, a low-slung many-drawered thing Liz got from Ikea. It's on Sean's side, which, unlike Kevin's half, is almost free of clutter — or I never would have noticed it. Up close, I see that it's origami, the little figure maybe four inches tall, folded out of brown paper. I don't know anything about origami, but this is not some simple cartoonlike rendition of an animal. It's sleek and sophisticated, more like a piece of miniature sculpture.

And when I pick it up, it feels weird. It's not made out of paper, but some kind of animal's skin. Which spooks me, somehow.

Was this always here? I don't think so. I would have noticed it.

But maybe not, I think, setting the little figure back on the dresser. After all, did I notice the boys' obsession with knights? No. And Liz was always taking them to workshops . . . of every kind imaginable. Although . . . there's no way Kevin or Sean made this thing. Their mother, maybe.

The thought of Liz hits me like wind shear.

Ohmigod. I've gotta call her. . . .

chapter 7

She gets in late the next morning, stumbling out of the secure area at National Airport, her good looks strained by tears. After a stiff embrace, I take her elbow, pivot her to the left, and introduce her to Christiansen.

Christiansen is here as a courtesy, to — as Shoffler put it — "help escort Mrs. Callahan to your house."

I told the detective to forget it when he first put forward this idea, but Shoffler talked me around, noting that uniformed policemen can really help get you through a media crowd. "A guy in uniform can be all business; hell, he can even be rude to reporters — and it just looks like he's doing his job. The squad car, the uniform — they'll help."

"Oh," Liz says, her eyes widening at the sight of the policeman. She throws me a wild glance, and I know what she's thinking — even though it makes no sense, even though I would be the one to tell her. She thinks Christiansen is here in some official capacity, to deliver bad news.

"Ma'am," he mutters, tilting forward in a kind of bow.

She waits, frozen, and when it becomes clear that Christiansen is not going to say anything else, she collapses into me, her face hot and damp against my shoulder. "Oh, Alex," she says. *"Alex?"*

I'm more or less holding her up as the crowd streams around us. We just stand there, Liz weeping against my shoulder. I'm not sure what to do. But then she steps back, bats at her face to dry her tears, and starts off toward the baggage claim area, moving so fast I almost have to run to keep up. We stand together, watching the suitcases tumble down the chute toward the conveyor belt.

I open my mouth to say something, but it falls closed of its own weight. What can I say? How was your flight? Sorry I lost our sons?

The telephone call to tell her what had happened was a nightmare, but this — this is so much worse. Instead of Liz arriving to the reunion I've been imagining, the jumping and excited boys and their beaming please-come-back-to-me-I've-changed father, this is how the love of my life reenters my world. She stands not twelve inches from me, enclosed within a force field of grief and anger. Of course she was scrupulous on the telephone, as I struggled to explain what happened. She did everything she could to reassure me it wasn't my fault, that I shouldn't think that way, that she doesn't blame me, of course she doesn't blame me.

But of course it's a lie. How can she not blame me? It's impossible.

"What happened to your face?" she asks in a neutral tone. "You look —"

"The search," I tell her with a shrug. "The woods."

"That's mine," she says, in a tight little voice. Her hand jerks up and points toward a green suitcase. The gesture is almost mechanical, as if she's a wind-up toy.

I don't recognize the suitcase. The sight of it — bright lime green with leather trim — makes me sad on a number of levels. It's one more thing acquired during our separation — the blouse she's wearing, the boys' new backpacks, and so on — and this accumulation of objects seems to emphasize the divergence of our lives. And then there's the stylish, buoyant look of the suitcase, which speaks of an alternate reality, Liz off for a jaunt to someplace chic.

Instead of here with me in this nightmare.

"It has wheels," she says, once I've fought through the throng and wrestled the suitcase off the belt. I carry it anyway, and if hefting its weight is not exactly a pleasure, it offers — like meeting the plane — a respite from my sense of uselessness.

Already, it's clear that as the machinery of disaster gains momentum, I am more and more peripheral to the effort. I've given my account of what happened a half dozen times now, tracked down the best and most recent photographs of the boys and given consent for the broadcast and distribution of their images. I've supplied detailed descriptions of their clothing. I've called all the neighbors to see if anyone spotted anything at the house — a car, the boys, lights, anything. (Yasmin Siegel confessed that she'd fallen asleep watching *The Sopranos*.) I've given consents: the phone may be tapped, phone records accessed, computer examined by experts, house searched.

In fact, I'm irritated that they haven't searched the house yet. I don't understand what's taking so long, as I complained to Shoffler over the phone right before I left for the airport. "Kevin was here," I told the detective. "He called from this telephone. He didn't get here on his own, that's for sure — which means that the kidnapper was here. You should be crawling all over this place."

Shoffler told me to relax. When there were jurisdictional issues — they had to liaise with D.C. Metro — it took a little while to get the wheels rolling.

I've surrendered my cell phone to a so-called communications technician dispatched by Shoffler. A woman named Natalie — the two of us went through the call lists, so I could identify the numbers, both of incoming and outgoing calls. I recognized all of the numbers. Krista, my assistant at the station. Liz. Cass Carter, whose son is in Kev and Sean's car pool to St. Albans day camp. Dave Whitestone, my producer. My folks. And so on. Natalie affixed an evidence number to my Nokia and gave me a receipt for it. She also provided a clone — a phone with the same number — in case a repeat call comes in from Kevin or Sean. Or from someone with a ransom demand.

I also talked to a kind woman named Shelley at the Center for Missing and Exploited Children, scanned a photo of the boys into the computer so that the organization might begin its national poster campaign. Another woman — Shelley's superior

— is supposed to call later to discuss other options and to offer advice.

Now I'm reduced to staying out of the way. I want to scour the earth for Kevin and Sean, but instead I'm immobilized.

We glide along on the moving sidewalk toward the parking garage. Behind me, Christiansen jingles the keys in his pocket. In front of me stands Liz, rigid with the effort of suppressing her terror.

When Christiansen turns the corner onto Ordway, Liz gasps. The little knot of reporters that began gathering early this morning has ballooned into a crowd. Two communications vans jam the alley on either side of the street, another sits in the Hokinsons' driveway, wedged up against their red Explorer. There are light towers, cables snaking across the lawns and sidewalks, camera and sound crews. A couple of well-dressed figures stand solitary within little established zones of space, prepping light and sound equipment for the stand-ups they'll do later. Neighbors stand in their doorways, too, gaping at the sudden occupation of the block. As the crowd catches sight of the squad car, there's a rush for position.

"Oh, shit," Christiansen says. "Pardon

my French, ma'am."

From Liz, a little moan.

I feel a jangle of dread, a weird sense of exposure. I've been part of scenes like this plenty of times, one more reporter in the press conference crush, or in a mob waiting to waylay some key figure in a story. With cable and satellite and the increase in venues for news, the size of these media mobs is getting out of hand. A couple of years back, I was part of the team covering the D.C. sniper case for the station, one of the more than nine-hundred badged for the press conferences held by the Rockville police chief.

I think — too late — that I should have warned Liz. And it's probably going to get worse. The story is going to be the top of the news, front page, lead story. The fact that I'm in the business, that I appear on TV, that my face is familiar to some, that I am (as Liz and I used to joke) "a third-string celebrity," will just stoke what is going to be a firestorm of coverage.

Liz cringes against me as the crowd begins to engulf the car. I know it would be a mistake — because a person shielded from the camera is automatically guilty of something — but it's all I can do to keep from throwing my jacket over Liz's head to protect her. She's weeping against me, really losing it.

"It's all right," I murmur. She takes deep shuddering breaths, trying to compose herself.

It's not working. Her hands are balled up into fists and she screws her knuckles into her eyes. "Just get us into the house," I tell Christiansen.

"How?" The tips of the officer's ears glow bright red.

"Walk fast, no eye contact, don't talk to anybody. Say 'excuse me.' Nothing else."

And that's what we do. I follow Christiansen as if he's a blocker on a punt return, yanking Liz left, then right into the momentary gaps the police officer creates. We somehow get through the blizzard of flashes, the mechanized chatter of camera shutters, the cacophony of shouted questions and comments.

"Excuse me!"

"Can you comment — ?"

"Excuse me."

"That's the mother; she looks —"

"Excuse me."

". . . know if there are any suspects?"

"Mr. and Mrs. Callahan, can you tell our . . . ?"

". . . parents of the boys have been separated . . ."

"Excuse me."

". . . possible the twins were trying to run away?"

"Fuck," Christiansen says, once we're inside the door. He's panting for breath, his ears on fire.

Making it inside and closing the door on the madness feels like a victory, but the sense of triumph lasts only a few seconds. Liz looks up at me, her eyes wet and out of focus. "Alex," she starts, but then she just stands there, swaying.

"Liz —"

"Alex!" she shrieks. She pummels my chest with her fists. *"Where are they? You have to find them!"*

chapter 8

We sit in the kitchen. "So there's no news . . ." she starts, and then her voice fades out.

"I'll call Shoffler — the detective. I told him we'd check in after we got back from the airport." I head for the phone. She doesn't take her eyes off me.

But Shoffler is in conference. I leave a message, then make Liz some tea. She sits like a rag doll, slumped and loose-limbed. I wonder if I should get her to a doctor.

"Did you call your parents?" she asks in a listless voice.

"They're on their way."

"My mom sort of . . . broke down," Liz says. "She's in the hospital."

"Oh, Liz . . ."

"She's all right, just — you know, she's sedated."

"I'm sorry."

"I begged my dad to stay with her, but he's coming. I couldn't stop him." She draws a sharp intake of breath.

She stirs the sugar into her tea for so

long, I finally put my hand over hers.

"Oh," she says, without inflection.

Despite the crowd outside, it's so quiet I can hear the white noise of the appliances: the hum of the refrigerator, the whine of the air conditioner. It feels almost as if we're hiding.

She rests her elbows on the table, holds her face in her hands.

"We'll find them," I hear myself say. She draws a deep, jittery breath, lifts her face up toward me.

"We will," I tell her, my voice fervent. "Liz, we'll find them."

She searches my face, but whatever she sees doesn't reassure her. Her face compresses into a red knot of torment. She lowers her head to the table, rests it on her crossed arms, and begins to sob. Inconsolable.

Liz is in the shower when the call comes from Claire Carosella.

"I'm returning your call," the efficient voice says. "I'm with the Center for Missing and Exploited Children. I think my colleague mentioned . . ."

"Right. She did mention that you'd call."

"At the Center," she begins, "we realize parents don't know what to do when this sort of thing happens, so . . . someone like me usually calls to offer advice."

"Right," I say, not knowing where this woman is going. Advice?

"First things first," she says. "The media. I'm sure they're already camped on your doorstep."

"Yes."

"Well, they'll drive you crazy," she says, "but really, they're your biggest ally. As soon as possible, you and your wife should go on the air and plead for the children's return."

"My wife — she's really . . ."

"I'm sure she's a mess. Believe me, I know. . . ." A pause. "But you've absolutely got to do it. It humanizes you as victims, both to the viewing public and to the abductor. Lots of these guys watch, you know. Sometimes, they even get involved in the search for the victim."

"Polly Klaas," I say, mentioning the name of a girl abducted from her bedroom in California and later found murdered. A man prominent in the effort to find the little girl, a guy who'd printed and distributed thousands of circulars and was appointed by the girl's grateful father to run a foundation dedicated to the search for her, had turned out to be a registered sex offender with a history involving young girls.

"Well, yes," Claire Carosella says, "that's one example, but —"

"It wasn't him," I interrupt, remembering the details. "It turned out to be a different guy."

"You've been doing your homework."

"Yeah."

My homework. In a couple of hours online, I've already learned more about abducted children than I ever want to know. Including the somber fact that most of them — more than half — are dead within three hours of their disappearance.

"Isn't there a chance these guys get off on the media coverage? The grieving parents, all that?"

A sigh. "Yes. That's one of the negatives." Another weary sigh. "But on balance, Alex, going on the air is way more plus than minus. Believe me, the tips, the calls to the hotline, volunteers, you name it — all these things get a big bounce after parental pleas."

"Hunh."

"The thing is, it can really help the investigation. And these guys — sometimes they just can't resist calling in. In which case they might say something that gives the police a lead. It's like pyromaniacs coming to watch the fire. They want to be a part of it."

"Okay," I tell her. "We'll do it."

"And just, you know . . . speak from the heart. Don't try to write out a speech and read it. It's better if you . . . if you just do it. The more emotional, the better."

"Uh-huh."

"Some parents choose to do it in a studio, but that means granting an exclusive — that's up to you. It can be somewhat less intimidating, and the lighting will be better . . . but . . . naturally it irritates the other reporters."

"Hunh."

"And it can come across as too . . . composed. I think just outside the house works best. Incidentally, do mention them by name — that's important. 'Kevin and Sean.' Not 'my sons' or 'my children.' "

"Right. Okay."

Her final advice is unsettling. "I feel I'd be remiss if I didn't mention this," she says, and then hesitates.

"Yes?"

"Some families hire public relations advisers," she tells me. "It's become quite common with victims groups, you know . . . the various disease associations, relatives of airline crash victims, that kind of thing. It's kind of segued over from that sector."

"You mean . . ."

"I know it sounds strange, but I'm told it can be a huge plus to have someone to interface with the media, and I am talking about a professional firm, Alex, not a friend. They can also help to maximize your exposure. I mean if the case drags on — they can help keep it in the news."

"I don't think . . ."

"Look, as I said, I'm only mentioning it because it's something to consider. It's how the Smart family kept Elizabeth's case front and center for so long. Even when everybody thought she was dead. Anyway, if you decide to go that way, I can give you a list of firms."

I thank her, but when I hang up, I feel as if I've stepped through a looking glass. My children are missing and they want me to do stand-ups and get a PR rep?

Shoffler calls to tell us that there's no news from the search parties, but that the switchboard is swamped with volunteers. The plan is to broaden the search.

"Great," I say, "that's great." If my voice lacks enthusiasm, it's because when I try to remember an instance of one of these big efforts actually locating the target of the search, I can't think of a single one.

"We're canvassing people who work at the festival, looking for anyone who saw your boys yesterday. So far, we're not getting very far."

"Oh?" This from Liz on the extension in the family room. "That's strange. Everybody notices the boys."

It's true. Identical twins hold a universal fascination. Now that they can tell time, the boys sometimes bet on how long they can be out in public before someone asks the inevitable question: "Are you twins?" Sean went through a stretch last year when he liked to answer no. He thought his deadpan denial hugely amusing, but it irritated people. We were all glad when he got tired of the game.

"Probably just haven't talked to the right folks yet," Shoffler says. "Anyway, there is something we've learned." He hesitates just long enough to unnerve me. I feel it in my chest, a little whir of anxiety.

"*What?*" Liz demands, with a note of panic in her voice. "What is it?"

"We ran the fair employees through a bunch of databases," Shoffler says. "Computer kicked out one thing of interest —

although right off I want to tell you I don't think this is going anywhere."

"What?" Liz says in a tight little voice.

"There's this fella runs a little shop — does face-painting, sells candles and magic wands, that kind of thing. Computer turned up a pedophile conviction."

"Who?" I demand. "What's his name?"

"Whoa," Shoffler says. "Just because he has a prior doesn't mean the guy's culpable here. We're checking out his account of his time and whereabouts, and so far it's holding up solid."

"Is he in custody?" Liz asks. "Does he know where the boys are? Can we talk to him?"

"We'll know for sure about him real soon," Shoffler says, "but like I said, Mrs. Callahan, I don't think he's involved. I just didn't want the press to spring this on you. Wanted to make you aware."

I know from the snuffling sound that Liz is crying again.

"I'll be by sometime today," Shoffler tells us.

"Jesus," Liz's father says as he plunges through the front door. "They're like a pack of vultures. Where's my daughter?"

She comes through the door from the

kitchen, gives a little cry, and then he takes her clumsily into his arms, patting at her shoulder. "Liz," he says, "it'll be all right. You'll see."

After a minute, they separate and he extends his hand to me. "Alex," he says. "Hell of a thing."

"Thanks for coming, Jack." It's an effort to address my father-in-law by his first name. What comes naturally is "Mr. Taggart," a form of address that the man himself, with his parade-ground posture and stiff manners, might prefer. Jack is a high-school principal. He's conditioned to expect deference from anyone younger than he is.

It is Liz who either mistrusts or fails to grasp her father's profound sense of formality, Liz who insists on the tokens of chummy intimacy. On their own, the boys would call Jack "Grandfather" and greet him with handshakes, but when Kevin and Sean were toddlers, Liz decreed that they should call him "Poppy." She insists on this, and also mandates hugs and kisses. To please her, everyone complies — but only when she's present. She looks on now, frowning, as her father and husband engage in something that — were it not so brief — might be called an embrace.

"Marguerite — this thing was just too much for her," my father-in-law says, stepping out of our statutory hug. He shakes his head, disappointment with his wife clear on his strong features. "High-strung," he mutters, "but" — he claps his hands together — "she'll be fine."

Marguerite Taggart is a sweet and warm woman, the yin to Jack's yang. Now she's under sedation in the MidCoast Medical Center in Rockland, Maine.

Liz may have wanted her dad to stay with her mother, but I can see that she's buoyed by Jack's presence. Jack Taggart is one of those supremely self-confident men who believes he can do anything. This clearly includes finding his grandchildren. He truly believes that once events have been placed in his capable hands, he can promise a positive outcome. It's irrational to put faith in Jack's can-do attitude, but Liz is not alone in finding comfort in his presence. I feel it, too.

My own parents are scheduled to arrive about an hour after Jack. I'd pick them up at the airport, but Shoffler and the search unit are due to come by and I don't want to leave Liz here to deal with them. On the other hand, although Jack blew through the crowd with no problems, my folks lack his imperious presence. They'll be swallowed alive.

When Dad calls from baggage claim, I suggest he tell the cab to come the back way. All these old blocks in Cleveland Park have service alleys that run parallel to the streets. "I'll unlock the gate."

"Okeydoke," my dad says. "Hey, I see the bags. We'll be there in a jiffy."

The plan doesn't work. My parents' arrival is heralded by a stampede from the front of the house to the end of the block and then down the alley and into our backyard. From inside we can hear the pounding feet, the ruckus of shouted questions. Jack and I rush out the back door, finding my mother — whose manners do not permit hanging up on a telemarketer — engulfed by reporters and microphones. A blonde with a predatory smile has seized Mom by the arm and wields her huge microphone like a weapon. With a deer-in-the-headlights expression, Mom's doing her best to answer questions. A few feet from the gate, Dad, grim-faced and tight-lipped, is trying to get through the crowd with his suitcases.

"Any word on the boys' welfare?"

"Were the boys upset over their parents' separation?"

"What about the suspect?"

"Was it a contentious separation?"

Once they spot me, the crowd of reporters abandons my parents and converges, circling in fast and instinctively cutting off exit routes, like a pack of dogs. The four of us barely avoid being trapped, blocked from reentering the house.

"Good Lord," my mother says once we're inside, letting out a weird little giggle. Her eyes are slightly out of focus, and when we hug each other, I realize she's out of it, so zonked on Xanax she feels boneless in my arms. Dad gives me a buck-up abrazo, but looks terrible. "We'll find them," he says firmly, but his voice is tinny and unsubstantial.

"We will," I say. "We *will* find them." Listening to myself, my voice forced but full of conviction, I realize I'm falling into a weird form of magical thinking. If only I can get the right tone and — like Jack — speak with unassailable assurance, what I say will come true.

Late that afternoon, we stand just outside the front door, elevated a few steps above the jostling crowd of reporters and cameramen. There's a forest of microphones, a sea of cameras. The hubbub of human voices rises and falls, supplemented by the mechanized chatter of the cameras. The lights flicker in their own crazed rhythm.

Liz stands next to me, flinching from the noise and dazzle. "I'm Alex Callahan," I begin. I plead with whoever has taken Kevin and Sean to return them, I plead with the public to be our eyes and ears, to call the hotline with any information.

I realize too late that I should have insisted Liz do most of the talking. Even to me my voice sounds polished and composed — my on-camera voice. I try to project my honest civilian desperation, but it doesn't work. I'm left with a feeling that I know quite well. It's hard to predict on-camera interviews, who will come off, and who doesn't work. Today, I fit into the second category. I'm left with the perception of having given a performance, and not a particularly good one.

Liz makes up for it. She can hardly manage a sentence without breaking down in the middle of it, but she goes on anyway, a forced march of bravery so moving I spot the glitter of tears in the eyes of some of the female reporters. At the end, she speaks directly to the boys. "Kevin? Sean? If you're watching . . . hang in there, guys. We love you. Daddy and I . . . we just love you . . . so much. And we're going to find you! Wherever you are. I promise! We'll come and find you. You just . . . hang on."

That's it, she's wrecked, she can't go on. She turns hard into me, ramming her face into my chest, crossing her arms over the top of her head as if she's expecting a physical blow. She sags against me, and I realize after a moment that I'm actually holding her up. Reporters continue to shout questions and the cameras continue their disorienting barrage of light as I half drag my wife back in through the door to our home.

It doesn't feel like much of a sanctuary.

Fortunately Liz is asleep when the two K-9 officers arrive at the door. Their task is to pick up an assortment of Kevin and Sean's dirty clothes, including the sheets from the boys' beds. Duchess — who wears an intricate leather harness — sits at her handlers' feet, breathing heavily while they divide the clothing into two plastic bags.

"Why are you doing that?" Jack asks, indicating the two bags. "Is one bag supposed to be Kevin's stuff and the other one

Sean's? Because I think you got things mixed up."

"Not exactly," the policewoman replies.

"Well?" Jack demands.

She strokes Duchess. "There's another dog," she says, almost in a whisper. "Corky. Another handler works him."

"Come again?" Jack says. "Could you speak up, young lady?"

Her eyes drift over to her partner and he takes over. "Duchess here is a tracking dog, pure and simple," he explains. "Goes by scent. I imagine you've seen bloodhounds in the movies?"

Jack nods.

"But there's another type of canine, sir, that's deployed in these situations, specially trained to detect . . . well, their expertise is to detect . . . remains, sir. They can even locate remains in ponds and streams — you know, underwater. It's amazing." He looks at the floor.

Jack's eyes snap shut, and for a moment, I'm afraid he's going to break down. "My God," he says, and looks at me. "Not a word to Lizzie about this."

"Cadaver dogs," the policewoman whispers. "That's what they call them."

chapter 9

Somehow we get through the day, a maelstrom of emotion, interrupted by what seems like hundreds of telephone calls.

I speak to Shoffler half a dozen times, but there's nothing new except his change of schedule; instead of "sometime today," he'll come by "sometime tonight."

On the advice of several friends, I call an investigative agency and talk to a guy I interviewed once for a story about the Russian mob in Brighton Beach. Before I get to why I'm calling, he puts two and two together: "Oh, my god, the missing twins. Jesus, that's you, I didn't think . . ."

He gives me the name of the firm's best missing-person investigator — a woman named Mary McCafferty. We set up a meeting for the following day. She gives me a list of information she'd like. "We're going to cut you a break," she tells me, "and do the work for half the normal rate."

But it's still not going to be cheap. Seventy-five dollars an hour instead of one hundred fifty dollars. Plus expenses.

I speak several times to Krista at the station — which, she tells me breathlessly, has pledged ten grand to a reward fund. The boys' pictures, an announcement of the reward, and the hotline number will be shown at the top of every hour.

I talk to a woman at the missing children's center. They've set into motion an e-mail "locater" search, which, through an elaborate network of electronic address books, might reach — with its attachment containing a picture of the boys, physical description, and hotline information — as many as three million people.

Friends and acquaintances call by the dozen.

At five o'clock, I realize that the boys have been missing for twenty-four hours. I don't mention this to anyone.

At six thirty, a bewildered Hispanic kid delivers the food Liz ordered from Sala Thai. My father regards the food with suspicion. Jack eats with gusto, encouraging his daughter to do the same: "Important to keep your strength up, sweetheart." My mother takes a bite of the Pad Thai and says to my father, "Really, Bob, it's just linguini."

It's seven, it's eight, it's nine.

Sleeping arrangements. I've been awake

for so long, I'm approaching an altered state of consciousness, although I can't imagine actually falling asleep. Liz bustles around, making up the sleep-sofa in the study for her father, changing the sheets in the master bedroom, which she has assigned to my folks. I trail her, carrying towels and sheets. It's her intention to sleep in the boys' room, but she stops in the doorway, frozen. "I can't . . . I can't sleep in here," she says. "Oh, God . . . Alex . . ." She begins to sob and I put my arm around her shoulder, but she stiffens under my touch, pulls away, composes herself. "I'll take the futon in the family room," she announces. "You get the living room couch."

She heads into the bathroom. I follow, with my stack of towels. She stands in front of the vanity and looks into the mirror; then her eyes slide down toward the sink. I see the expression on her face in reflection for a moment before she turns and I see the puzzled frown straight on.

"What's the deal with these dimes?" she asks.

The vanity has a faux-marble top with a backsplash. On the upper edge of that backsplash and perfectly centered between the faucets rests a row of Liberty head dimes. Seven of them, precisely aligned.

"I don't know," I say.

"Do these belong to the boys? Did they start a collection?"

"I don't think so."

But the ambiguity is only notional. I've never seen the dimes before — and I would have seen them. It's my habit to stand and watch Kev and Sean brush their teeth, to make sure they stay at it for more than two seconds, to see that they rinse their toothbrushes and sluice down the spit and toothpaste. It's not that dental hygiene is such a big thing with me. My vigilance is due to Liz. I knew I'd be called to account for any evidence of a lapse. No way I would not have noticed a line of coins on the sink. And the sight of them spooks me. They seem like some kind of crazy sign or message.

"Someone put them there," I tell Liz.

"Who? What?"

"The kidnapper."

"Oh, God. Alex . . . ?"

"Come here for a sec," I say, pulling her toward the boys' bedroom. "I want you to take a look at something." I point out the little origami rabbit on the dresser. "Does this belong to Kevin or Sean? Because I never noticed it before . . ."

"No," Liz says, "I never saw it before." She looks at me with a little worried frown. "*Alex* . . . that rabbit. The dimes. What does it mean?"

"I don't know."

Tears well up in her eyes, but she shakes me off when I try to comfort her. I follow her back to the bathroom, where she blows her nose, splashes cold water on her face, buries her face in a towel.

When I hear the loud rap at the door, I'm in the family room down on my hands and knees, still trying to get the rickety futon frame to fold down. Jack and my father have been taking turns on door duty, and I hear my father's husky voice, and another voice, in counterpoint. I'm still extricating myself from behind the futon when my father and the detective arrive at the door.

"How you holding up?" Shoffler asks me.

I manage a sort of shrug. Shoffler himself looks terrible. He wears a crumpled linen sports jacket, one button dangling by a thread. A battered pair of khakis rides low on his hips, forced there by his belly. His weary eyes make it clear he needs sleep. A nap in the car on the way to

Ordway Street, in fact, would explain the spiky explosion of hair on the right side of his head. "The press gives you too much trouble," he says, "I can get D.C. to post an officer."

I shrug. "I'll let you know."

"That the kind of thing you do?" he asks, nodding toward the front of the house.

"I've done it," I say. "It's just their job."

"Bob — do I have that right?" Shoffler says, looking at my father. He hooks a finger in his belt and hitches up his pants.

"Yes, you do. Robert J. Callahan." My father gives a little whinny of high-pitched laughter, a sign of nerves to those of us who know him well.

"You mind calling the others to come in here?"

A gush of fear blooms in my chest. "You have something? You have . . . news?"

Shoffler shakes his head, and bends to help me, yanking on one of the futon frame's recalcitrant legs. The whole thing unfolds with a crash. "There you go," he says.

Between us, we manage to maneuver the awkward futon into position. "My son had one of these doohickeys when he was at Bowie State," the detective says. "Slept on it once. Pretty comfortable."

Once Liz and the others are in the room and seated, Shoffler tells us he's going to give us an update on what's been happening. The search in the woods outside the fairgrounds proceeds, he tells us, with more volunteers than they can "shake a stick at." The hotline is swamped with calls, but it's going "to take time to sort things out." The questioning of fair employees, he says, "is slow, but it's coming along. As I told Alex earlier, we're having some trouble finding reliable witnesses who remember seeing the boys, but we're making progress."

An image of Kevin and Sean at the fairgrounds, laughing at a comic juggler, swims up in my mind. I shake my head, as if this motion might dispel the picture. As the hours go on, I can no longer think of the boys without a panicked rush of loss. It's like falling off a cliff, over and over again.

The one bit of real news Shoffler offers is that the candle-selling pedophile has been cleared of suspicion. "Although the fair, of course, has closed him down. So he's not going to be selling any magic wands to any little kids for a while. But as for abducting your boys, he can account for every minute of the time in question."

"Well, that's a relief," Liz says, pressing her hands against her thighs.

"I thought if an alibi was too rock solid, that was suspicious," Jack puts in. "In and of itself."

Shoffler exhales. He doesn't dismiss Jack's comment, but responds patiently, as he has to every question asked. In ten minutes, he's managed to charm and reassure Liz and my mother and to impress Jack and my father. He has a knack for listening that would put most reporters to shame.

"Too good an alibi?" he says. "Well, there's really no such thing, Jack. I know what you mean, but in this case, we have a whole boatload of witnesses as to this guy's whereabouts."

"And what was he doing?" my father asks. "If you don't mind my asking."

Shoffler pats at the explosion of hair on the side of his head, manages a weary smile. "He wasn't at the fair all day. He spent the entire afternoon from one to six at" — he opens his notebook, pages through — "the Bayside Motel in Annapolis, where he was participating in a defensive driving course." He looks up at them. "After that, he went to" — again he consults his notebook — "a support group potluck for persons who've recently lost a parent — his mother died three weeks ago. This potluck was also in Annapolis. Trinity Episcopal Church." Shoffler closes his notebook.

"So this guy — he's out of the picture," Jack says.

"Yes."

"Well, that's good," Liz says again, throwing a glance at me. "Isn't it?"

"Definitely," Shoffler says. "It eliminates a possibility, and that's always positive. Means resources can be focused elsewhere. So —" He rubs his hands together. "You folks have any more questions?"

"There's been no ransom call," my dad says with a worried glance my way. "Isn't that, I mean — why do you think that is?"

"Well, it's early days," Shoffler tells him, "but I don't expect you're going to get one."

"*No?* But, but — why not?" Jack demands.

Shoffler screws up his face, sighs. "First off, if you're after money, why take *two* kids? It's not like it's a bake sale, if you see what I mean."

"I'm not sure that I do," Jack says.

Shoffler shrugs. "Two kids'd be twice the trouble, but they wouldn't get you twice the payoff. Desperate parents — my opinion is they'd pony up just as much for one child as for two. And then" — he hesitates, but in the end doesn't tiptoe around it — "fact is, there's plenty of rich folk in the world. Somebody with a profit motive? I think they'd go for parents with . . . ah . . . greater resources than Alex and Liz here. Unless" — he looks inquiringly from Jack to my father to my mother — "the boys' grandparents . . . ?"

"I'm a high school principal," Jack says. Uncharacteristically, he follows this statement with a nervous laugh. His relative lack of means is the only subject known to make Jack defensive. "Maybe Bob here is one of those secret millionaires next door." He laughs again, and looks at my father.

"No," my father says. "I'm not saying we" — he looks at my mother — "couldn't come up with a good piece of change if we liquidated everything. Which we would do, of course, but it would take time. But —" He shakes his head, conceding Shoffler's point.

"Well," Shoffler says, "you see what I mean." His hands float up into the air and then come back down on his thighs with a slap.

"What about a nonmonetary reason?" my father asks.

Shoffler frowns. "Such as?"

"My son, the kind of stories he does —" A glance my way. "He makes enemies."

Shoffler raises his eyebrows, looks at me. "That so?"

I get that rush in my chest, the adrenaline burn of alarm. I hadn't thought of this. The idea that whoever took the boys did so because of me — it's sickening. I tend to go for edgy pieces. Gangbanging, money laundering, arms trafficking. Stories like that. So maybe . . .

"My father's right," I tell Shoffler. "I didn't think of it."

"Well," Shoffler says. "If you can come up with anybody who might take a grudge that far . . ."

"But why go after the kids? Why not me?"

"Just get with your files and see if anything jumps out at you. Make a little list for me. Can't hurt."

I promise to do that, after which Shoffler looks at each of us in turn. No one seems to have anything else to say.

Jack gives in to a mighty yawn. "Excuse me." He stands up. "Well, thank you very much."

"Would you like some iced tea?" my mother asks, also getting to her feet. "Or coffee?"

"Actually," Shoffler says, "I know it's late, but we'd like to conduct the search now."

"The search?" Liz asks. "What search?"

"The search of the residence," Shoffler says. He shoots a glance at me. "Your husband and I have talked about it. He thinks the kidnapper was here. In this house. That maybe we'll find something. Anyway, it's routine."

"I don't *think* he was here," I correct Shoffler. "He *was* here."

"Did you tell them about the dimes?" Liz says. "And that rabbit?"

"What's this?" Shoffler asks.

When I explain, he nods, pulls out the notebook, makes a notation. "We'll take those into evidence."

"I don't get it," I tell Shoffler. "There's no question Kevin was here. He called me from this number," I say. "I turned over my telephone to you guys. You know that."

Shoffler nods in a noncommittal way, hitches up his pants. "Right. And we've asked Verizon for the records."

"What?"

"Just to backstop the log on your cell phone. Make sure the call from Kevin wasn't forwarded, you know, from somewhere else."

"But —"

Shoffler ignores me. "It's late and we'd like to get started," he says. "I'm guessing it will take a couple of hours. So you all — you're welcome to — go for a drive or something."

"A drive?" my mother says, in the same incredulous tone she might have used if the detective had said "a swim" or "a manicure."

"Some folks find it upsetting," Shoffler explains to her in his patient voice, "strangers going through their house. Their things." He shrugs. "If you decide to stay, you'll all have to remain in this room until we're done with the rest of the house. Then we'll finish up in here." He makes a clicking sound, snapping his tongue away from the roof of his mouth. It seems unnaturally loud.

"Well, I don't want to go for a *drive*," my mother says.

"I think we'll stay put," I say.

"Good enough," Shoffler says. "In that case, we could cross something else off the list. Get everybody's fingerprints."

"What?" Jack says.

"Strictly routine, Mr. Taggart. We need the prints of the people who have been in the house, so we can exclude them. Eventually, we'll have to print everyone else who's been in here — housekeeper, babysitter, handyman — for the same reason." He looks at his watch.

"Why can't this be done tomorrow?" Jack asks, his arm around Liz's shoulder. "My daughter is exhausted."

Shoffler wags his head. "I know. It's very late — believe me, I'm aware of that. But I'm sure you understand that if there is any evidence here, anything that might provide a lead, we want to know about it right away. Not only can we act on it sooner, the longer we wait, the more the scene becomes contaminated. Plus, the team's already here, outside, ready to go —"

"They're outside right now?" I hear myself say. I don't know why this bothers me, but it does.

Shoffler looks at his watch. "You mind if we get started?"

chapter 10

We sit there for an awkward moment, not knowing what to say, until Jack grabs the remote and turns on the television.

It's impossible. What could be appropriate? He scowls as he blips from one hopeless choice to another. Baseball, crime shows, sitcoms, a *Frontline* program about the teen fashion industry.

"Dad," Liz says.

Jack turns the television off. But when it goes dark with its electronic fizzle, we can hear them in the living room, conducting their search. It sounds like they're taking the place apart. The counterpoint of conversation, the sounds of doors and drawers being opened, the audible evidence of the search — all this disturbs me. Even though I pushed for the search, it still feels like an invasion of privacy.

And suddenly the word *invasion,* which with its military connotations always seemed too forceful for this usage, seems perfect. Listening to these strangers pawing through my family's belongings makes me feel as if

I'm under attack, my territory violated. I hate the sound of their footsteps, the murmur of voices, the occasional spurt of laughter. It bothers me so much that I lift the remote from the end table, press the power button.

A mistake. I've caught the top of the ten o'clock news. There's a collective intake of breath as the photo of the boys flashes on the screen, the announcer saying: "No news in the case of the missing Callahan twins . . ."

"Oh, God," Liz says, as I punch the television off.

It's almost a relief when a jittery redhead with bad skin and green fingernails arrives to take our fingerprints.

We all endure this woman's bad temper as, one at a time, she calls us to the seat next to her. Using the coffee table as a platform, she presses our fingertips into an ink pad and then rolls out each one onto a prepared card. As she rolls my left pinky and then lifts it straight up from the file card, I can't shake the feeling that there's something sordid about the process. The card contains nothing but the minimal information required to identify me, that and the oblong blobs left by my fingertips, each with its own intricate pattern of whorls and lines.

I am given moistened towelettes to remove the ink from my hands while my mother takes my place. Maybe it's because the Xanax has worn off, maybe it's the half a dozen cups of coffee she's downed since her arrival. Whatever the reason, she can't seem to allow the technician to manipulate her fingers. She keeps twitching, moving the fingers herself. She apologizes and the tech issues an exaggerated sigh as she rips each messed-up card in two and tosses it into the wastebasket.

"Relax," she tells my mother for what must be the tenth time, "let me move your finger. You're rolling it — see, you're *smearing* it." Her tone of voice varies between accusing and patronizing. "Let me manipulate your fingers. *Don't* roll . . ."

"I'm not rolling," my mother says. "I'm trying not to."

"You *are*."

"Stop bullying her," I say. "This is voluntary, correct?" My mother casts me a grateful look, but she's beginning to sniffle.

"Let's try again," the fingerprint bitch says, filling out another card with yet another exasperated sigh.

This time, it goes well for a minute or two, but then, Mom twitches or something.

"You're doing it again!"

My mother breaks down, begins to cry.

"Leave her alone," my father says, getting to his feet.

"Excuse me," the tech says, extricating herself from her seat and marching toward the door. "I don't get paid enough to put up with this grief."

"I'm sorry, Mom," I say in an automatic tone.

"Do you want some water, Glenna?" my father asks in an anxious voice. "Alex — do you think we could get some water in here?"

"Sure." I drag myself up from the couch and speak to the policeman posted in the hall. I realize — and the thought fills me with guilt — that I am tired of my parents, that I wish they would go home. Jack, too. I know they've come because they *had* to come and lend whatever support they can. I guess I'd be hurt if they hadn't come. But it feels as if Liz and I have to take care of them.

Shortly after the policeman brings the water, Shoffler shows up. He stands in the threshold and raps his knuckles against the inside of the doorjamb. "Can I have a word with you, Alex? With you and Mrs. Callahan?"

There's something about the look on Shoffler's face that freezes my heart. First of all the latex gloves he's wearing — they're all wearing them — provide a chilling, clinical note. I stand up fast, as if there's a rope attached to the top of my head and someone's yanked me to my feet. "What is it?"

"You can speak freely right here," my father says, with a little inclusive sweep of his hand. "We're all family."

Shoffler holds his hand up, palm toward my father like a cop stopping traffic. "Just the parents," he says, with something that's more like a grimace than a smile.

Liz is gray. We follow Shoffler upstairs into my study, where a uniformed officer, also gloved, sits on the corner of my desk holding a clipboard. Shoffler introduces the man: "This is Officer David Ebinger."

Shoffler explains that it's the custom, post-O.J., to have a single officer handle evidence, from tagging and bagging, to checking it in and out of the evidence room, to introducing it in court. "We have to establish chain of custody," he says, in a matter-of-fact way, "in case there's a court case somewhere down the line."

We nod. We understand.

And then Shoffler closes the door. "We

found something," he says.

I can't say a word.

On my desk sits a brown cardboard box about the size of a shoe box. Its flaps are open, splayed to the sides, and taped to it is a white tag with writing on it. Shoffler nods to Ebinger and then, using the eraser end of a pencil, extracts from the box a crumpled and badly stained piece of clothing. Once he's got the whole thing clear of the box, I see what it is: a yellow T-shirt. The stain is reddish brown and I know instantly that it's blood.

Liz moans. I put my arm around her and she leans in to me, turning her face in to my chest. She can't look, but I can't stop looking. Shoffler is trying to gently shake out the piece of cloth suspended from his pencil. It must have dried in this crumpled state, and it's so stiff his efforts don't accomplish much. For some reason I feel compelled to watch, filled with dread that the shirt will slip off the pencil and fall to the desk and that I must not let this happen. Finally the folds of fabric in one part of the bunched T-shirt lose their adhesion. It's like a clenched fist opening, and suddenly I can see what the bunched folds hid, a palm-sized flat expanse of the T-shirt.

I don't need to see any more.

What's visible is the cartoonish drawing of a fish tail, the tail of what I know to be a whale, the interior of which I know to be printed with the word NANTUCKET.

"That's Kevin's," I say. I seem to speak without volition. "Sean has a green one." I can't take my eyes off the shirt. I try to concentrate on the fabric, exclude the image of Kevin *in* the shirt. There's a weird metallic taste in my mouth. Liz is shivering in my arms.

"Where did you find it?" I hear myself ask.

"Could you confirm that, Mrs. Callahan? I mean the identity of the shirt?"

Liz stiffens, lifts her head away from my chest. She turns her head, takes a look. She makes a terrible little sound. Her hand flies up to her mouth. She manages a few choppy nods.

Shoffler presses her. "Are you telling me the shirt belonged to your son Kevin?"

"Yes."

"Where did you find it?" I ask again, but again Shoffler doesn't answer. He maneuvers the shirt back into the box, pushes the flaps shut with the pencil. Ebinger meticulously tapes it closed.

"There's one more thing," Shoffler says.

"Would you follow me?"

Shoffler leads, Ebinger follows in our wake. I try not to speculate on the fresh horror he's going to show us. I concentrate on looking at the back of Liz's head, the slight sway of her dark ponytail. We enter the boys' room. I can hardly breathe.

"We decided to leave this in situ for the moment," Shoffler says, levering open the door of the closet with his pencil. "Can you explain this?" he asks, using the pencil to point to the top shelf. He moves aside, allowing us to peer into the closet. There, next to Candyland and Sorry is a small glass mixing bowl full of a clear liquid. It's on the very edge of the shelf, ready to topple.

"What is it?" Liz asks. "Is it water?"

"We're not certain yet — but, ah — as I said, if you can tell us what it's for, that would help."

Liz looks at me, but all I can do is shrug. I have no idea what a bowl of liquid is doing on the top shelf of the boys' closet.

"Did they have a pet or something?" Shoffler asks. "I mean a frog, a bug . . . a fish? That would make sense."

"I don't think so," I tell him.

"Hunh," Shoffler says, "you don't think so." He turns toward Liz. "Mrs. Callahan?"

Liz just shakes her head and frowns and gives me a funny look.

"We'll take a sample of the liquid and print the bowl. Is it your bowl, by the way?" He looks from me to Liz.

"I don't know," I say. "I guess so."

"I don't recognize it," Liz says.

"Hunh," Shoffler says again. "Well, Dave is going to deal with this," he says, nodding toward the closet, "and the crew can take on the family room. You can have the run of the rest of the house now." He removes his gloves.

"Detective —"

"It shouldn't take long," he says, ignoring me, "and then we'll be out of your hair. I expect everybody's pretty tired," he continues, "especially the grandparents."

"The shirt," Liz squeaks, "does that — ?"

"Sorry," Shoffler says, retreating into formality, "the shirt is evidence, and questions about it will have to wait. It would be premature to speculate. We'll send it to the lab and then I'll be in a better position to discuss it."

"But —"

He's moving toward the door now, walking past Liz and me. There seems to be no choice but to follow him out into the hall. We pause before returning to the family room, so that the two policemen coming out of my study can get to the front door. Each of them carries a large cardboard box sealed with evidence tape.

"What's that? What are you taking?"

"I think it's your computer."

"My computer?"

"Relax, Alex. It's routine. The kidnapper was here, right? Naturally we have to remove some items to examine them. Detective Ebinger will give you a search warrant inventory when we're finished, and you should look that over. As for the computer, what if the boys have been in touch with someone over the Internet? We have to examine that possibility."

Liz turns on me. "You did have parental controls on that thing, didn't you, Alex?"

"They never used the computer."

"Alex!"

"They never went near it! I don't even think they knew how to turn it on." This is probably true. The Apple engineers disguised the iMac's on/off switch so well that when I bought the machine, I had to call the shop to ask where it was.

"You promised me."

"Liz —"

Shoffler interrupts. "Alex," he says,

"would you be willing to take a polygraph test?"

"What?"

I say *what,* but I heard him. I also know what it means. Murder — even the murder of children — is often a family affair. When children go missing, the parents are automatic suspects. I can hear Officer Christiansen's voice during our walk back to the Jeep in that deserted field outside the festival gates. "Nine times out of ten, it's a parent."

Who could forget the Susan Smith case? The smiling faces of her sons blanketed the news for days as their distraught mother begged for their return, the return of boys she herself had sent rolling into the cold water of a lake, belted into their car seats. How could she do it? I wondered — everyone wondered — did she watch the water rise, did she watch them go under? I also remember a couple in Florida who made tearful appeals for the return of their adorable daughter, whose mangled body was later discovered buried in their backyard.

Would you be willing to take a polygraph test? It is in this company — Susan Smith, the tearful infanticidal Florida couple —

that I am being placed.

So I know. Asking me to take a polygraph test means that the bloody shirt . . . or maybe they've found something else in the house . . . makes them think I might be involved in the boys' disappearance. And, of course, I also know that they're wrong.

Before I can answer Shoffler, he does that traffic cop thing with his hand. "You're not *required* to take the test," the detective says. "It's strictly voluntary — you understand that, right?"

"What?" Liz says. *"What?"*

I just stand there. Anger bubbles up in me. "I'll take the test," I say, "but it's a waste of time. I don't get it. There had to be hundreds of people who saw my kids at the fair. And Kevin called me, he called me from here. Your guy — Christiansen — he was in the car."

Shoffler screws up his face, looks at the ceiling, as if he's getting some kind of information from up there. Then he nods, makes up his mind about something. "Look," he says, "the phone call? You say that was your kid — but no one else can confirm that. It could have been anyone. Even if the call did come from here." It seems as if he's going to say more, but he changes his mind and just shakes his head.

I know what he's thinking though, and the word goes off in my mind like a cherry bomb: *accomplice*.

"It's just like that shoe you spotted out by the fence," Shoffler says. "You know? I'm not implying anything here, but the thing is — who spotted it?"

"What shoe?" Liz asks in a panicky voice. "There's a shoe?"

"We found a child's shoe at the fairgrounds," Shoffler says. "According to your husband, it belongs to one of your boys."

"Kevin," I say. "One of Kevin's Nikes."

"You can understand why we'd like you to take a test," Shoffler says in what I guess is meant to be a soothing voice, "because . . . the thing is, what we've got, it's all . . ." He stops there, ending with a little shrug. He doesn't say it, but I get the message. I could have put the shoe there, outside the jousting ring, then pointed it out to Shoffler. An accomplice could have made the phone call from this house to my cell phone. There's been no ransom note, no telephone call. Shoffler himself said it: *Why take two kids? It's not like a bake sale.* There's no outside corroboration for my story. It all begins and ends with me.

"Somebody had to see us there," I say. "I

mean — it's crazy. Thousands of people saw us."

"Well, as for the fair visitors," Shoffler says in a conciliatory tone, "I'm sure you're right. For certain we got plenty of volunteers claiming to remember you." He makes that clicking noise with his mouth. A regretful click. "But of course the thing's been all over the tube. Most of the folks who have come forward weren't even there during the right stretch of time. Now, I'm sure we'll eventually find plenty of reliable witnesses who saw you and your sons and can confirm the time frame." His hands shoot up in a what-can-I-do gesture. "But until we do, my advice is — take the test."

"Of course I'll take the test," I say.

"Good," the detective says. "I'll schedule it."

My parents and Jack have materialized in the hall behind the detective. "They told us to go to the kitchen," my mother says.

"What's this about a test?" Jack asks.

"They want Alex to take a polygraph," Liz blurts out in a shaky voice.

"A lie detector test?" my father says to Shoffler. "What the hell is that supposed to mean?"

Shoffler holds out his traffic cop hand. "It's routine," he says. "Exclusionary."

"Like the fingerprints?" my mother puts in.

Shoffler nods.

My father squares his shoulders. "Look, Detective Shoffler," he says, "be frank with me: Do we need a lawyer here?"

"This is all on a strictly voluntary basis," Shoffler says. "If your son wants —"

"No," I say, interrupting the detective. "Dad — Jesus! No lawyer — I don't need a lawyer."

"It's not . . ." my father starts, "I don't mean . . ." He shakes his head. I see that he's holding my mother's hand tight, their fingers intertwined, knuckles white. "It's just, I don't like this is all, Alex. I don't like the way this is going."

"I'll set it up for the morning," Shoffler says.

For a moment, the false accusation gets to me — to be accused of such a thing. I can write the sound bites myself, imagine the breathless but somber delivery:

"More developments in the case of the missing Callahan twins: Police found a blood-soaked T-shirt in the father's house."

"Police have requested that the father take a polygraph test."

But my wounded outrage about being accused, the flare of sadness — these emotions persist for only a few seconds. They barely register against the despair that's enveloped me since Shoffler displayed Kevin's blood-drenched T-shirt. The one glimmer of hope came from a thought that in itself was so hideous I hate to admit to it: *there was only one T-shirt, not two*. Maybe two kids *were* too much trouble. And it was Kevin's shoe, too. Maybe Sean . . .

I'm sinking.

It isn't that consciously I've put much into believing that Shoffler and the authorities will track down whoever took my sons, will find Kevin and Sean and bring them home. Yet on some level I invested more in that idea than I realized. I put faith in the professionalism and energy of the authorities, in their manpower and resources, in helicopters, search grids, canine trackers, evidence technicians, and databases.

But if the request that I take a polygraph means — and what else can it mean? — they think I played some active role in my sons' disappearance, then there's no hope. The authorities are so far off the track that I may as well put my faith in the yellow ribbons neighbors have begun to string around the trees up and down Ordway Street.

chapter 11

The polygraph test is scheduled for this morning at eleven. Despite my innocence, I can't help worrying. How can a machine designed to measure galvanic response (and I have only a vague idea what this is) distinguish kinds of stress? How can a mechanical device separate anxiety about telling deliberate lies from anxiety about taking the test, about being falsely accused, about the fate of my missing children?

Mostly, though, the test is a distraction — almost a welcome one — from the horror of the T-shirt. And although I don't look forward to the walk to the car, especially since Shoffler failed to keep news about the "child's blood-soaked T-shirt" from leaking to the press, in a way I can't wait to get out of the house. Hour by hour, the atmosphere becomes more suffocating, a bell jar of anguished waiting.

Every time the phone rings — which is at least once every five minutes — we wait, suspended between hope and fear.

Mostly fear. We're relieved when the call

offers no information about the boys, when it's just another call from the press or the police, from a friend or a stranger wanting to help. The cliché turns out to be true. No news is good news; no news feels like a reprieve.

My parents and Liz may be incensed over the accusations against me, but with Jack I'd have to say the jury's out. He's not sure. In some ways, this is easier to take than my mother's constant litany of affronted woe.

My father wants to go with me to the police station, even Liz makes the offer, but I won't put them through it.

At this morning's press conference, which we all watched in the family room, Shoffler refused to answer questions or comment about the bloody T-shirt and warned against "leaping to conclusions."

Still, I know what to expect when I step out the door.

And then it's time. Christiansen arrives with a fellow officer to escort me to the squad car. Although I'm not in handcuffs or shackles, *escorting* doesn't begin to describe how I'm hustled down the steps and propelled through the shouting, strobe-dappled crowd.

I'm not under arrest yet, but the body

language of my companions makes it clear what this is: a perp walk. I fight against my natural inclination to avoid eye contact. It's not easy. Reflex alone makes me want to turn my head and avert my eyes from the constant explosions of light. I work to keep my head up. By the time we get to the car, I'm blind from the dazzle.

Christiansen pushes me inside. I'm being transported to the Park Street station for the polygraph. D.C. is involved now because there are "jurisdictional questions to be resolved, dependent on the location and the nature of the crime." This is the way Shoffler explained it at this morning's press conference, for which, Christiansen tells me, they badged 318 representatives of the media.

Like most authorities, Shoffler didn't explain what he said — despite pleas from the press.

I got it, though — along with the millions of Americans who watched various "experts" deconstruct Shoffler's statement. It comes down to this.

Scenario 1: I murdered my kids at home, disposed of their bodies, then drove sixty miles to Cromwell, Maryland. I then wandered around the fairgrounds for a couple of hours to establish my alibi before reporting the kids missing. Jurisdiction: D.C.

Scenario 2: I murdered my children in Maryland, somewhere in the vicinity of the Renaissance Faire. Jurisdiction: Anne Arundel County.

Scenario 3: The boys were kidnapped from the Renaissance Faire (this has now been referred to by at least one broadcaster as "the father's version of events"). Jurisdiction: Anne Arundel County in conjunction with the FBI.

The police station has a kind of played-out atmosphere that against all odds calms me down. It's so different from the adrenalized energy at home. It reminds me of the DMV.

I get the sense that most of the people who work here, from clerk to detective, see enough barbarity on a regular basis that it's blunted their emotional response. No matter how unthinkable a crime — even the murder of children — there's a precedent, a number for it in the criminal code.

It's all procedure. There's a process to deal with every conceivable type of human wrongdoing, a process that doesn't leave much room for passion or outrage. While I'm here, everyone — if not exactly polite — at least treats me with professional disdain, interested only in advancing that process. I'm here for a polygraph test; the idea is to get it done and move on to the next chore.

Just like getting fingerprinted, though, there's something sordid about the procedure. I feel trapped, caught in a lose-lose situation, the lie detector test a not-so-modern version of the test given to the Salem witches. As I remember it (from a History Channel special), if the accused woman, weighted down with stones, managed not to drown — as a normal person would — it signified guilt and she was burned as a witch.

The test is the same. Just being asked to take a polygraph counts against me. I won't fail the test, but as someone who's covered a lot of court cases, I know it's possible the result will be "inconclusive."

If I pass, that won't help. It's just that refusing it would have been worse. *Passing* means nothing because no one actually trusts the results — which, I am reminded, as the technician asks me to take a seat, are not "admissible in court." He offers a thin smile.

"Kind of makes you wonder why they bother," I hear myself say, instantly irritated by my nervous chatter.

He shrugs. "The results can be instructive," he says, "even if not on the evidentiary level."

We both know why they *bother* with lie detector tests. They can be instructive in many ways. It means one thing if someone agrees to take the test, another if he hires his own technician, who might frame a slightly different set of questions or put them in a more client-friendly way.

Gary Condit took the test, but hired his own tech. Same with the parents of JonBenet Ramsey. I remember these deviations from the accepted path of innocent behavior. So does everybody else.

For the most part the test is a form of pressure, pure and simple. You have a suspect, you squeeze him, make him nervous in every possible way. We've all seen it a million times. That's what Shoffler wants: to squeeze me.

The technician squirts gel onto the sensors and attaches them to my skin. The gel is very cold.

The polygraph man himself also seems cold — even mechanical — as he explains the procedure. After a long pause to check his machinery, he begins to ask me his list of prepared questions.

The inflection of his voice does not vary,

whether he's asking me routine establishing questions ("Is your name Alex?" "Do you reside in North Dakota?" "Is the shirt you are wearing blue?") or the ones at the heart of the matter ("Did you kill Sean and Kevin Callahan?" "Do you know the whereabouts of Sean and Kevin?")

There is a long interval between each question while he adjusts his machine and makes notes. I catch myself holding my breath when I'm answering the questions and can't stop myself from mentioning this. The technician offers a weak smile. "That won't matter," he says, in a way that does not reassure me.

And then it's over. I'm handed a foil-wrapped wipe to remove any residue of gel from my skin. I roll down my sleeves expecting to return to the squad car and be driven home.

Instead, Shoffler materializes, with a young African-American man he introduces as Detective Price.

The three of us go to Price's cubicle. On the monitor, tropical fish swim through waving aquatic vegetation. The gray fabric walls of the cubicle display a dozen or more photographs of a little smiling boy.

"Tell me something, Alex," Shoffler asks, "you mind going through your story one more time? I'd like Detective Price to hear it — he's been assigned to assist us with the case."

I shrug. I don't see the point, but once again, why not? "Fine."

"Thing is, Detective Price has some special training in . . . ah . . . questioning people. What I hear is he's got a real gift for tickling the memory bank. What I hope is maybe you'll come up with something that will help us find your sons."

"Some kind of lead," Price says in an earnest baritone. "That's what we all want."

This is bullshit and all three of us know it. Shoffler's looking for inconsistencies in my story. Which means that's what he thinks it is — a *story*.

"Whatever you want," I say.

A heavyset woman with huge round earrings raps on the side of the cubicle wall. "Yoo-hoo, need you to sign something, Jason." She beckons with one red-nailed finger. "Come to my parlor please."

Shoffler studies the array of photographs pinned to the cubicle walls. "Cute kid," he says, and then he lets out a regretful jet of air. "Jeez, I'm sorry."

"What about the ticket?" I ask him.

"What?"

"Ticket to the fair. One adult, two children. I showed it to you. I think I *gave* it to you, didn't I?"

"Yeah."

"It's got the time right on it, when we went in. One adult, two kids."

Shoffler shakes his head, his face showing a kind of get-real look. "Alex — you do realize this ticket means nothin'." His hands rise up, fall down. "You could have bought a ticket for one adult and ten kids, you know what I'm saying?"

To my surprise, I'm embarrassed.

Acoustics.

Liz and I did the backpack thing right out of William and Mary. In London, we went to St. Paul's Cathedral and climbed halfway up the dome to the Whispering Gallery. Our guidebook noted an acoustical anomaly: someone halfway across the vast dome could whisper against the wall and the sound, if unimpeded, would travel around to anyone listening on the opposite side. Liz insisted we try it out, and we took up our positions, waiting several minutes until no one was in the way. I still remember the shock of Liz's voice in my ear, so intimate and immediate, when I could see her only as a small shape across a distance of a hundred yards or so. "Meet me back at the hotel," she whispered, "and I'll show you a good time."

Through some trick of acoustics, I now hear Detective Price's voice, although I can't even see him in the crowded and noisy space of the police station. His words float to my ear, precise and clear. "No, that's what I'm telling you. That's why we're going for it. The guy is *not* lawyered up — you believe that? Not yet, anyway."

He sits across from me, straddling a chair, arms making a kind of platform upon which he rests his handsome head. "You must be sick of this," he says, with a sad swivel of his head. "I can only imagine."

Price is good, I have to acknowledge that. I was expecting — I don't know — gamesmanship, I guess. Good cop, bad cop with Shoffler, I don't know. Some kind of heavy manners.

It's not like that. It's just me and Detective Price in the room. Shoffler is nowhere in sight, although I don't doubt he's behind the long mirror against the opposite wall.

I give my permission for the use of a tape recorder.

We start by going through my account of Saturday one more time, in great detail.

Then we move on to my finances.

"It's tough, isn't it, running two separate households on more or less the same income?"

I admit that it's a strain, financially, but tell Price that Liz and I are getting by.

"I understand you were late with your support payments on two occasions."

I nod. "That's true. But it wasn't because of the money. I was abroad. On assignment. You can check with the station."

"Abroad," Price says. His face twitches when he repeats the word, as if he just got a whiff of something unpleasant. "Abroad," he says again. "I see."

He says nothing for a good long minute or two. I look at my feet and resist the urge to fill in the silence. Price rocks back on his chair, then tilts his head and looks at me. "The preliminary separation agreement takes a good chunk out of your salary, right?"

I nod.

"Your house — that's a pricey neighborhood, isn't it? If you don't work things out with Liz, you're going to have to sell, isn't that right?"

I shrug. "That's true." And then, before

I can stop myself: "I don't care about that. It's not important to me."

I hesitate. I don't like the way I'm trying to explain myself to this guy. I don't like the way he refers to my wife by her first name. He's never even met her.

"So will you lose the house?"

I suddenly get angry. "What are you saying? You think I killed my kids because I don't want to move out of Cleveland Park? Is that what you think? *Jesus*."

He makes a conciliatory gesture. "Okay, new subject. Did the boys have insurance? Some policy out there? Because if they did, it would be best if you told us now."

"Insurance? You mean medical insurance?"

Price shakes his head. "I mean life insurance."

"Life insurance? They're six years old!"

Then I get it, and my voice, angry and too loud, shows it. "Now you're suggesting I killed my kids for insurance!? What — and after a decent interval, I'm going to cash in and move to fucking Brazil! Are you out of your mind?"

"No," Price says, his voice calm and reasonable. "No one's suggesting anything of the sort. We're just talking about the pressures you're under, that's all, we're just exploring that area. Personally, I think it's far more likely that someone like you — you simply lost your temper, the way you did just now, and it went a little further than you intended, you know . . ."

Of course, I go ballistic. *"Look,"* I say, my voice shaking. "I didn't kill my children."

"Mr. Callahan. Maybe we should take a break here. Maybe you *should* consult an attorney."

"I don't need a break and I don't need a fucking attorney."

"Did Detective Shoffler tell you that someone saw you in the parking lot, opening your car — and this was after you reported the boys missing."

"I was checking to see if the boys went to the car when they couldn't find me. The security guy — he suggested it."

It goes on like this. One hour, two hours, three, four. We're into hour five, when Price, after asking me if I need to use the facilities, excuses himself to do so. When he comes back, he brings me some water and suggests we go over the whole story again.

We do. "Remind me," he starts, "whose idea was it to go to this festival? You come up with that?"

"No," I tell him, "I've told you. It was

their idea. It's not my kind of thing."

"What is your kind of thing?"

It goes on.

"You say you heard Kevin's voice on your cell phone," Price says when we reach that point. "He said one word: 'Daddy.' So what I want to know is — how you could tell it was Kevin? They're identical twins, right?"

"They're my kids. I could tell."

"You could *tell*." Price makes quotation marks in the air.

"That's right."

He looks as if he's about to challenge this, but then he smiles. "I guess I can accept that." He shakes his head. "Must have been rough, though," he says with what seems to be genuine concern. "Tantalizing." A regretful sigh. "Just that one word, and then he never called back."

"No. That was it."

"Boy," Price says, then suddenly veers off in another direction. "Why don't you tell me about the night *before*. Hmmmm?"

"I don't see —"

"Do you *not* want to talk about that?" He frowns and then apologizes, as if he's inadvertently hit a sore spot.

"No, I don't mind talking about it. I just —"

Price shrugs. "Look, you never know when something's gonna come up that will help."

I nod.

"Okay, so the night before — Friday night — you said you had a lot of work to do. So, let's talk about dinner, okay? You cook, or did you eat out?"

"We ate out. Pizza."

"What pizza? Where?"

"The Two Amys — on Wisconsin."

"Anyone see you?"

"Sure. The waiter, other customers."

"You pay with a credit card or cash?"

"Probably a credit card."

"You don't remember."

"I don't remember."

He waves the significance of this away, tosses me a smile. "I don't always keep track of that kind of shit, either."

Jason Price has a powerful charm and he uses it all to persuade me that he wants to be my friend, he really does. And the way to get in tight with my new friend is to tell him what he wants to hear. And what he wants to hear — not that he'd hold it against me, he's had some bad moments with Derrick, he wouldn't lie to me — is that I did it. I lost it, we all do, it's the human condition. Nobody is under control 100 percent of the time. And so on.

I'm making it sound hokey and easy to dismiss, but it isn't like that. It's an almost religious yearning, the impulse to confess. If only I could confess, I'd be cleansed and reborn, I could start over.

As the hours slide by, I begin to slip into a dangerous apathy. I want to stop talking. I want to sleep.

I've read more than once about survivors pulled back from the brink. There's a point where the will begins to fade. Just before freezing to death, the victim of hypothermia is said to get warm and sleepy; the drowning person, to find himself immersed in a burst of light. I take it from such accounts that oblivion can be enticing, a welcome respite from struggle and pain.

We're going over the journey through the fairgrounds yet again when someone raps on the door. Detective Price frowns, says "excuse me one moment," gets up, opens the door a crack, conducts a brief conversation with someone else. Although this discussion is conducted at the volume of a whisper, I can tell it's an argument. Then, without a word, he leaves me alone.

I wait in a kind of dull reverie, checking my watch every few minutes. Ten minutes go by. Twenty. Half an hour.

When Price comes back, he launches into a whole new line of questioning, one that baffles me.

"What is your religion, Alex?"

"What?"

"Your religious conviction. Your faith."

"I'm not very religious."

"Are you an atheist, then?"

"No, not exactly. What does this have to do with anything?"

"Bear with me, okay? Say you had to check off a box, for instance — would you check off *atheist?*"

"No. I'm sort of a lapsed Catholic. I — I don't know. I'd check off *Christian,* I guess."

"You guess."

There are questions about what I think about animal sacrifice, about a piece I once did about Santería in south Florida, about my spiritual convictions, my opinion on religions such as Wicca.

"Look," I say finally, "where are we going with this? I don't understand the relevance."

"You don't like this line of questioning?" Price asks, a surprised frown on his face.

"I just don't get it," I tell him.

"It's not idle curiosity," he says. "I can

assure you of that."

And looking at him, at the professionally disappointed expression on his face, I finally realize that no amount of cooperation on my part is going to exonerate me. I'm trying to prove a null hypothesis — and you just can't do that. No matter how many questions I answer correctly, Jason Price is interested only in answers that point toward my guilt. And since I'm not guilty, there's no reason to sit here and endure this.

I tell him I want to go home.

"You refuse to submit to further questioning."

"I don't see the point."

"You refuse. Is that what you're telling me?"

I shake my head. "You don't quit, do you?"

Jason Price offers a thin smile. "Is that a yes?"

I decide to oblige him. What can it matter? "Yes," I say. "I refuse."

Price gets up. He leaves me alone in the room.

chapter 12

A rap on the door jolts me out of a half-sleep. I don't know how much time has passed, but it's Shoffler, not Price, who steps into the room. "Let's go," he says.

I know right away that something's happened. His attitude toward me has changed, but in a way I can't read. He turns off the tape recorder, and I follow him out to his car. It's a big white Ford, a Crown Victoria. It's daytime — morning. I spent the night in the interrogation room.

It scares me when Shoffler holds open the door for me. Why is he suddenly solicitous of my feelings? *Because: He feels sorry for me.*

When he gets in and fastens his seat belt, I brace myself, rigid against the expected somber tone, the terrible news, the very worst news. It isn't until we've gone a couple of blocks that I realize I'm holding my breath.

"The test came back," Shoffler says, shaking his head.

"What?" This is not what I'm expecting,

and my relief is immediate and profound. "You mean the polygraph test?"

"No," Shoffler says. "No — the lab test. The test on the T-shirt." He lets out a jet of air as he steers the car around a corner.

"And . . . what?"

"Chicken blood," he says, with a quick look my way. "The shirt was soaked in chicken blood."

"Chicken blood!" I repeat, elated. I'm not sure what it means, but it's good news, I know that much. The blood was not human blood. It wasn't my *kid's* blood.

"UmmmHmmmm," Shoffler says.

I realize now what Jason Price was getting at with his questions about religion and animal sacrifice. My elation fades.

"Look," Shoffler says, "we pretty much, well, we also came up with some solid witnesses who saw you at the fair with the boys."

"Huh."

"Coupla fair employees," Shoffler goes on. "The guy who runs the Jacob's ladder — he remembered your boys real well. Told us one of the kids climbed the ladder like a monkey."

"Sean."

Shoffler nods. "Yeah, well for a while after your kid got to the top, there was a big line to try the ladder — older kids who figured if the little guy could do it, it must be a piece of cake. At a buck a try, the guy who ran the concession was grateful, so he had a good reason to remember."

"He just sort of came out of the woodwork?"

"Had the Sunday and Monday off, so we didn't get to him until this morning. He's a local, doesn't travel with the fair. And then after we questioned him, we wanted to check him out." A sigh. "Make sure he doesn't know you, doesn't know Liz, doesn't know the kids — that kind of thing. Actually, we got a number of fair employees who saw you and the kids. The guy who runs the archery concession — he remembers you and your boys real well. And there were others."

"Hunh."

"After we found that T-shirt, we had to check, you understand? Because if you went to the fair to set up an alibi — well . . ."

"I guess."

"Look" — Shoffler is irritated and makes a dismissive gesture with his hand — "The chicken blood, all the people who saw you — none of that lets you off the hook."

"No?"

"Think about it. Even if you're at the fair with the boys, who's to say you didn't take them somewhere afterwards, you know? — then go back to Prebble yellin' about how you can't find your kids. The chicken blood? I don't know. Maybe you got a secret life." A blue Mercedes SUV cuts him off, and he reacts by hitting the horn. "Jesus, look at that guy. I should stick on the bubble. Anyway, what does get you off the hook is we got your afternoon pieced together now from stand-up witness to stand-up witness, got you covered from the time you dropped off the tape at the TV station with the kids in tow to the time you showed up at security saying the kids were missing." He pauses. "So . . . looks like I owe you an apology, Alex."

We're sitting at a light. My euphoria lasts about as long as it takes for the light to turn. Yes, it feels good that I'm no longer a suspect. But the kids are still gone. It's still the same nightmare.

I say nothing.

"I'm sorry about the polygraph test," Shoffler continues, "and that whole routine with Price. I apologize. I really do."

"You thought I did it."

He shrugs.

We turn onto Klingle Road and head toward Connecticut. I look out the window, shake my head. "And in the meantime, whoever took my kids has all the time in the world . . ."

I think of the kidnapper with my kids, in my *house,* that creepy folded rabbit, the line of dimes, the shirt soaked in blood. And me in the interrogation room — and all the while the trail getting colder.

I rant on about this, and Shoffler just lets me go at it until finally, it seems pointless to continue. Out the window, a couple of little kids holding balloons from the zoo walk past with their mother. *If only we'd gone to the zoo.* I try to suppress these useless excursions into rearranging the past, but they pop up at least a hundred times a day. I press my eyes shut.

After a while, Shoffler says: "This man with the dog, at the jousting ring. Got a couple of witnesses claim they saw him with your boys."

My heart goes cold. "You think that's the guy?"

"Well . . . we don't want to get ahead of ourselves. The tall man, the dog with the ruff — all that was in the news, so we take everything with a grain of salt. Still, we start asking if anyone saw the missing twins with this guy? And of course people *did* see this. Or at least they" — he makes quotation marks in the air — "think so."

"They think so."

"Lucky for us, somehow it never got into the news what kind of dog it was — so that gives us a kinda litmus test for the witnesses. We know it was a whippet, so if they saw a man with a German shepherd or a dachshund . . ."

"Right."

"I was gonna ask you about what kinda look you got at the guy? You remember his face?"

I hesitate. I can bring the scene up in my memory, but what I was looking for was Kevin and Sean, to reassure myself they were still where they were supposed to be. As soon as I spotted them in the crowd of cheering kids, I relaxed. "I don't know," I tell Shoffler. "I didn't really pay attention. I noticed his costume, and the dog. I thought he worked for the fair."

"I'd like to put you with a sketch artist — see what you come up with. I'll set it up."

The light changes and we turn onto Connecticut. "I've got a press conference at five," Shoffler says. "You want to join me? You and Liz? I mean it's your vindication. You maybe ought to be there to take questions."

There's no maybe about it. I know what Claire Carosella would tell me. If it will maximize airtime, Liz and I will stand in front of the crowd of reporters all night.

I know from experience what it will be like. They'll shout each other down for the right to lob questions at us. The questions will be either rhetorical ("Are you relieved that suspicion has been lifted from your shoulders?") or impossible to answer ("Do you feel the police are getting closer to finding your boys?").

"We'll be there," I tell him.

•

In the next two days, energetic friends and neighbors rally around. Now that I'm no longer a suspect, the floodgates are open again. The household is inundated with food — casseroles, cookies, salads, enormous baskets stuffed with every imaginable edible.

Ordway Street is aglow with yellow ribbons. Connecticut Avenue is decorated, too, for blocks in both directions.

A courier brings handmade cards from the boys' fellow campers at St. Albans: Magic-Marker flowers, carefully printed words of support, cramped and juvenile signatures.

The accumulation of teddy bears and flowers left at the curb gets to me. They remind me of roadside displays at crash sites, the posthumous tributes in Oklahoma City, the heaps of flowers and stuffed animals that followed Princess Di's accident, the mounds of commemorative tribute outside Ground Zero. Funerary offerings.

The police established a hotline and although they discourage the idea of a second one, a tag team of neighbors can't be stopped. Jack organizes the volunteers who run this "totline," coordinating their shifts. Unlike the official hotline, this one promises a reward plus confidentiality.

My old friend Ezra Sidran, a computer genius, sponsors the construction of a website: findkevinandsean.com. Liz's friend Molly launches a drive to enroll volunteers to monitor the site. Within two days it's pulling in almost four hundred hits an hour.

Since I've been exonerated, the station revives the reward fund, with Krista herself doing stand-ups to make appeals. Fox tops up its original seed money with another five grand. The station's accounting firm contributes time to receive and tally contributed funds. Within a few days, the fund holds more than $90,000.

A trio of Liz's old running buddies organizes the printing and distribution of thousands of flyers. For the most part, we're captives in the house, but we're told that the boys' faces are on every conceivable storefront, bus shelter, telephone pole, each flyer with its little fringe of tear-offs imprinted with the hotline number and Web address.

I have a conference with Mary McCafferty, the private eye I hired to help search for the boys. She explains to me what she's done, which is mostly to "troll for clues" by interviewing dozens of our friends and acquaintances — and new friends and acquaintances of Liz and the boys up in Maine. This has produced "nothing so far." Recently, she's been concentrating her efforts on household help: plumbers, babysitters, plaster repair guys, dishwasher installers, painters (I gave her the entire file of home-repair receipts). "It's amazing how many times it turns out to be someone like that."

"But not in this case."

"Not so far."

I work with a police artist named

Marijke Wilcke, trying to dredge up the image of the man with the dog. Since I just caught a glimpse of the guy, I'm not optimistic. Shoffler insists "Dutchie," as he calls Marijke, is "real good at coaxing details outta eyewitnesses. She's just about a genius."

We have trouble right away, trying to establish the shape of the man's face. The fact that he was wearing a ruff, too, creates problems, not only because it makes it hard for me to determine the length of his face, but also because it obscures the conjunction of neck and shoulder, his jawline, even his ears. The neatly trimmed goatee and mustache don't help, either. Despite Marijke's skill at translating my vague impressions onto the page, the result is vague and generic. The man stares blankly back from the final image, neatly groomed hair and trimmed goatee and mustache, just as I remember it, but the rest is just a guess.

Shoffler stops by to take a look.

"What do you think?" Marijke asks.

"Looks like they're all on the same bus."

"What?"

"Marijke and Larry — he's another sketch artist — they been through this with three other eyewitnesses who saw this guy with your kids." To Marijke he says: "Go on. Give him the tour."

She brings up in sequence five versions of the man with the dog, all of which prominently feature the goatee and sharply trimmed mustache. Apart from that, the sketches vary in head shape and other features. "Facial hair," Marijke sighs, "especially when it is trimmed into geometric shapes and clean lines — it's just so dramatic it makes the other features fade. What you remember is the facial hair. Maybe," she says in her slightly accented English, "it's even pasted on."

Shoffler shakes his head.

"And that ruff around his neck — that's another problem."

Marijke flicks back to my sketch. "You are happy with this one?" she asks me.

I shrug. "I guess."

When she taps her mouse a few times, the hair and the beard and mustache disappear. Clean-shaven, the man could be anybody.

"I make a composite from all of them," Marijke says, "then I do one with the facial hair, one clean-shaven, okay?"

The official position shifts. With the boys stipulated as the victims of a kidnapping, an FBI agent is assigned to the case.

Shoffler tells me ahead of time that Judy Jones is very young but very smart. "A rookie, but a real firecracker."

We gather in the family room. Shoffler introduces her and she explains to us that the Bureau's involvement in kidnapping cases has been routine since the Lindbergh case.

Liz sits next to me and holds my hand, although there's nothing intimate about this. We're like two strangers at the site of a disaster, our touch the instinctual clutch for human contact. Liz and I present a united front in public — and that includes sessions like this one. But except for moments when she breaks down and needs — literally — a shoulder to cry on, she's formal and distant, clearly uncomfortable with our forced reunion. I've yet to catch sight of her, for instance, in her bathrobe.

"The depth of the Bureau's involvement varies," Judy Jones says, carefully making eye contact with each of us. "Since we are satisfied with police conduct in the investigation, our role will be limited to support."

Jack immediately protests. "What — the FBI's so hung up on terrorists a couple of kids don't matter? Don't my grandsons deserve your full attention?"

I think the limited role for the Bureau is

a plus, but Jack doesn't see it that way. From the way he goes on about how the boys deserve the best, it's clear that despite the memorable series of FBI screwups over the past decade (Ruby Ridge, Waco, the spy Robert Hanssen, the embarrassing repression of leads in the 9/11 attack, the shocking errors at Bureau labs), Jack harbors fantasies of Bureau efficiency and excellence that go back to Eliot Ness.

Jones assures us that the Bureau's limited role is not because the FBI is "preoccupied with homeland security. We're prepared to lend whatever support Detective Shoffler requires and requests."

"How can you be satisfied with the police conduct?" Jack persists. "They thought Alex was the guy and while they're putting him through the wringer, the real guy's making tracks." He throws up his hands.

"I understand your feelings. With hindsight, we're all geniuses. But you have to understand that there's nothing in the conduct of the case that warrants criticism. As soon as he was summoned, Detective Shoffler took steps to secure the scene — a very difficult scene to secure, by the way. He immediately launched a vigorous search and inquiry. In the time since the boys disappeared, he and his team have questioned a large number of witnesses, some of them more than once. He's made a good liaison with the District police. He's pursued the case by the book, and that includes" — she glances my way and offers a tiny sympathetic grimace — "suspecting and questioning Mr. Callahan."

"How's that?" Jack says, his face red with belligerence. "They waste their time with Alex here, and boom — no one's even looking for my grandsons. Everyone thinks they're dead."

Jones looks down at her fingers — the nails are bitten raw. "In the field of criminal justice," she says, "we are all to a certain extent students of history. We have to rely on known precedent. In suspecting Mr. Callahan, Detective Shoffler was going with history. The truth is that most child abductions and murders are committed by parents — especially when those parents are separated." She hefts the police file. "This kidnapper *didn't* go by the book. You just don't come across many cases — I couldn't find a single one — where a kidnapping occurs many miles from a victim's home and yet the kidnapper returns to that home, where he has one of the victims place a phone call to a parent, a phone call that is not a ransom plea." She shakes her head. "It's all very risky behavior."

"What about the T-shirt?" I ask. "Do you have any theories about that?"

She sighs and glances at Detective Shoffler. "There's nothing in the database, really nothing. Maybe some kind of animal sacrifice. We're looking into that."

Shoffler grimaces. "What I think is maybe the T-shirt was just to throw off pursuit. Not that we let up on other suspects or possibilities. You got two kids missing, the search is really relentless. But until that lab test came back, it was natural to focus certain resources on Alex." He wags his head sadly. "I think the T-shirt was deliberate and it worked like a charm."

"A red herring," Jones says, "almost literally. Except the fish on the T-shirt was a whale instead of a herring."

Liz groans and her head droops.

"This guy is too fucking cute," my father says.

"Detective Shoffler has asked me to pick up a couple of threads in the investigation," Jones tells us. "First, that folded rabbit — I've already checked into that."

"Really — what did you find out?" I ask.

She shrugs. "Not much. We ran it by an origami expert. He said it was cleverly constructed and of high intermediate level, but that's about all he could tell us. It's now with a second expert, but I'm not very confident this lead's going anywhere. Like any other subculture you get into, from skydiving to candlepins — origami has more devotees than you'd think possible."

"What about the material?" Liz asks. "That skin or whatever it is."

"Apparently it does feel like skin. It's called elephant hide. But in fact it's a special kind of paper used in origami."

"Really."

"It stands up to being folded wet, the expert explained. Very commonly available and pretty much the paper of choice at a certain level, especially for animal forms. I'm afraid tracking the source of the paper does not look promising. The Internet alone has dozens of sources."

Liz looks as if she's going to start crying.

"The other area Detective Shoffler has asked me to pursue," Jones says, "is the question of Mr. Callahan's possible enemies. I've got a copy of the list Mr. Callahan supplied, and when we're done here" — she shifts her gaze to me — "I'd like to go over it."

My mother sticks up her hand, as if she's in a classroom. Her face is bright red.

"What if it's because they're *twins,*" she blurts out. "I keep thinking about that Nazi doctor . . . his experiments." She presses her hand to her mouth. "I'm sorry," she says, looking at Liz and me.

My father puts his arm around her shoulder. "I thought of that, too," he says.

This is a possibility I try to keep out of my head. I can't handle it, can't stand the idea of some modern-day Mengele doing things to the boys. They'd be better off dead. And so would I.

"I checked on twins," Judy Jones tells us, with a negative shake of the head, "and I can tell you that in the past twenty years, there are very few cases of twins being kidnapped. Or twins going missing. None at all that seem relevant to this case."

"What about those boys out in L.A.? Lopez? Some kind of Hispanic name." This from Jack.

"The Ramirez twins," I say.

"It sounds like Alex knows why that case isn't relevant," Jones says, with a nod my way.

"Police caught the kidnapper with the bodies of the boys," I tell them. "Then he committed suicide."

"That's about as closed as a case can get," Jones says. "So . . ."

* * *

Liz's mother, Marguerite, flies in from Maine, and nearly requires hospitalization again after fighting in through the press crowd.

Although, already — just one week after the abduction — that is beginning to diminish.

Compassionate strangers keep on volunteering for the search teams — which continue, weather permitting, to comb the area around the fairgrounds. When we can, we join them — Liz, Jack, Liz's mother, my father, and me. Outfitted in cutting-edge gear donated by Tenleytown Outdoor Sports (a friend of a friend of mine owns it), we drive the hour and a half to Cromwell and then separate, according to police direction, each of us joining a different search team.

Mom's eyesight won't allow her to stumble around in brambles and ravines. She stays behind to help with the Power-of-Prayer outreach group launched by one of her friends, working a vast network of e-mail circles.

The single telephone in my study has been joined by half a dozen other receivers, spillover lines installed by the authorities. "If the kidnapper does call," my mother explains to one of her group, "we don't want him to have any trouble getting through."

The phone never stops ringing. When we're at home, we all pitch in to answer calls, logging name, number, and purpose of call on printed information sheets.

Shoffler stops by one afternoon, now ten days after the disappearance. Everyone else is busy so we talk alone.

First he tells me he's getting a lot more information about the man with the dog. "What we're getting is that this guy had kids around him all the time. It's the dog, right? It's a very cute dog. It works like a magnet for this guy. A kid magnet."

"That's what I saw — a bunch of kids petting this dog."

"We got some confirmation from one of the ticket sellers at the gate. He remembers the boys leaving with a man and a dog."

"Remembers them leaving? Really? Where's this ticket seller been?"

"He's kind of a reluctant witness. Has a rap sheet. He wasn't coming forward to volunteer, that's for damn sure. We got to him the second time around. We're going through the whole employee roster again, see — and this time we ask did he see a tall man with a dog and two kids *leaving* the park. Well, this kid, basically a kind of nervous Nellie, a law-abiding citizen except he likes to smoke pot, you know — he worries about it. What if he keeps his mouth shut? Would that be lying? Would that be obstruction? Would that be a parole violation? So, he comes forward."

"Huh."

"I was skeptical, too. How can he remember this? Thousands of people coming and going every single day — half of 'em dressed like Friar Tuck or King Arthur. And we're talking about more than a week ago now."

"Ten days."

"Right. So anyway, here's what the guy tells me. He doesn't really remember the twins, just two kids about the same size; he didn't really look at 'em. What he remembers is that the group struck him as weird."

"The group?"

"The two kids, the man, the dog. I ask what does he mean. He's got knights and princesses up the kazoo, he's got boatloads of Goths and . . . this little group strikes him as weird? Weird how? Weird why? And what he tells me is he noticed that the man was in costume, the *dog* was in costume — but the kids were not. That didn't make sense to him. Usually, he said, it's the other way around."

"Hunh."

"When he said that, it rang true, you know? It's not the kind of thing you'd make up. Plus, he nailed the dog."

"Said it was a whippet?"

Shoffler pulls out his notebook, puts on his glasses. He's very attached to his notebooks, and he writes everything down. Sometimes he'll refer to notes several times in the course of a conversation. He's got hundreds of notebooks. He jokes that one day he'll write his memoirs.

Now he finds what he's looking for. "Yeah, so here it is. I ask him what kind of dog the tall guy has, and he tells me it's 'one of those fast dogs. Like a greyhound, but not as big.' "

"There you go."

"So then I ask him what the owner was wearing. And he says: 'I told you — a costume.' I keep at it: what *kind* of costume? He tells me his sister got him the job, he's not into this Renaissance shit. Then he points out the obvious — people don't come to Renaissance fairs dressed up like cowboys or superheroes."

"Right." I can tell Shoffler is excited about this, but I can't see where he's going.

"The guy's getting real tired of me," the detective says, "but I press him. Can he be more specific? Well, the tall man wasn't a king. He wasn't a knight. The guy didn't know *what* he was. His costume — it had this ruff, same crazy neckware as the skinny dog. And then he tells me the guy wore some kind of tights and he had a *flute*.' " Shoffler looks up at me, peering over his reading glasses. "I say hold it, he had a *flute?* Cause I got that from one other source, but I didn't make much of it. The kid brightens, you know, like he's just had a realization. 'I think that's it,' he tells me. 'The guy wore this jacket, you know, four different colors. And the flute. That's what he was supposed to be: the Pied Piper.' "

Shoffler closes his notebook. He looks pleased with himself, but I feel a skitter of dread down the back of my neck. How did the fairy tale go? The way I remember, the Piper got rid of the village's rats, but the town wouldn't pay up. He piped a tune and all the children followed him. And then — didn't the children disappear?

chapter 13

I always know how long it's been since the boys disappeared. I don't have to do the math; it's instantly available. Today, as I drive my parents to the airport, it's been twenty-one days, eight hours and change.

I suggested they go home (as Jack and Marguerite did a week ago) and it didn't take much to get past their token resistance.

In the terminal, my mother hugs me for a long time, then dabs at her tears. My father gives me a manly abrazo. I linger outside the security bay and watch a bald man with bulky shoulders pull my mother aside for extra scrutiny. Stripped of her bright yellow linen blazer, she stands with her arms outstretched so he can pass the wand around her. He does this so slowly and methodically, her arms begin to shake from the effort of holding the position.

This is how unreliable my grip on my emotions has become: One second I'm just observing the bald man harass my mother and the next I'm incandescent with rage. It takes a real effort not to bust through the security gate and go after the guy. I'd like to take him down. I'd like his head to hit the floor. I can already hear the mantra — "I was just doing my job" — but I don't buy it. If he's trying to focus on likely terrorists, he's wasting everybody's time and money harassing my mother. He's not "just doing his job"; he's on a power trip.

As the days roll by, the media hoopla continues to fade. Kevin and Sean are relegated to the occasional news update. The calls and e-mails, volunteers and donations fall off too. The hotline grows lukewarm, the yellow ribbons start to tatter and fade, the posters of the boys disappear from store windows, displaced by announcements of choral music programs, missing dogs, Run for the Cure bulletins.

Meanwhile, the police are doing "everything we can" — which isn't much. At least for a while, there continue to be leads, and each one causes in me a brief hope before Shoffler declares it a dead end.

He drops by one night with packages of Chinese food. He tells us they've been working hard on the subculture of Renaissance festivals, "looking for the tall man, circulating everything — sketches, descriptions, the dog, the whole shebang. You wouldn't believe how many medieval enthusiasts are out there."

"How many Pied Pipers can there be?" Liz asks.

"You shouldn't think of him that way," the detective cautions between bites of lo mein. "The costume might have been deliberate — you know, a disguise. It's like guys in uniform. Say we have a burglary, a bank job — whatever. Man's in a UPS uniform, mechanic coveralls, maintenance man blues — that's all anyone remembers."

"So what about the guy," I ask, "the tall man? You getting anywhere?"

Shoffler makes a face. "So far," he says, "nothing but Elvis sightings."

Cromwell. Most days, I drive out to join the core volunteers, the ones who continue to show up every single day, even in the stultifying heat, to search. I make the long drive willingly; it feels good to get out of the house and do something.

Although I realize, one day, struggling through the underbrush in the area outside the fairgrounds, that I'm participating in the search with no hope of finding any trace of the boys — but also with no fear of doing so. I don't believe I'm going to see a small crumpled form, the clothing intact, the flesh melting into the leaves and sticks. Liz is different. When she makes the trip, she searches with a stricken intensity that conveys all too well what she expects to find.

Me — I think the boys are with The Piper, whoever he may be, and although by now the dangers of "denial" have been pressed on me many times and I know I may be fooling myself, I still think Kevin and Sean are alive. This makes searching with the volunteers in Cromwell almost a kind of ritual, a form of devotion to the cause of finding the boys, like saying a prayer or making a pilgrimage.

Some of the Cromwell volunteers alarm me. I wonder about their ardor for the task, their willingness to wade into yet another patch of the poison ivy–choked, bug-infested terrain. By now, I've grown to know many of them. Although most have just latched on to this search the way others might fasten their efforts to fund-raising for breast cancer or lobbying for a new playground, there's something unsettling about a few of them. The dark fervor in the eyes of one man disturbs me, as does the quasi-religious devotion of a couple of women.

I wonder what the rest of their lives are like, that they can afford this huge investment of time. Once in a while, I find myself thinking one of them might be involved with the abduction, an accomplice, reporting back to The Piper. Although I feel guilty for harboring such thoughts, I've compiled a file of their names and addresses, their jobs and marital histories, their quirks and hobbies. I've turned it over to the P.I., Mary McCafferty.

The situation between Liz and me continues to deteriorate. During the first few days after the boys were abducted, what happened was so terrible, we took some comfort in our common loss.

That's long gone, replaced at first by a Jack-like formality from Liz that's slowly segued into something even less friendly. When we're in the same room now, she can't seem to stay in her chair. When our eyes meet, hers skid away from mine.

Behind it all is the undeniable fact that at rock bottom, she blames me. This comes up more and more, in the form of "if only" scenarios.

I tell myself it's the same in the aftermath of any disaster: Once over the shock, the loved ones of victims look around for a way in which the event could have been prevented. I remember this from many assignments, the anguished faces of mourners after preventable disasters (the Rhode Island nightclub fire, the Florida Valujet crash, the explosion of the shuttle): "It's such a tragedy because *it didn't have to happen.*" It plays out in our legal system — suits are filed before the flames die down. The litigation of blame.

In this case, there's no need for inquiry or reconstruction. I'm the embodiment of "human error." And as the agent who could have prevented the catastrophe, I am slowly becoming — in the heart and mind of my wife — its cause.

We attend a fund-raiser sponsored by the Center for Abducted Children. It seemed impossible to refuse, but the event itself is tough to stomach. Liz and I sit at the dais, along with other celebrities of misfortune. Some of the parents wear laminated photographs of their children pinned to their chests like identity badges, a heartbreaking gallery of winsome smiles and sparkling eyes.

Dozens of strangers offer help and sympathy but there's something about all this that sets my teeth on edge. In some cases, I get the impression that it's a weird kind of stardust they're really after.

The main speech is delivered by a single mother named Melinda. She tells the harrowing tale of her eight-year-old daughter's abduction in the simple but powerful way of a born storyteller. She makes all the right pauses for effect. Eight years after the girl went missing, her remains were discovered buried in a neighbor's yard.

"All told, about one hundred children a year are kidnapped and murdered by strangers," she tells us. "Despite the saturation coverage such abductions and murders get from the media, that makes it one of the rarest of crimes. A child is more likely to be hit by lightning." She pauses. "Some of us have been hit by that kind of lightning." She crosses her hands over her heart, according a sad nod to some of us seated at the head table. One of the women lets out a lone sob. "When it does happen," Melinda tells us in a husky voice, "it's lightning fast. 74 percent of these kids — my daughter Bonnie was one of them — are killed within three hours of their abduction.

"Of the children who were abducted," Melinda continues, "the vast majority, seventy-six percent, were girls, with the average age being eleven. In eighty percent of the cases, the children were grabbed within a quarter mile of their homes. So don't feel your child is safe in your front yard, or riding her bike down your block. It's the same with car accidents, most of which occur within a mile of home. The vast majority of other types of accidents occur in the home as well. Our homes, ladies and gentlemen, may be our castles — but they are not fortresses."

While she pauses for effect, I think: *Kevin and Sean* don't fit. They're not girls, they're much younger than the average age, they were more than fifty miles from home. *And there were two of them.*

"So we need the resources to act fast, too," Melinda says. Her timing, as she launches into the plea for funds, is impeccable. I'm not surprised to learn that she's pursuing a new career as a motivational speaker or that she's written a book, *Keeping Our Children Safe*, full of pointers about how to protect children from predators without at the same time scaring them silly. The book is available outside the banquet room. Ten percent of the proceeds go to the center.

After the public departs, there's a prayer circle for parents and relatives of the missing. We sit on folding chairs, holding hands. My neighbor clutches mine with such a ferocious grip, I almost lose feeling in my fingers. After the minute of silence, we take turns reciting aloud the details of our personal catastrophes.

I walk out when I realize that most of those in the circle are in fact grieving. They've come to share coping strategies for what they regard — except for the ritual nod to an unlikely miracle — as the permanent loss of their children. Like the parents and spouses of MIA victims lost in Vietnam, they no longer seek their "loved ones." What they're after is something else, something always referred to as "closure." In other words: the remains. Evidence of death.

"I can't stay here," I whisper in my wife's ear. "They think their kids are dead." When I stand up to leave, she comes with me, but not because she wants to. "Excuse us, please excuse us," she mutters as I yank my hand out of my neighbor's and careen toward the door.

In the car, her eyes are hard and unforgiving. "Who do you think you are, Alex —

judging them about how they were handling their loss?"

"They think their kids are dead. I don't."

Liz bursts into tears.

That night, she makes the announcement: "I'm going back to Maine," she says. She looks at her fingernails and, once again, starts to cry.

The next day, she's gone.

Work. Although Al told me from the moment he heard about the boys that I could forget about work for "as long as it takes," last week I got an e-mail asking me to "clarify" my plans. Either I should come back soon, at least on a part-time basis, or I should request a formal leave of absence, one that specified a time frame and a date of return. The fine print noted that given the circumstances, the station would continue to provide benefits even if I did choose to remain on "compassionate leave." Benefits, yes, but since my absence would require the hiring of a replacement — no "remuneration."

Almost everyone agrees that returning to work is "the best thing." The basis for this conclusion is some sketchy if universal notion of work as distracting and therefore therapeutic. It boils down to this: If I'm too busy to think about my missing sons, I'll be less depressed.

I doubt this.

Getting up, getting dressed, the old familiar commute — it seems so strange to resume this routine. And the station itself feels like foreign terrain. TV stations are crazy places, loud and frantic with energy, everyone always careening toward or recovering from a deadline. Me? I feel inert and idle amid the hive of activity. I exist within a kind of insular bubble created by everyone's elaborate courtesy. Voices lower when I walk by, glances slide away, no one knows what to say to me or how to act in my presence. I can see the wheels turning — should I mention it, or not? When I explain that nothing they can do or say could make me feel worse, they feel rebuffed.

One day, after I return to work, Shoffler drops by. He arrives with a six-pack of Sierra Nevada and a huge soggy pizza. "Health food," he says, with his high-pitched stuttery laugh. "Stick with me and you, too, can be a fat slob."

I'm glad to see him. In fact, I can't think of anyone else I'd rather see at my door — except my sons. For openers, Shoffler is just about the only person in the world who's always ready to talk about the one thing of actual interest to me. Besides, he's cynical, funny and, I've come to realize, very smart. We usually end up going over and over the busted leads to see if there's something we missed: the origami rabbit, the whippet, the witnesses who saw the man getting into a black panel van, the latest Elvis sightings, the chicken blood, the "enemy" list of folks I'd attacked on the air. Shoffler checks his notebooks — he's on his third now. The case file, he tells me, is seven binders thick. Each case, he's explained, starts with a single three-inch loose-leaf binder. The binders — which Shoffler has allowed me to look at — contain copies of every piece of paper generated by the investigation: report, witness statement, interview, crime scene photo, forensics tests, search warrant, search warrant inventory, evidence receipt, and so on.

We eat the pizza, watch an O's game, and shoot the breeze for a while before he gets around to the reason for his visit.

"I hate to tell you this, Alex," he starts, then stops. He's uncomfortable, tapping his fingers against the top of the pizza box, jiggling his foot. At the look on my face, he pushes his hand toward me. "Don't worry. It's not about the boys. There's nothing new. It's about . . . me: I've been taken off the case."

"What?" Shoffler is known as a bulldog, who never lets go, who sacrificed two marriages to work, who spends any spare moment pounding away at his cold cases. "What do you mean? You don't ever close a case. You're famous for that. *Taken off the case?* Why?"

A big sigh. "Here's the deal. It's not just you — all my cases are being reassigned. There's this new thing been in the works ever since 9/11 and it's finally happening: Metro Area Counter-Terrorism Unit." His hands fall open, like a book. "Officers from every jurisdiction, plus a coupla Bureau designates, folks from Customs and INS. I'm the guy from Anne Arundel. Look, I'm sorry."

I say nothing. It's a real blow.

"Your case has been handed over to a young detective named Muriel Petrich. I may be a bulldog, but she's as smart as they get. And ambitious. That's a good combo."

"Right."

"Look, I know. . . ." He shakes his head. "You can count on me to keep my hand in, right? And call me anytime, any reason. You get an idea, a lead, whatever, I'll do what I can. But give Petrich a chance — she's a tiger."

"Right." I can't keep the bitterness out of my voice. I feel Kevin and Sean are being abandoned.

I've fallen into the habit of sleeping in the family room. Half the time, I crash on the futon, dozing off while still in my clothes, to wake at two or three or four, the TV still playing, the lights still blazing. Tonight, as soon as Shoffler leaves, I clear away the beer bottles and pizza debris, I put all the dishes in the dishwasher, turn it on, wipe the counters. Then I make the rounds of the house, turn off the lights, lock the doors, then strip down to my underwear and get into bed.

This is the white iron bed Liz scrimped and saved for. She ought to have it in Maine. It seems terrible that I can't picture where she lives or the things that surround her, that I should be in the midst of all the objects she so lovingly accumulated. The bed: I remember nights when one of the boys or even both would come in at night, waking from bad dreams, or lonely or sick, and stand at the foot of the bed and say,

"Mom?" Not "Dad," never "Dad," I can't fool myself about this. It was always Liz they turned to because she was always there. I remember weekend mornings when the kids came in to wake us, piling onto the bed, the four of us launching into a brand-new day.

I lie in the dark. Every now and then, a car turns up Ordway and a pair of lights slides up the wall and across the ceiling. I lie in the dark and come to a decision. Going back to work, stumbling through the hours in a preoccupied fog — I can't do that.

I'm going to find my sons.

chapter 14

When I turn in my resignation, everyone tries to talk me out of quitting. I should give it more time, etc. I guess they think I'll fall apart entirely without the structure of work.

Big Dave wags his huge head and turns my written resignation over, placing it facedown on his desk. "I'm going to call this a leave of absence," he says. "Let's say three months."

"I can't promise that," I tell him. "I don't know how long it's going to take."

When Dave says something he really doesn't want to say, he lowers his head, furrows his brow, and peers up at you, something like a giant turtle. I prepare for some kind of ugly comment when I see his head go down, but what he says is this: "What are you planning to use for money?"

Dave is familiar enough with my financial situation to realize this is going to be a problem. We're close enough that he's been to the house a few times for Liz's carefully crafted dinner parties. He knows we're not rolling in it and that the separation has been an additional hardship.

"Look, if you get pressed," he says, "just ask." The way he squeezes this offer out tells me it's causing him pain.

I thank him. "I've got a little set aside," I say.

In fact, I'm not sure what I'm going to do about money. There's no way I can ask Liz to let me open an equity line on the house, for instance. Technically, according to the terms of our separation agreement, I can't even take a leave of absence because it diminishes my ability to provide support for her. I have to find a way to search for the boys *and* keep up the support payments for Liz. I can't leave her short.

I'll have to hit up my father for a loan — even though, like everyone else, he'll think leaving my job is a mistake. I've got a couple of friends, Michael and Scott, good for a few grand.

And that's how I'm going to have to do it. Beg. Borrow. Whatever it takes.

"I still think you're making a mistake," Dave says, shaking my hand. I can tell, though, that behind his discomfort, he's relieved that I'm off his hands.

* * *

It starts with Dave, but it doesn't stop there. Everyone tells me I'm making a mistake. What can I do that hasn't already been done? What goes unsaid is that most of them think I'm chasing smoke, that my children are dead and that I should face that likelihood — while not abandoning hope, of course.

Miracles do happen. Elizabeth Smart comes up a lot.

Even Shoffler tries to dissuade me. "Alex," he says, sounding like a disappointed parent. "Don't do it. I've seen it before, and I'll tell you, it's nothing but heartbreak. You do this and you're gonna burn yourself out — emotionally *and* financially."

"So what?" That's the thing. The second I decided to abandon the idea of "work," I couldn't believe I waited this long to do it.

The detective sighs. "Most of these cases, if they get solved — which most of them don't, I'm sorry to say — it's something coming in from the outside, you know? You can investigate the hell out of it and still get nowhere. And then some guy mutters something to a cell mate, or the perp gets caught in another jurisdiction committing a similar crime and the computer makes the match, and there you go."

"I know that."

"I know what you're thinking — that you're gonna bring more energy and focus to the search than any professionals could and so you'll succeed where all the rest of us have failed. You think that just because you *care* more, you'll find your boys. What I'm saying —"

"I will find them," I interrupt. "Or I'll find out what happened to them. And if it burns up all my resources, if it burns me out — so be it."

Shoffler lets out a long sigh, but doesn't speak for a long moment. In the background, I can hear people talking, phones ringing, the clacking of computer keyboards. "Well," he says finally in a weary voice, "keep in touch."

Kevin and Sean. Sean and Kevin.

In many ways, I'm much better equipped for the task of searching for them than most parents would be. I'm a reporter: finding out things is what I *do.*

But before I start asking questions, or seeking advice, the first thing I do is try to think about the *why,* not that I haven't thought about it a thousand times. Still . . .

I go over it all again.

Starting with The Piper. By the time the cops were done, they'd found more than a dozen witnesses who saw them — the boys and The Piper — heading out into the parking lot.

The Piper. I still think of him that way, despite Shoffler's caution about the costume being a disguise. The problem is that he has no dimension for me. He's an idea, not a person. He's not real.

But he *is* real. He's a man who lives somewhere, who buys groceries, drives a car, wears a particular kind of socks . . . and he kidnapped my sons. Since I don't know enough about him to have a real image of him, I have to concentrate on what I do know. And on what he did. He took my kids and he had a reason for it.

MOTIVE, I write at the top of my yellow pad. And then I think about the possibilities.

Profit? The absence of a ransom note would seem to rule that out.

Retaliation? Did someone abduct the boys in retaliation against me, for some story I did? True, my work put me in contact with some bad people, but Shoffler looked into this angle and ended up discounting it. In revenge crimes, the perpetrator almost always sends a signal to let the victim know. The "smirk factor," Shoffler called it. "This guy's real cute — with the T-shirt and the phone call and all that, but we still got no smirk factor. If the guy getting even with you doesn't let you know he's settled the score, where's his satisfaction?" Shoffler and I worked at it, trying to connect the clues the Piper left behind with one of the investigations I've done, but there didn't seem to be any connection.

Sexual predator? This is the default position, but I don't really buy it. Why grab two kids — which would only make the abduction more difficult? And then — why return with them to the house, why call my cell phone, why deliberately confuse matters with the bloody T-shirt? Sexual predators are impulsive and opportunistic. Or so they say. Going back to the house, leaving mementos — that was premeditated. Not a classic pattern.

Kiddie porn? Cute blond twins. Were they abducted by a ring to make a film or procured for sale to someone with a twin thing? Shoffler looked into this — *hard* — but it didn't go anywhere. For one thing, most children caught up in the murky world of kiddie porn are not abducted but "purchased" from relatives or foster parents. And a high-profile kidnapping that was sure to provoke a storm of media attention was unlikely in a subculture that preferred the darkest corners. Still . . .

Religious wacko? There was really nothing to suggest that.

Medical experiment? Shoffler rejected the Dr. Mengele Theory on the basis that there were virtually no cases on the books of pairs of twins going missing. But suppose Kevin and Sean were the initial pair?

I sit for a long time trying to think of other possibilities. In this world of delayed childbearing and infertile couples, it's conceivable that the boys were abducted by someone desperate for children. Someone stalking the fair, who saw his chance and went for it. I mull this over for a while, the idea of an obsessed wannabe parent.

Whoever it was, he or she would have to be a total recluse, living outside of society — because there's been no credible sight- ing of the boys since the day they were abducted. And what about the dimes? The T-shirt? The phone call? How would any of that fit into the would-be parent scenario?

A recluse. An obvious thought occurs to me, but one that never occurred to me before. Unlike Elizabeth Smart, there's no way someone could wander around with identical twins in tow, not without arousing suspicion. *So wherever they are, whoever's got them, if the boys are alive, Kevin and Sean are hidden from view, isolated.*

I glance over my list of possible motives: profit, retaliation, sexual predator, kiddie porn, religious whack-job, Dr. Mengele, wannabe parent. Stripped down like this, the bare list gives me a chill. The least terrifying motives suggest reckless lunacy; the most alarming are truly evil.

I take a deep breath. Beneath the list of motives, I write a second word: CLUES.

Origami rabbit.

Chicken blood.

Row of dimes.

The abductor's mementos. Judy Jones established that the rabbit was folded of standard material, bore no fingerprints, was of high-intermediate difficulty. And that was about it.

Still, The Piper left the thing on Sean's side of the dresser. Why?

The chicken blood. It was possible that the blood-soaked T-shirt was a ruse to focus suspicion on me, but that was only an assumption. The chicken blood might have some other meaning. The police lab did establish that the blood came from a breed of chicken common in the commercial poultry business.

The dimes. The lab checked them for prints and struck out. There was also an attempt to source them — but it turned out that although you don't see many "Mercury" dimes in circulation, there are millions of them out there. They were minted for almost thirty years, from 1916 to 1945, at which point the FDR dime replaced the Liberty head design. The police and the FBI had also looked into mint marks, and the dates of the coins left by the abductor, but there was no discernible pattern.

Still, the coins were placed deliberately; the Piper took the trouble to line them up. They must have some meaning.

There are other clues. For instance, the dog. The Piper used the cute little dog as a kid magnet. Shoffler checked into whippets and told us that the breed was rising in popularity. Lots of whippets out there. But how many can there really be? I never see whippets out for a walk.

And then there's The Piper himself — his costume. Was that just a disguise, or did it, too, have meaning? I needed to check into the fairy tale of the Pied Piper. And what about the costume — where do you go for Piper gear? I got just a glance, but it seemed pretty elaborate. And what about the ruffs? One for him, one for the dog. Where do you *buy* a ruff? Did Shoffler check that out? And if so, what did he find out?

Under CLUES, I add:

whippet
Piper: fairy tale
costume
ruff

I'm going to need a look at Shoffler's files. Only I guess they'd be Muriel Petrich's files now.

I pick up the phone and call Petrich. She's not in. I leave a message and try her home number. Instead of a crisp message or the voice-mail robot, I hear a young child's voice, a child who has trouble pronouncing the letter *R*. "Hi, you've weached the home of Petew, Muwiel, and Bwittany. If . . ."

The sound of the little girl's voice, so sweet and vulnerable and proud of herself, is more than I can handle. It's like stepping off a cliff. What I've lost. I hang up.

I have an impulse to call Petrich back. I want to tell her to get the kid's voice off the voice mail. As she would know, anyone can get the address from a criss-cross directory. Is she crazy? Advertising to random callers that there's a child in the house?

I take a deep breath, retreat from my impulse and my proxy vigilance. Despite her job, Petrich still lives in a world that seems like a friendly place. She knows — but she *doesn't know,* not really — that it can all evaporate in an instant.

chapter 15

It doesn't make sense to get into the dimes or origami without at least looking at the police files first to see what they've got. So until Petrich gets back to me, I hit the Internet.

And once again, I descend into the world of missing children. I've been to a lot of the sites dealing with abducted children before; maybe there's something I've missed, some angle I've overlooked.

I'm back in Milk Carton Land, accompanied by sidebar ads for private eyes who suggest they can find the missing children. I'm engulfed by the faces of the vanished — including the smiling faces of Kevin and Sean.

I correct myself. No one "vanishes." It's not a magic act. These kids were abducted. The man who went to the Renaissance Faire dressed up as the Pied Piper is the one who ripped my sons out of my life . . . and into his world. And I'm going to find out who he is and why he did it.

I visit a website maintained by the IRE — an organization of investigative reporters and editors. At first, it doesn't seem relevant. Most of the database on kidnappings concerns the online world — as in "Dangers of the Internet." There are dozens of stories about intrepid cops and FBI agents working stings in chat rooms.

But this can't have anything to do with my kids. Some six-year-olds have amazing computer skills, but not Kevin and Sean, whose access to computers is strictly controlled by Liz. Anyway, they're just learning how to read; they don't know how to spell or type. There's no way they could get into a chat room, let alone make some kind of arrangement to meet a stranger.

But some of the articles in the IRE's archives scare the hell out of me. One concerns a churchgoing couple who ran a "foster home" in rural Illinois — from which they sold children to pedophiles. Another is about some killer nerds in Idaho who abducted a ten-year-old with the intention of making a snuff flick. It's one nightmare after another, each one darker than the one before.

A second site reminds me that there are fewer than one hundred kidnappings by strangers each year and that small children are not the usual targets. Teenagers are. Girls older than twelve make up more than half the cases. I scan through the dozens of websites that one of my search requests prompts, each representing a missing child. It's depressing, clicking through this forlorn catalog of faces. And the websites themselves seem remote outposts in the vastness of the world, like the photos on milk cartons: HAVE YOU SEEN THIS GIRL?

Shots in the dark.

The sites for certain children — findkevinandsean.com is one of them, I'm glad to see — surface over and over again while I browse. There are also paid ads for missing children that show up on the right of my screen. I make a note to check with Ezra, my computer-genius friend. How much does that kind of thing cost? Now that the boys are relegated to the occasional news update, maybe a paid ad connected to search terms such as "abducted child" would be worthwhile.

And maybe it's time, after all, to get a PR person. Someone who might line up a special on *20/20* or *Dateline*, keep the boys in the news. The Smart family managed this after their daughter had been missing for several months, an hour-long special flooded with images of their missing child. The special, which I watched at the behest of Claire Carosella from the Center, made it clear that the police had fastened their attention on a handyman, an ex-con who died several months after the kidnapping. It was a believable theory, bolstered by some suggestive evidence about a car — although the dead man's wife insisted on his innocence.

Even with the suspected man dead, the Smart family continued to lobby for attention to their daughter's case. Maybe they were just hoping to find her remains, but there was a lesson to be learned. *Don't get too tied to a theory.*

On an impulse, I plug *twins* into the search field along with a couple of my other key words: *abduction, missing, disappeared, children.*

Google kicks out more than a hundred thousand sites.

I specify *missing twins.* Still more than thirty-three thousand listings. I scroll through for twenty minutes or so, only to learn that virtually all of the stories are about Kevin and Sean.

I log on to Lexis/Nexis, using my password from the station. I enter the search terms *missing twins* and restrict the search to news stories published before the date of the boys' abduction.

The list includes more than a thousand stories, but once I get into it, I see that in real terms there are only three stories about abducted twins.

The Ramirez boys. The press raised this case within hours of the story about Kevin and Sean breaking because the similarities were so striking. Julio and Wilson Ramirez were abducted from a rec-center gymnastics class in West L.A. Not only were the Ramirez boys identical twins, but at the time they were abducted, they were seven years old — almost the same age as Kevin and Sean.

I thought of them in the very first hour of this nightmare, sitting on Gary Prebble's bench outside Faire Security.

It happened just about a couple of years ago. The boys disappeared and there was a massive hunt — although not so massive as to keep criticism from surfacing about how much greater the effort would have been if they'd been Anglo kids.

Three months after their disappearance, the killer was caught red-handed, so to speak. He was apprehended at a ramshackle cabin in the mountains not too far from Big Sur. The bodies of the dead boys were found at the cabin — one in his refrigerator, neatly packaged like cuts from a side of beef, the other suspended in a well shaft. The killer was taken into custody and promptly identified himself to the authorities. He turned out to be Charley Vermillion, a sexual psychopath who'd been released from a Louisiana loony bin about a month prior to the boys' disappearance. Vermillion was cuffed and Mirandized and slapped into a squad car. But before the squad car made it to the local lockup, he was dead, having chewed a cyanide capsule he'd taped under the collar of his shirt.

So the Ramirez case was closed, and with the perp dead, there wasn't any way it could be relevant to my boys. Thank God. Both the FBI and Ray Shoffler explored the notion of a copycat crime — but it didn't go anywhere.

The second set of sites involves the Gabler twins. This is a false hit, though, because the Gablers were women — and Vegas showgirls, at that. The story showed up because one of my search terms was *children* and the newspapers reported that the Gablers had recently appeared in a musical revue at a place called the Blue Parrot. The revue was called *Children of the Future*.

They disappeared about three years ago and turned up a month later, their decomposing bodies recovered in the usual "rugged area" twenty miles outside Vegas. The press photos show the Gabler twins alive, side by side in skimpy costumes, their long legs in fishnet stockings, smiling faces encased in futuristic headdresses. It's hard to see how they could possibly have any connection to my boys.

Which leaves the Sandling twins: Chandler and Connor. I'm familiar with this one, too — the one with the happy ending. The way I remember it, the mother was implicated in the abduction of her kids — although never prosecuted, as I recall. There was something about a boyfriend, too.

Because of the mother's alleged involvement, I never really focused on the case. I'm willing to take a second look now, because it's just occurred to me: Who else do I know wrongly suspected in the disappearance of his children?

I take a look. Initially, it's as I remember. Unlike me, Emma Sandling was not an upstanding member of the community but a vagabond for whom "unconventional lifestyle" would be an understatement. A heroin addict who'd been through countless rehab programs, she wasn't much of a mother. Her kids were often cared for by friends or relatives, and they'd been in foster homes more than once.

Some of the news stories mention an incident connected to one of Connor and Chandler's foster-home stays; terming it "the first abduction." Reading on, I decide that calling that incident an *abduction* is unfair, a major (and misleading) exaggeration. It seems to boil down to Emma Sandling's having returned the boys a couple of days late from an authorized visit — due, she contended, to car trouble.

Then there was the "live-in boyfriend," plus the fact that at the time of the abduction, Sandling and her two sons were living in a tent in a state park near Corvallis, Oregon.

The boyfriend — whom Sandling insisted was "just a friend" — was a drifter named Dalt Trueblood. Sandling had met him in rehab, and when she bumped into him at the library in Eugene, she'd invited him to stay in her tent for a few weeks. It turned out Trueblood was a parole violator, although Sandling claimed she hadn't known that.

If child protective services were not happy to learn that home to the Sandling boys and their mother was a tent, they were even unhappier to know that a wanted felon was sharing that space. When the boys disappeared, Trueblood did, too — and until he turned up a few weeks later (drunk and disorderly, directing traffic with a red cape in downtown Portland), it was not unreasonable to think that the Sandling boys might be with him.

Between her addicted past, her lifestyle, and the missing boyfriend — when the boys "vanished," suspicions settled on Sandling. The idea seemed to be that she and Trueblood were in collusion, that they'd intended to present some kind of ransom plea — although this never happened. As for Trueblood, when the police arrested him in Portland and questioned him, he said he left Eugene because the kidnapping "spooked" him.

The circumstances of the kidnapping were simple enough: Sandling took her boys to the McDonald's in Corvallis, intending to treat them to a Happy Meal. She left them in the ball pit while she went to get the food. No other kids — or adults — were in the play area. Nine adults — six of them senior citizens holding a book-group discussion — sat in the main area of the restaurant. When Sandling came back with the food, the kids were gone.

Unfortunately for Sandling, the adults and staff in the restaurant remembered seeing her, but none of them saw her children. Some of the stories display diagrams of the McDonald's, marking the location of customers and staff; these make it clear that Sandling and the boys had to cross the sight lines of other customers and the staff to get to the play area. Apart from the nine customers, six McDonald's employees were behind the counter when the boys disappeared. Two cars were in the drive-through lane. No one saw a thing.

It didn't help Sandling's case that at the time she reported her sons missing, she was known to leave them for hours at a time in the public library while she worked cleaning houses.

What followed was predictable: an explosion of recriminations within the Oregon child-protective bureaucracy and a police investigation with a tight focus on Emma Sandling. The judge who a year earlier had reunited the boys with their cleaned-up mom was condemned on all sides. Social workers who'd attested to Emma Sandling's newfound reliability were subjected to second-guessing of the most vituperative sort. There was a lot of chest-beating about how the twins — Chandler and Connor — had fallen through the cracks ("chasms," according to the Portland paper) of the system. There were calls for investigations and the wholesale reform of the child-welfare system.

If my experience is any guide, Emma Sandling must have been subjected to some heavy interrogation, although she, at least, seems to have had the wit to ask for a lawyer. She was not charged but held "for questioning" for thirty-two hours.

The boys showed up eight weeks later at a shopping mall near Eureka, California. According to a feature story in the *Sacramento Bee*, the boys had been riding in a small motor home for "a long time" when the driver stopped for gas. It was the kind of RV — a truck and trailer, really — where the driver's cab is separated from the passenger compartment. The boys waited for the driver to let them out. They wanted to tell him it was too hot in back; they wanted ice cream; they wanted to pee. But the driver didn't come. They banged on the side of the trailer and yelled; then one of them threw himself at the door and, to their surprise, it fell open.

They climbed out. One boy wanted to go

into the convenience store attached to the gas station, find the driver, and get money for ice cream. But the other boy had come to doubt the story their abductor told them. He was worried that he and his brother never left the compound where they were being kept. This trip in the RV was the first time. He wanted to telephone their mom's best friend, Phoebe. So he and his brother ran toward the shopping plaza, went inside, and looked for a pay phone. They were old hands at making collect calls, but the pay phone wouldn't work. So they went into a gift shop to ask if they could use the phone to make a collect call. The clerk recognized them and called the police.

By the time a squad car came to the scene, the RV was gone.

In the aftermath, press coverage of the happy reunion of Sandling with her sons was muted. There was cynical speculation about how that RV door "fell open," about Sandling's successful efforts (enlisting a helpful lawyer working pro bono) to protect the boys from aggressive interrogation by the authorities. Against this kind of negative stance on the part of the police and the larger community, it was not surprising that despite a wave of testimonials from employers, personnel at the school the boys attended, and friends about how Sandling really had turned her life around — it took several months and a lawsuit for her to regain custody of her sons.

I expand my search and pull down everything I can about the Sandling case; a couple of hours later, I'm convinced that my whole impression was biased by coverage that scapegoated Emma Sandling. Shoffler seemed to have bought into that, too, along with Judy Jones of the FBI — at least they never talked as if the case was relevant, despite its obvious parallels to my own.

The parallels — six-year-old twin boys kidnapped from a public place — are so striking I can't stop reading the clips. Maybe there's something I overlooked when I bought into the assumption that Sandling's sketchy personal history meant she'd somehow rigged the kidnapping of her own sons. Reading through it all, though, there's no evidence that anything other than what Emma Sandling said happened did, in fact, happen. Trueblood had an alibi. No other accomplice surfaced. Sandling never once changed her story. And although the gift store clerk was allotted a portion of the reward, none of it ever trickled down to Sandling.

I spend the next two hours talking to the police stations in Corvallis and Eureka. At first, when I introduce myself and explain my area of interest — the Sandling case — I get the runaround. When I push it, the reaction surprises me: I get stonewalled.

Using names published in the newspaper accounts of the kidnapping, I hunt down the telephone numbers of Emma Sandling's clients, her social workers, her lawyer, and anyone else whose name I can prise out of the media coverage. I reach about half of them and I get the same reaction. They don't know where she is. They can't help me.

I push myself out of my chair, realizing that it's dark outside and I've been hunched over the computer for hours. I intend to continue my pursuit of Emma Sandling, but I know I should eat something. I've been losing weight steadily since Liz left me; people are beginning to remark on it.

I head for the kitchen to forage, although I know there's not much left. In the fridge are a couple of dried-out pieces of cheese, a moldy cantaloupe, and a half gallon of milk that proves to be sour. A rotisserie chicken I failed to wrap is now as desiccated as a mummy. The freezer holds nothing but shrunken ice cubes and a single frozen pizza. I look on the pizza box for the pull date and find it under an encrustation of frost crystals. The date, faint and purple, is more than a year ago.

Even this depresses me. The pizza has been in the freezer since before my bust-up with Liz, since before my life disintegrated. It was probably bought as dinner for the boys. I have a moment during which I elevate the pizza to some kind of talismanic status. I find I'm reluctant to throw it away. I shake my head, upend the milk in the sink, and toss everything else.

I've been eating out most of the time. That's got to stop; it's too expensive. I tell myself I'll go shopping tomorrow, get some TV dinners. And some healthy stuff. Apples. O.J.

For the first time since the boys were kidnapped, I pull on my running shoes and head out into the humid Washington night. I'm way out of shape, but running is a relief. I enjoy the sensation of moving, of the sweat collecting on me, of the labored rhythm of my breathing. I like the way the cars rumble past, the haloed lights in the mist, and how my attention focuses on basic issues: where to put my feet, how to angle my run to pass pedestrians most efficiently, how to time street crossings in such a way that I don't have to break stride.

I go out for about fifteen minutes and then head back. I stop at the 7-Eleven on the corner of Porter and Connecticut, breathing hard, sweat pouring off me as I dig out the five-dollar bill from the key pocket of my shorts. It, too, is damp with sweat.

The clerk is the one Jack started calling Slo-Mo — as in "Oh, no, it's Slo-Mo." She's a shy, thin woman, little more than a girl, with beautiful features. She does everything at such an exasperatingly deliberate pace that customers who know her have been known to turn around if they see more than one person in line.

"Two Jamaican beef patties," I tell the clerk. These will be dinner: tasty, if greasy, meat pastries.

The clerk looks at me with enormous brown eyes and then looks down at her hands.

"You the man who children is gone," she says.

"That's right."

"My uncle — he know these thing from

the other world." She presses one finger to her forehead. "He say your boys all right."

"Your uncle? What other world? Does he know where the boys are?"

"No, no." Her fingers twist together and she looks to the side, eyes cast down. "It's — what you say? — spirits world. He say your boys not there, still in this world. I tell him that you live near this shop, that you come in here many day. My uncle say this — your boys all right. I think myself you like to know." She fashions her facial expression into a shy smile that is also a kind of shrug.

"Thank you." And I mean it. I'll take whatever glimmer of light I can find in the world. "Thank you for telling me."

"You welcome." She pauses. "Spicy or plain?"

I toss the change into a big glass jar set out to collect funds for a child named Belinda, who has leukemia. Another shot in the dark — like the websites, like the milk cartons, like all of it. When it comes to children, you can't go with percentages or probabilities; you do what you can, whatever you can.

"Thank you for telling me what your uncle said." My gratitude is heartfelt; it's amazing how this unsolicited bit of encouragement lifts my heart.

The Madonna of the cash register rewards me with a beatific smile.

chapter 16

"Hang on," Shoffler says, "we're just breaking up the huddle here." I hear voices, the chime of elevators, Shoffler exchanging parting comments with someone. Then he's back. "So what's up?"

"The Sandling twins."

If I didn't know the detective so well, maybe I wouldn't notice, but I catch the hesitation and the sudden holdback in his voice. "So — what about them?"

"The more I read the more it sounds like Kevin and Sean. The parallels are compelling. And I can't understand why you and Judy Jones dismissed the case as irrelevant. Pretty much blew it off."

Once again, there's that hitch in his voice, a guarded quality. "We checked into it, Alex. We *did*. Look — that kidnapping took place a whole continent away. You got the ages of the boys and the fact they're twins. That's it."

"That's *it?*"

"Apart from that, there didn't seem to be a connection." Shoffler clears his throat.

"The mother, you know — she wasn't exactly a pillar of the community."

"Look, Ray — I've read everything I can find about the case. And far as I can tell, Emma Sandling may not have been Mother Teresa but there's no evidence she had anything to do with kidnapping her children."

"That's your opinion. Maybe there's stuff you don't know about."

"Must be. Because as far as I can tell there wasn't exactly a full court press to hunt down the kidnapper once the kids popped up in Eureka."

"You're wrong," Shoffler says. "There was an investigation. A thorough one, too. But the mother wasn't exactly helpful."

"You mean —"

"I mean Emma Sandling was not cooperative. She *said* it was to protect the boys, but not everybody bought that. Look — the kids are safe and sound; it's a happy ending. For a few days, that was big news, a miracle. But after? There's no perpetrator, no charges, no *story,* no trial. All you got is the boys themselves and a police investigation that goes nowhere. Why? Because for whatever reason — whether she's involved somehow or she genuinely wants to protect her kids — Mommy won't talk and she won't let her kids talk."

"She could have made a buck or two out of the media, that's for sure."

"True, and that could mean she's on the level. Or maybe it's just damage control. The more the thing gets looked at, the more her part in it is exposed to the light of day."

"*If* there was a part."

"Okay, *if* there was a part. But the consensus out there was that she had a hand in it, that it was some kind of shakedown that got screwed up. After which, Mother Sandling made herself scarce."

"I don't think so."

Shoffler says nothing for a moment. Then he says: "Why not?"

"Because the more I look at it, the more I get this creepy feeling that whoever took the Sandling kids is the same guy who took mine. They got away, so he took my kids to *replace them*."

"Hunh." A pause. "A 'creepy feeling'?"

"It's the same pattern. Come on, Shoff."

"There's gotta be a boatload of twins on the West Coast. Why would this guy come all the way across the country?"

"I don't know, but the point is I'm looking at this Sandling thing and it sounds so much like my boys. I figure I'll take a closer look. But I *can't,* because for one thing, Emma Sandling? She's *gone;* she might as well have fallen off the face of the earth."

"You tried to find her, hunh?"

"I did. And finding people is one of my job skills. If you're a reporter, you've gotta have sources and you have to find them whether they want to be found or not. But I can't find Emma Sandling."

"Hunh."

"And while I'm trying to track her down, I'm also talking to the cops out there in Oregon. Well, no, that's not accurate. I'm talking *at* the cops out there in Oregon."

"I don't —"

"I call both jurisdictions — Corvallis, where the boys went missing, and Eureka, where they stumbled out of that trailer. Eureka — they tell what they can, which is not much. But Corvallis? I get *nothing,* Ray. A stone wall. The cops flat out won't talk to me. They give me some bullshit about 'privacy issues.' "

"So this is why you called me." He lets out a sigh.

"Yeah. I thought you might be able to talk to them out there. Let them know I'm not gonna be a problem."

There's a long moment before he answers. "I'm sorry, Alex. I can't help you. I wish I could, but my hands are tied."

"Your hands are tied? We're talking about my *sons*. Ray, you can't —"

But the detective is no longer on the line.

Two hours later, I'm outside Shoffler's place in Greenbelt, Maryland, waiting for him to show up. The house isn't what I expected — although I'm not sure what that was. I knew Shoffler worked seventy-hour weeks, that he'd burned through two marriages. I guess I expected a crash pad but the tidy rancher in front of me is neat and homey, with a picket fence and well-kept flowerbeds. There's even a grapevine wreath on the door.

At first, I sit on the porch, but at dusk a cloud of biting gnats drives me back to my car. I wait, listening to the O's game on the radio and periodically cranking up the air when it gets too hot.

I'm jolted out of my doze by a deep metallic concussion that seems to take place inside my skull. The sound is actually a rap on my car door, a fact that I realize when I open my eyes to see Shoffler looming next to my window.

He's not happy to see me. He stands in a predatory, almost threatening stance, half in shadow, illuminated by the sickly green of the streetlight. He looks terrible, irritated but so exhausted that my eyes flick to the dashboard clock to see what time it is: 3:32 a.m.

A film of moisture coats my skin. My mouth is cotton, my lips dry and cracked. My shirt is glued to the leather seat and makes a little sucking noise as I sit up and reach for the door handle. But Shoffler pushes his big hand against the Jeep's door and scowls at me.

"Go home, Alex."

"No."

"Just go home."

"I need to talk to you."

He pivots on his heel and moves toward the front door; he's inside before I can get out of the car. I ring his doorbell, which actually goes *ding-dong,* at least a dozen times. I can't believe it. I've been sitting in the driveway for six hours. Back in the car, my impulse is to lean on the horn, cause a ruckus, force Shoffler to deal with me. But remembering the look on his face, I decide against it.

I've spent a lot of time with Shoffler in the past few weeks, and every minute of it

I've been attuned to him with the rapt attention of a lover, always on the lookout for telltale signs: *Has he heard something? Does he have news?* I've become adept at reading the clues of body language — vocal inflection, gestures, and facial expressions.

I also know that cops and military types put a lot of stock in respect. If I lean on the horn and get in Shoffler's face in that public way, I won't get anywhere. He might even have me arrested. I move my car two blocks away and set the alarm on my cell phone to wake me at six. The detective won't catch me dozing again.

When he comes out the door at 7:44, he looks surprisingly jaunty for a man who got — at most — four hours of sleep. And then he sees me, as I step out from behind his Crown Vic.

His shoulders drop. He wags his head. "Jesus, Alex."

I just stand there. The Crown Vic's door locks snap open.

"Get in," he says.

"What?"

"Get in."

It's already hot outside, the sun a white blur behind the dull haze of sky. The interior of the car is stifling. It stinks, too, of old take-out food and stale cigarette smoke spiked with pine air freshener. I've spent enough time with Shoffler now to know this about him: he drinks coffee all day long, he chain smokes when he can, and he eats most of his meals in the car.

He backs out of the driveway, lowers all the windows. I think at first that we're heading out for coffee, Dunkin' Donuts or the 7-Eleven, but before long we're on Route 50, rolling along in a rush of white noise. The detective remains silent next to me. After a few minutes, he fools with the controls and all the windows slide closed, with the exception of his. He punches up the air, and lights a cigarette, inhaling with a long greedy pull. It's out of habit — not out of deference to me — that he exhales out the window. He's pissed and the irritation comes off him like a force field.

"Where are we going?"

"I got a meeting," he says, "on the Hill."

"But —"

"You wanna talk? This is the time I got. You want to get back to your car sometime before midnight? That's your problem."

"Okay."

I have to resist the reflex to apologize, or at least say something that might lower the tension in the car. It's better this way, with both of us pissed off. This way there won't be any bullshit.

We're on 95 now. Shoffler plunges in and out of dense traffic, his driving style fearless and so aggressive I have to work not to push my feet against the floor. He smokes his cigarette all the way down to the filter, stabs it out in the crowded ashtray, then flips the lid closed.

It's not actually out, and within a minute a thin fringe of smoke — and the acrid smell of burning filters — seeps out from the seam of the ashtray. After a couple of minutes he opens the ashtray again and dribbles some cold coffee into the smoldering mess. There's a sizzle as the liquid hits the filters, followed by a new and terrible smell. "Aromatherapy," Shoffler says. He shoves the ashtray shut and taps his fingers against the exterior of the car. "Look," he says after a while, "I'm not really pissed at you."

"You're not?"

"You know why? Because you're right."

He yanks the big car into a momentary gap in the left lane, earning a long complaining beep. He sticks his hand out the window, middle finger raised. "My daughter tells me I lack maturity — that's how she puts it. I tell her this *is* maturity for me: I give these jokers the finger now instead of pulling 'em over." He rolls his shoulders, pats his breast pocket looking for a cigarette, knocks one out, lights it. "So — Mother Sandling."

"Yeah."

"It's like the Sniper case. Everybody's saying the sniper is a white loner — white, white, white. White guy in a white van. Now, you may not know this, but as the thing is going down, some of the guys in the District — I'm talking about African American police officers — they don't think so. They've got the idea — from eyewitness testimony, from voice tape — that this guy's a brother. They also think he's driving a converted cop car, a blue Crown Vic or a Chevy Caprice — what they call a *hooptie*. Some of the yo's are partial to recycled police cars — whether out of a sense of irony or just because these babies do *go*. But the point is, do the rest of us hear any of this? Why is it that no one, in any of the briefings, says one word about a black guy in a blue sedan who calls himself *we?*"

I shake my head.

Shoffler stabs his cigarette into the mess of crumpled butts. "Is it because Montgomery County happens to be involved in a lawsuit about racial profiling?"

"You're kidding."

Shoffler wags his head. "Now, in the Sandling case — we got a lawsuit there, too, more than one. Jones and I — we did see the parallels, you know. Jones gets on the horn to Corvallis. And what happened? Were they helpful, did they extend every courtesy? No. They more or less told us to get lost."

"She's the FBI and they blow her off?"

"They're polite, they *want* to accommodate us, but yes they blow her off. Like a fucking hurricane."

"Why."

"Li-ti-ga-tion. Here's the deal: Emma Sandling has some issues with the way her boys' case was handled. She's suing the police out there — about the length of time she was detained, about the conduct of the investigation, about the follow-up, about every damn thing. There are suits about misconduct and another one over lifestyle profiling."

"What's that?"

"They're saying that the equal protection clause in the Constitution should cover class and lifestyle issues, the same way it covers race, religion, gender, and ethnicity."

"It's a *constitutional* issue?"

"Yeah. Think-a-that, hunh? Now, the cops out there — they don't trust Sandling. They still think it's about covering her ass; they still think she was *involved*. So why — ask yourself — would Sandling be anxious to talk to anybody connected to law enforcement? The cops thought she did it. Her kids were taken away from her — and it took her months to get them back. The only reason she succeeded was because a sympathetic judge figured that leaving the boys in the library and living in a tent was not really neglect. Given welfare reform and the unemployment rate and the lack of child-care alternatives for Sandling, what's she supposed to do? Anyway, when Jones called, trying to get Sandling's phone number, she got nowhere."

"Sandling wouldn't talk."

"Right. Sandling won't talk, the cops won't talk, the lawyers won't talk. We asked."

"Did she know about Kevin and Sean?"

Shoffler swings his big head in my direction and just looks at me. "What do you think? You think she coulda missed that story? Maybe if she lived on Mars. No, the thing is your boys' kidnapping brought the whole thing back. It terrified her."

"How do you know?"

"We had a conference call: me, Jones, Sandling, and her lawyers. The lawyers are a big help, as you can imagine — keep telling her she doesn't have to talk to us, doesn't have to answer this question or that. But we really whacked away at this woman; I mean, we laid on the guilt as thick as we could. Here were two boys in peril, her boys might have information helpful in the investigation, how could she as a mother . . . blah, blah, blah."

"And?"

"Nothing. We did not get to first base. Wherever she's living now, no one knows who she is. And she wants to keep it that way . . . which is understandable. She's worried about some kind of leak, that her boys' case will end up all over the news again, they'll be outed in their new place. Maybe the perp will come back for another round — to which Jones says, '*not* if we catch him.' But Sandling is *not* interested; she won't say boo. The lawyer follows up by warning us not to mention the Sandling case to the media."

"You're kidding."

"He called Jones's supervisor at the Bureau and my chief in Arundel . . . just to reinforce the warning."

I just sit there, in a funk of anger and impotence. I'm pissed at Sandling, her lawyers, the cops, everybody. And what's worse, I'm sick at heart. I take a few deep breaths, fighting off a sort of interior collapse.

"You okay?" Shoffler says.

I shrug.

"I can do two things for you," Shoffler says. "First — and I doubt this will do you a hell of a lot of good — I can get you a copy of the sketch. The one they did working with the Sandling kids. Jones got that out of them. I wasn't supposed to make a copy, but I did. Anyway, it was published in the papers at the time. Anyone asks, that's where you got it."

"Does it look like The Piper?"

He shrugs, holds up one hand. "Who knows? Not really. More facial hair than our guy. Kind of fogs up the features." He sighs. "Second thing — and you could get this on your own, so I'm just saving you some time here — Sandling's maiden name is Whalen."

"You think that's the name she's using?"

"I wouldn't know," Shoffler says, flashing me a grin. "I was constrained from pursuing the matter."

He drops me off near the White House. "Take the MARC Train from Union Station," he advises. "New Carrollton stop. A cab'll take you the rest of the way. Cost you ten bucks, max."

When I open the door the next morning to go out for the paper, there's a manilla interoffice envelope inside the screen door. I'm not expecting much, but I'm still disappointed when I see the sketch.

The face is expressionless, as real faces never are. The lack of expression somehow robs the features of coherence and makes the image ambiguous. Even mug shots have some animation — that supplied by life itself, I guess. I take the sketch to my study and line it up with the sketches Marijke made, one from my glimpse of The Piper, the others produced by sessions with other eyewitnesses. There's something about the eyes, maybe, that looks the same from sketch to sketch. Apart from that, it's different men with facial hair. The faces gaze down on me, inscrutable, almost mocking: *you don't know who I am*.

Mary McCafferty taps one pink fingernail on her desk and looks at me with her large brown eyes. "Finding her shouldn't be a problem," she says. "She may not have had an address, living in a park — but she had a car, which means a driver's license, insurance. She apparently had a library card, and I'll bet she had a doctor for those kids. There will be school records, maybe traffic and parking tickets, grocery shopper cards. Believe me, unless you really work at it, you're in a thousand databases these days. And what are the chances she severed every connection to her past?" McCafferty shakes her head.

"Really."

"She may be using a different name — but you say it's her maiden name, so chances are she kept her social, and then . . . well, then it's a piece of cake. I might have something by tomorrow. E-mail okay? Or should I fax you?"

"E-mail's fine."

"We're all set," she says, getting to her feet. She hesitates, shakes her head. "But mine's the easy part. *You* still have to get her to talk to you."

"I know."

"My guess is this woman's pretty quick to call the cavalry," she says. "Don't get arrested."

chapter 17

McCafferty comes through. Emma Sandling, neé Whalen, lives in Florida. The next morning, at seven a.m., I'm on a Delta flight to Daytona Beach.

The drive into town from the airport takes me past the enormous Daytona International Speedway. Then I'm coasting along Highway A-1-A, a sun-bleached strip flanked on both sides by an unending succession of fast-food outlets, motels, miniature golf courses, and bowling alleys. Everything's paved. The only flora, apart from the landscaped oases in the elaborate mini-golf parks, is the occasional windlashed palm. Every once in a while, between the giant hotels and condos on the oceanside, I catch a glimpse of why all this exists: white sand and the hard glitter of the Atlantic.

After several miles, I spot the landmark I've been looking for, the huge sprawl of the Adam's Mark Hotel. My room at the Drop Anchor Inn is a block away on the other, less desirable, side of the road. Its giant anchor-shaped sign advertises VACANCY SPECIAL WKLY RATES AARP AAA STUDENTS SENIORS.

According to the Weather Channel, the difference in temperature and humidity between Washington and Daytona Beach is incremental, but that's not the way it feels when I step out of my rented Hyundai Sonata. Heat radiates from the pavement, so dense and humid and hot, it's like an assault. A stiff offshore breeze is no cooling zephyr, either. It's like a blast from a giant hair dryer.

The room is what you'd expect for thirty-two bucks a day: the dark stripes of cigarette burns mar several surfaces, television and lamps are bolted to their tables, and I had to put down a twenty-dollar deposit for the remote. Stale cigarette smoke suffuses every fabric behind an olfactory haze of air freshener. But the room is big, with an air-conditioning unit that seems to be up to the task. And it has a telephone, so I can plug in my laptop.

Emma Sandling, now Susie Whalen, works near here, right on the famous beach itself. She operates a concession stand called the Beach Bunny, a couple hundred yards from the Adam's Mark. She's also a part-time student at the Daytona Beach

Community College, halfway through a program in "respiratory therapy." Her boys currently attend the fifth in a string of free vacation Bible schools, this one sponsored by the Word of God church in Ormond Beach. Whalen drives a red '84 Subaru wagon with Save-the-Manatee plates. She and the boys live in a tiny rental apartment in Port Orange, where she gets a break on the rent in return for janitorial work, which includes mopping down the halls and stairs and keeping the laundry room and storage area clean. All per an e-mail from McCafferty, who billed me for just two hours. "Glories of the information age," she noted.

I sit on the bed and after a minute, stretch out and stare up at the textured ceiling. Ever since I received McCafferty's e-mail, I've been trying to figure out how I'm going to get close to Emma Sandling.

My plan is to go to the Beach Bunny, rent a chair and umbrella, buy a tube of sunscreen, and chat her up. I'm good at this kind of thing; most reporters are.

I pay for a day ticket, put the receipt on the dash, and turn my car onto the beach, falling in line behind a black Explorer. We roll along the sand at the posted ten-miles-per-hour pace. To my right, an endless parade of buildings and parked cars, the sparkle of hotel and condo swimming pools. To my left the white beach, the forest of umbrellas, towels and beach blankets and people, the expanse of ocean and sky.

I spot the van where Emma Sandling works, which is easy enough. It's under a huge inflated rabbit — dressed in a bikini. The thing bobs and snaps against its guy wires in the stiff breeze. A short line of customers stretches out from the service window, skinny teenaged boys in board shorts, bulky retirees. A deeply tanned girl peels away from the window with a paper basket of fries.

And then I'm past the van, my first glimpse of Emma Sandling that of a figure inside the service window, counting out change. I exit next to the Adam's Mark and make my way up A-1-A to the entrance ramp for a second pass. This time, Sandling is outside the van, clipboard in hand, talking to a couple of boys holding lime green boogie boards. She's a small woman with coppery hair pulled back in a loose ponytail. She wears pink shorts and a white halter top and flip-flops. A flash of a smile, an impression of freckles, and I've cruised past again.

The guy at the entry point recognizes me this time and waves me through. About a hundred yards from the Beach Bunny, I nose the Sonata into a space between a white pickup and a rusting Blazer.

"Help you?" She has an engaging smile. Dimples.

"Just a bottle of water."

"Sure thing. The small one or the one-liter size?"

"I'll take the liter."

"That's good," she says, pulling a bottle of Dasani from the cooler behind her. "It's hot out here. You want to stay hydrated."

She puts the change on the counter, looking past me to the woman next in line, but I hesitate, immobilized by her nonchalance and vulnerability. "Somethin' else, sir?" she asks with a little frown.

"No, I'm all set," I tell her, and move out of the way.

I find an open spot on the uncrowded beach, stretch out my towel on the hard sand, and watch the waves roll in, the endless ebb and flow. Little kids play tag with the leading edge of the water, build sand castles, present shells to their mothers. Gulls cry, planes cruise by overhead, hauling advertisements. Women intent on tanning lie inert on their towels, like basking sea lions. Teenagers in bikinis squeal as they tiptoe into the water. Behind me, a parade of cars crawls by at the subdued pace of a funeral cortege.

I sit there with the sun beating down on my back and the image of Emma Sandling in my mind. My skin feels too hot, and when I close my eyes, there's a sort of thudding in my head, like a heavy door slamming shut over and over. By the time I get back to the car, the thudding sensation is gone and in its place is this single depressing thought: *It won't work.*

I must have been kidding myself — because how could I ever have thought it would work? Sure I can get close to Emma Sandling, maybe even make friends with her. But what about when I get around to the subject at hand? When her new friend starts talking about the abduction of her sons — an incident she's gone to such lengths to bury in the past?

The interior of the car is so hot I have to put my sandy towel on the seat. The steering wheel burns my hands. Back in the motel, I take a look at my notebook, reviewing the information McCafferty sent about Emma Sandling's schedule. I jot down a few questions I want to ask. Then I stare at the ceiling for a long time thinking about how I can get Emma Sandling to talk to me.

Finally, I get into my shorts and T-shirt and head out, running along the sidewalk flanking A-1-A in a trance of heat and motion. Maybe running will spring an idea loose. I go half an hour out and half an hour back, then drag myself back into my icy motel room. Take a shower.

I think about it. I do have some leverage over Emma Sandling. She's in hiding. I know where she is. I could expose her. She'll understand that. She's got a life here; she won't want to pick up stakes again.

But leverage doesn't exactly amount to Plan B. Not really. There's only one thing to do: throw myself on her mercy.

Thanks to McCafferty's e-mail, I know Emma's schedule. She'll close the Beach Bunny at five, then drive to Ormond Beach to pick up the boys from vacation Bible school. Some fast food, I'd guess, and then she'll drop the kids at the baby-sitter's in Port Orange, leaving just enough time to get to her seven o'clock class at the Daytona Beach Community College. That goes until nine-thirty, after which she picks up the kids and heads home. A long day.

I could just show up at her apartment, but I sense that I'll do better if I can talk to her without the kids being around. She won't feel as threatened. If I had more patience, I might wait for the morning, wait at the Beach Bunny before she opens up. But I'm impatient. If I can find her car in the parking lot at the community college, I'll wait for her there.

In the meantime, I check my e-mail. There's one from Petrich, appending the police files about the dimes and the origami rabbit. I read these over, but the only new bit of information is a paragraph-long expert opinion from an origami scholar.

> Without destroying the specimen, I cannot examine the folding techniques, but from exterior study, it is my opinion that the specimen is a modified Lang rabbit, a piece of moderate difficulty adapted from one of the many rabbits created by noted origamist Dr. Joseph Lang.

I try watching television, but that drives me crazy — ads and laugh tracks and news bites like fingernails on a blackboard. Turning it off is worse; I'm left with my own adrenalized dread and the glacial passage of time. After a while I head to the beach and walk, somewhat soothed by the crash of the surf. Still, I check my watch every few minutes.

At nine, I'm heading down Clyde Morris Boulevard, the sky a streaky pink above. I turn onto International Speedway Drive, then hang a right into the college's huge parking area. The lot's half empty now, but it must have been crowded when Emma got here, because I find her red Subaru way out on the periphery. I'm sure it's hers because of the Save-the-Manatee plates, but I check the number against the one on McCafferty's e-mail anyway. Yes.

It's nine-fifteen. I park a few spaces away from the Subaru. I listen to the radio for a while, but after a few minutes, I have to get out of the car. I'm edgy and restless. But then I feel conspicuous just standing there, so I gravitate toward a small strip of vegetation that separates the parking lot from a service road. This is where I wait, in the midst of palmettos and reedy bushes, muttering to myself as the leaves rustle and clatter in the breeze.

I realize what I'm doing: I'm rehearsing.

It's as if I'm practicing a stand-up before the camera rolls. I know it's stupid, as if there's any right way to say what I'm going to say — but I keep trying out different phrases anyway, because it fills my mind.

"Emma — my name is Alex Callahan. We have a tragedy in common . . ."

"Emma Sandling, I need your help."

"Emma . . ."

It's full dark now. Light fixtures stand at regular intervals in the lot, each creating a cone of light that's alive with orbiting bugs. More cars depart. In this section, only a dozen or so remain.

A figure approaches, but soon I know it's not her. It's a kid, baggy pants and earphones. He shuffles toward his rusted-out Toyota and then drives away.

Five minutes later, I see her, hurrying in my direction. It occurs to me it might seem creepy, the way I'm standing in the bushes, so before she gets too close I walk toward my car. I have the vague idea of opening the trunk, to give me an excuse for standing outside the car. At the last moment I change my mind and open the hood instead. Instantly, this seems like a mistake.

She has her keys out and she cuts a wary glance my way before opening her door.

I feel paralyzed.

She rolls down the window — manually. She turns on the ignition. The car sounds as if the timing is off. It's idling too fast. By the time I can get myself to move, she's fastening her seat belt. I approach her, holding my hand up.

"Excuse me?" I say.

"I'm sorry, but I'm really in a hurry."

"Wait." And then I blurt out, in my newscaster's voice: "We have a tragedy in common."

My rehearsed words sound strange, very strange — even to me. Emma frowns, as if I've spoken in a foreign language and she's trying to translate what I said.

"I'm Alex Callahan," I say, talking too fast now, my words tumbling over one another. "You've seen it on the news. My sons Kevin and Sean have been abducted. Your tragedy's over, Emma, but mine is ongoing. I need your help. I need —"

It's the sound of her name, I think, that really does it. Nothing else I said really sank in until I used her name. The name she doesn't use anymore.

I see the realization hit, recognition followed a nanosecond later by horror. Then she's gone, driving away in a pebbly screech.

I blew it.

But the truth is I don't feel panicked because I know she can't get away from me. Not really. I know where she's going. But just for this moment, I can't seem to move, can't seem to get my breath. The air presses in on me, heavy and dense. I'm still standing in exactly the same place when *she comes back*.

She stops her car, opens the door. Light spills out the open door and she sits there, in its illumination. "Look — I'm sorry," she says. "I didn't feel good about it. There's a lot of negative energy — me being the one person who could really sympathize with you, but instead I did everything I could to keep away. . . ."

Her voice trails away and for a minute or so she doesn't say anything. The sound of the traffic seems to be getting louder, gathering force.

"And when I saw about your boys on the television — oh, God." She takes a shuddery breath. "I knew it was him, I just knew it. And I thought — I actually *thought* . . . I thought . . ." Her voice is falling apart now and she's starting to cry. "I thought . . . *good,* now he won't come back. He's got what he wants." She chokes in a sob. "I'm sorry."

"Hey," I start, "that's okay. I under—"

"No, it's not," she says, interrupting. "I'm so ashamed of myself." A sigh. "The thing is," she says, "when the kids showed up in Eureka — you'd think everybody would be sooooo happy. But they weren't, not really. There was this big deal about how it was a miracle and all, and wasn't it wonderful — but it's like it wasn't *enough* for them. The happy ending was good for . . . like . . . forty-eight hours. After that, they wanted to get back to tragedy and disaster, the nastier the better. And it was so hard. The kids came back, and then they took them away from me."

"That must have been unbelievable."

She shakes her head, taps her foot, taps out a cigarette and lights it. "I'm trying to quit," she says. "I never smoke around the boys."

"That's good."

"You have to understand," she says, "I'm still afraid they'll find some way to take the boys away. You know?"

"I understand."

"See they still don't believe I'm innocent. They never believed that Dalt just *left,* just spooked when I called from the police station and told him what happened. He'd had a kind of messy past; he spent some time in prison. I knew that, but

I didn't know he was on parole. And then when they couldn't find him — they fixated on this theory. They just wouldn't believe the truth — that he took off because he was afraid. They were always thinking they'd find the kids buried somewhere. Or Dalt would turn up and confess that he and I had sold my kids as sex slaves or something."

"Really."

"Really. And when the boys came back, it's like they wanted the boys to be fucked-up. The fact that they were fine, really — I mean *more or less* fine — was a disappointment. And they just would not leave the little guys alone. They just kept picking away at them. I don't know. I guess I wouldn't have trusted me, either."

"Look, I have a lot of sympathy for you. But the reason I came looking for you is because I'm desperate. I think whoever took your sons has my sons now."

She looks away from me, and when she looks back, I see that she's crying. She holds her face in her hands. "I know."

"So —"

"I just don't think I can help you. Part of it was that the police fixated on me and Dalt, but part of it was that they had no leads. The CCTV at the gas station had some footage of the trailer, but no license plate. A bunch of people at the gas station saw the guy, but he was wearing a uniform — coveralls and a cap, like a maintenance man. He didn't show up on the station's video."

"Will you talk to me? Just tell me about it."

She looks at me. "If I can do it without turning my life into a *National Enquirer* story — yes. I don't know what I can tell you that's going to help, but . . ." She shrugs.

"Thanks."

She heaves a sigh, looks at her watch. "The babysitter's going to be worried. Not to mention I've gotta get those boys to bed. Why don't you come to the Bunny tomorrow?"

I don't know why, but I play innocent. "The Bunny?"

"I saw you there — Orioles cap? You bought a bottle of water." She taps her temple. "Too bad I didn't see the guy who took the kids. I never forget a face."

chapter 18

I help Emma during the times when she gets slammed with customers — handing her cans of soda, restocking the backup cooler, minding the window while she rents out a board or sandcrawler. We talk during the slow periods. Between the roar of the surf, the roar of the generator, and the hum of the refrigeration machinery and air-conditioning, it's so noisy inside the concession stand that we conduct our conversation at a volume just short of shouting.

By midmorning, we've each recited our basic stories. To me, there's little question that the man who abducted her sons is the same man I think of as The Piper. But Shoffler was right. The parallels are broad. There's no real detail, let alone evidence, to link the two cases.

We compare notes on what it was like to be suspected of responsibility for the disappearance of our own children. "With me, you can figure it would happen," she tells me. "I mean, I'm a junkie — recovered, yeah, clean for three years now, but so what? You're always this far from a relapse." She pinches a tiny space between thumb and forefinger. "You gotta turn that space into — like — titanium. That's what I'm trying to do."

"I like your chances."

She shrugs. "The thing is — with me, it was like they thought it was a shakedown of some sort, I was trying to get money, that's what was behind the kids' disappearance. But with you? I don't get it."

"My wife and I were separated. Anyway, The Piper — he made it happen. He left this bloody T-shirt in the closet and for a couple of days, anyway, they thought I killed the kids."

"Oh, that's *right* — I remember that. The chicken blood."

"And that bowl of water — that was part of it, too. I don't know what they thought — I was keeping the boys locked up in the closet?" I shake my head.

"What bowl of water?"

"There was a bowl of water up on the shelf in the closet in the kids' room. Way up high. I don't know what it was doing there. It was the same closet where they found the T-shirt."

It's not really a gasp — it's more like she's stopped breathing — but there's no way to miss the sense of alarm coming off Emma Sandling.

"What?"

"It really is him," she says.

"What do you mean?"

"What about dimes? Was there a row of dimes?"

"Yes. They were lined up on the bathroom sink. How . . ."

Emma puts a hand on my forearm. "There was a row of dimes right down the middle of Connor's sleeping bag. I thought Con did it himself. But then Amalia — she lived in the tent next door — she took one look at those dimes and she freaked right out. I mean she practically turned white — and Amalia, she was very dark-skinned. She was the one who noticed the water, too — a bowl up on this little shelf I had, you know, rigged to the side of the tent."

"Why did she freak out? What does it mean?"

"Well, that's what I wanted to know, but Amalia — first she tells me not to touch anything, she's like too hysterical to explain anything. Don't touch the water, she says, don't move the coins. And she is *serious* about this, like it's life and death, you know? And I don't get it. I'm like — what's this about? She tries to explain it to me, but her English isn't all that good. What I get out of it is that it's some kind of voodoo thing, and the bottom line is I should *not* mess with it. Did I say she's from Haiti? Hang on."

She waits on a contingent of teenagers, ringing up Cokes and chips, a tube of sunscreen, a Life's a Beach T-shirt. A girl giggles and says, "Come *on,* Kevin, stop it!" *Kevin.* The name, just the sound of it, transfixes me. *Kevin. Sean. Where are you?*

There's a lightness, an uneasiness in my chest. It's because the police removed the water and the Liberty head dimes as evidence. In view of what Emma just told me, I can't get over the feeling that this could hurt the boys. And maybe it has.

Emma slides the window closed, comes back, sits on the stool, pushes her bangs back away from her forehead. The air-conditioning inside the van can't quite keep up with the heat, and we're both covered with a film of sweat.

"So this Amalia — you still in touch with her?"

Emma shakes her head. "Never saw her again. Right about then is when the cops came and they cordoned off the tent with police tape. I wanted to stay there — I was still thinking the boys might show up —

but they took me down to headquarters. They started questioning all the other people in the park, too; they blocked the exits. Amalia and her guy Bertrand — they were illegals, you know. She worked in the Comfort Inn. He was a roofer. Lots of people like that live in the parks. You know — the working poor. Campsites are way cheaper than rent. Anyway, Bertie and Amalia — they sure didn't want to talk to the police. Amalia just clammed up. Didn't see anything, hear anything, know anything. When the police came back to her about those dimes, because I mentioned it — and this was, like a week later — Amalia and Bertie were long gone."

"So you never found out what she was talking about?"

"Well, I found out it was some kind of curse — which I'd already figured from the way Amalia acted. But that was about it."

"She told you not to move them, not to even touch them?"

"Right."

"The police seized the bowl of water from my house. And the dimes. As evidence."

"Oh, me, too. In fact, they just about destroyed everything in my tent — including the tent — testing for blood and all. You should see what I got back when they finally returned my worldly possessions. They made a list, you know, when they took it all. I guess they have to."

"The search warrant inventory."

"Right, yeah — that. Well, some of the things I didn't get back at all. It was marked down on the list: tested to destruction." She makes little quotation marks in the air, then shakes her head. "The dimes were in a little baggie. I threw them in the ocean, afterward, you know, when I got the boys back. One by one."

I take over the window while she goes outside to sign out two beach umbrellas. I sell two ice-cream sandwiches and a rocket pop.

"I don't get the voodoo connection," I tell her. "The guy who took my kids is white."

"That's what my boys said — the guy wasn't black. I couldn't really figure it out, either. One of the detectives told me they were thinking maybe it was a child-kidnapping ring."

"Emma?"

"Please try to call me Susie."

"I'm sorry. Susie?"

She's sitting on the stool, her legs crossed, swinging a leg from which one flip-flop dangles. I notice that her toenails are painted five different pastel colors, like tiny jelly beans.

"Can I talk to the boys?"

"Oh, Jeez," she says. "I knew it would get down to this."

"I just think maybe there's something — I don't even know what — but something they know that might help me."

She sighs. "I just don't want to *revive* it all, you know? What if they tell you something and you want to tell the police? And then the police question them again — and it leaks out." She sighs again. "I really don't want to move and have to start all over again." She tilts her head back and stares at the ceiling. Behind the roar of the generator, the wind kicks up outside. A spray of sand ticks against the van. Above us, the balloon-rabbit snaps against the guy wires. When Emma looks back at me, I see the glitter of tears.

"I guess I shouldn't ask."

"How can you not ask?" she says. "I know that." She balls up her hands and rubs at her eyes with her knuckles, like a child. She takes a deep breath and fills her cheeks with air, like a cartoon depiction of the North Wind — then exhales, all at once, a tiny explosion. Compassion finally overwhelms her instinct for self-preservation. "Okay," she says, pressing her eyes shut as she says it, as if she doesn't want to witness her own assent.

Emma sets the ground rules and makes me swear "on my children" that I will adhere to them. I will call the boys by the Florida names (Kai and Brandon). I won't press them too hard if they don't seem to want to answer. The session can last only fifteen minutes and whatever they say is for me only. And so on. It amazes me that after all she's been through, she still places so much value on someone's word.

We meet the following night. My first sight of Kai and Brandon almost takes my breath away. It's not that they look like my boys. They don't. But they share the habits of twinship, the way they look at each other, play off each other, interrupt one another, finish each other's sentences, check to the other with their eyes for assurance in the midst of speaking.

I'm braced for a horror story, but what they tell me is almost reassuring.

"Where were you?" I ask them, first of all, looking from one to the other. "What was the place like?"

"It was a big house." Brandon looks at

his brother, who gives him a little nod.

"Really big."

"With a humongous lawn."

"Lotsa trees. Like in a forest."

"What kind of trees?"

Kai looks at Brandon and shrugs. "I think pine?"

"Yeah," Brandon agrees, looking at his mother. "Like in the Grand Tetons."

"We stayed there for a couple of months," Emma explains. "I worked in Jackson at a restaurant."

"They had *buffalo burgers,*" Kai says, knotting up his face in disgust. "Gross."

"Were there other people there, at this big house, I mean — mowing the lawn or doing the chores — or just the man who took you into his car at the McDonald's?"

"Just him. I mean there were other people sometimes, but we couldn't meet them. We had to stay in the big room. Doc told us."

Doc. I don't like the sound of that. *Doctor* Mengele. Papa Doc. Baby Doc.

"But we didn't have to be quiet or nothing."

"Or anything," Emma corrects.

"Or anything. We could play Nintendo even."

"Why couldn't you meet anyone?"

" 'Cause they might tell, and then Mommy" — he shoots a look at Emma — "might get into trouble and we'd never see her again."

"When the man approached them at McDonald's," Emma explains, "he told them that he was a friend of mine, that I had to go back into treatment, that I couldn't stand the idea of telling the boys —"

"Doc told us she had a relapse," Brandon says.

"He told the guys it would break my heart to say good-bye," Emma explains. "He said I was staying in the ladies' room until they left. He told them I'd come for them as soon as I was better. But if anyone *knew* they were staying with him, he wasn't authorized — so they'd have to go back into foster care and child services would never let them live with me."

"Ever again," Kai says in an earnest voice. "That's what he told us."

"Now we have a code," Brandon elaborates, "so we know if it's true from Mommy or not."

"Don't tell him!" Kai warns.

Brandon glares at his brother, then turns to me with an apologetic smile. "We can't tell anyone or someone might find out and then they could trick us."

"That's a good plan." I can feel my fifteen minutes ticking away. "So what did you do all day? Play Nintendo? Watch TV?"

"Nuh-uh. No TV. We played Nintendo a lot. And Ping-Pong."

"Uno and Yahtzee, too."

"Mostly we did training."

"Training?" I look from one to the other. "Like what?"

"Exercises," Kai says, and begins to list them in a kind of singsong rhythm as he counts them off on his fingers. "Push-ups, sit-ups, stretching, gymnastics —"

"Both of you?" Dr. Mengele jolts into my head along with phrases like *muscle biopsy, cardiac development, VO max.*

"Uh-huh."

"Did he *test* you — like on machines or anything?"

"Nuh-huh."

"We had contests sometimes, though," Kai says. "Mostly I beat."

"Not every time," Brandon protests.

"We did gymnastics a lot," Kai says. "You know, somersaults and stuff."

"And backwards somersaults. Want to see?"

"Alex doesn't have time for that," Emma

cautions. "Apparently, they did this for hours every single day," she adds. "Balance beams, vaults. It made me wonder if Doc was some kind of crazed would-be Olympic coach."

"We climbed up ropes, too," Kai says, with some animation. "Right to the ceiling. We did that *a lot*. It was hard. It was for making you strong."

"What kind of ropes?"

Kai and Brandon look at each other and shrug. "Just ropes," Kai says. "They were thick and they hung down from hooks in the ceiling."

"The knotted ones were more easy."

"Yeah, the plain ones were really hard to climb at first. 'Member, Bran? — we could just about get a couple feet off the floor."

"We got better."

"So this was . . . where, in a gym . . . in this big house?"

"Yeah — it was in the basement. It was a really, really giant room."

They nod earnestly. "Yeah. Like the Y or something."

"How high were these ropes?"

They look at each other. "Real high."

"As tall as this ceiling, or . . . ?" The rooms in Emma's apartment might have eight-foot ceilings.

"No," Brandon protests. "Much higher . . . like really high."

"Hunh. So, did this man . . . did he . . . *do* anything to you?"

"Like what do you mean?"

I'm not sure how to put it, and Emma dives in. "No," she says. "None of that."

"None of what?" Kai demands.

She hesitates. "You told me he didn't hurt you."

Brandon shakes his head. "He didn't hurt us. He *liked* us."

"He liked you. So . . . was he . . . *friendly?*" I ask.

Emma shoots me a look, but lets it go. The boys shake their heads, bored now, beginning to fidget. "Nah," Kai says, "he was just . . . he was just . . ." He looks at his brother, but Brandon shrugs. Neither one of them seems able to characterize their captor's manner. "He was just kind of regular," Kai says finally. "Mostly, he left us alone except when we were training."

"So what made you stop trusting him?" I ask Kai. "At the mall. What made you try to call your mom's friend?"

"I don't know," Kai says, frowning. "He just — I don't know." He shakes his head.

"Kai's very intuitive and a little wary," Emma says with a wan smile. "Brandon's more of an optimist."

"What's that mean, Mom?" Brandon asks.

"It means you hope for the best, sweetie."

"Is . . . *tootive* good, too?" Kai asks.

"*Intuitive*. Yes, K-man, it means you're smart and alert, not to what people *say*, but to the way things feel to you." She turns to me: "They've been in care a lot, and there's a lot of BS in the system. It doesn't exactly foster trust." She shrugs. "Brandon's the exception."

"Ooooooh," Brandon says. "Mom said *BS*."

The fact that their captor didn't exploit the boys is a huge relief, but I can't get any kind of fix on his intentions toward them. Did he kidnap . . . a family? *Sons?* What kind of a relationship did they have with him? "This guy Doc — did he eat with you?" I ask.

"Nah — we got our own cereal and stuff for breakfast, and for lunch we made our own sandwiches. He made dinner — stuff in plastic boxes that he heated up in the microwave."

"It was okay," Kai says. "The food. Healthy stuff. No junk food."

"And you never saw anyone else?"

Brandon swings his head back and forth. "Nope."

I'm trying to think of what else to ask when Kai volunteers something. "Sometimes he did tricks for us, remember, Bran? In the beginning?"

"Tricks?" Emma frowns. This seems to be new to her. "What kind of tricks?"

"Yeah, with cards and stuff," Brandon says. "You know — *magic* tricks."

"And coins."

Coins.

"Did he . . . line up the coins?" Emma asks.

Brandon makes a face. "Noooooo. He like . . . pulled them out of the air, made them disappear."

Kai claps his hands. "Like that."

Emma taps her watch. The reminder propels me into the kind of question I never ask as a reporter, an open, expansive question that almost always draws a shrug.

"Can you think of anything else . . . about the house or the man or . . . I don't know . . . anything that happened while you were there?"

"We told the police," Brandon says, really bored now. "Over and over and over."

"I know, but if there's anything that

might help me find the man again — could you tell me?"

"He lied," Kai says. "Mommy never told him to take us. She was just in line getting our food."

"I know. So if there's anything —"

Kai heaves a sigh. "Okay. Concentrate, okay, Bran?"

They both shut their eyes and screw up their faces in exaggerated expressions of deep concentration.

Kai opens his eyes and shrugs.

"I think that's enough," Emma says.

Brandon opens his eyes and turns to his brother. "Did we ever say about the dogs?"

Kai shrugs.

"Dogs?" I ask.

"Skinny ones," Brandon says. "You could see the bones. But they weren't hungry. He said they were supposed to be like that."

I thank Emma at the door, so profusely that she's almost embarrassed. "I don't see how it helped much," she says. She bites her lower lip. "I hope it helped. I hope you find them."

I can hear the boys in the room behind us, and the sound of their voices sets off a throb of loss. I can't seem to move and there's a kind of awkward silence. Emma clears her throat. Obviously she doesn't want to close the door in my face, but she's got homework to do and boys to get to bed. "Well," she says, "good luck."

"They're lucky to have you," I say at last. "They're lucky to have you for a mother."

She scratches an eyebrow with her pinky, then gives me a wry look. "Thanks," she says, and shifts from foot to foot, "but they were born addicted to smack, you know — so I've got some ground to make up."

"Well, for my money you'll do it and then some," I say.

This avuncular platitude seems to make her nervous. She wants me to leave. The truth is I'm having trouble moving because I'm depressed by the prospect of heading back to the Drop Anchor.

"Well," Emma says. My hesitation on her doorstep is only adding to her second thoughts.

It's with some effort that I toss a little salute and turn away from her door. Yes, I've confirmed my guess that the abductor of the Sandling boys is the same man who took my sons, but where does it get me? Am I any closer to finding them?

chapter 19

Back in D.C., I consult my notebooks and throw myself into the pursuit of my "leads," such as they are.

The dimes. If Emma's friend Amalia was correct about the connection with voodoo, I know where to start. One of the producers at the station — Scott — did a piece about voodoo last year. He was somewhere down in Florida, where there's a significant Haitian population.

"Hey, Alex! Miss you, man. How's it going?"

"I'm hanging in."

"If I can do anything, you —"

"Matter of fact, that's why I called. Remember that piece on voodoo? I have a question and I thought you could tell me where to go with it."

"A voodoo question? Sure. If I can't answer, I'll know where to point you."

"The person who took the kids left some mementos behind in my house."

"Wait. Weren't your kids abducted from some fair?"

"The kidnapper brought them back to the house and he left some things behind. I'm not sure the police ever released any of this."

"*Voodoo* mementos?"

"Some of them. I think so, anyway."

"Jesus! Dolls?"

"No. Coins. A row of coins. And a bowl of water, placed up high."

"You know — that reminds me of this case at a nursing home in Cocoa Beach. The SEIU was trying to organize some of the help in a series of nursing homes down in that area. In one of them, the nursing home management retaliated by leaving voodoo . . . *messages,* I guess you'd call them . . . all over the facility. The janitorial staff was mostly Haitian, right? And these warnings, or whatever they were, took the form of patterns of coins and bowls of water in weird places. Ended up the management was charged with unfair labor practices! Intimidating the workforce, you know? Because those coins — they were curses. And those bowls of water — those were for the spirits to drink — implying that there were spirits *around,* you know. Thirsty ones."

"No kidding."

"The coins in your house — were they dimes?"

"Yes."

"Winged Liberty dimes — with the wings sort of coming out of Liberty's head?"

"How did you know?"

"Because those dimes are the coin of the realm in voodoo. I couldn't squeeze any of this into the program, but it was fascinating stuff. First off, because of those little wings, most people call the things Mercury dimes. So it's possible all of these superstitions are based on a misunderstanding. Because the head on that dime is supposed to be Lady Liberty. Anyway — Mercury was the Roman god of crossroads, of messages, of games of chance and sleight of hand. The god of magic. The way that fits is that Haitians believe some of the *houngans* have supernatural power — can do magic, in other words."

"What's a *houngan?*"

"That's a priest, a voodoo priest. Getting back to those Mercury dimes, the voodoo equivalent of Mercury is called Legba."

"The voodoo equivalent? There's an equivalent?"

"Voodoo's a very syncretic religion. It just appropriates bits and pieces from everywhere. Probably why it's still rolling on. So Legba, he's also related to St. Peter — guardian of the gates, right? This figure —

Mercury, Legba, St. Peter — it's all about access and thresholds."

"So how do these coins get to be curses?"

"Now that, I don't really know, but those nursing home workers would not even go into some of the rooms, they were that spooked."

"Hunh."

"I guess the Mercury dime can go either way luckwise, because people down in Louisiana and Florida wear the things around their necks on chains. Supposed to attract money."

"Really."

"Plus the dimes are used in mojo bags."

"Mojo bags?"

"Don't knock it. I got one made up when I did the story and maybe it's coincidence, but my life's been *happening* ever since. So for a mojo bag, you need a Mercury dime. You need a couple of roots — the kind would depend on what the *houngan* decides. Mine had a St. John the Conqueror root. I remember because I liked the name."

"Hunh."

"Anyway, the *houngans,* they know the right kinds of roots. So you get the Mercury dime, the roots, some sugar; you wrap it all up in a two-dollar bill; you wrap *that* up in a red flannel bag; you tie it all tight. Then to get your mojo *workin'*, as it were, you have to anoint the bag with the menstrual blood or urine of the woman you love. That part was a little tricky with Christine."

"I'll bet."

We talk a little longer, and I thank him, and in case I need to know more about voodoo, he gives me the name of an academic at Florida State.

I compile a list of medieval festivals. I know from previous forays that there are more of these things than you might think.

Lucky for me, the very first site Google kicks out — a Directorie of Faires — turns out to be a huge help. By clicking on the center of the elaborately tooled leather cover of the "book" that constitutes the homepage, I get access to an extensive list of events: *Faires, Festivals, Reenactments, Feasts, Pageants, Jousts,* and so on. Listed in chronological order, the faux parchment pages inside the "book" provide a wealth of information. Each separate fair or festival has links that contain details about the year in which the event or festival is "set" (1567, 1601, etc.), how long the particular venue has been in operation, the number of stages for performances, the number of booths selling goods and food, maps, weather information, hours, and admission prices — along with telephone numbers and other contact information about the management. There is even a "weapons policy" for each event, declaring whether or not weapons should be "peace-tied" (whatever that means).

Apart from two hundred and nine "major events," the directory also lists the artists and companies that drive these festivals, a mind-blowing catalog that encompasses everything from "birds of prey demonstrations" to fire-eaters and "baudy" comics.

Craftsmen and vendors have their own "page"; among the listings are purveyors of leather drinking vessels, "chaine maille," and juggling sticks.

Using the directory as a guide, my routine is to spend a few hours every day on the telephone with people who run the events. Most have to be won over, coaxed away from the instinct to be defensive and uncooperative. I understand why they don't want to talk to me. I'd definitely dodge calls from some desperate guy floating the notion that my fantasy world is the stalking ground of a kidnapper.

But mostly, I win them over, at least to the extent that they agree to post the Wanted poster in private employee areas.

I made the poster at Kinko's. Under the classic banner WANTED, it displays an array of the different sketches of the Piper (including the one created by the police artist who worked with the Sandling twins). Beneath the sketches is a brief description of the abduction of my sons, the circumstances and date, along with what's known of the Piper's physique, costume, and dog. Finally, there's contact information and the promise of a reward.

I send several packets a day — a cover letter and several copies of the poster. I use FedEx — even though it's expensive — for the sense of urgency implied by overnight delivery. I log the mailings into my computer, in which I've set up a file for each venue, so I can track follow-up calls and e-mails, responses, and the actions taken. Links to my calendar remind me when to follow up.

As soon as I finish with all of the events in the Directorie, I plan to tackle the vendor and artist lists. In the meantime, I take breaks from the medieval world to plan a similar campaign in the canine realm.

Maybe I can get to the Piper via his dog. I'm shocked when my first Google search — *whippet* — produces more than thirty-seven thousand sites. Lots of redundancies, but still, there are more whippet breeders, whippet clubs, and whippet fanciers than I'd ever imagined.

"Oh, yes," gurgles the woman from Whippet World, "they're *wonderful* pets, energetic but *pliant,* and so . . . just great looking, don't you think? Can I help you find a puppy? Is that why you called?"

My simple explanation — that I'm trying to find someone who was seen with a whippet — just confuses and worries her.

"This is all you know about the man, then — that he had a dog? Did the dog *attack* you?"

I explain who I am and why I'm trying to locate someone via his whippet.

"Oh," she says, her voice gone flat, all the enthusiasm evaporated. "Oh, dear. Well — I don't know. If the man doesn't *compete,* it will be awfully tough to find him. If he does compete, or even if he once did, then maybe there's a chance. But if he just bought a whippet from a puppy mill or even from a breeder, or acquired one through adoption — I don't know."

"Compete? You mean at dog shows?"

"Well, that's a possibility. Whippets are really, really on the upswing in hounds. We have great hopes for one of the boys at this year's Westminster, as a matter of fact."

"How many dog shows are there?"

"Oh, my *dear,* you can't imagine. But I think you'd be wasting your time looking in that direction. I wouldn't guess that an individual such as you're describing — well, one wouldn't think he'd seek out the *spotlight* by going to dog shows, particularly if he used the dog as — it's so painful to even *think* of this — as some kind of lure."

"So —"

"What might be worth a go is to look at other types of competition. No danger of press coverage there. Lots of whippet owners compete — we just seem to relish the battle, you know! And if your fellow was one of these, someone might recognize him. You did say you had a sketch you could distribute?"

"Yes."

"You might try that, circulate it amongst some of these groups."

"What are we talking about? You mean racing around a track?"

A fruity laugh. "Good Lord, not much of *that* going on these days. Mind you, I don't say you can't find old-fashioned oval racing if you really look for it, but coursing is *far* more popular — that's a form of racing in which the dogs chase lures. They're sight hounds, you know — whippets are — they chase on visual cue. Coursing usually involves obstacles and a convoluted path. We use white plastic bags for lures — *mun*dane but *hu*mane, as we say. Whippets are also great Frisbee dogs, and they truly excel at flyball and flygility and . . ."

I let her go on . . . and on . . . and at the end she promises to put a link to my poster on her website and to send me a list of whippet groups and breeders.

The packet arrives two days later by Priority Mail. The list inside provides the names of four hundred thirty-four groups and more than two hundred websites she suggests I might contact. *There will be some overlap, of course,* she notes on a Post-it. *Whippet owners are real joiners!*

I've still progressed through only forty-two events in my list of the medieval events. Now it would seem that exploring the whippet angle will require another huge effort. I feel overwhelmed, daunted, depressed. This is obviously the kind of manpower-intensive activity the police should do. Should have done. In my opinion.

The Elizabethan neck ornament known as the ruff provides another avenue for research. From my roster of vendors, I pull down a list of those involved in sewing and selling Renaissance garb — ruffs, bumrolls, doublets, farthingales. The catalog of dealers expands every time I talk to one of them. The market for ruffs extends beyond Renaissance festivals to drama companies, minstrels, troubadours, jesters, choirs, and circuses (where clowns and various animals wear ruffs). Not unlike the amazing number of medieval festivals and whippet fanciers, ruff-making turns out to be a cottage industry in its own right. You can buy them by mail or over the Internet or at the festivals themselves.

"I'm sorry, but we do most of our trade in cash," a woman from Carpe Diem Rags tells me. I make a few calls a day, but what looked like a narrow and promising angle now looks like it could consume months of my time.

I wake up in the middle of the night and think: *gym equipment*. How many people have ropes hanging from their ceilings?

Whatever the answer may be, I find out

the next day that you can buy ropes anywhere. The same rope suspended from ceilings for upper-body work is also used to tie off boats, to scallop along the edge of floats and docks for "impact cushioning," as handrails on gangplanks, for decoration in nautically themed restaurants. It can be purchased in marine supplies stores, also online and through mail order. It's available at Lowe's and Home Depot. An ordinary rope can be converted to a climbing rope with the addition of a cable-bight at one end, from which it can be suspended from the ceiling. And old climbing ropes seldom die. They migrate from first-rank health club and big, well-funded high school or gymnastics academy to church-sponsored gymnasiums and community center gyms . . . and from there to every kind of gimcrack fitness palace.

Emma comes through. The Corvallis police send their files on the Sandling case, which include copies of relevant files from Eureka. I pore over these for hours, and they do supply a few leads — names of fellow residents of the park where Emma and the boys lived in their tent, Dalt Trueblood's CV, names of the parents of Connor and Chandler's friends. I follow these leads, I talk to these people, but I find nothing new. How did Shoffler put it? I'm chasing smoke.

I spend hours a day, grinding away at my lists, working the telephone, getting my packets ready for FedEx. I go online at least four hours every day, too, following up on the e-mails still coming in via findkevinandsean.com.

The trouble with these computer sessions is that they wear me down. Hope flares and leads abound, but they all deteriorate into what Shoffler calls "Elvis sightings." It's a tightrope walk — trying to remain open-minded and alert without being too hopeful. The continuum of disappointment is wearing me down.

In the first three weeks, the findkevinandsean site was a great source of positive energy. There was a kind of buoyancy in knowing so many people out there were pulling for us. A vigilant public was anxious to help and we got a constant supply of reinforcement and even potentially useful information.

I still get well-wishers every day and the occasional query as to where contributions should be sent. The boys are the subjects of thousands of prayers and prayer chains. But apart from these and daily postings from a few women who have made it an avocation to troll missing children's sites looking to enable miracle reunions, the website has devolved into a magnet for wackos.

Well-intentioned wackos predominate, amateur and professional psychics mostly, along with practitioners of more eccentric forms of divination — all of them eager to offer their services, some for a fee, some for free. There are writers who want to write books about the boys, earnest types who've received messages in their dreams, adherents of various religious sects offering a spiritual haven to me and Liz.

And then there's what Liz calls "toxic spam." Badly spelled and syntactically twisted, these are e-mails that bristle with dark hints and bizarre innuendos or, worse, spin out some deeply disturbed fantasies in which the boys star as victims in nasty psychodramas.

There are death threats, too, for Liz and myself, along with cynical offers to market artifacts of the boys' childhood: artwork, clothing, baby teeth. We always turned over to the FBI the ones that seemed downright threatening, and I continue to do so, but just going through them on a daily basis is depressing.

* * *

Days pass when I hardly go outside. I spend fourteen, sixteen hours a day toiling at my lists. On the phone, sealing up packets, trudging through cyberleads. Despite my earlier intentions to be healthy and keep the house organized, I'm living on pizza and bagels and beer. The house is a wreck. My clothes are loose and the face in the mirror is haggard and gray. And disheveled. I'm letting my beard grow, and my hair. My gums bleed. My right hand — my mouse hand — develops a persistent cramp. Most of the time, I work with a kind of mindless determination, but once in a while, a bleak mood settles over me and I admit to myself that none of this work seems likely to get me one step closer to Kevin and Sean. The day comes when, for a moment, I allow myself to think about what it would be like to just . . . give up.

And that's worse — the chasm of emptiness — much worse than the feeling that I'm mining blind veins. Maybe what I'm doing is useless, but I'm doing *something.* I keep at it, working with the despairing energy of an underprepared student cramming for finals.

Because I can't shake off the feeling that time is running out.

chapter 20

"You look like shit."

Shoffler. It's Saturday night and the detective has dropped by unannounced. My heart does a little loop-de-loop at the sight of him — does he have *news?* — but I calm down when he hoists aloft a six-pack of Sierra Nevada.

"Gonna let me in? I even brought your favorite yuppie-scum brew."

"Hey." I hold open the door.

He screws up his face at the state of the living room. "Where's Martha Stewart when you need her?" and follows me into the kitchen, which earns another frown.

Shoffler pulls out two beers, holding them by the necks, then sticks the carton in the fridge. "Something's evolving in there, chief."

"You didn't tell me you were promoted to the housekeeping police."

At this lame attempt at a joke, Shoffler manages a polite little laugh: "Heh!" He twists off the caps, hands me one of the beers, then plunks himself down at the table. He raises his bottle, tips it toward me. "Cheers," he says.

I reciprocate. "What's up? How's the new gig?"

He makes a disgusted face. "It compares favorably with gum surgery."

"What do you mean?"

"I mean that essentially it's an exercise in crowd control — that's the bottom line." He tells me that if there's a terrorist incident in D.C., my best bet is to steal a canoe or rowboat. "Paddle out on the Potomac."

"You call that an evacuation plan?"

"Don't get me started." He takes a long pull on the beer. "What's up with you?"

"Not much."

He raises his eyebrows at that. "So why do you look so played out?"

"Maybe it's my total lack of success."

"But what about Sandling? No leads from the files?" We've talked on the phone a couple of times since my trip to Florida, so he knows about my meeting there and that Emma Sandling got her lawyers to send me the police files.

"I'm sure it was the same guy . . . or someone working with him, but beyond that I got nothing useful. At least so far."

"Nothing?"

"Jack."

"Hmmmm." He gets up, ambles to the refrigerator. "Another beer?"

"Why not?"

"So if you got nothing, what you been doing?"

"Come to headquarters," I tell him. We migrate to my study, and I give him a quick tour through my lists, the stacks of Wanted posters, my online pursuits. He nods.

We head back toward the kitchen, where Shoffler hits the fridge again. "You?"

"I'm all set."

He sits back down at the table and makes a gesture in the direction of my study. "What you're doing — it's like digging to China with a teaspoon. You know that, right?"

I shrug.

"You haven't spared much time for . . . housekeeping, I can see that. Or grooming, for that matter. You look like hell."

"Thanks. That why you're here?"

"Matter of fact, I was going to drop by anyway, but *yes.* I got a call from a concerned party — your neighbor, Mrs. Whoosey, the one with the dog."

"Mrs. Siegel."

"Right. I told you doing this shit would burn you out and you *are* burning out. I mean — look at this." He gestures at the room. "It looks like Baghdad. And look at *you*. This is fucked up, Alex."

"Thanks for the concern."

"Yeah, well, I feel like I owe you. I never should have bit on that T-shirt." A frown of self-disgust takes over his face for a moment and he seesaws his big head in a slow, rueful way. "He suckered us."

"So this is . . . what? Some kind of damage control?" I'm sorry as soon as this comes out of my mouth. My voice had the self-indulgent tone of a sulky teenager mouthing off to his parent. And I didn't mean it. I like Shoffler and I know he's here out of simple human concern. And the truth is, it's a relief to have him in my kitchen. My personal contact with humans has pretty much dwindled down to brief exchanges with Damon at Whatsa Bagel and Consuelo at Vace's Pizza.

Shoffler doesn't so much stand up as vault to his feet, instantly offended. "You know what? Fuck you." He slam-dunks his almost full bottle into the trash can, then stalks toward the door.

I follow him, unable to think of anything to say. When he gets to the door and turns around to face me, I see that his face is bright red. It makes me feel terrible.

"That was out of line, Ray. I'm sorry. I don't know . . ."

He pushes my apology away. "I consider you a friend, Alex. I came here as a friend. And that shit you're doing" — he slowly wags his head — "it's good to do, don't get me wrong. Who knows? Maybe you'll get something. But if you do, it will be like winning the lottery. In all my years, I have never seen that kind of legwork pay off. Ever."

I put my hands up, straight up, as if I just got busted and I'm surrendering. "I can't just sit here."

"You been keeping notebooks? You've been writing stuff down?"

"I'm your disciple there. I'm on number five. But I've been through them, Ray, over and over. I can practically recite what I've written down. I don't think there's one thing in there I haven't followed up on."

"Tell you what. You go out and get a pizza, and some more beer wouldn't hurt, either. And while you're doing that, let me take a look."

I shrug. "Okay."

When I get back, we have to clear space on the table for the pizza and search for napkins. It's been so long since I've been shopping that paper napkins are long gone: there's not a single paper towel left in the house, either. I end up in the dining room, extracting two pale green damask napkins from the armoire, where Liz keeps our linen, such as it is. The sight of the napkins, the feel of the fabric, sets off a small explosion of memories about the special occasions when we used these things. Christmas, Thanksgiving, the boys' birthday.

Shoffler tucks a napkin into his collar, separates a slice of pizza and more or less inhales it. "Damn," he says, taking a long pull of beer. "Burned the roof of my mouth. I always do — I missed that lesson on delayed gratification."

"Kevin always burned —" I stop myself. I jump on anyone who refers to the boys in the past tense. And now I'm doing it myself.

Shoffler nods, then taps notebook number three, which I see is separated from the rest of the stack. "Here's what I'd go after," he says. "The Gabler twins."

"The showgirls?"

"Showtwins. You went as far as you could with the Sandling boys, so next, I'd say check out Carla and Clara — and by the way, you kidding me? What kinda parents go and do that kind of thing?" He shakes his head, picks up another piece of pizza.

"But, they're women. Adults. *Showgirls*. I don't see how —" I shrug.

"Think outside the box a minute," Shoffler says. "I'm going through your notebooks and what I see is twins who disappeared. Just like the Sandlings. Just like yours."

"Except they didn't come back."

"Right, right, right. They were killed, so you don't want to think there's a connection."

"They weren't just killed. I never really took much of a look at it, but weren't they mutilated or something?"

"Something like that — all the more reason for you to shy away from any connection to your case. But what I'm saying is that there's a parallel. So maybe you should check it out. Go out there."

"To Vegas? Why?"

"If it's me? Because you can gamble all night and the food is great." He lets out a high-pitched laugh, but then gets down to business. "I'm serious. I can see what you think of this, but I'm telling you . . ." His voice trails away and he resets himself in the chair. "Look at it this way — your instinct to follow up on the Sandlings was right, okay? *Twins.*"

"But they were the same age, they were kids —"

"But now you're making a lot of assumptions. You're thinking it's about kids — and maybe it is. But you shouldn't assume that. What if it's about *twins?* It always struck me as odd — taking two kids. That didn't sit right. You wanta get your kids back? — you gotta have an open mind. Because you don't know. It might be about kids. It might be about twins. Or it might be about something else, something we can't even guess yet. But your sons are twins who disappeared and the Gablers are twins who disappeared."

"I don't know."

"So what — you think it's a waste of time," Shoffler says. "Like you've got something better to do?" He gestures toward the study. "Like you're hot on the trail?"

I shrug. He's right. I don't have anything better to do, except stay in lockstep with my e-mails and phone lists.

"Look, it's a lead. You might not like it, but like the man says, if you didn't have this lead, you wouldn't have no lead at all. I'm telling you. How many sets of twins who disappeared popped up in your research? I'll tell *you* because I went the same route." He counts them off on his fingers. "One — you got the Ramirez boys — but the guy who popped them popped himself. Nothing there. Then you got the Gabler girls. Then you got the Sandling boys. Maybe looking into the Gabler twins is a waste of time. But maybe not."

"I don't know."

He picks up the notebooks in one hand and holds them aloft, as if we're in court and they're evidence. "I looked through these, I gave them a good hard read. And the only thing that stuck out — and this is a professional opinion I'm giving you now, after my eighteen years as a detective. The only thing that stuck out was the Gablers. That's the only unturned stone."

"This is . . . I mean, is this a *hunch?*"

"Don't underestimate that shit."

I shrug. "If you think it's worth a shot." I'm in what-the-hell territory, but it isn't that simple. Maybe I'm agreeing to the trip as a way to make up for my earlier rudeness. Maybe Shoffler is selling me on Vegas and the Gablers because he thinks it will be good for me to get out of town.

"Anyway, it's cheap as hell this time of year," Shoffler says. "And I'm wired into the homicide squad there."

"I hear you're wired in everywhere."

He makes a cynical face, but behind it I can see he's pleased to hear that assessment. "Yeah," he says, "I'm AT&T. For all the good it does." He shakes his head. "No evacuation plan — can you believe it? We got this high-falutin' antiterrorism task force and this is the major policy decision so far. It's like the opposite of evacuation. We're talking about a military cordon — *keeping D.C. residents in.*"

"People will go nuts if it leaks."

"Oh, it's gonna leak. I might dime the *Post* myself." He pulls a hand back over his forehead. Under what, for lack of a better word, you'd call bangs, his forehead gleams a startling white. "Anyway . . . Vegas," he says. "There's this guy out there, friend of mine — Holly Goldstein. He'll get you the file on the Gabler girls."

"Holly?"

"Ha! Yeah — that's the nickname of a nickname. Hollywood Mike Goldstein. Everybody just calls him Holly. I'll give him a heads-up."

chapter 21

Vegas. I've never been to Vegas before. It just never happened. But like everyone, I guess, I had a full-blown notion of the place — equal parts glitz and sleaze. As it turns out, my mental Las Vegas pales before the real thing.

The initial mile out of the Avis lot from McCarran Airport *is* sleazy, as torn-up and funky as any disreputable stretch of Route 1. Tired motels and seedy casinos vie for space with down-at-the-heels wedding chapels and fringe commercial enterprises. The Hearing Palace. Leonard's Wide Shoes. The Laughing Jackalope. This last is a motel-casino right out of a B movie. In fact, you wouldn't get away with inventing The Laughing Jackalope. It's too seedy. The sign features a sinister rabbit decked out in a green tuxedo lounging against a fan of cards.

I pass a giant billboard advertising MICROSURGICAL VASECTOMY REVERSAL. (Is there a big market for this? The sign lists four locations.) Then I hit the first big hotel-casino, the sheathed-in-gold Mandalay Bay.

It's unbelievably huge, bigger than any structure in the D.C. area except maybe the Pentagon. And it's the first of many of these monsters. I'm reduced to gawking as I drive up the Strip in my rented Ford. Each hotel is like a separate theme park, a huge and lavish stage set. Mandalay Bay, Luxor, New York New York, Paris, the Bellagio, Caesar's Palace. A tidbit from the flight magazine said that the light from the Luxor's obsidian pyramid can be seen from outer space. The gigantic faces of Vegas-centric celebrities loom everywhere on massive billboards. David Copperfield, Lance Burton, Penn and Teller, Wayne Newton, Cirque du Soleil, Céline Dion.

Lights, billboards, crowds. It's Times Square on steroids.

But I'm not staying in one of these nouveau palaces. Priceline found me a bargain at the Tropicana. It's still huge, but compared to the new places, it seems almost petite. I drive around to the self-park lot and go into the hotel through the casino.

Which is so crowded it's hard to walk. A barrel-vaulted stained-glass roof sprawls above endless ranks of slot machines. Four women in bright green sequined costumes sing and dance on a stage-lit elevated platform. Lights flash, twinkle, pop. The air is filled with Nintendo tunes, a constant beep and boink of canned melodies interrupted by the occasional grace note — a cascade of coins as a machine pays off. Every pop phenomenon — movie, sitcom, celebrity, popular toy, ethnic emblem, nursery rhyme — boasts a slot machine counterpart. Falsetto choruses burst forth at regular intervals, caroling signature phrases. "Wheel of Fortune!" "Come on Down!"

By the time I fight my way through to the registration desk, I need a sensory deprivation chamber.

"Welcome to the Big Sleazy," Holly Goldstein says when I get him on the phone. "I pulled the files on the Gabler case. Got some time at three if you're not tapped out from your flight."

I tell him I'll be there.

"Grab a pencil," he tells me. "Folks expect we're right near the Strip or in old Vegas, but we're way out of town. In fact, if you're on the Strip, technically you're not even *in* Las Vegas. You're in Paradise."

"What?"

"Yeah. With a capital *P.* The developers incorporated the Strip as a separate jurisdiction called Paradise."

"Really."

"Yeah — in which case, you could say that the Las Vegas P.D. is a long way from Paradise. They stuck us out here in the burbs, like a bunch of dentists. It's about a thirty-minute drive, depending on traffic." Goldstein gives directions in the sonorous voice of an anchorman or voiceover specialist. Even his laugh is mellifluous, a liquid chortle. Shoffler told me that Goldstein was in showbiz before he turned to law enforcement. "That's what the 'Hollywood' is about. Holly did a cop show about twenty years back and his true vocation called him."

At two fifty, after driving through miles and miles of subdivisions and strip malls, I turn into what does, in fact, look like a suburban office park. The complex isn't even a stand-alone cop shop. The Las Vegas P.D. shares its headquarters with Happy Feet Podiatry, the Bahama Tanning Salon, Nauticale Pool Services. Finally, I spot a clutch of white vans marked CRIME SCENE, and a set of doors identified as CRIMINALISTICS, and I figure I'm in the right area. A man wielding a leaf blower turns it off to speak to me, but shrugs when I ask him where to find Homicide. A colleague, mulching a shrub, points over his shoulder. *"Por aquí."*

In the reception area, two women tap away on computers. The wall behind them displays a large super-realistic photo of woodlands, a country-style wreath with fake birds and eggs, and some children's drawings. One woman asks my business, then buzzes Goldstein and tells me to wait, gesturing toward a tiny alcove just big enough to hold two chairs. I sit, facing a framed engraving of a wooded path. The gilded inscription reads: YOU'LL NEVER WALK ALONE.

Goldstein is a tall, handsome man in his early fifties, with silver hair and jet black eyebrows. We shake hands, and he delivers what amounts to a testimonial to Ray Shoffler. "Ray's ears must be burning," Goldstein concludes, "but I kid you not, the guy is really something. Old school. We get all hung up now in technology and it's great, okay? Our case files are ten times as thick as they were even ten years ago — we get that much data. And it can help, especially in court. But to solve a crime? Nah. Sometimes you get lost in all that crap; it works against you. Take 9/11. The information was there, but it got lost in the data stream. Ray cracked a case for me one time strictly on a hunch."

"I'm here on one of his hunches."

"There you go," he says, with a dip of the head. "Hey, Cindy," he calls out. "Open Sesame."

I follow him through a metal gate that swings open with an electronic growl. We make our way through a warren of tiny offices, edging past a crew working with a huge camera and boom mike. They seem to be in the process of photographing a piece of paper. "Cold case," Goldstein says, with a nod toward the cameraman. "They're assembling documents. You can't afford to slap these things in a scanner. You gotta preserve the original — so they have to be photographed. The deal is we just elected a new sheriff. One of his campaign promises was to go after the cold cases."

"Like the Gablers?"

He shrugs. "All of them, supposedly. But with the Gablers, I don't know. Thing is, they're kind of an orphan case."

"What do you mean?"

We arrive at a conference room. Goldstein gestures toward one of the dozen chairs arrayed around a wooden table. "Let me explain how we work here. First of all, we got a huge area to police. Clark

County and the city of Las Vegas — it's more territory than the state of Massachusetts. Eight thousand square miles." He nods toward the huge satellite photo of Las Vegas and environs that occupies one wall. "And growing. Fastest growing city in the U.S. The workload can be a bitch. We're supposed to work these cold cases in our down periods — which is a joke around here."

"You have a lot of murders?"

"Less than you'd think. We average maybe a hundred fifty homicides a year. And hardly any of our work comes from the Strip. The big casinos have a huge stake in safety — and there's lots of surveillance. Tourists don't get popped — that's quite rare. And they don't come to Vegas to pop each other, either. Most of our business is the same as anywhere else. Husbands and wives, boyfriends and girlfriends. Meth labs, drug deals gone sour."

"So the Gablers . . . what do you mean they're orphans?"

He slaps his hands down, one at a time, on the two binders on the table in front of him. "Clara and Carla. Carla and Clara. They're orphans two times over — or would that be four? For openers, they're actually orphans — their folks got killed in a car crash down around Searchlight. The girls were seventeen."

"That's terrible."

"Cars kill *way* more people than guns. It's not even close! I mean, forty thou a year get killed in cars, just here, in the U.S. That's like a coupla jumbo jets crashing every single week. Anyway, the Gabler girls — not only are they orphans, but their *case* is orphaned, too. See, the way it works is every detective *owns* his cases. The investigating detective — once it's his case, it's always his case. The guy who ran the Gabler investigation was Jerry Olmstead. He had the desk next to mine, which is why I know as much about the case as I do. Anyway, Jerry had his thirty-five in, high blood pressure, the wife was antsy. So he retired, moved to Lake Havasu. A month later, *to the day* — his ticker goes off."

"Jeez."

"So that's how the Gablers became orphans the second time around. And it's not good when a victim loses his or her investigating detective. You get attached, you know what I'm saying? Right from the get-go. It's your case; it's your baby." He leans toward me, his face earnest. "It sounds like bullshit, but we really feel — I mean we detectives — we really feel like we're working for the victims. Soooo —" He shrugs. "With Jerry gone, the Gabler case has no built-in advocate. It's a pretty high-profile deal, so maybe the guy who inherited the case will take it on, now that the sheriff's got a hard-on for cold cases. But I doubt it, I really do."

I don't say anything. I'm thinking about Shoffler's move to the task force.

"So why didn't *you* inherit the Gabler case?"

"Didn't want it. Tough case. And I was slammed, anyway. On account of the Mongols."

"The what?"

"The Mongols. Motorcycle gang. Them and the Angels had a war down in Laughlin. Lotta people killed. Lotta witnesses to interview. I was in court for months.

"But look," he says, shifting gears. "I checked to see who has the case, and it's Moreno's. Pablo Moreno. He's a pretty good guy. He's in court this week, but you can give him a call on his cell." He tells me the number, and I log it in my notebook.

"So this Moreno — he's working the Gabler case?"

Goldstein shakes his head. "No. Like I said, maybe he'll pick it up now that there's this push, but I wouldn't put money on it. Like all of us, he's got dozens of cold cases to choose from. And the Gabler case has a strike against it."

"What's that?"

"No one's beating the drums. Sometimes you have a murder and ten years later, Mom or Dad is still making it their business to call and follow up with us. And I mean every single day. But the Gabler girls? Uh-uh. No one making noise at all. Sort of the opposite."

"What do you mean?"

"The murder was so . . . grotesque, you know? And these girls, they worked on the Strip. Well, two blocks off, but close enough, y'know? And the Strip — that's our bread and butter. Horrific unsolved crimes are not the publicity you want. Not exactly." Goldstein frowns. "My way of thinking — the sensational aspect of the murders actually works against the case being pursued. It's bad for business. Too . . . visceral, you know what I'm saying?"

"I guess."

"Let me put it this way. Here in Vegas, we got guys with man-eating tigers, we got disappearing cars and people, we got roller coasters will scare the living shit out of you. We got showgirls up the kazoo. Heck, every two-bit casino — even some restaurants — has beautiful waitresses with their asses and tits hanging out all over the place. But it's all . . . packaged, you know. The death-defying magic shows, the rides and all — it's thrills and no spills. And as for the showgirls, that's sanitized, too. Sex without fluids, as someone put it. Not that we don't have call girls and prostitutes — Jesus, it's frickin legal here. You've seen the booty boxes?"

"Yeah." He's referring to metal boxes that stand on many streets amidst the boxes vending *USA Today* or the like, but inside are the details and photos of many of the town's prostitutes.

He shakes his head. "Most towns have real estate sheets in those things, you know? Homes for sale. We got hos for rent. Anyway, the Gabler case — showgirls massacred! — considering all it had going for it, the story actually moved to the back pages pretty damn fast."

"Hunh."

"No family — that really hurt, I think. So anyway, the case just kinda faded away."

"So it's okay if I look at the files? Moreno won't mind?"

He holds out his hands and rolls them

open in the direction of the binders. "All yours. Not that there's a lot in there. I mean — no one reported these girls missing for more than two weeks."

"Jesus."

"Well, you know, it's *Vegas*. New people pouring in all the time. Other people pouring out." He thumps the notebooks again. "Clara and Carla," he says, with a rueful shake of his head. "Even after their roommate gets around to wondering if something happened to them, it's another week before there's any evidence of foul play. Up to then, nobody's even *looking* for these girls. That's what you'd figure, you know? They took off for L.A. or Maui or just went back home. Whatever. I mean, apart from each other, they had no family, no one really paying attention that they're missing. In the meantime, the trail's gettin' *way* cold. I mean — two weeks is a lifetime."

"This evidence —" I say. "You're talking about . . . when the hiker found them?"

"Right. *That* poor sonofabitch. He had to be hospitalized! They had to helicopter him outta there. But he didn't *find* them."

"No?"

"Not exactly. Not *them*. He just found half of Clara, right? The bottom half."

chapter 22

Goldstein is right. After an hour and a half with the files, I don't know much more about the murders than I did from the news stories.

The last time anyone saw them, the Gablers were working the topless show at the Blue Parrot. The personnel director at the Parrot, one Clay Riggins, left three messages on the twins' voice mail, ascending in irritation level — and then gave up. The messages provided the police with a probable date for the girls' disappearance. And no, Riggins didn't call the police, figuring the girls just blew town or got a better gig somewhere else. From Jerry Olmstead's interview with Riggins: *They were identical twins, you know? Not that hot, but they were learning a few makeup tricks and getting better at dancing. There were angles you could work with them, you know?*

Tammy Yagoda, a twenty-three-year-old showgirl at the Sands, had been the Gablers' roommate. She was the one who reported them missing. She hadn't seen them for two weeks — and that time frame meshed in nicely with the date of their first no-show at the Parrot. Tammy told the police that the last time she saw them, the twins were fine. They were working at the Parrot, they were taking dance and speech lessons. The thing was, Tammy had more or less just moved in with a new boyfriend, Jaime, so it wasn't until she went back to the apartment to get some clothes that she realized something was wrong. The stench from the litter box hit her as soon as she opened the door. Romulus and Remus, the two Burmese cats who belonged to the Gablers, were ravenous. Yagoda reported that the twins adored the felines; they never would have left the cats like that. So she knew something was wrong.

She was right about that.

Red Rock Canyon is a popular tourist site about twenty miles from Vegas. A well-marked thirteen-mile scenic drive leads the visitor through the Mojave Desert landscape. Dramatic rock formations form a backdrop for native fauna (bighorn sheep, desert tortoise, wild burro) and flora (cholla and barrel cactus, manzanita, Joshua tree). The rocks bear pictographs and petroglyphs, the work of Paiute Indians, dating back at least a thousand years. It isn't just tourists who love the place — the locals do, too. It's a haven for the hordes of native Vegas hikers, mountain bikers, and rock climbers. The brochures and maps encourage everyone to "Leave No Trace."

Josh Gromelski, solo hiking in an isolated area behind Icebox Canyon, stumbled upon more than a trace. He'd scaled the walls of Icebox and had entered an area behind it, which led to a much smaller canyon known as Conjure Canyon. Free climbing, he nearly tumbled to his death after setting a handhold that, when he pulled himself up, brought his face about four feet from the torso and legs of what turned out to be Clara Gabler. Gromelski had a GPS system and a cell phone in his backpack. He lasted long enough to call in his gruesome discovery before tossing his Clif Bars and going into shock.

I can see why. The crime-scene photos are stomach-turning. I force myself to take a second look, although I don't know why. Like other photos I've seen — the piles of naked Jewish corpses being tipped into mass graves, the gas-bloated bodies at Jonestown, the fallen Taliban fighter on the road outside Tora Bora, his pants pulled down and a crowbar jammed up his ass — the first glance is indelible. Like other sights I've seen in person — the carnage in Kosovo, where I beheld a pregnant woman with no head — some things don't require a second look.

The photo of Clara Gabler's lower half joins what has become, over the years, a gallery of horror in my head, a place where such images — the ones you wish you'd never seen — are imprinted forever. The trunk is severed at about the waist, the legs splayed apart, one of them slightly bent. The upper cavity is like some obscene bowl, the edge of skin and subcutaneous fat at the cut comprising the container that holds a gnawed mash of red pulp.

Despite the damage done by predators, the lower half of Clara Gabler did not deteriorate much in the dry Mojave air. Except for the tattered flesh still visible where the body was severed (*wildlife,* the crime scene report noted, *removed the organs*), the torso and legs look like the lower half of a doll. The shapely legs are encased in fishnet stockings, the feet — slightly turned in — are still shod in patent leather sandals with four-inch heels. A scrap of gold-sequined fabric — like the bottom half of a bathing suit, but shredded and twisted at the waistline — covers Clara's lower trunk.

The identity of the legs and torso was not established until later, although it didn't take long to find the other half of Clara Gabler once the police went looking. It was only twenty yards away, wedged into a rock crevice, apparently dragged there by coyotes. This is the half with a face, a face with nibbled sockets for eyes. Looking at it is difficult: the freakish way her body suddenly stops, just below the rib cage . . .

Carla was found about fifty yards away, facedown in a little gully. According to the reports, animals and birds had been feeding on the bodies for approximately two weeks before the hiker found them.

Carla Gabler met death in a more conventional way than her sister. She was shot, execution style, behind the right ear. It's almost a relief to sift through the photographs in her file, and I have to remind myself that she, too, was murdered in cold blood. The crime-scene photograph shows Carla in her costume: fishnet stockings, high-heeled sandals, gold-sequined panties, jewel-encrusted bra. She was facedown on a rock when shot. Between livor mortis, predator damage, and the exit wound made by a .38 caliber bullet, her face is unrecognizable.

If the photos are brutal, the text offers no refuge. The dry prose of the autopsy report notes that Clara was cut in half by a saw powerful enough to slice through her spinal column. *The incision passes straight through the soft tissue of the abdomen, slightly above the umbilicus, severing the intestine at the duodenum . . . continuing through the intervertebral disk between the second and third lumbar vertebrae.*

But it's even worse than that. According to the medical examiner, *injury to subject's trunk occurred premortem.* The cause of death was exsanguination.

The language of the report fails to blunt its meaning. Clara Gabler was alive when she was cut in half, alive when her murderer sent her soul howling into the next dimension.

In other words, I tell myself, the butchery wasn't carried out in an effort to make the body more compact for disposal. It was an act of sadism.

But not, apparently, the result of a sex crime. Neither woman had been molested. In fact, according to the medical examiner, there was no evidence of recent sexual activity on the part of either one. Various documents in the files — Q and A's with Yagoda, Riggins, with other residents of the Palomar Apartments, where the Gabler girls lived, and with fellow employees at the Parrot — explored the notion that maybe the twins did a little hooking on the side. "Hey," Goldstein said, "they're identical twins, it's Vegas, they're *showgirls*, fah Chrissake. A few three-ways, to help make ends meet? It wouldn't exactly surprise anyone." But according to Yagoda, Carla and Clara — while not virgins — were not "like that." "Not at all," Goldstein says. "Didn't even go out that much. In fact, Yagoda said the Gabler girls *worried* about just that kind of thing. The twin thing. They hated it when people joked about three-ways — which happened, you know. They didn't even like to double-date."

Yagoda made the formal identification of the girls. For the record she stated that when the Gabler twins were alive, she could tell Clara from Carla with ease, through mannerisms and figures of speech. But now . . .

Distinguishing identification was eventually made through dental records. Both girls were cavity-free, but Clara chipped a tooth when she was nine and subsequently paid for a porcelain veneer — and this allowed investigators to determine which corpse was which.

The reports also make it clear that although, postmortem, predators may have dragged the corpses a few yards, the Gabler girls were not killed elsewhere and then dumped in Conjure Canyon. They were killed not far from where they were found.

I go through the binders again, first Clara, then Carla, taking notes. I spend a couple of hours plowing through the brutal eight-by-tens, looking at the sketches, reading every single document. And when I'm done, I have to say I feel sick, and tired. And it looks as if I've wasted my time.

Still, I'm in Vegas and I know that when I get back, Shoffler's going to ask me — did I do this, did I do that? I can almost channel him: interview Tammy Yagoda, go to the Blue Parrot, visit the crime scene, find out where the costumes came from. And so on.

Goldstein nods his head when I tell him this. "You should speak to Chisworth, too. Barry Chisworth. He's the M.E. worked the case. Bright guy. Probably noticed stuff didn't make it into print."

"Like what?"

Goldstein shrugs. "Who knows? A guess at the weapon, a hunch about the murderer — but nothing really substantiated by evidence. Guessing is not part of the M.E.'s job, and they don't speculate on paper for good reason: anything they put down has a good chance of ending up in court. They're real careful to confine written remarks to what they can back up. But of course they *do* have opinions. You get a good M.E., like Chisworth, he might pass his take on the thing on to the investigating officer. Which in this case, unfortunately, would be the late Jerry Olmstead."

I write down Chisworth's name, and the number for the M.E.'s office.

"But you can cross off the costumes," Goldstein says. "I can tell you where they came from — the Parrot. What's his name — Riggins — he was pissed about that. Jerry could not believe it. Here's this brutal double murder and this bozo's pissed about his costumes. We thought he might ask for the undamaged one back."

"So why the costumes? Why were they wearing them?"

Goldstein shakes his head. "They were probably on their way to work. Apparently they liked to dress at home, do their makeup, too. Didn't like the dressing room scene at the Parrot." Goldstein's digital watch emits a little chirp, and he stands up. "Hey, I gotta go."

He sticks out his hand. I thank him for his help.

"My pleasure. And if there's anything else — just call me. You planning to head out to Conjure Canyon at some point?"

"Maybe. I'm not sure what I could really see." I don't say what I'm thinking — which is that I don't see the point of any of this, that I don't see how the Gabler case can have anything to do with Sean and Kevin, that I believe it's make-work, suggested by Shoffler to get me out of the house.

I can thank the detective for that, at least. Now that I'm not doing it — the long days and nights with my lists and phone calls, the constant and obsessive prowl through cyberspace — it seems like motion without direction. A gerbil wheel.

Goldstein shrugs. "In the gospel according to Ray, you always go to the scene. You never know how it's going to speak to you." He scoops up the files. "On the other hand" — he squints at me — "don't try traipsing up to Conjure Canyon in your street shoes. In fact, you might consider hiring a guide. It's rugged out there. And this time of year, you gotta get an early start or the sun will eat you up."

Goldstein has a point about the sun. It takes five minutes of open doors and maxed-out air to cool down the car to the point where I can touch the steering wheel. I can see why the locals are so vigilant about window sunshields. It may be a dry heat but it hits you like a strong safety. I drive past a bank thermometer. A hundred and five.

Back at the Tropicana, a Bulgarian acrobat performs on the elevated stage. He stands on one hand on a wobbling tower of blocks, earning a splash of applause from the gathered crowd. Most of the Tropicana patrons don't even look, transfixed by the plink-plink boing-boing of the slots.

Up in my room, I flesh out the notes I took at the police department and then make a to-do list:

1. *The Blue Parrot/Riggins*
2. *Yagoda (roommate)*
3. *The M.E.: Barry Chisworth*
4. *Conjure Canyon*

Might as well do it by the numbers. With a little luck, I can knock off the first three today and head out to the canyon early in the morning. But I'm not optimistic. As I reach for the phone book, I've got to say that this unturned stone of Shoffler's doesn't feel a whole lot different from the gerbil wheel.

Two young women, identical twins, dressed in provocative costumes. One butchered, one assassinated. Shoffler may be famous for his hunches, but he's got to be wrong this time. This doesn't have anything to do with my kids. It *can't*.

chapter 23

The Blue Parrot is only a couple of blocks off the Strip, but it's several steps down from the splendor of the big casinos. Even from the exterior, the down-at-heels look hits me: A few nonfunctioning tubes in the gigantic sign give the neon parrot a disheveled look, as if it's molting.

I pop for valet parking, handing my keys to a distinguished-looking man in his sixties. He gives me an austere nod along with a bright blue claim ticket. It occurs to me that Vegas is the ultimate service economy, so there are lots of men like this — dapper retirees who look as if they ought to be sitting in boardrooms.

At six p.m., the place seems tired and dingy, only a couple of its tables going, stage curtains drawn, the place mostly empty. A few hardy types slam away at the slots, but at this hour most of the patrons are there for the $3.99 Early Parrot Dinner.

A fatigued woman in a cheetah-print micro-dress sighs and shows me into the boss's office. This is a ten-foot box, paneled in fake wood, with a scrofulous magenta carpet and a particleboard desk from which the veneer is beginning to separate and curl. Clay Riggins, fifty, bald, with the permanent squint of a smoker, has seen better days himself — although a big diamond stud in one ear speaks of a certain bravado. He's on the phone, a Diet Dr Pepper in his hand. He raises it by way of hello and continues his conversation. Which concerns pool maintenance.

I stand there for more than five minutes, counting the number of empty Dr Pepper cans in the room (fourteen) and wondering what I can possibly learn from Riggins. What do I even *hope* to learn? *Something,* Shoffler says in the back of my head. Or maybe not. The detective would tell me that the process can be circuitous. *This guy, maybe he says something and later you put it together with something else.*

Riggins finally hangs up. "Sorry 'bout that," he says, with a little grimace. "These days, you gotta ride herd on every single thing, know what I mean?" He shakes his head. "So you're here about the Gabler sisters."

"Right."

"Well, I don't mind talkin' to you, but I

hardly knew these girls, know what I'm saying?"

"They worked for you for eight months," I point out.

"Yeah yeah yeah, but plenty of people work for me. I didn't really know the two of them — didn't even know where they lived."

I'm not sure what to ask him. "Were they . . . good at their job? What did they do, anyway?"

"We gotta stage show — bird theme. They more or less came out in their costumes, took their tops off, and shook their tits along with a dozen other girls, while one of the dancers or singers did her thing in the middle. And no — they weren't very good at it. They had the twin thing going for them, and that was about it."

"Hunh."

"Truth is, they weren't that pretty," Clay Riggins tells me. "I kept telling them, they needed a little work, a little less nose, a little more boob." He barks a laugh. "Then" — he seesaws his hands in the air — "maybe I showcase them a little more. As it was . . ." He expels a dismissive puff of air and taps his hands on the desk.

"So what did you think when they didn't show up for work?"

"Now, that," he says, as if this never occurred to him before, "was not like them. Dependable — yeah, I give 'em that. Never missed a single day of work."

"So — weren't you surprised when they didn't show up? Didn't you think something might be wrong?"

He frowns, pushes the air with his hands, as if shunting this notion right back to me. "Nah — this is *Vegas,* son."

"So what did you think?"

"Truth?" He fingers his earring. "I thought they went home. Took jobs in Wal-Mart or the Dairy Queen or whatever. I thought they were like a lot of girls come here — hoping to meet Prince Charming or catch the eye of some Hollywood director or whatever damn thing these girls think. I thought maybe they figured out it wasn't going to happen and decided to bag it. They were on the shy side — maybe didn't want to come and tell me in person. That's what I thought." He shrugs and drains his Dr Pepper. "But maybe not."

"What do you mean?"

"Tammy? Their roommate — she's the one brought them to me. A good kid, Tammy. Works at the Sands now. Anyway, the twins told her they had an audition, thought they had a line on a new job."

I sit up straight. This is new. "What audition? Where?"

Riggins shrugs. "I don't think Tammy said."

Tammy Yagoda lives with her fiancé, Jaime, in a new condo five miles out of town toward the Hoover Dam. The living room contains a huge television and an overstuffed couch. "We just moved in," Tammy apologizes. "It's going to be soooo great! Good thing we're minimalists — right, honey?" She gives Jaime a megawatt smile and asks him to get me a chair.

Jaime brings in a beat-up straight-backed chair from the dining alcove. The two of them twine together on the couch as we talk, trying to keep their hands off each other. But failing.

"Tammy's been through all this a million times," Jaime warns me. "She can't think of anything she has to add."

Tammy looks up at him adoringly — her champion. "I still can't believe it," she tells me, her features clouding. "They were such sweetie pies, really nice girls." She twists her pretty face into a grimace. "It was so horrible."

Jaime gives her a buck-up hug and a peck on the cheek.

"How were they *nice?*"

"In just about every way," Tammy says. "Do anything for you. Plus" — she looks at Jaime — "they were, you know, a little *naive*."

"What she means," Jaime puts in, "is they were sexually inexperienced."

"Jaime!" She gives his thigh a little girly slap.

"Hey, he asked," Jaime says. "Why not say what you mean? Now, I didn't know these girls, but from what Tammy told me, they were like . . . off the truck."

"He's right," Tammy says, with a sigh and a sad little shake of her head. "They were soooo naive. Like they believed guys when guys said they weren't married."

"You told me they didn't even know what a blow job was. Thought it involved blowing air on someone's dick. You had to explain it to them."

"Jaime!" Another slap.

"I mean, what planet were they living on, you know?"

"So they didn't date much."

"Oh, no," Tammy says. "I lived with them for almost a year and maybe they each had a couple of dates. Don't get me wrong: they weren't virgins, but they were like — they had to be in love to have sex with someone, you know? That kind of cuts down on your social life here. They hated doing the topless thing. They couldn't wait to get out of that."

"No old boyfriends, no stalkers they were worried about, no admirers, no one . . . uh . . . romancing either one of them?"

"I met Jaime a couple of weeks before they went missing and it was" — she looks at her fiancé — "it was love at first sight. So maybe they met someone in that two weeks, 'cause I was *busy*." A chuckle from Jaime. "But far as I know, there was no one."

Jaime rubs her thigh and kisses her neck. I feel like a voyeur.

"Guys came on to them, of course, all the time," Tammy says, "but they never brought anyone home. They weren't like that. And I taught them to be careful. Coming home from the Parrot, there's a guy escorts you to your car; they're real good about that. But even so, I told them — don't ever get into your car without looking in the backseat. Always check behind you."

"How about a guy with a dog — a whippet? You ever see anyone like that?"

"No. Clara was afraid of dogs. They were cat people."

I ask if the twins were into medieval festivals or Renaissance fairs.

"What's that?" Tammy asks.

"You know, Tammy," Jaime answers, "one of those things with knights and shit. Like *Excalibur*. My cousin Wilson dragged me to one of them a couple years ago. I thought it was dorky, but Wilson — he loved that shit." He rubs Tammy's thigh. "It might be the kind of thing those girls'd be into."

"I don't think so," Tammy says. "They weren't like . . . historical." She brightens. "They did go to see *Harry Potter*. . . ."

I ask Tammy's opinion: What does she think happened to them?

Tammy shivers and looks at Jaime. "I don't know. Some psycho. I mean, what else? It has to be. Someone who followed them from the Parrot. Found out where they lived. Stalked them." She squeezes her eyes shut. "Gives me the creeps."

Jaime agrees. "I wouldn't let Tammy go near her apartment — not after she found the cats abandoned like that. Even before the cops discovered the bodies, Tammy knew something terrible happened. She just *knew*."

"That was sad, too," Tammy says, turning her woeful gaze toward Jaime, "about the cats. I tried to find a home for them, but they had to go to the shelter."

"Clay Riggins mentioned some kind of audition," I tell her. "You know anything about that?"

"Yeah! And that's soooo sad, too, you know? They were so stoked about that. They worked their butts off — speech classes, dance, Pilates, got their teeth whitened. And it looked like it was all about to pay off. And then . . ."

"What kind of audition was it? I mean, what was it for?"

Tammy shrugs. "Some kind of magic show."

"A magic show? Hunh. You know anything else about it?"

Tammy shakes her head. "This is just like . . . like two days after I met Jaime. Clara told me about it when I called to tell her where I was — because I knew they'd worry, you know? She said she thought they really had a shot. She was excited, but . . . I was on my cell, at work. I didn't get any details."

Ezme ("with a *z*") Brewster, the owner and resident manager of the Palomar Apartments, greets me with a "Howdy." She's sixty, or maybe even seventy.

Reading glasses suspended from a rhinestone chain rest on her chest. In one hand, she holds a TV remote; in the other, a lit cigarette. She gestures with the cigarette toward the color TV in the corner. "Come on in, honey, but hold your fire for a minute. I'm watching something."

From the television, Maury Povich says: "Let's find out right now!" The camera flips to a black teenager, head hanging to reveal intricate cornrows, then to a shot of a smiling toddler.

"In the case of two-year-old Devon," Maury says, opening an envelope, "Donnell — you *are* the father."

An overweight woman jumps up and does a kind of victory dance, then shakes her fist, cursing out the kid with the cornrows — who now wears a kind of shit-eating grin. Little bursts of pixilated fog cover the woman's mouth as she shouts expletives.

Ezme hits the *power* button. "Rotting my damn brain," she says, stubbing out her cigarette. "But what the hell. I'm not gonna solve the conflict in the Middle East at my age. So you're here about the Gabler girls?" She makes a sad face, shakes her head. "How can I help?"

"I'm not sure." I explain to her who I am

and that I'm checking out murders involving twins.

"Oh, my God, of *course*. You poor man. Those little boys. I saw you on TV. Terrible thing. And you think there's some connection with Clara and Carla? Good Lord. . . . Well, they were some of the best damn tenants I ever had. A real damned shame. Paid on time, kept the place neat as a pin, no male visitors. I was in the hospital when they disappeared. Electrolytes out of balance or some damned thing. If I'd been here, I damn sure would have reported them missing a lot sooner than happened."

"So you saw them regularly."

"Every single day. They were homebodies, those two. Rare in this town."

I ask her the usual set of questions about tall men, skinny dogs, medieval fancies. She shakes her head: no, no, and no, not so far as she knew.

"Did you know anything about an audition for a magic show?"

She nods. "That was another damned shame. They worked like dogs improving themselves, spending all their hard-earned money on this kind of lesson and that kind of lesson. They finally get a shot, and then —" She heaves a sigh, which turns into a prolonged coughing fit.

"Who was the audition for?"

She taps her head. "It was a new act, just getting started. There was to be some weeks of rehearsal. Clara did tell me the name of it." She sighs, looks at the ceiling. "But I don't really remember. The Meressa Show? Marassa? Malessa? Some kind of name like that — reminded me of *molasses*. The audition was at the Luxor, I think — or maybe it was the Mandalay Bay."

I ask for her take on what happened.

She lights a cigarette. "Some wacko lured 'em out to Red Rock, killed 'em for fun. That's what I think."

"I guess that's the theory."

"What else could it be? The police dug back into their high school days and their hometown and all, and they didn't find a thing. It didn't seem to be personal, either, know what I mean?"

"You don't think so?"

"I don't. Nobody claimed it. No sexual motive. What I think is they were killed more or less for fun."

"Maybe."

"Watching television as much as I do," Ezme says, "you get a good idea what people can get themselves up to. Between the reality shows and the news, I'd say we're closing in on the Romans. Except — when we get to the gladiator stage, Barbara WaWa will interview the guy before he heads out into the ring. And the gladiator will thank everybody in creation who got him the chance to die on television. His manager. His hair stylist. His personal trainer."

"Can I see the apartment?"

"Oh, honey, there's nothing to see. A couple with a baby lives there now."

"What about the girls' belongings?"

"I left the apartment right like it was for three or four months. The girls didn't have much stuff and what they had wasn't worth a bean, but I couldn't bring myself to clear it out. Police finally tracked down some cousin out in North Dakota. This cousin — she didn't want nothing. Not one thing. Kinda sad, isn't it? Didn't really know the girls. Didn't want to bury her kin, neither. The girls are planted here, courtesy of the state. I finally gave what was useful to the Purple Heart. They came and fetched it, see."

I'm out of questions. I thank Mrs. Brewster and turn toward the door.

She stops me with a hand on my arm. "Oh, Lord. And them in their little costumes. You think it was this audition, don't you?" She sucks in a breath.

"The audition? What do you mean?"

"Isn't that what you're thinking? That some crazeball *lured* them, used their hopes and dreams to suck them in — had them put on their costumes, speak their lines, and go through their routines, and then . . . like he had them *try out* for their own murder." She sucks in her breath, which launches another spate of coughing. Mrs. Brewster's eyes close briefly, as if she might be uttering a silent prayer. "That's *dark*," she says. "That's downright *evil*."

When the skin on the back of my neck stops crawling, I squeeze out a thank-you to Mrs. Brewster for her time.

Standing next to the car as I wait for it to cool down, I think Ezme Brewster is probably right. The Gablers auditioned for their murderer. But the thing is: So what? I can't see how it has anything to do with Sean and Kevin.

Back at the Tropicana, I have two messages. The first is from Liz. "Alex, what are you doing in *Las Vegas?*" Her voice is shrill and disapproving. Then she's all business: "Please give me a call."

The second is from Barry Chisworth, the

medical examiner. He says he'll be happy to talk to me and leaves a string of numbers.

Liz is not easy to talk to these days. She knows it's unfair, she's trying to work it through with her therapist — but she can't get past focusing all her negative feelings on me. She feels guilty for letting the boys come to stay with me — and indulges in endless versions of the what-if game. So whatever remnant of blame that's not on me, rests on her. Whoever abducted the boys doesn't even fit into her picture. She let the boys come. If she'd refused . . . if only she'd let me take them on the trip to the beach. . . .

I force myself to call.

"Hello?" Her voice is tremulous, tentative.

"Hey."

"What are you *doing* in Las Vegas, Alex? Are you *gambling?*"

"I'm following a lead that Shoffler suggested."

"Really? He's not even connected to the case anymore."

"He didn't ask to be transferred. He continues to take an interest."

"What lead?"

My mind spins. I'm not going to tell her

anything about the Gabler twins, that's for sure. I doubt the connection anyway, and what happened to the women is too gruesome to raise with Liz. "A bad lead. It didn't go anywhere."

"Well, you shouldn't be in Vegas. My dad's been thinking about it. You should be canvassing the houses near Shade Valley Road. That's the most likely —"

"Liz. The police checked those homes. Over and over."

"My dad's convinced!" Her voice is shrill, out of control. We go on for a while. The tone continues to deteriorate. "I'm still expecting my spousal support," she says. "Whether you have a job or not. I'm not supporting trips to Las Vegas. I mean it, Alex: The check better be on time."

I tell myself this sour bitch isn't really Liz. She doesn't want to feel the loss and terror, so she's sticking with anger.

"Liz."

"I mean it, Alex. Don't ask me to cut you any slack. Just don't even try."

I wish I could say the perfect thing, something to comfort and buoy her, something to give her hope. But the descent of my wife into this petty bitterness makes me so sad I'm afraid if I open my mouth, I might break down. I hang up.

She calls back four times. The escalating level of fury and vitriol will be recorded on my voice mail.

chapter 24

At his suggestion, I meet Barry Chisworth at Rumjungle, an elaborate bar-restaurant in the lower level of Mandalay Bay. Like most of the other restaurants I passed on my way (the French Bistro, Red Square, etc.), this one has a theme. I'm just not sure what it is. Sheets of water cascade down the walls. Flames dance from an open pit. A safari fantasy, I guess. With water elements.

Chisworth is a stocky guy in his fifties, with the overdeveloped shoulders of a weight lifter. He has one of those little tufts of hair between his lower lip and his chin. "Thanks for giving me an excuse to get out of the house," he says, with a crunching handshake. "I live alone, of course, but still . . ." He laughs at his own joke and I join him. "Try a mojito," he suggests, holding up a tall glass. "Hemingway's fave. Slammin' little drink."

I usually stick to beer, but I get the feeling Chisworth will be disappointed if I reject his suggestion. "Why not?"

"Two more of these bad boys," he tells

the bartender, and then turns back to me. "So . . . you want to know about the Gabler girls." He leans toward me. "I want to make it clear that I won't go on the record. Whatever I say — it's strictly background."

"You got it."

"Well, it was some case. I see a lot of stuff — but that one was . . . definitely *something*."

He fingers the tuft of hair, which he does often, as if it reassures him. It reminds me of the way Sean used to touch his blanket.

Sean. When I think of one of the boys in this incidental way — and this happens dozens of times a day — it's like a trapdoor opens in my mind. And at first, I fell through it, fell into a kind of tumbling despair. But over the past couple of weeks, the thought of my sons, the fact that they're missing — it doesn't hit me the same way. I almost have to work at it, concentrate on my loss to feel it. And it occurs to me that somewhere deep inside, I'm getting used to it.

The waiter serves up the two mojitos, and Chisworth checks his glass toward mine. "Cheers."

"You know," he says, "I always figured the guy who did those two girls was more than a one-shot wonder, so to speak. You find anything yet?"

"My interest is more specific." I explain who I am.

He does a double take. "I thought you looked familiar." He fingers the tuft. "But . . . Jesus, how can there be a link between your sons and the Gablers?"

I shrug. "Identical twins."

"Twins, yeah, but . . . not the same *kind* of twins. I mean, these were showgirls. Nice girls, maybe, but working a topless show, all the same. It's hard to figure how the same psycho who snatched them would have any interest in . . . what? . . . male first-graders."

I shrug.

"Well, for what it's worth . . . a couple of things bugged the hell out of me."

"Really."

He leans toward me. "You've got this girl. Cut in two. Now the animals had been at her wounds for two weeks, so that wiped out any chance of establishing what kind of implement was used to sever her torso. You can conclude it was something sharp, probably metallic, but that's about it. On the stand, and therefore in print, you can only present evidence and conclusions. In this case" — he shakes his head — "the soft tissues were really tattered. Even the bone had been nibbled on."

My heart lurches.

"Metal fragments from wounds of that magnitude would normally be present. And they would help narrow down the type of weapon. With Clara Gabler, animals consumed those fragments. Any spatter evidence was also compromised by insects and wildlife."

"Two weeks is a long time."

"Any other climate, actually, and the remains would have been pudding — so in that sense, the remains told me quite a bit. Now, keep in mind that I've seen a lot of wounds. Hell, I've *made* a lot of wounds. And while I couldn't testify to this, I'd say beyond *my* reasonable doubt that Clara Gabler was cut in two by a power rotary blade — a sweep from left to right across the torso. Good-sized blade. Maybe like so." He puts down his mojito for a moment and holds his hands about a foot and a half apart in the air. "Fine kerf and hard enough to cut through bone without making too much of a mess. I say that because there wasn't much splintering."

"And these saws, saws like this would be . . . available? You could buy them?"

"Oh, sure. We're just talking about a

table saw. You could get it at Home Depot. But the thing is, to use a big table saw like that in the wilderness, you'd need a generator. Either that or an old-fashioned takeoff from a vehicle driveshaft to run the thing. And a platform to work on. And you'd have to get all that gear up there, way up past Icebox Canyon. A few ATVs, maybe one good off-road vehicle like a Land Rover, and you could do it. They're illegal in the area where the bodies were found, but hey, it's not like the Mojave is fenced in. And there's a relatively easy way in from the direction of Death Valley. We found tracks, but that's the thing — we found lots of tracks.

"But here's the thing that got to me about it: Why bother schlepping a rotary saw and a generator and some kind of table up there? Why call attention to yourself by breaking the law with ATVs and so on if you're going to commit murder? That's what I couldn't figure. I mean if you're going to mutilate someone — a chain saw would be very efficient."

I see what he means. "So — why would someone go to all that trouble? In your opinion."

"I just couldn't get my head around it." He shrugs, takes another sip of his mojito.

"Of course, whoever murdered the Gablers is obviously a whack job, so I guess there's no reason the method should make sense."

I gesture to the bartender for another round.

"Pretty good drink, huh?"

"It is." This guy, I think, wasn't kidding about getting out of the house.

He talks about Hemingway and *"Kooba"* for a while, his trip to Havana, his opinions about the embargo. It takes me a while to bring him back to the subject at hand.

"You have any other flashes on the Gabler case?"

He pulls on the tuft of chin hair. "Oh, yeah — and this also really got my head in a wringer. You read the autopsy report, right?"

"I looked at it."

"So you know this chick, Clara, was alive when this . . . took place?"

I nod.

"There were traces of sawdust on her body. Back of her calves, back of the head, soles of the shoes, fingers. Pine dust. But no defensive wounds, no injuries to fingertips or toes."

"A coffin?"

"It's possible. I just mention that. Maybe the guy was going to bury them but changed his mind. But here's what I really thought was weird: You get this massive injury to Clara Gabler, who was alive at the time it was inflicted. Yet I found no sign of restraint. No abrasions, no tissue damage to the wrists or ankles. And no visible damage from a struggle to get free, no defensive wounds at all, no flesh or dirt or wood beneath the fingernails. Nothing."

"And that means, what? Drugs?"

"That's what I thought, but I found nothing. Zip."

"So what does it mean?"

"It means she was not restrained and, as far as I could determine, she wasn't drugged. The woman is cut in half, but she's not restrained. You tell me — how do you pull that off? Just lay down there, honey. Okay, now don't move. This won't hurt a bit." He shakes his head.

Something dark begins to crawl around in the back of my mind, but whatever it is — I can't get a fix on it. "So maybe she didn't know it was going to happen."

"Maybe. But I told you. I ran all kinds of tests. First I'm looking for sedatives, opioids, tranquilizers. No. And no muscle relaxants. I even scanned for paralytics. Nothing. I came up blank."

"How about the other Gabler — the one who was shot?"

"She was executed," Chisworth says. "Plain and simple. Prone, on the ground, facedown. One shot, back of the head, gun just far enough from the skull to avoid a mess. That got me, too, tell you the truth."

"What do you mean?"

"The comparison. I mean Clara's death involves a lot of trouble and hassle. Dragging a lot of equipment up to an inconvenient spot. And then, with her twin it's just the opposite. No muss, no fuss. All business." He drains his mojito. "Why?"

At seven the following morning, I'm in the car with my supplies: two bottles of water, sunscreen, Orioles cap, and sunglasses. That third mojito was definitely a mistake. I continue to regret it as I head out to Tropicana Boulevard. The hard morning light bounces off the polished curves of other cars and makes me wince. It helps when I hang a left on Charleston and point the car due west — away from the sun. I'm on my way to the Red Rock Canyon, the site where Carla and Clara Gabler were murdered.

I drive through miles of terrain flat as a communion wafer. If God didn't make it that way, Asplundh or Caterpillar picked up the slack. Eventually, actual subdivisions give way to future subdivisions, some of them nothing but an expanse of bulldozed dirt and a Southwest-style entryway landscaped with a few good-sized cacti. *Upper One Hundreds! Low Two Hundreds. Low Four Hundreds. Only four left!* This is boomtown. I could see it on the satellite map in Holly Goldstein's office: the city metastasizing toward the surrounding mountains.

To the west, development stops just short of Red Rock Canyon — one of a number of parks and conservation areas on the way out to Death Valley and the California line. I can see as I approach how beautiful it is: a desert basin backdropped by a crenellated escarpment of red sandstone. Five dollars at the booth (which opens at six a.m.) gets me onto the thirteen-mile scenic drive. The ranger gives me a brochure that covers the flora and fauna, the trailheads, and a little history of the area. There's even a simple map of the drive and the trailheads. "Icebox Canyon?" she replies when I ask. "Park in the lot at milepost number eight. And take plenty of water. Won't be an icebox today."

There's already a car in the lot, a Dodge pickup with a pair of bull's horns fixed to the hood. The bumper sticker reads MY

KID CAN BEAT UP YOUR HONOR STUDENT. I guzzle half a bottle of water, stick a fresh bottle in the pocket of my cargoes, and follow the sign to the trailhead.

Within fifteen minutes, I give up on the idea of actually going to the spot where the Gablers were found. That is in a small canyon above and behind Icebox, a place called Conjure Canyon.

I've done a good bit of rock climbing but not much since my college days. None at all since a year or so after the boys were born. And I didn't come here prepared to follow in the footsteps of the hiker. No climbing shoes, for one thing. And free climbing the almost vertical upper wall of Icebox would not be a good idea for someone whose last climb was years ago.

I'd been thinking I could find a way around, a way to circle in. Now that I'm here, I can see that the terrain is so rugged, it would take me hours. I'd need hiking boots, a backpack, a lot more water. I decide to settle for getting close enough to the crime scene to get a feel for the place.

Right away, a couple of things bother me. First of all, I see what Chisworth meant. If his hunch about the rotary saw and the generator is correct, the killer had to drag a lot of equipment to a very inconvenient site. A site that happens to be close to a very popular hiking area. Sure, most tourists probably just make the standard trek, the one outlined in all the guidebooks — to the floor of Icebox and back to the parking lot. But the area around Icebox is popular with rock climbers — that's why Josh Gromelski was climbing there. There's lots of wilderness around this part of Nevada: why pick a spot with so many potential witnesses? And with all the outdoor enthusiasts in this part of the West, the killer must also have known that someone would stumble upon the remains of the Gabler twins. Sooner rather than later. Why not pick a place just as inaccessible but less popular?

The first twenty minutes, I'm crossing flat desert, walking past cholla cactus, creosote bushes, and Joshua trees. The walk is relatively easy, although it's rocky and I have to watch my step. Then I begin to get into rougher terrain. Before long, I wonder if I'm going the right way. This may be a popular hike, listed in the brochure as moderate, but the trail's not well marked. It's not a national park, I tell myself; it's a wilderness area. Suck it up.

Sometimes, I'm forced to climb over rocks and boulders. A few times I have to backtrack because I took a wrong turn and ended up on a cliff edge. Ten minutes later, I roll an ankle. It hurts, but it's not serious. A little farther on, the terrain is so rough I don't know if I'm still on the trail.

I'm still enjoying the effort of the hike, but I realize I'm out of shape and unprepared. I should have popped for a guide . . . or at least a topo map.

The sun will become an issue before long. I can feel the heat behind the temporary cool, waiting to lock on as soon as the sun gets a direct shot at me. Already, the air is warmer, and sunlight lasers off the rocks, slicing in through the open sides of my sunglasses. When I'm not in shadow, the rocks are warming up right under my hands.

Once I reach the floor of Icebox Canyon, the sun becomes less of a problem and I decide to climb a little way up, picking a route toward a shelf of rock where a piñon tree twists out of the stone. It's a tougher climb than I thought it would be, and by the time I get there, I'm huffing for breath and glad to sit down. Right away, I can see that I'm not the first to find this spot. A crumpled Juicy Fruit gum wrapper nestles against the piñon's roots, and someone's jammed four cigarette butts into a crevice.

I pull out my bottle of lukewarm water and tear off a bite of Clif Bar.

So here I am, only slightly the worse for wear, perched on the side of the canyon that Josh Gromelski chose for his climb. I look up, toward the place where he found the remains of Clara Gabler. But the crime scene is not — how did Holly Goldstein put it? — it's not *speaking* to me. I finish the Clif Bar, thinking *so what?*

So the killer chose an inaccessible spot. So he cut Clara Gabler in half while she was alive. So he used a rotary saw. So he went to a lot of trouble to haul a bunch of stuff to a remote site. So the girls were auditioning for a magic act. So what? What does any of this have to do with Sean and Kev?

I pick up the Juicy Fruit wrapper and the four cigarette butts and twist them up in the Clif Bar wrapper, then stick the trash in my pocket along with the empty water bottle. Picking my way back down toward the canyon floor, I can't believe I'm here, in the wilderness outside Las Vegas, chasing . . . I don't know what. What am I *doing?* Liz is right. This is just another version of the gerbil wheel. I'm wasting time. I'm wasting money. This whole trip is self-indulgent.

I'm mad at myself, descending a tumble of boulders at a reckless speed, jumping from rock to rock in a knee-jarring, risky way, going down toward the canyon floor as fast as I can.

And then it hits me. Hits me with so much force that I lose concentration for a moment. The next thing I know I'm putting my foot down wrong, and then I'm falling, careening through space. I touch off one boulder, and then manage to launch myself toward a flat rock. A clumsy three-point landing rips the skin off my knees. I'm sprawled on a ledge above a twenty-foot drop-off. I watch my sunglasses cartwheel down the rocky slope, then lower my head and close my eyes.

I stay there for a few moments, the rock hot against my cheek, as a rush of sensation sweeps up my forearms. The prickly residue of adrenaline may come from the fall, but the fall itself came from the realization that hit me during my reckless descent.

Where were the Gablers found?

Conjure Canyon.

What were the Gabler girls auditioning for?

A magic act.

The crime scene photos of the women's

bodies pop into my mind's eye, the upper and lower halves of Clara. Clara Gabler, cut in two. *Severed by a power rotary saw,* Chisworth guessed, *a sweep from left to right across the torso.*

In other words, not cut in half. *Sawn* in half.

They were on stage. That's why they were wearing their costumes. It was a *performance.*

During which Clara Gabler was sawn in half. The blood seeping out of the box was real, the screams not the work of an actress but cries of pain and terror. Sawing a lady in half. And then the real live girl emerges, her two halves magically reunited.

Only in this case the trick was: there was no trick. There was a double. A twin.

I sit on my ledge, staring across the desert, across the sprawl toward the Strip. I pick gravel out of my shredded palm, doing my best to keep my mind focused on the Gabler girls. So Ezme Brewster was right. It was entertainment. A live show.

I stand up, ankle aching, rivulets of blood running down from my knees. My mouth is dry, my head hurts, the world before me seems to shimmer in and out of focus. I'm dehydrated. I squint against the glare, look for the best way down, start off toward the desert floor.

But motion doesn't do the trick. I can't keep my thoughts from cohering forever. I can't really hold off the memory of the Sandling twins telling me their captor did tricks for them. What kind of tricks? Card tricks and coin tricks. "He made coins disappear." *Magic tricks.*

Card tricks. Sawing a lady in half.

Twins in the first case, twins in the second.

Stumbling along the desert floor toward the parking area, I feel like a blind man on a cliff. I'm trying to hang on to my confusion and ignore the jolt of foreboding that hit me on my way down from the piñon tree.

But when I reach my car, open the windows, stand outside in the blast-furnace heat, there's nothing for it. I can't hold it off. The link is tenuous on the surface, but in my heart I know that Shoffler's hunch was correct. There is a connection between the Gabler twins and the Sandlings and my sons, and the link is *magic*.

For the first time since the boys disappeared, I have an inkling of what might be in store for them and it drops me into a bleak despair. If I'm right, and the man who grabbed them is the same man who killed the Gabler sisters, The Piper isn't just a killer, but a sadist. And not just a sadist, but an entertainer with a gift for pain and misdirection.

My sons are the raw material for a murder artist.

chapter 25

I put in a call to Shoffler to tell him that I think his hunch may have been right on the money, that the link between the Gablers and my sons is one that we never would have come up with in a thousand years: magic. I want to talk it through with the detective, get his advice. But it turns out he's in France for some kind of security conference. I leave a message.

I can intuit some of his advice, anyway. While I'm in Vegas, I should try to determine if The Piper worked here as a magician and follow out whatever other local leads I have.

Turns out, if it's about magic, Vegas is the place to be. After three days, I've seen more doves and lighted candles materialize and disappear than I can count. It's beginning to seem routine to me that a man in a tuxedo snaps his fingers and a dove or a duck — or a goose! — flutters into existence out of thin air. Or that he might turn a top hat upside down, thump it to show it's empty, even call a volunteer to thrust a hand into its vacant interior. And then, with a wave of his wand, voilà! A rabbit. A real rabbit, which hops around on the stage, bewildered.

I've seen scarves and ropes and pieces of paper torn into shreds and restored to amazing intactness with the help of a few magic words. I've witnessed feats of mind reading, miraculous escapes, levitations, and dozens of transformations (a shred of paper into a bird, a ball into a rabbit, a doll into a woman, a piece of rope into a snake).

Any number of times, I've seen leggy beauties disappear, after which they step out, preening and smiling, from impossible and unexpected locations — the rear of the theater, for instance. At the San Remo, Showgirls of Magic (topless in the evening) are just what they sound like: leggy beauties doing tricks with cards and coins and, yes, bunnies.

After the shows, there are opportunities to buy merchandise; shops sell mementos of the performing magician, along with standard tricks and magic kits, reproduction posters, biographies of Houdini, books about magic.

It's in these shops that I show my sketches of The Piper to magician clerks and cashiers, who perform card tricks and sleight of hand while they make change. I tell them the man in the sketch is a magician. Do they recognize him? A couple "think so," but no one can put a name or place to the memory.

I'm getting myself a beer before the Lance Burton show when a bear of a man approaches me. "Boyd Veranek," he says, "with a *V.* Pleased to meet you. Watch this."

I get it — the guy's going to do a magic trick. I don't want to be his audience, but it's crowded and without being rude, I can't get away from him. He cups his huge pawlike hands together and pulls them slowly apart. In between his palms, a paper rose hovers and trembles in midair. He abruptly jerks his hands wide apart and the flower drifts toward the floor. He plucks it out of the air, holds it by the stem, and with a little bow, presents it to me.

It's made from a Lance Burton napkin, its petals ingeniously scalloped, the stem tightly coiled paper. Veranek beams at me.

"You just made this . . . here? That's pretty good."

"Works better with the ladies, I guess," Veranek says with a smile. "Hey — I saw you at Showgirls of Magic, saw you at

Penn and Teller. Figured you're a fellow illusionist. Am I right?"

"Not exactly — but I can see that you are."

Veranek smiles, shrugs. "You might say. I'm a retired engineer. I used to do magic as a hobby, but it's become a second career. I do kids' parties, bar and bat mitzvahs, the occasional cruise or trade show. Helps, given what happened to my portfolio. Now, *that* was a disappearing act." He laughs and I join him. "So if you're not a magician," he says, "you're what? A magic junkie?"

I tell him that I'm a private investigator. That I'm looking into a murder. I no longer bring up my kids if I can help it, hoping to sidestep the predictable sequence that follows disclosure of my nightmare. Recognition and the obligatory expression of sympathy give way to fascination and then to a barely disguised repugnance. The fascination is easy to understand: it's the instinct that makes us stare at car crashes. The repugnance is similar to what cancer victims or the disabled must recognize: Despite the fact that whatever is wrong is not contagious, there's nevertheless a fear of contagion. A terrible thing happened to me: No one wants to catch my bad luck.

"A murder?" Boyd Veranek squints at me, as if he's not sure whether I'm joking or not. "And all of these magic shows fit into this investigation . . . how? If you don't mind my asking."

"I think the killer is a magician."

"Oh, boy. There goes the neighborhood. A professional? An amateur?"

I shake my head. "Don't know. But I have some sketches. Mind taking a look?"

"By all means." He squints, studies the sketches, shakes his head. "The murder was here? In Vegas?"

"Nearby. It was about three years ago. Showgirls murdered out in the Red Rock Canyon. You might have heard of it."

He frowns, but any memory of the murders has been replaced by some fresher brutality. "Boy. I'm hitting all these shows to see if I can get a new wrinkle or two for my act, and you're doing it . . . *wow* . . . to track a killer."

I nod.

"You really want to know about magic — you ought to talk to Karl Kavanaugh," Veranek says. "He lives here in Vegas and he knows everything."

"Who is he?"

"He's a magician, although he doesn't

perform much anymore. He works for Copperfield — who has a museum of magic here."

"Really."

"It's a private museum, but the point is Karl knows everything about magic — A to Z. He's a magician's magician. He might be able to help you. Might even recognize your guy."

"You have his number?"

"I don't. Not on me. He's probably in the book — Karl with a *K*, Kavanaugh, also with a *K*. If not, give me a call, because I can probably track down his number for you. I'm at the Luxor. Veranek, with a *V*."

"Okay, thanks a lot."

It's only a few minutes until showtime and the crowd begins to drift into the auditorium. I'm about to join them when Veranek thrusts a glass into my hands. "Here comes my wife. Would you hold this for a sec?"

He's fiddling with his program, doing something fast and furious with his hands. Moments later, a sweet-faced woman squeezes through the crowd and appears at his side.

"There was a line," she says, "in the little girls' room."

"I'd say you just got out in time," Veranek says. "Look what you picked up in there. Must have come outta the plumbing." He plucks something from her shoulder and holds it in his cupped hand. An ingeniously fashioned frog crouches there. Somehow, he makes it jump.

"Oh, *Boyyyyyd.*" The woman giggles like a teenager.

I stare at the frog, which reminds me powerfully of the origami rabbit I found on the boys' bureau.

A jolt of paranoia hits me. This guy approached me, not the other way around. He looks nothing like my sketch of The Piper, but he is tall. He makes folded animals. He does magic tricks.

"That's amazing," I hear myself say. "That frog, that's really good."

"Nah — it's not very good. I'm way rusty. Mostly I do balloon art these days. Origami's kind of faded. Too bad, in a way. Folding has a very long history in magic. It kind of figures — you know?"

"What do you mean?"

"For one thing, it requires dexterity," Veranek says, "and if nothing else, magicians are good with their hands. Also — it's a transformation. Just a few folds and you turn a flat piece of paper into a bird, an animal. People *like* that. But you don't see much folding anymore. It's all balloons these days." He smiles. "Same idea, though."

I feel a sense of pressure in my head, as if I'm underwater. "Can you do a rabbit?"

"Boyd," the sweet-faced woman says, "I don't want to miss the beginning of Lance."

"Don't worry, honey; I can make a rabbit in thirty seconds flat."

And he does. With impressive manual dexterity, Veranek tears the back of his program into a square. Seconds later, he's transformed it into a cute little bunny. It looks nothing like the rabbit I found in the boys' room. I tell myself that it proves nothing, not really, but my suspicion of Boyd Veranek evaporates.

The lights in the foyer begin to flash.

"That's amazing," I say, admiring the rabbit perched on the back of Veranek's hand.

"Boyd," his wife says. "Come on."

Veranek executes a little bow and — I don't see it happen — makes the rabbit disappear.

chapter 26

Karl Kavanaugh *is* in the book, and I arrange to meet him the following morning. He suggests the Peppermill, which he tells me is on the upper Strip across from Circus Circus.

The restaurant occupies a shaggy shingled building, vintage Seventies, that seems to be crouching between its massive neighbors. Inside, blue velvet banquettes are shaded by faux cherry trees.

Kavanaugh waits for me just inside the entrance, a tall graceful man in a blue suit. "I'm in my sixties," he told me on the phone. "I wear aviator sunglasses."

We shake. Kavanaugh's hand is large and strong, with long, elegant fingers.

"Boyd likes to lay it on," he says. "But I'm no magician's magician or whatever he told you. What I would claim is that I'm a student of magic."

A young woman escorts us to a table. She wears a short pleated jumper and white blouse, a kind of sexualized version of a Catholic school uniform.

"Do you perform here in Vegas?" I ask him.

"No. I'm retired, more or less. I came here — well, I came here because I was following the craft."

"What do you mean?"

"Well, some industries stay put," Kavanaugh says, "geographically speaking — like the motion picture industry, or maybe steelworking or shipbuilding, but magic keeps changing its capital. And right now it's here in Vegas."

"And before?"

Karl's eyes brighten. "At the turn of the century, it was New York," he says, "which makes sense. The stages were there, theatrical agents, gossip columnists, magic shops, vaudeville. Not to mention the big audiences. Remember, movies didn't exist yet, so live entertainment was the *only* entertainment. So you'd get someone like Houdini, he'd draw huge crowds. As would his competitors and imitators. There was no copyrighting or trademarking back then, so there were plenty of Howdinis and Hondinis and Houdins — and they drew big crowds, too."

"Howdinis? You're kidding."

"Not at all. That's one reason so much advertising from that era harps on establishing identity: 'the one and only.' The genuine! The real! The authentic! There was room for all these competitors because magic was flourishing. But then the movies really started to come on, and vaudeville began to die out. And a lot of magic acts went down with the ship."

"How come?"

"Magic couldn't make the transition to film. It just doesn't play on the screen. Not the big screen, and later down the road — not on TV, either."

"Hunh."

"So then the epicenter of magic relocated to Chicago. This was in the twenties and Chicago was where all the rail lines met, the home away from home for fleets of traveling salesmen. You had the merchandise mart, and all that. Magicians got a kind of second wind working trade shows — still probably the biggest employers of magicians."

"Trade shows? You're kidding."

"Oh, no. Because trade shows are essentially *live entertainment*. Say you're trying to attract attention to your booth. Nothing like a magician. People *will* stop and watch."

"Where else do magicians work these days — besides Vegas and trade shows?"

"Cruise ships — there's quite a bit of work there. Birthday parties, bar mitzvahs, adult residences." He taps his fingers on the table.

I start taking notes. There must be associations for cruise ships, for trade shows, for magicians. I could paper them all with the Piper sketch.

"And Ren fests," Karl adds. "They hire a good many magicians."

"Ren fests? What's that?"

"Renaissance festivals. Pretty popular."

Renaissance festivals. It's one of those moments when the past crashes in on me. My head fills with vignettes of the day at the fair: the look on Sean's face as he bore down on his brass rubbing, Kevin's slightly alarmed expression as he stared at the falcon perched on the leather-gloved arm of its handler . . .

I concentrate on writing in my notebook.

Karl must see something on my face, because he asks if I'm okay. I mutter about jet lag and the moment passes and he's talking again about magic's geographical journey. "So, magicians congregated in Chicago for a while, say 1930 to 1962, then the whole scene moved to L.A."

"Why L.A.?"

Leo shrugs. "A well-known magician

bought an old mansion there and opened a club. Called it the Magic Castle. Eventually, the Castle drew more and more magicians out to the West Coast. And L.A. became the new epicenter of magic."

"Who was this magician?"

"Mark Mitchell — probably doesn't mean anything to you."

I shook my head.

"That really points up the decline of the art," Karl says, with a sad shake of the head. "I mean to me, as a student of magic, the deterioration of its status is quite remarkable."

"It's changed? Magic shows seem quite popular here."

"Maybe so, but that's an anomaly. Going back into history, though, magic was once the highest of all the arts, its performers famous the world over. Back in the day, attending the performance of a magician inspired awe and wonder. That, alas, is gone. Today, the word *magic* retains its elevated status only when used as an adjective to describe something else."

"What do you mean?"

"If a performance is sheer magic, a work of art magical, a meal so memorable the chef is called a magician, this is still high praise indeed. But magic itself, as a performing art, is no longer even considered an art, but a series of cheap tricks — or more expensively staged illusions."

"You're right."

"And its leading lights from the past are all but forgotten. Like Mark Mitchell, of the Magic Castle. I know you've never heard of him, but how about Dai Vernon?"

I shake my head.

"Just as a test: Apart from Houdini and the guys working Vegas today like Copperfield, give me the names of a few famous magicians from the past."

"Let's see." I frown, concentrate, look up at him. "Mark Mitchell and . . . Karl Kavanaugh!"

Karl laughs, a big happy sound that makes me like him.

"Well, not that you really care about all this, but I'm close to the end now," he says. "New York, Chicago, L.A." He ticks them off on his elegant fingers. "And then in eighty-five or so, when Vegas started to take off, magic relocated here."

"Why Vegas?"

"Because magic is at its best live and in person, and the oddity of Vegas is that it's the one place in the country where stage acts flourish. Not just theater, but music, dancing, stand-up, and . . . magic. That's why I said the popularity of magic here was an anomaly."

I thought about what he said, about live acts being so popular in Vegas, about all those gigantic billboards advertising the shows of shopworn stars and celebrities I'd never heard of. "Why *is* that?"

The waitress takes our orders. Kavanaugh orders lemonade. I order a club sandwich and coffee. "Watch out," he says. "That sandwich will be the size of an aircraft carrier."

"Mr. Kavanaugh," the waitress scolds, "maybe your friend has a better appetite than you."

"I warned you," Kavanaugh says. "So where were we?"

"You were telling me why magic is so popular here."

"Right. Well, it's not just magic, it's all live acts. People can't gamble all the time, and just as no one comes to Vegas to buy a lottery ticket, no one comes to Vegas to go to the multiplex, either. It's a unique place. Look at the big hotels. They don't even need signs. They *are* signs. They're like Hollywood sets, backdrops for the tourists and conventioneers to play against. The old guy from Scranton, the couple from Huntsville, they come to Vegas and suddenly they're starring in their own movie. The glitz is everywhere and so are they. Because they aren't just in Vegas, they're also in Cairo, Paris, Venice, and New York New York — only with showgirls, slots, and free drinks. They pay to see live shows because that's what you *do* in Vegas. You take in a show." He opens his hands in an expansive gesture. "The ladies like it. And magic is popular because it works so well on stage." He leans toward me with a shy smile. "In fact, I have a theory about it."

I make a gesture. "Please."

"We're all so jaded by filmed special effects that almost nothing can really break through and startle us anymore. We look at something really mind-blowing, some stunt or effect that was actually quite difficult to pull off — but it doesn't blow our minds. Not anymore. We don't even care how it's done."

"It was done with computers, with stuntmen, whatever."

"Exactly. That's why magic doesn't play well on television, because *anything* can be done on film. I mean in a way, what is a movie but an extended magic effect? We're seeing a reality that we know is not real. When we see something on film, we know it's fake. But when you see something in real time, with your own eyes, you still trust your senses. So even the simplest trick provokes amazement. I can do a card effect and watch mouths fall open. Magic is still *magic* in other words, when people see it up close. It still provokes wonder. It still gets that response every magician is after: 'How'd you *do* that?' And by the way — I never tell."

"Never?"

"Almost never. It's too disappointing. Some *very* complex devices and mechanisms enable certain magical illusions, don't get me wrong. And back in the day, magicians were on the cutting edge of technology and mechanical invention. There are some amazing automata from the eighteenth and nineteenth centuries, just wonderful stuff. So I don't want to minimize the role of ingenious devices. But pretty often the secret to the most amazing effect is something simple, even crude. Some wax, a string, a magnet. You hate to pull the curtains aside like that. That's not why people come to magic shows."

"Why *do* they come?"

"They come to be deceived, to be fooled, to be amazed. That's where the pleasure is — not in finding out that something astounding was enabled by a secret latch or a mirror or an accomplice in the audience. The pleasure comes in being deceived — except that you can't figure out how it happened."

"Okay . . ."

"Now, someone like Houdini, a real showman, he used to press the point. Before one of his escapes, he'd insist on being examined naked — usually by the police — to prove he literally had nothing up his sleeve. They'd inspect his gym shorts, or whatever he was going to wear for the performance, before they escorted him onto the stage. Fortunately, this was in the days before the cavity search."

"You mean —"

"Yup. Something up his keister. That's the suspicion — although this is not to disparage Houdini. He was an astonishing athlete and he trained as hard as Lance Armstrong."

"Nobody trains that hard."

"Maybe I'm exaggerating, but he trained like hell. For instance, he had this one effect where he was cuffed and wrapped in padlocked chains and then lowered into cold water — icy water, mind you. Now, sure — he had to have some kind of file or pick to get those locks open. But still — he's upside down in thirty-five-degree water with his hands and feet cuffed, and wrapped in heavy padlocked chains. So he had a pick — he still has to spring all those locks. Years before, he'd practiced holding his breath until he could do it for three and a half minutes. Amazing. And to get ready for these cold-water escapes, he trained by sitting in a tubful of ice cubes every night for weeks until his body could tolerate the shock, until he could still function" — Kavanaugh wiggled his fingers — "in the freezing water. That kid David Blaine recently did something of the sort. Encased himself in ice for several days — actually an endurance feat more than anything else. That kind of thing also has a long and honored tradition in magic. Being buried alive. In fact, all kinds of physical feats used to be part of the magic shows. Water spouting. Stone eating. Walking on coals. Interesting to see Blaine revive that aspect."

"Blaine?"

"You don't know him? You should check him out — he had a few TV shows. *Street Magic* was the first, I think. Anyway, very impressive."

"But . . . you said it yourself. Magic doesn't play on the screen."

"Blaine did something really innovative:

He concentrated on the audience. He shows himself doing the effects for small groups — one, three, four people, that's all. And watching their response is fascinating. They go nuts, absolutely crazy, they are *transported.* They literally can't believe their eyes. It's wonderful stuff. Some of them actually cover their eyes, as if they can't trust themselves to look at the world anymore."

I add this to my notes: *David Blaine.*

Kavanaugh sighs. "I could go on all day. So maybe you should tell me what you really want to know."

"I'm not sure what I want to know." I tell him I'm investigating the murders of the Gabler twins, and that I think the murderer may have been a magician.

He steeples his hands and rests his chin on the point. "I remember the case. Dreadful. But what makes you think a magician was responsible?"

When I tell him what I've learned, he leans back. I hear a sharp little intake of breath, and his expression is serious, even grave. "Oh, my Lord," he says. "The lady sawn in half. Sweet Jesus — it's like an in-joke."

I show him the Wanted poster with the sketches of The Piper. His face contorts. "I don't know. Maybe. You mind if I keep this?"

"No problem."

He folds the poster precisely in half, then runs a nail along the crease, then folds it again, and slips it into his pocket. "I'm not sure I agree with you — that a magician committed the crime. I hope not. Maybe just somebody with a repulsive sense of humor. If it is a magician — you'll find there are certain characteristics many of us share. Would that kind of thing be helpful to you?"

"Please."

"Well, most magicians take up the art as children. And there are a couple of reasons for that. It takes a long time to develop the dexterity a magician needs, for one thing. And many tricks take a *really serious* amount of practice. It's like . . . oh" — he looks at the ceiling — "*skateboarding*. Even a simple skateboarding skill — and I know this, because my grandson is a devotee — takes hours and hours and hours to master. Same thing with magic. An adult would be daunted by the amount of time it would take to master — well, let's say a faro shuffle."

"What's that?"

"If you cut the deck in half and shuffle,

cut and shuffle eight times, interleaving each card, at the end you've restored the deck to its original configuration."

"And people can do this?"

"Oh, sure. I could do it by the time I was ten years old. And I can still do it. But it took a lot of practice. So much practice that an adult would just give up. But kids — they'll put in that time."

"Hunh."

"So if you have more than one suspect, you might want to find out if one of them did magic tricks as a kid."

"Let me ask you something — are there any tricks that use kids as their . . . subjects?"

"Well, at kids' birthday parties, sure. You get volunteers from the audience. But if you mean the magician's assistant — the assistant is almost invariably a young woman, the better to inject a little sex appeal into a show. And scantily dressed women do work quite well for the purposes of misdirection — I can tell you that from personal experience. People *will* look at them. In the past, children were very commonly used as assistants. And they would perform all the roles that women do today — I mean they'd be levitated, locked in cabinets, or put into urns or baskets, then transported to distant spots or transformed into animals and back again."

I force myself. "Sawn in half?"

Kavanaugh frowns. "Maybe. I can't give you a date, but I believe that illusion is relatively recent. I've only ever seen or read about it being performed with women assistants."

"Hunh. Anything else about magicians I should know?"

"Well, actually, I've been thinking about *your* fellow. If he is a magician, I'd say he's a student of the art, someone aware of the history."

"Why do you say that?"

"Well . . . just what he did, with those girls, you know. I mean dismemberment and restoration have been part of the magician's stock-in-trade for centuries, but nowadays you only see antiseptic tricks. You might see paper — or money, or rope, or fabric — torn or cut into pieces. Or maybe the magician has someone in the audience write something on a piece of paper — which is then torn to shreds before eventually being restored to wholeness. A twenty-dollar bill, somebody's tie — that's enough for today's audiences. Even the standard sawing-the-lady-in-half is bloodless. She's smiling the whole time.

No one believes she's being injured — or even in danger of being injured. Someone, I read — can't remember who — thought the trick was actually a thinly disguised display of sexual sadism." A shrug. "I don't know about that. It's still very popular. But certainly, it's bloodless. My point is that tastes change. Audiences used to love gore."

"What do you mean?"

"Audiences still love violence, don't get me wrong. Danger — someone else's danger — makes us feel more alive. But in terms of magic, audiences don't enjoy blood and gore the way they used to. We've all become squeamish. Plenty of people who love their steaks and burgers find hunting, for instance, barbaric. You wonder what they'd think of a slaughterhouse."

"They'd be vegetarians."

"Exactly. But that squeamishness — that's a new phenomenon. There was a time — and it wasn't long ago — when people routinely enjoyed watching beasts rip each other, or human beings, to bits. In the Old West, or in Merry Old England, public executions were extremely popular. People came early to get the best spots. They probably had the equivalent of tailgate parties. In performance magic, it was the same. Just for example, there was a popular trick in Houdini's day called Palingenesis. The posters would show the magician with an enormous sword. And the day's flyer would advertise: *Man to Be Cut Up Today. Come one! Come all!* During this show, a man would be chloroformed — supposedly — and then dismembered, and I mean the bloody parts strewn around the stage. The audience sees this happening, mind you. The poor man's various parts are collected, a rug or cloth placed over him, the magician speaks his potent words or waves his powerful wand and — presto! — the man jumps out, restored to health and wholeness."

A wave of nausea rolls through my stomach.

"And that was far from the only such act. Dismemberment tricks are ancient. In India it used to be popular for conjurers to cut off children's tongues — that was a standard. Ripping apart birds, cutting up snakes — street magicians in India probably still do this kind of thing. They would show the blood; they might even dip stones into it. Then once the bird — usually a bird because they're cheap and dramatic — was restored to life, they'd sell the stones as lucky amulets, imbued with the life force."

"Wait a minute — you don't mean it was real blood?"

"Oh, yes. Well, not in the case of the children's tongues. But the birds? Certainly. It's my opinion — if you have time?"

I nod.

"I believe these tricks go back to ancient days. Dismemberment and restoration to wholeness and life — it's the power of life and death, isn't it? Magicians didn't start as mere entertainers, you see. They used to fill a much more elevated role in societies. This is the common theory, in any case — that today's magician was yesterday's priest or shaman."

"Really."

"Religion and magic have always been mixed up together. That's because magic explores that region between the natural and the supernatural, between life and death, between reality and illusion. And religious figures have, I suspect, always employed magical devices and tricks to focus the attention of adherents and enhance their apparent power. There's no question about that. Good Lord, there are sketches on papyri that show the ancient Egyptians used hydraulic devices to make temple doors open mysteriously."

"Open sesame?"

A chuckle. "Quite right. And there's solid evidence the priests in Greece used speaking tubes to make the statues talk at Delphi. It does make you wonder about weeping and bleeding statues. Even the 'magic words' have quite religious roots."

"What do you mean?"

"Well, *abracadabra* — that comes right from the Jewish Kabbala. So words, symbols — the Kabbala is a mystical text about . . . to some extent . . . the power of words."

"Really? So *abracadabra* means something."

"Absolutely. And *hocus-pocus?* — that's even more shocking. Some scholars believe that *hocus-pocus* is a corruption of *Hoc est meum corpus.*"

My blank look conveys my lack of understanding.

"No Latin, eh?"

I shake my head.

"Well, I don't know how religious you are and I don't want to shock you, but it's believed that the magician's phrase *hocus-pocus* — which we perceive as so much nonsense — descends directly from the words of the Christian Eucharist: *Hoc est meum corpus*. 'This is my body.' "

"No."

"For that matter, Jesus of Nazareth was quite openly referred to as a magician in the early days of the church. And his miracles — the loaves and fishes, water into wine, even the resurrection of Lazarus from the dead — these are in the form of standard street magic of the era. There are Roman frescoes from the second century showing Jesus with a magic wand."

"I don't know what to say."

"The point is that magic has rather deep and surprising roots. Think about it: If you didn't know you were being manipulated in a magic show, you'd think you were witnessing miracles."

"I guess so."

"In fact — do you remember the spiritualists? In the twenties?"

"I've read about it. Madame Blavatsky and so on."

"Exactly. Ouija boards, seances, that scene. Well, there was a lot of interest at that time in communicating with 'the other side.' After a failed attempt to get in touch with his mother — during which, instead of speaking to him in Yiddish, she addressed him in English, which she did not speak — Harry Houdini launched a campaign to debunk the spiritualists. He saw them as taking advantage of the grief-stricken and desperate, and as getting far too well paid for second-rate magic tricks. He set out to demonstrate that most supernatural manifestations were actually common magic effects — made much easier by the fact that the entire audience was made to sit in the dark holding hands."

"Did he succeed?"

Kavanaugh shrugs. "Not really. What Houdini didn't count on was that people *wanted* to believe, and so they did."

"I had no idea magic had anything to do with religion."

"Oh, yes. Sitting across from you is the defrocked descendant of a high priest," he says with a smile.

"And you think the man I'm looking for — if he's a magician — he might be aware of this aspect of magic."

"I think he might be a student of magic's history, yes. The dismemberment of that girl is what makes me think so. There's a trick — I think I was talking about it when I got sidetracked on magic and religion. Wasn't I talking about the trick with the birds?"

"Right. A bird was torn apart."

"That's right. And as I said, I'm sure this is still routinely performed in India. Here's how it works. There's a traditional magic device called a dove pan — it has a hidden compartment for a secret load. So at the beginning of the trick, the magician opens one compartment and out comes a bird. Fluttering and so on. A little business with the bird and then the magician tears it apart."

"*Actually* tears it apart?"

A shrug. "Or cuts it apart. A bird would be sacrificed, in any case. Usually a white dove if the magician could afford it because blood shows up so well against the white feathers. It's very dramatic. The audience is encouraged to handle the dead bird. Stick their fingers in its wounds, as it were."

"And then?" I feel light-headed. Cold and clammy, as if I'm coming down with something deadly.

"The magician closes the pan, passes the hat amongst the spectators, begging them to contribute to his mental effort — it takes a lot out of him, harnessing the life force. He exhorts them also to focus their own energy on restoring the bird to life. A failed attempt or two to build tension, a secret confederate who doubts the magician's ability heckling from the crowd. Then a big show of concentration, a few magic words, and . . . presto!"

"Presto?"

"The magician opens the pan — this time exposing the hidden compartment — and out comes the live bird, fluttering with life."

Kavanaugh misinterprets the look of horror on my face. He thinks I'm confused. He thinks I don't get it.

"It's just like those girls killed up in Red Rock, you see? One is sacrificed, then the other is produced, vibrant with life. That's the second desirable thing about white doves: They all look the same. From the point of view of the audience, two white doves are identical. They're *all* twins, you might say."

A rush of pressure. I'm standing in the path of a freight train but I can't move. *They're all twins. They're all twins.*

Kavanaugh leans toward me. "You okay?"

chapter 27

I spend a couple of days going to magic shows in increasingly seedy venues, shopping my sketches of The Piper. I question the girls who work these shows. Did they know the Gablers? Do they recognize The Piper? Did they ever audition for a magic show three years or so ago? The thought of murder and magic intertwined does not cut through their boredom. They go through the motions of looking at my sketches, but they're thinking about something else: a cigarette, a boyfriend, a chipped nail.

During the day, I work the phones, pestering every vendor or renter of ATVs and generators in the Vegas area to check their records for the time frame around the Gabler murder. "Three years ago?" one guy tells me. "That's a lifetime here, man. Half of the places in business didn't even exist."

Even when I tell people who I am, a move forced by the indifference I meet, most of those I talk to are wary and defensive — or just too busy. If I were a cop, they might help me, but as it is . . . no. They cite "privacy issues," liability, understaffing, poor records.

I check my e-mail and my messages at the Las Vegas Public Library. Shoffler is still in France, so I call Muriel Petrich. She listens to me talk about my breakthrough. She takes notes, asking me to repeat certain things. She promises to get on it, promises that the police will paper every magician's association and trade-show booking agency with The Piper's sketches and so on. But I can tell from the way she's talking to me that either she's not convinced that my breakthrough really amounts to much or that my case has slipped down on her list of priorities.

"Why do I get the feeling that you're just going to go through the motions?" I ask her.

"Come on, Alex — is that fair? I'm going to take the obvious steps, but" — a sigh — "I don't know what else I can do here. What do you want me to do?"

"Show some enthusiasm."

Another sigh. "Look, I've got a family over in Severna Park — a quadruple murder. Maybe this didn't make the news in Vegas, but it's a pretty big deal here. They were asleep, in their beds. So that's wrapping me up pretty good right now."

Now it's my turn to sigh. "That's . . . horrible. I'm really sorry."

"Look, Alex. I'm on it, this magic angle. I really am. I promise I'll do what I can."

I check in with the people I've interviewed: Tammy Yagoda, Ezme, Riggins at the Blue Parrot. Have they thought of anything new? They haven't.

I call Pablo Moreno and explain my interest in the Gabler case. I tell him I think the perp was a magician. He listens. He's polite. He'll look into it. He might have some time available next week — he's rotating off the active crew.

And then . . . that's it. I've got what I think is a great lead, I think I found out something important about The Piper, but I don't know what else to do about it.

I find myself in the casino, submerged in the cacophony of the slots, chatter, laughter. A sequence of beautiful smiling women in scanty outfits bring me beer. For an hour or so, I hang around the craps table, watching a big redhead named Marie on a roll. She plays with such happy-go-lucky zeal and joy, it's painful when she starts to lose. I drift away toward the slots.

After a few false starts, I settle down at the Lucky Leprechaun, and quickly fall into the rhythm. Insert money, pull, wait for the symbols to snap into place. I'm thrilled when the little cartoon man in green clicks his heels together, gives me an Irish wink, and tumbles over his pot of gold — sending noisy cascades of coins into my machine's waiting tray.

I feed money into the machine, pull, watch the wheels spin. Again. Again. And again.

Another beer? Why not.

I visit the casino's handily located ATM, while asking another player to watch my machine.

Insert money, pull. Again. Again. Again.

Another beer.

Feeling bloated, I switch to a more compact beverage. Scotch.

Back to the ATM again. Max out my card for the day. My remaining balance? — $920.

Nine hundred and twenty dollars. I tell myself that's not much, that I'm almost broke, that I should take the cash in my pocket and quit while I'm behind. I don't listen.

I know I must be drunk but I don't feel it. I feel a tremendous sense of clarity as I focus on the leprechaun, waiting for his jaunty little dance, his exaggerated wink, his smiling turn toward the pot o' gold.

At one point I have three plastic tubs of coins, but I keep recycling them, fighting my fatigue, the ache in my back, the whine of conscience. I'm mechanical now, the way I push the coins back into the steel slot over and over until finally, there's only one coin left.

I no longer want to win. It seems important, even imperative, to lose. Sometime during the past few hours, my brain made a bargain with fate. From "lucky at cards, unlucky in love," I concocted a different formula. Unlucky at gambling, lucky in life.

I need to lose my last quarter to save my sons.

The coin feels warm, almost alive as I push it into the cool metal slot. I pull the metal arm, and wait for the wheels to stop turning. And then it happens: one, two, three shamrocks align themselves across the bar. The leprechaun dances and winks, and tumbles his pot of gold. The screen blinks on and off: WINNER WINNER WINNER. The machine bleats a tinny version of "When Irish Eyes Are Smiling." A small crowd gathers to watch my payoff cascade endlessly into the tray.

* * *

I'm determined to lose all my money. It's not easy and I have no idea how long it takes. Casinos aren't big on clocks, and there's no hint of daylight to cue the gambler's circadian rhythms. I finally lose my last dollar to a mean-looking pig who wallows in his cartoon sty as the screen flashes GAME OVER.

The hangover is so bad I feel weak and out of focus. I step outside the Tropicana into a wall of heat. The glare of the fading sun as I drive toward McCarran Airport almost kills me. The cheery music from the ranks of slots at the airport is so irritating it propels me into a little trot. Bad idea. Something inside my skull seems to be sloshing around. There are ominous clicks and a stabbing pain behind my eyes. I take refuge in a quiet corner and force myself to drink a bottle of water.

My plane is, appropriately enough, a red-eye, so I get in at dawn. The drive home soothes me, the familiar monuments, the practiced route. The brilliant flowers and green trees and grass seem jungle lush after my sojourn in the desert. On the river, sculls glide along the placid water.

The house has that stale, uninhabited smell. Liz used to light candles when we returned from vacation. I consider giving her a call, but what would I say? Now that I'm home, the connections between the Gablers, the Sandlings, and our boys don't seem so solid.

Murdered Twins. I spend a few hours online, trying different search engines to see what turns up. But I'm going over old ground, and these searches don't find anything new.

The only other murder of twins — apart from the Gablers — was the one in southern California. I remember it from my early forays online: the Ramirez twins, Wilson and Julio. I never paid much attention to the case, despite the fact that the victims were seven years old and twins. The perpetrator was dead.

But I can hear Shoffler telling me not to make assumptions. And Holly Goldstein explaining how certain facts or insights never make it into police reports, let alone into the news. For instance: Barry Chisworth's hunch that a rotary saw had been used to cut Clara Gabler in half.

So maybe there was an accomplice in the Ramirez case — a suspect whose name hadn't surfaced. Maybe the police didn't have enough to charge him, and now, he's back.

At first, it's not promising. The killer was a man named Charley Vermillion. According to the police, he'd been released from the Port Sulfur Forensic Facility about two weeks before the Ramirez boys went missing. *Forensic facility* means nothing to me, although *released* suggests some kind of incarceration.

I look it up. A forensic facility in this case is an asylum for the criminally insane. Port Sulfur is in Louisiana.

A story in the *Times Picayune*, accessed through Google, reveals that Vermillion was captured after an anonymous tip. According to the same report, he was holed up with the bodies of the children in a ramshackle cabin near Big Sur. One corpse was found in the refrigerator. The body had been pierced dozens of times, then butchered and neatly packaged in plastic bags. Vermillion had apparently cooked and consumed parts of the dead boy. The other child, also dead, was found suspended by the feet in a fifty-foot-deep well.

Taken into custody, Vermillion killed himself in the squad car by ingesting a cyanide capsule taped to his shirt collar.

That's about as solved as a case can get.

Ten minutes later, I'm talking to Harvey Morris, a detective in Big Sur who worked the case.

"Wasn't much work to it," Morris tells me. "We got a tip and we just went where the informant pointed. And there was old Charley with a fridge full of body parts. He surrendered without a fuss, just seemed confused and talked about going home. He's in the squad, we've secured the crime scene, and we're ready to go to the station. All of sudden the sonofabitch starts making these noises like he's strangling. I think he's having a heart attack or something. He turns red, bright cherry red. Starts convulsing. We call an ambulance, and give him CPR but . . . he croaks."

"When did you find out he'd poisoned himself?"

"Not like — until the next day. We didn't see him take the pill, you know? I thought a stroke or something — what do I know? But the medico guessed cyanide and the autopsy confirmed it. That and a shitload of Valium. No wonder he was no trouble. Forensics found tape residue on the underside of his shirt collar. He was all ready to sign off, you know?"

"Hunh."

"For the sake of form, you try to tell yourself it's terrible a guy like that offs himself. Don't get me wrong — it *was* terrible for me because it happened on my watch. There was an inquiry; I was put on administrative leave; I had to go through a whole load of crap. But what I think? I think killing himself was the best thing Charley ever did."

"So, what was — ?"

But Morris isn't finished. "The guy was a psycho, right? Louisiana didn't want to let him out of that bin, but some do-gooder forced their hand. He goes on trial here and what's gonna happen?"

"Insanity plea."

"Absolutely. He woulda been slam-dunked right back in the bin, *our* bin this time. And do Mr. and Mrs. Ramirez get any satisfaction? I don't think so. The guy *ate* their kids. And before he cut that one kid up, he stabbed him dozens of times. They like . . . reassembled what was left of the body, you know, put the pieces together. Apparently that poor kid was *run through* with a long, sharp blade, and I'm saying he was stabbed front to back, side to side, every which way. I mean — the kid was a pincushion." A disgusted snort. "Vermillion goes to trial, Mom and Dad have to sit there and listen to that crap."

He pauses, and I can hear him take a deep breath — almost like a sigh. "I get upset," he says, "because there were suggestions that I could've stopped the guy, you know? But Jesus, he's *cuffed* — he gets at the pill, like . . . with his mouth. You frisk somebody, you don't look for a *pill* taped under his collar, you know what I'm saying?"

"Maybe at the station you'd find it."

"You got that right. Maybe there you would find it, because you'd process him, get him into coveralls." He pauses. "So you got questions?"

"I was wondering about the cause of death."

"Technically, cardiac arrest."

"I mean the Ramirez boys."

"Well, no surprise there. The one we found in the freezer? Loss of blood. All those stab wounds, right? There's a technical term for it —"

"Exsanguination."

"Bingo. Bled to death."

"And the second boy? The one they found in the well?"

"The best we could figure that was that he was put in there for preservation. Like you'd hang a side a beef. It was cool down there and Vermillion only had so much room in his fridge."

"Was he dead?"

"Oh, he was dead, all right. Been dead a couple of days. But I don't think he suffered. He was shot in the head. Single shot. Thirty-eight caliber."

Just like the Gablers.

One dismembered, one shot in the head.

"This tip you got? The one that led you to Vermillion's cabin. Didn't you wonder about that?"

"Oh, sure we did. We tried to run it down, but you know — Vermillion's only out of the bin a short while and he's runnin' in what for him is foreign territory. It's not like he's got a lot of friends and acquaintances we can question. We figured a drifter. Maybe someone he hitched a ride with."

"You're probably right," I say and thank Morris — who invites me to call again "anytime."

But he isn't right. He's dead wrong.

Whoever killed the Ramirez boys also killed the Gabler twins — and that was not Charley Vermillion. It couldn't have been because Vermillion was dead when the Gabler murders took place.

So whoever killed the Ramirez twins is

the monster who kidnapped the Sandling boys. And abducted my sons.

Anonymous tip, my ass.

chapter 28

I know one thing. I can't just show up at the Port Sulfur Forensic Facility. If I waltz in there asking questions about "Cannibal" Charley Vermillion, I won't get past the door.

Even if the hospital did everything by the book, when an institution for the criminally insane releases an inmate who then goes out and butchers a couple of kids — there are consequences. And, in fact, as I learn from a *Times-Picayune* story, heads did roll. But the top guy — Peyton Anderton — managed to hold on to his job. Meanwhile a ten-million-dollar civil suit brought against the institution by the parents of the Ramirez twins is still winding its way through the courts, virtually guaranteeing everyone's silence. I'd guess that no one's talking to anyone.

After a long run through Rock Creek Park, I decide to call Anderton. I'll tell him I'm with *Countdown* and pitch a story that he'll want to see on television. Like . . . how difficult and dangerous his job is. How forensic facilities — not just in Louisiana, but nationwide — need more funding. Better facilities. More staff.

That ought to get me through the door. Unless . . . he recognizes my name.

So I call him. And of course he's flattered by the attention. A little wary, maybe, but —

"No camera crew?"

"No," I tell him. "To start, I thought we'd 'talk about talking,' see if we can find a comfort level. Keep it off the record and then, down the line . . . if we can work it out — great! And if we can't, well, it's no big deal."

"I should tell you up front that if it comes to going on camera, I'd have to think about it."

I'm reassuring. And flattering. "You have a good voice for it, but we're a long way from any shooting."

"Good, because I'd have to clear it, you know, with the powers that be."

I don't say anything.

I can hear the wheels turning at the other end of the receiver. Finally he says, "Looks like I have a window Thursday afternoon. If you can be here at three o'clock?"

"I can do that."

"I'll tell the gate."

★ ★ ★

Louis Armstrong Airport, New Orleans. Along with every other locale in the States, New Orleans had commoditized itself, with jazz and voodoo and Mardi Gras ruling the T-shirt and trinket trade. The voodoo connection — the coins — seems more evidence that I'm on the right track. If I can get Peyton Anderton to talk about Vermillion . . .

The woman at the Alamo counter is friendly, asks where I'm headed, do I need directions?

"Port Sulfur."

"Say where?"

"Plaquemines Parish." I pronounce *Plaquemines* so it rhymes with *nines*. She corrects me.

"Plak-a-*mihn*," she says. "And we don't bother with that *s*, no." She slides my license and credit card back to me, pulls out a map, and marks the route with a green pen. "Follow I-10 across the river to 23. You get to Belle Chasse and then you just head on south. The highway follows the river all the way." She folds the map and hands it to me with a smile. "Now, why you want to go there for? You got all the city, Cajun country, and what-all, and you gonna pick Plaquemines?" She cocks her head. "Must be here on business and not pleasure."

"No fun in Plaquemines?"

"Not unless you really like to fish; you don't go to Plaquemines for fun, no. Oil and gas and fish, that what they got down there. Oranges. Also, it's scary."

"Scary? What do you mean?"

"Plaquemines give a bad name to Louisiana a while back — and that ain't so easy, know what I'm saying? And I don't know it's really changed all that much. You take me — I'm half black. I just wouldn't go there. No, thank you."

"Why not?"

"You heard of Leander Perez?"

I shake my head.

"Back in the day, he ran that place like . . . I don't know. He was like a dictator and people like me, we were slaves there. Vote? Forget it. Black people couldn't vote. Hell, they could hardly drive. It was all . . . like . . . juke joints and lynchings. . . ." She shakes her head, plunks down the car keys. "Row seven, space twelve."

I scoop up the keys and I'm about to leave when she adds something. "You ain't no person of color, but you're a Yankee — so y'all be careful."

I promise I will.

"And wear your seat belt. They'll bust you for that in Plaquemines."

An hour later, I've made the turn at Belle Chasse. It doesn't seem scary except for an excessive number of patrol cars, but it does seem . . . boring.

Sprawl gives way to orange groves and back to more sprawl. Land carved up into ten-acre parcels, bright For Sale signs everywhere, big McMansions under construction.

And then I'm past the sprawl, driving down a new four-lane highway through undeveloped countryside. I pass an occasional cattle farm, a few little towns, and not much else.

The names are a trip in themselves: Concession, Live Oak, Jesuit Bend, Myrtle Grove.

There's not much to see. On the river side, the levee blocks any view, and as far as I can tell, the Gulf side is just flat country. I know that there are oil rigs out there, and a big deepwater port, but all I can see is low-lying trees and reedy vegetation and, once in a while, a lone house. I read in one of the guidebooks that the area had been hit hard by hurricanes a few years back, with many old houses destroyed.

West Point a La Hache, Diamond, Happy Jack, Magnolia.

And then I'm there: Port Sulfur. I read in a guidebook that the town got its name from a sulfur mine out in the salt marsh.

Downtown is a gas station/convenience store. Across from this stands the Port Sulfur High School (home of the Mighty Broncos), along with the library, sheriff's office, and Department of Human Services. Half of these establishments are housed in trailers.

I pass the gas station and follow Anderton's directions, turning right a mile past town on Louisiana 561. After the specified two point seven miles, I see the small sign for the Port Sulfur Forensic Facility and turn up a long drive. I can see the hospital, an ugly rectangle of yellow brick — but in front of it is a fine old plantation house, with white pillars and a verandah, and glorious live oaks. Surrounding both structures is a fence strung with concertina wire.

The guardhouse windows are occluded by condensation. The man inside slides open his window with some reluctance, then asks my business. I spell my name for him and he slides his window shut again. He studies his clipboard, running his finger down a list, finds what he's looking for, then laboriously fills out two bright orange visitor's passes. He slides open his window and passes them to me. "Clip one on your shirt," he tells me, "and place the other on your dashboard. Turn them both in when you leave." He raises the gate and retreats to the comfort of his air-conditioned cubicle.

I know from his CV that Dr. Peyton Anderton is forty-three years old. But with his round baby face and rosy skin he still looks like a boy pretending to be a man. Even his mustache has the look of being pasted-on for the senior play, and I'm sure he grew it to make himself look older. He wears a seersucker suit and a bright smile.

"Mr. Callahan!" he says, shaking my hand with an enthusiastic grip. "Glad you found us." He's wearing some kind of cologne.

It's a big room, and still has the graceful dimensions of another age and use. High ceilings, generous windows, heavy moldings. A ceiling fan turns overhead. Several antique maps of Louisiana grace the walls behind Anderton's desk, and a set of beautiful wood-and-glass display cases line the walls. "Some of the artwork," Anderton says, following my gaze, "created by the patients. We've had some talented folks here."

We sit in a pair of easy chairs, drinking iced tea and talking about the challenges the workforce faces in what he refers to as "the facility."

"For myself, it's not so bad," he says, after we've been shooting the breeze for fifteen minutes or so. "Down here in the administration building, where I spend most of my time, it's quite pleasant, as you can see."

"It's beautiful."

He beams with pride. "It tends to surprise folk," he says. "The main building is a whole different story. It's what you'd expect of a facility that's a hybrid of hospital and prison. Security for the patients and staff is a priority, of course, and it doesn't exactly make for a comfortable ambience."

"And the work — do you find it gratifying?"

He thrusts his chin forward and nods sadly, then gives me a look that is meant to be frank, but again has a rehearsed quality. "Not really," he says with a sigh. "Most of our patients fall into two categories. Many are here for pretrial evaluations — to see if they're capable of standing trial. The rest are insanity acquitees."

I must look puzzled because Anderton explains: " 'Not guilty by reason of insanity.' *Not guilty,* see what I mean? The point being, our patients are here to be treated, not punished. And we *do* treat them. But I'm afraid we don't cure too many."

"Because . . . ?"

"Because their illnesses are often chronic — like diabetes. We can manage that disease with insulin and diet, but we can't cure it. It's the same with schizophrenia or bipolar disorder. And that can make the job very frustrating."

"Ah."

"So long as the patients are monitored and taking their medication, they're not a threat to themselves or anyone else. But when they're released — and we *have* to release many of them at some point — we have no means of keeping track of them *or* their meds."

"Isn't there some kind of . . . parole?"

"Conditions might be set for release, yes. There might be a period when they're required to continue outpatient therapy. But it's a gray area. It's not like they're on parole, not in a criminal sense. If they don't show up for therapeutic sessions, if they go off their meds — we have limited resources to force compliance."

"When you say you 'have' to release them —"

He shakes his head. "There, once again, we have limited resources. Overcrowding is a huge constraint. When the population reaches a certain size, we tend to progress patients through privilege levels because we simply don't have the staff to enforce the more restrictive confinement."

"Privilege levels?"

"That's the way it works in most places like this. Can a patient exercise without supervision? Without sign-out? Can he join the general population for meals, or is he confined to his room? Can he take a shower without supervision? Without some kind of reward system, we simply couldn't encourage good behavior."

"And the ultimate reward is to be released."

"Exactly. And we *have* to release people. The courts have held that unless we have clear and convincing evidence that someone is mentally ill and dangerous to himself or others, we can't keep him here. He can be antisocial and capable of all kinds of things, but if he isn't crazy, he gets a bus ticket. Because he has a right to freedom even if he's a *nasty* sonofabitch." He pauses and adds: “Foucha versus Louisiana, 504 U.S. 71.”

I smile encouragingly, and make a note, wondering how I’m going to bring up Cannibal Charley without putting a bullet in this conversation. But Anderton is on a roll.

“You see the problem,” he says, leaning forward with a confidential air. “Guys in here, like guys in prison, have all day to file writs. They get some starry-eyed baby lawyer to help them appeal for release on the grounds that their constitutional rights are being violated. The release committee meets. It doesn’t want to let a guy go — everyone knows the asshole in question is going to get into trouble. But that’s not enough. Maybe we don’t want to, maybe it’s against our better judgment, but the courts are not interested in educated guesses. Lots of times, we have to release. We have no choice.”

I decide to take a flier. “It’s like that guy a few years back,” I tell him. “What’s-his-name . . . ?”

Anderton laughs. “Which guy? I’m telling you this happens every month.”

“The one who killed those little boys out West.”

Anderton sags and lets his head droop.

"Charley Vermillion," he says in an exhausted voice. "You see? We could turn every patient into a Nobel Prize winner and we'd still have Charley Vermillion thrown in our faces. He's exactly what I'm talking about."

"What do you mean?"

"Charley Vermillion had a personality disorder that was chronic and probably incurable. He was a violent pedophile. And that made him a danger to the community. No question about it. But here, in the context of this facility, with the right medication . . . he was a model patient."

"So you felt he could be trusted?"

"In the context of this facility? Absolutely. He had every privilege. Of course," Anderton says with a chuckle, "we don't have children running around."

I return the chuckle. "So how did he get here?"

Anderton frowned, trying to remember. "Attacked a child. I think it was in a restroom. As I recall, the boy's father intervened and Charley cut him up pretty bad."

" 'Cut him up'?"

"With an oyster knife. That was his job. Shuckin' oysters in the Quarter."

"And he was acquitted?"

"Drug-induced psychosis."

"So he got off."

"Well . . . he spent nineteen years at this address, so I wouldn't say he 'got off.' But the point is we didn't have a choice. Charley Vermillion was disturbed, and he could be violent if he didn't take his meds. But he definitely knew right from wrong when he walked out this door."

It made sense, except for one thing. "It took . . . *nineteen years* to decide that?"

Anderton shrugs. "He petitioned for release."

"He waited nineteen years to petition for release?"

"Nope. Someone put a bug in his ear. Probably another patient."

"Any idea who?"

Anderton frowns, and instantly seems on guard. I've struck the wrong chord. The question was too specific. "I'm really not at liberty to talk about individual cases," he says in a stiff voice.

"I'm sorry, of course you can't. I understand. It's just a pretty dramatic example of what can happen —"

"There are patient confidentiality issues."

I can't stop myself. "Yes, but in this case Vermillion is dead, isn't he?"

A mistake. I regret it instantly. I try to

change the subject, ask about Anderton's training, his doctoral thesis, his prior experience. I suck up to him, doing my best to reestablish our earlier chumminess, but the doctor is now on guard.

I urge him to think hard about going on camera, and this revives his mood a little, although he reminds me that he'll have to consult with his "masters."

"And my comments, I'm afraid, would have to be restricted to general discussion or hypothetical cases."

I tell him that's not a problem, that I'm going to be spending a couple of days in the area, maybe I could buy him lunch and we could talk some more.

Another mistake. I see it in his body language. He clasps his arms around himself; his lips flatten into a line.

"A couple of days here? The closest motel is all the way down in Empire and I don't think you'd like it."

"I meant I'll be in New Orleans. It's not a bad drive."

"Well," Anderton says. He stands up, looks at his watch. The interview is over.

I'm getting to my feet, thinking that the interview has been something of a bust, and wondering what I'm going to do next. Probably I should call the Ramirezes. They filed a suit, maybe they learned something in discovery. And then there's the lawyer who helped Vermillion petition for release. That petition would be in the public record. I could get the lawyer's name, try and track him down, see what brought him to Vermillion's case.

I'm mulling this over as I get to my feet and follow Anderton toward the door. And then I see something in the display case along the wall — and the hair stands up on the back of my neck.

Inside the case is an arts-and-crafts exhibition of artifacts made by the patients as a part of their therapy. There are small sculptures, weavings, pottery, drawings, beadwork, each piece identified with a date — going back to the 1930s. And among the *objets* is a set of origami figures, a whole menagerie, each one a stunning little sculpture. A rhino, an elephant, a lion . . . and a duplicate of the rabbit I found on Sean's dresser.

A second later, I'm standing in front of the display case with my fingers pressed against the glass. In front of the origami figures is a little paper tent of thick stock, like a place card at a table.

1995

I can't speak. There's a hammer in my chest. Finally, I hear myself speak. "Who made these origami figures?" I ask him. "Was it Vermillion?"

"Oh, no. Good Lord. Charley wasn't interested in art. Not at all. Works such as these are far beyond Charley's capabilities." He hesitates and now his voice is suspicious. "Why do you ask?"

I can't take my eyes off the rabbit. And I'm not sure what to do. Anderton is wrapped in his bureaucratic armor now. If I tell him the truth, will that get through to him? Will he identify the patient who folded the rabbit?

"Dr. Anderton, I have to confess something to you . . ."

I know after thirty seconds that it's a mistake. Anderton is less interested in what I'm telling him than he is angry at my deception and irritated that the documentary was a ploy. I blunder on, pleading for the name of the inmate who created the origami menagerie. I explain about finding the little rabbit on my son's dresser. I spell out my theory that Charley Vermillion was not the real killer of the Ramirez twins, that the man who folded the rabbit was the real murderer.

He shakes his head. "That sounds like

kind of a wild theory to me," he says. "I mean, these showgirls and all? I don't know how you can make all these connections."

I tell him if my boys die, I'll consider that he has blood on his hands.

But Anderton won't budge. He cites "the sanctity" of medical records, the "holy pact" of patient confidentiality.

"Just tell me one thing," I plead. "Whoever it was, he's not still in custody, is he? How long was he here? When was he released?"

"That's three things."

I say nothing.

Anderton presses a finger against his chin and stares into space, as if searching for a reason to deny my request. In the end, either he can't come up with one or he suffers a momentary spasm of compassion.

"No," he tells me. "The inmate in question is not in custody. Came to us in 1983. Released in 1996."

"What did he do? What was he in here for? What's his name? We're talking about my sons here. Please."

Dr. Peyton Anderton wags his head sadly. "I'm sorry, Mr. Callahan."

I want to throw him into the display

cases and knock him out and then ransack his office. But I don't. I get control of myself. "Thanks for your help," I tell him, and step through the doorway. Two huge orderlies wait outside in the hall and I realize that at some point Anderton summoned help. A silent alarm or something.

"You do understand I'd like to do more," Anderton says. He's still behind me, still hitting the "my hands are tied" note as I head down the steps and push out through the big front door.

chapter 29

I wait twenty minutes in the tiny Port Sulfur library for a shot at one of their three computers — which are occupied by kids checking their e-mail. I try chatting up the woman at the front desk, but she turns out to be not chatty. I ask her if she remembers the case involving Charley Vermillion.

"No," she says.

I expand on it, identify him as a former patient at the asylum down the road.

"No," she repeats, and returns to her magazine.

When time's up for one of the kids, I use my allotted twenty minutes to snag a bargain room at the Crescent City Omni. Then I e-mail Muriel Petrich to request that photographs of the origami rabbit be either sent to me at the hotel, or scanned and e-mailed. In the few minutes left before the library closes, I use the copying machine to copy the listings for attorneys in the Plaquemines Parish telephone book, and I establish that the parish seat is in Pointe a La Hache.

Which is across the river. That's where the courthouse is, and that's likely where the petition for Charley Vermillion's release was filed. When I ask one of the kids waiting to check out a book how to get to Pointe a la Hache, he tells me there's a free ferry that goes across the river every half hour. I can catch it a few miles north. Look for the signs.

I sit in my car, cell phone in hand, and look at the list of attorneys-at-law. It may not be a good idea to pick a lawyer from the yellow pages, but I don't have much choice. I call three of them before I get to Hawes, Halliday, and Flood. Lester Flood can fit me in at three forty-five tomorrow afternoon at his office in Belle Chasse. My intention is to petition the court for release of the identity of the man who made the origami rabbit in Peyton Anderton's display case.

I head north toward the ferry, but once I get there, I realize there's no point in making the crossing today. It's too late. The courthouse will be closed. I drive back to New Orleans and check into the Omni.

My room is on an air shaft, but the price is right and the parking is free. Once I've checked into the hotel, I call Petrich. I don't really expect her to be in, but I want to leave a phone message to reinforce my e-mail request for a copy of the photos of the rabbit. Turns out, she's working late.

"Where are you, Alex? What's up?"

"New Orleans."

"New Orleans? You find something?"

I don't know why, but I'm reluctant to tell her about Vermillion or the rabbit in the display case. It reminds me of how Liz didn't want to tell anyone she was pregnant before she got past the three-month mark. As if announcing the news might tempt fate and put the pregnancy in jeopardy. "Maybe. I'll let you know if anything pans out."

"You do that," she says. She promises to scan the photo and send it as a JPEG before she leaves work.

I head out for gumbo at a sandwich place down the block, watching my budget, and then take a walk through the Quarter. I end up on Bourbon Street. It's very crowded and the heavy air smells faintly of decades of whiskey and vomit. I stand outside one club, and the music spilling out sounds so great I go inside. What the hell. A beer.

The blues. The guy up front is hunched into the microphone, his body a coiled instrument of woe. *Oh, my heart it starts a-hammerin', and my eyes fill up with tears.*

It ought to be the perfect music for me, a conduit for my misery, but it isn't. I sit there and drink, but nothing happens. I can't feel the music. I can't even taste my beer. I last about ten minutes and then I'm out the door.

When I get back to the hotel, it takes me a long time to fall asleep, and when I do, I have a dream in which everything I touch disappears.

In the morning, I grab some free coffee from the lobby, plug in my laptop, and log on using Liz's AOL account. Her password is the twins' birthday, 010497 and that stops me cold for a second. I check off five New Orleans area telephone numbers for AOL to try. It takes almost twenty minutes before the server finds a connection.

I go to my Yahoo! account and see that Petrich came through. I hit the key to download the JPEG file she attached to her message and wait for it to come up. The blue bar expands across the bottom of my screen, and then, there it is. Even in two dimensions, the rabbit is impressive and powerful. I made no mistake — it's identical to the one in the display case in Anderton's office. There's an evidence tag affixed to the rabbit. A stamped rectangle on the page bears the words: *Anne Arundel County Police Department Evidence Room.* There's a signature (*Sgt. David Ebinger*) and date (June 1, 2003).

At nine, when the hotel's "office suite" is available to guests (for a fee), I print out a few copies of the photo of the rabbit.

My plan is to give one copy to the lawyer, Lester Flood, in hopes that he'll be able to use the photo as evidence, that he'll be able to compel the release of information from the Port Sulfur facility.

I'm about to leave when I decide to e-mail Judy Jones at the FBI. Maybe the Bureau can help. It takes me twenty minutes to hammer together a message about what I've learned, explaining how I came to discover a rabbit identical to the one found on my son Sean's dresser in the display case of a Louisiana asylum.

When I'm finished, I look over what I've written. I'm dissatisfied. I *know* that the connections linking the Ramirez murders to the abduction of my sons (by way of the Gablers and the Sandling boys) are solid. I know that the "anonymous tip" was bogus, that the man held responsible for the murders of the Ramirez boys was not the man who actually killed them. I know that the man who made the rabbit in the Port Sulfur display case took my sons. But on paper, no matter how much I tighten and clarify my account, it all seems . . . insubstantial.

I fire off my final version, but in the end I know it doesn't make it. Showgirls? Magic? Calling into question a double murder that was solved to everyone's satisfaction? The little folded rabbit doesn't seem strong enough to support the weight of all that.

In the car, I take a look at the map. Plaquemines Parish is a peninsula divided by the Mississippi River. The courthouse in Pointe a La Hache is on the west bank. I plan to go there first, looking for the petition for release that freed Charley Vermillion. I've done courthouse document searches before. It's time-consuming work, and tedious. It can take days. But I should be able to get a few hours in before it's time for my appointment with the lawyer.

My guidebook confirms what the kid in the Port Sulfur library told me: Ferryboats run back and forth across the river. I head for the one that crosses from Belle Chasse to Dalcour.

My guidebook also noted that the courthouse in Pointe a la Hache is more than a hundred years old, having survived any number of hurricanes. Old as the courthouse is, I just hope the place has air-conditioning.

It takes me less than an hour to get to Belle Chasse, and I'm lucky, catching the ferry five minutes before it leaves. Every other vehicle on board is a pickup truck. The river is wide, the water a turbulent roil of chop and current. The ferryboat's powerful engines point the craft upstream against the drag as it muscles its way toward the far shore.

The houses on this bank seem older and more refined, but otherwise the drive is much like yesterday's. Small towns remarkable mainly because the speed limit plummets for a mile or so. A levee concealing the river. Citrus groves. And not much else.

In twenty-four minutes, I arrive in Pointe a la Hache. It's not hard to find the courthouse — which is by far the largest structure I've seen in Plaquemines. But it's a burned-out shell, surrounded by yellow crime-scene tape, much of which is lying around on the ground tangled in the weeds. A grove of skeletonized live oaks hulk above the ruined building like so many demons, their ropy trunks and gnarled branches charred black.

A construction trailer sits to the side, bearing a sign that reads PLAQUEMINES PARISH PUBLIC WORKS. A rap on the door summons a red-faced man in a battered yellow hard hat.

He looks me up and down as if I'm from another planet. "Yup?"

"What happened to the courthouse?"

He fails to keep the smirk off his face. "Burned down."

"When did *that* happen?"

"January twelve, two thousand three."

"What a shame." The sight of the fine old building in ruins depresses me. Where are the records now? Did they survive?

"Shame and a half is what it was," Hardhat says. "Stood more'n one hundred years. Lasted through I don't know how many hurricanes. Served its citizens well. Betsy came through here at a hundred forty miles an hour and that wind brought half the river with it when it got to this bank. Lots of folks rode out the storm in the courthouse, up top there. It was the high ground, you understand. A hundred years and then —" He snaps his fingers. "Gone."

"Is there a new courthouse?"

But he's not finished.

"Nature couldn't destroy the place, but man could. And did."

"You mean it was arson?"

"Right," he says, with a knowing nod. "And that's according to none other than the Bureau of Alcohol, Tobacco, and Firearms. They found accelerant residue. Big-time."

Arson. "But why?"

He wags his head. "They's a hundred years of history in them files. Least there *was*. Some say that's it, some old record somebody wanted permanently lost. Deed or some-ut."

"But there must be electronic records."

He laughs. "For the past few years, they is. But for the other ninety-five or whatever, nossir. Those records is solid gone."

Maybe I can still find out the name of Vermillion's lawyer. That case is recent enough to fall within the time frame of "the past few years."

"Myself," Hardhat says, "I'm partial to 'tother theory about the arson."

"What's that?"

"Well, they been tryin' to move the courthouse for years, to some more *convenient* location. But the dang pop-u-lace keep votin' the idea down." A laugh. "I think it gon' move now."

"Move the courthouse? Why?"

"Your lawyers, judges, court reporters, and what all. Long time they been wantin' it on the east bank, in Belle Chasse. Belle Chasse an easy drive from N'Awlins. Not like gettin' down here where you got to hassle with the ferry and all. Rumor is, the lawyers got tired of haulin' they ass way down here to conduct they bidness. How much money it take to get somebody throw some kerosene in there and toss a match? This *is* Louisiana."

"They going to rebuild it?"

"Don't think so."

"So where do they conduct court business now?"

"Temporary courthouse," he says. "Bunch of trailers."

"Where are they?" I ask, looking around.

"Oh, that's why I think they gon' get their way. They didn't even bother to put the temporary courthouse here. Those trailer — they over there in Belle Chasse," he says with a chuckle. "It more *convenient*, you see, for the *interim*."

chapter 30

I find the temporary courthouse in Belle Chasse — a half-dozen trailers in the park- ing lot of an abandoned shopping center. Each trailer bears an identifying sign: TRAFFIC COURT, JUVENILE COURT, and so on. When I find the right trailer, the one housing records, the clerk of court tells me I'm out of luck. All the files pertaining to the Port Sulfur Forensic Facility were destroyed in the fire.

"I was told there were computer records for the last few years. I'm just trying to get the name of a lawyer connected to a case."

She's a white-haired woman with bright brown eyes. She gives me an ironic smile. "Supposed to be electronic backup, but it never took. They got a new system now. Gentleman who installed the old system got hisself indicted."

"I see."

"We got four months of records and that's about it. You might find something about your case in the newspaper, though. *The Peninsula Gazette* right here in Belle Chasse is the paper of record. I b'lieve they required to publish filings."

I mull over the dates as I follow the courthouse clerk's directions to the *Gazette*'s office. The Ramirez twins were abducted May 4, 2001, two weeks following Vermillion's release from Port Sulfur. The petition for release would be earlier — and maybe a lot earlier.

I can start in late April and work my way backward. I'm not looking forward to it. Searching through newspaper morgues is about as tedious as it gets. But I've got three hours to kill before my appointment with Lester Flood, so I may as well make a run at it.

But not right now, it seems. As I approach the newspaper office, a young woman with dark spiky hair is locking the door. She's wearing a halter top, cut-off jeans, and flip-flops. The halter top displays most of a large spider tattooed on one shoulder.

"Will you open again this afternoon?"

The girl cocks her head and sizes me up. "Why?" she asks, in such a way that the word has at least two syllables. "You want to place an ad?"

I explain that I want to look through the morgue.

"Excuse me?"

"I mean the old newspaper files."

"Ohhhhh. Yeah, I knew that." She taps her head. "I heard my daddy say that one time. He's not here. He's fishing. So what are you looking for?"

"I'm looking for notice of suit. The courthouse records were destroyed in the fire, so this is my only hope."

"Huh. Your only hope. *The Peninsula Gazette* your only hope? I wish Daddy *was* here." She smiles at me. A surprisingly sweet and shy smile. "I'm Jezebel," she says. "Jezebel Henton."

"Alex Callahan."

She shakes the keys. "Well, Mr. Callahan — I *could* let you in. Of course, I'd have to stay there with you. How long is this going to take?"

I shrug. "It could take a while."

"Hunh." She looks at me.

"I have an appointment at four-thirty."

She twists a ring on her pinky. "Well, since I have to sit there, I think it's only fair if you pay for my time, don't you?"

"I guess so."

"So you pay me ten dollars an hour," she says, " 'cause otherwise, I could just go watch TV, right?"

"Right."

"Plus," Jezebel says, "I'll help you look.

I'm experienced — so that's why I'm worth ten bucks an hour. I've done courthouse searches for Pinky Streiber."

"Who's Pinky Streiber?"

"He's a private investigator," she says. "You've never heard of him?"

"No."

"He's legendary," she insists. "He really is. So —" She sticks out her hand. The fingernails are a shiny black, the polish half chipped away. "Deal?"

She takes me upstairs. I explain what I'm looking for. "What I really need is the name of Charley Vermillion's lawyer. I'd like to talk to him . . . or her."

"That should be on there with the published notice, although sometimes they just list whoever in the firm took it over to file it. And right away I can save you some time," she says, selecting a key and opening an oak door. "The paper only publishes arrests and suits once a week. Wednesday."

Jezebel finds it at 3:48. "Binnnnnnnngo!" she shouts, and then continues in a revved-up voice. "Am I good or am I good? January ninth, 2000. Case number four-nine-six-eight-seven Division A: Charles Jimmie Vermillion vs. Port Sulfur

Forensic Facility, et. al., filed by Francis —" She stops suddenly. "Oh, shit. Pardon my mouth."

"What's it say?"

"Filed by Francis Bergeron," she says. "Frankie Bergeron. I hope you don't need to talk to him real bad."

"Why?"

"He's dead — that's why. Car crash. Over by Des Allemands. Single car accident. Went flying into the bayou. Frankie was a very aggressive driver, so you can take your pick: Some kind of road rage incident, or was he just going too fast and misjudged the curve? No witnesses ever came forward. Hey — what's the matter?"

I shake my head. "Every time I think I'm getting somewhere with this thing, I hit a dead end."

"Well, Frankie Bergeron sure is a dead end, but Pinky says there's always another way to find something out."

"That would be the courthouse."

"Oh, yeah. This was your last hope. I am so sorry, Mr. Callahan."

"Maybe Bergeron's firm would have records," I say, more to myself than to Jezebel. "Do you know who he worked for?"

"Lacey and Bergeron. Right here in

Belle Chasse. You could call Mr. Lacey. I'll get you his telephone number. Don't call him after say . . . oh . . ." She twirls a Rolodex, tapping one thumb against her lower lip and then writes the number on a Post-it. "Don't call him after three. Maybe two. He drinks a little."

She hands me the Post-it. Her handwriting is clear and beautiful. We spend a few minutes replacing the cartons of newspapers we've been going through, Jezebel locks up, and I fork over thirty-five bucks. "I almost feel bad about taking this," she says. "I mean, Frankie Bergeron. . . ."

"Deal's a deal."

She folds the money in half and then in half again, then pinches it between her thumb and forefinger. "Then again, I don't think this thirty-five dollars would really cheer you up all that much, am I right?"

I shake my head. "Thanks for the help."

She pushes the money into the back of her jeans, then sticks out her hand. "Well, then, good luck, Mr. Callahan. Maybe things will turn around. Pinky says they always do in an investigation if you just keep pounding it."

"I hope he's right."

"Where's your appointment?"

"Tupelo Street."

"Where you going, if you don't mind my asking?"

"I'm going to see a lawyer. Lester Flood."

She considers that. "First year back from Tulane, but Les is a good enough guy." She looks at her nails. "Tell him Jez Henton says hey. You know how to get there?"

Jezebel's directions deliver me within four minutes to the offices of Hawes, Halliday, and Flood, which are housed in a charming old brick building on a street that — judging from the proliferation of shingles — is obviously the preferred location of the legal establishment in Belle Chasse.

I wait ten minutes, and then I'm shown into Lester Flood's office. It's charming in that southern way, highly polished antiques, beautiful but worn rugs, and very high ceilings. There's a collection of snow globes on a side table.

Flood doesn't look much older than Jezebel. "Mr. Callahan," he says. "Les Flood." We shake hands and he gestures to a chair.

"Now," he says, "what can I do for you?"

It takes me fifteen minutes to tell him. He jots down notes on a yellow legal pad, and occasionally asks me to spell a name or clarify something. When I'm finished, I give him a copy of the rabbit photo. He regards it for a moment or two, then slides it to one side. He taps his pad with his pen.

"I don't know," he says, pressing his lips together. "I can take this on; I *will* take this on if you decide to go that way, but . . ." He shakes his head. "I don't know. The court requires strong evidence and a pressing need to compel disclosure of information about a hospital patient — which this individual was." He winces. "I have to say I don't like our chances."

"Why not? This *is* strong evidence. And there sure as hell is a pressing need. My sons."

He drums his fingers on the legal pad. "I am sympathetic to your position. I might even agree with you. But there are a lot of suppositions in your theory."

"Such as?"

"Well, for starters — you don't *know* that the abductor of your children left the origami rabbit on your dresser. You never noticed it before they were abducted, but it could have been there before, am I right?"

"I don't think so."

"You a hundred percent sure?"

"I am now."

He nods. "Yeah. Sure you are. But that's reversing things, isn't it? The argument will be that your son could have gotten the thing elsewhere. From a kid, a neighbor, who knows?"

"But he didn't."

He nods. "You understand I'm playing devil's advocate here. I agree that the rabbit is unusual, and that finding a replica of the one found in your house at the facility in Port Sulfur is suggestive. Especially given the links between that facility and the Ramirez murders and the parallels between the Ramirez case and your own. But there's an awful lot of dots to connect in there. And there are no rabbits in either of the other cases. So it all could be coincidence, which is what the defense will argue. There were no prints on the rabbit found in your home, right?"

I nod.

He presses his lips together. "You also know that there's another suit out there against the Port Sulfur facility."

"The Ramirez family."

"Yes. And the facility felt it was in good standing there. They appealed the lower court's decision to release that fellow. Lost the appeal. They had to let the guy go. What else could they do?"

"We're talking about Vermillion."

"Right, Vermillion. We might not like it, but releasing men like that is compelled by law. Now, you can argue — as the attorneys for the Ramirez family do — that the man should not have been released. But that's hindsight and a fallacy. *Post hoc, ergo propter hoc*. 'After this, therefore because of this.' He killed two kids, therefore you shouldn't have released him. And anyway, why blame the facility: They didn't really want to release. To complicate everything, the whole thing's in a mess right now because the defense records went up in smoke. I heard that the Ramirez legal team has actually agreed to share its files with defense so that the case can continue."

"Really."

"Yeah. But probably what's going to happen is that the state . . . and the facility . . . will settle. In the meantime" — he shakes his head — "I can't think the court's going to jump at the chance to get into this again and compel disclosure of *anything* by the facility. At least not until this other thing's settled. For one thing, if what you suggest is true, it would mean that whole suit the Ramirez family brought would kind of be gazumped, wouldn't it? I mean you are suggesting that Vermillion didn't kill those boys?"

"That's right."

Lester Floyd raises his hands, palms up. "That would give it a hell of a twist." He smiles. "Like I said, I'm willing to try to compel disclosure."

"I'm really in a hurry."

"I'm even willing to hurry," Flood says. "I just don't like our chances real well, and I want you to know that ahead of time."

"I understand you're telling me that success is not likely, but I've got to try."

"Okay. Fine. Let's do it."

We discuss money. My bank account has been temporarily replenished by a five-thousand-dollar cash advance from Visa. I write Flood a check for his requested retainer: a thousand dollars.

I drive back to New Orleans in a somber mood. I finally get a lead and where does it take me?

Scorched earth.

Charley Vermillion had a cyanide capsule taped to his collar and committed suicide upon his capture. An arsonist burned down the hundred-year-old Pointe a la Hache courthouse containing records about Vermillion's suit petitioning release from custody (after nineteen years). Francis Bergeron, the lawyer who filed that suit, drove off a bridge into the bayou and died. The electronic system designed to store court documents imploded, so there is no record of the court proceedings involving Vermillion.

Can all this be coincidence?

chapter 31

In the morning, I put in a call to William Lacey — formerly the partner of Francis Bergeron. He "doesn't see any harm" in telling me that his partner's work on behalf of Charley Vermillion was pro bono.

"Did he do a lot of pro bono work?"

"Frankie? Hell no, and I don't know what put the bug in his ear about Vermillion. It's not like mental health was a special cause. Frankie didn't have too many causes. He was looking to run for office down the road, you know?"

"So you don't know how the case came to his attention."

"No idea. Tell you the truth, I thought it was out of character. It was a risk — and damned if it didn't backfire. Of course, he did get to argue in the court of appeals, and that was always kind of in the cards. So maybe that was the point. Exposure."

I ask him if I could take a look at the case file — that the courthouse record had been destroyed.

"Hmmmmm," he says. "I really couldn't

do that. There are attorney-client issues."

"But in this case, both attorney and client are dead."

"Point taken," he says, "but I'm afraid it's a moot one. I turned Frank's files over to the district attorney. You aware there's a suit pending over Vermillion's release?"

"The parents of the Ramirez boys."

"Bingo. And who the hell wouldn't sue when the state, in all its wisdom, releases a wacko who utilizes his constitutional rights to kidnap and murder a couple of kids? That's a damn worst-case scenario and a half."

"So the district attorney is . . . where? Belle Chasse?"

"Now he is, sure. But that's the point. My understanding is Frank's files went up in the fire. It's right after the parish court took custody of those files that the place burned down."

That leaves the rabbit.

I stare at the image on my computer screen. Shoffler looked into it and I did, too, but at the time the little paper creature represented only one of several leads. Now it's all that's left.

I look through my notebooks.

Paper folding practiced by Leonardo. Mathematically based. Connections to 19th-century stage magic.

A note in the margin, added later, reads: *paper folding a kind of transformation. Balloons more popular now.*

Traditional form: no gluing or cutting allowed — only a square of paper.

This makes origami an ideal hobby, I realize, for people confined to prisons or mental institutions.

Facility requires a mind adept at geometry and abstract thought. Popular with physicists and mathematicians.

Origami jargon: overland folds, blintzed, waterbomb, stretched bird bases.

Diagrams shared freely on Web. Complex diagrams.

Judy Jones: rabbit made of special origami paper, elephant hide. Folded wet.

Petrich: expert identified rabbit as "modified Lang."

Online, I type *origami Lang rabbit* into the Google bar. It kicks out more than a thousand sites. Dr. Joseph Lang created many rabbits, but after two hours of going through the listings, I've seen dozens of Lang rabbits and modified versions of same, and not one of these bunnies looks much like the one I found in the boys' bedroom. Maybe Petrich's expert found a different Lang rabbit from the ones I've seen so far.

Or maybe — he made a mistake.

When I type in *origami rabbit,* Google kicks out thousands and thousands more listings, although many turn out to be repetitious. I slog through for another hour and a half, but I still find nothing that looks like my rabbit.

But I do learn that the origami world is very chummy and active on the Web. It abounds in competitions and exhibitions, and there is much critiquing of origami books, commentary on sources of material, exhibition of new creations, and trading of folding diagrams. Maybe the origami cybercommunity can tell me more about my rabbit. Judging from the menagerie in Anderton's display case, the Piper wasn't a novice, but pretty deeply into the hobby.

Maybe he had access to a computer at

Port Sulfur. Maybe he communicated with people in the subculture. It's possible someone will recognize his work. Or even identify him.

I plug *origami* into Google and make a list of two dozen website addresses. I compose an e-mail requesting help in identifying the rabbit in the attached JPEG file. I send it out.

And if this doesn't work, well — Anderton knows who made the rabbit. If I have to, I'll put the question to him — hard.

I've been in a zone, sitting there hunched over the laptop for so long that when I stand up it's painful. I do some shoulder rolls and stretches.

I should call the folks. I should call Liz. I haven't spoken to my parents or my wife in more than a week, dodging the worry and concern from the folks and the hostility from Liz.

At least I should call and check my messages.

It's the usual suspects.

Big Dave at the station. *Alex! Something's come up that I think you'll be interested in. If you're ready to come back, we're ready for you. It's a real opportunity, so . . .*

The folks, "just checking in."

My friend Scott, still trying to cheer me

up: *Heyyy. Hi, Alex. Well, here's the deal: I'm putting together this . . . ah . . .* badminton *tournament. It's for charity, of course, although we're not expecting a* huge *crowd. Anyway . . . it's Brad and Jennifer, Tim and Susan, Bill and Hillary, myself and Demi — she's got one hell of a defensive lob, in case you weren't aware. Charlize Theron needs a partner . . . So . . . if you're interested, buddy, give me a call, okay?*

Liz. *Where are you now, Alex? We need to talk.*

I don't want to talk to any of them. I tell myself I'll return the calls tomorrow. I head out for a jog. Stepping out the door from the air-conditioned lobby into the humid air, I'm surprised there isn't a thunderstorm in the doorway. The air feels so dense it's almost like running through water. I head out along the waterfront until I get to a dock area and a security fence stops me. On the way back, I pick it up as I cruise around the perimeter of Lafayette Park. A crowd sways and claps to the music from the bandstand, a free concert, some kind of funky salsa blues. I'm dripping wet by the time I get back to the Omni, and I fog up the mirror in the elevator.

After a shower, I pop a beer and sit back

down in front of the computer. It's only been an hour or so, but already I have eight responses to my e-mail plea. Most of them suggest links I might check, but one of them (folderman@netzero.com) recognizes the rabbit as the winner of a competition at the Prospect Hill branch of the Philadelphia Public Library.

> The Prospect Hill Origami Society sponsors an annual competition, posing a different figure challenge each year. This year, it's the shark; 1995 was the year of the rabbit. It isn't one of the big folding competitions, but the entrance fee is trivial, so you get a lot of students and the like. The rabbit in the photo you're circulating was the grand champion in 1995, and we were all irritated when the creator was identified only by his first name or something. No address. Clearly the guy was a spectacular talent and some of us wanted to communicate with him, but there was no information about how to do so. Get in touch with George Esterhazy — he's the president emeritus of the group. He's retired now but still very engaged with folding. Cheers, I hope this helps.

Folderman appends Esterhazy's phone number and e-mail address. I shoot him a fervent thank-you, then send my original e-mail to Esterhazy along with a copy of Folderman's message.

A few minutes later, I call Esterhazy. He might be one of those guys who checks his e-mail once a week. At least I ought to bring it to his attention.

"Esterhazy," the reedy voice says.

"Mr. Esterhazy, my name is Alex Callahan. I don't know if you've had a chance —"

"Yesss. I got your e-mail. And of *course* I remember that brilliant little rabbit. Byron B. Very frustrating."

"Byron B.? What do you mean?"

"That was his name — all the name we ever got. As I was saying, it was very frustrating. Some on the committee wanted to strip the championship from him, but I was against it. Wouldn't have been right. It was a blind competition, you know, and his rabbit was head and shoulders above the other submissions."

"Excuse me, but how was the rabbit submitted, if you didn't know the identity of the person who made it?"

"Turned out the fellow who sent the piece was an occupational therapist at the . . . wait, I'll remember."

"Port Sulfur Forensic Facility in Louisiana?"

"Yes! A madhouse! Not unknown, of course. Jules Kravik — a famous folder — he was deeply disturbed and lived most of his life in a mental institution."

"Hunh."

"With this Byron B. fellow, we might have been permitted to communicate except that by the time the competition was judged and we were ready to inform the winners and announce results, he'd been released. And our attempts to persuade the institution to pass on the news of victory and the small cash award were very firmly rebuffed." A sigh. "So that was it. I was a bit surprised that he didn't resurface in the origami world — clearly a talent, very innovative use of the stretched bird base. But that was it."

I'm so excited I barely have the manners to thank the man before I hang up.

Byron B. might not be much, but it's something. It's not like the facility in Port Sulfur is a detox center or a rehab facility with patients checking in and out at will. It's an institution for the criminally insane. Which is to say that, whoever Byron B. is, he fucked up badly and in a very public way — otherwise he wouldn't have been in that particular bin for so many years.

And he hadn't checked in of his own volition. Which meant that somewhere in Louisiana, there was a court-order committing a man named Byron, last name initial *B.*, to the Port Sulfur Forensic Facility. Depending upon what the guy had done, there might even be a news story. Thanks to Anderton, I know the year: 1983.

Ordinarily, I might not select a private investigator on the advice of a thirteen-year-old girl, but nothing about my life is ordinary anymore. Jezebel Henton is happy to give me Pinky Streiber's name, which she spells for me, and his number, which she apparently knows by heart.

"Thanks, Jez."

"One thing about Pink maybe you should know?" She hesitates.

"What's that?"

"Just 'cause it kinda startles people. See, Pinky — the reason that's his nickname? He's an albino."

I meet Pinky Streiber at his office in the French Quarter. A hard-looking blonde in a red linen sheath sits at the reception desk. She tells me to take a seat in what has to be one of the hippest offices I've ever been in. Jazz on the sound system. Paintings and antique furniture and a scatter of big plants. Tall ceilings and rotating fans. Huge windows with white shutters. Pinky Streiber is doing all right.

Five minutes later, he's shaking my hand and leading me to his dimly lit and sparsely furnished inner sanctum. He sits behind a slab of polished wood, which has nothing on it but a red telephone. I sit on a red leather Barcelona chair. Streiber wears sunglasses and his skin is dead white. There's a familiar smell in the air, but I can't quite identify it.

"Sunscreen," Streiber says, as if he's read my mind. "I'm drenched in it. That's what you smell. Coppertone Sport 48. And I apologize for the sunglasses, but I only take 'em off at night."

After he understands the task, Pinky says, "Well, it's labor-intensive, but even so, it's just legwork. If we can get a million hamsters hopping on keyboards long enough, we'll eventually get a copy of 'Gunga Din,' *n'est-ce pas?* The question is: How big is your budget?"

I shrug. "Don't hold back. Whatever it takes." For the time being, I'm just going to keep writing myself more of those checks the credit card companies send in the mail. Eventually, I'll hit up my dad. And then . . .

"I'll give you a break, seeing as how this ain't exactly a run-o'-the-mill divorce case, but I'll still need a retainer, let's say five hundred dollars. And just so you know, I don't do courthouse searches myself. I've built up a kind of motley crew of paralegals, retired folks, teenagers, and the chronically underemployed. You say go, I'll turn 'em loose on this and they will hit every single courthouse in Louisiana until they find that commitment order."

"Great."

"I pay my subs twenty bucks an hour. Now, this could take a lot of hours. Or a few. You never know."

"Right. I understand."

"Ohhhhh-kay. So it's Byron B. Commitment order to the Port Sulfur Forensic Facility. Entered the system in 1983." He writes this down. "That's it, right? That's all you got. You know when he got out?"

"Ninety-six."

"Okay, then, that's all I need."

"I might as well help," I tell him. "If there's somewhere you don't have enough bodies, I know how to search records."

“Dynamite. You just earned yourself a stint in St. John the Baptist Parish. Parish seat’s in LaPlace. My number one sub there just had a baby and my backup took a job at the new Target.” He pronounces the word as if it’s French: *Tar-zhay.* “It’s not far from here, actually. Highway 10 will take you right to it.”

“Okay.” I pull out my wallet, extracting a dog-eared check.

“Becky will deal with that. We do take Visa and MasterCard,” Pinky says. “Some folks like to get their miles.”

chapter 32

Days in the LaPlace courthouse, nights in the local Comfort Inn. Poring through the records, I drink gallons of coffee and work to keep the name Byron in the forefront of my mind. It would be easy to run right by the citation the way I've missed my turn and driven right past Ordway Street on my way home from work.

The third day, I'm on my way back to the motel when my cell phone rings.

It's Pinky. "You in your car?"

"Yes."

"Pull over."

"What?"

"I'm excited and chagrined and a little disappointed, my man," Pinky says, with a little bray of a laugh.

"What?"

"This search coulda really helped out with the unemployment statistics here in Louisiana."

"Pinky."

A sigh. "Yeah. Deal is I hired a woman to work St. Mary's Parish. She's off visiting her sister in Houston until today, but she's worth waiting for because this lady is really smart. Schoolteacher. Anyway, the assignment from me is waiting on her fax machine when she gets home. Bingo. She calls me right off. Turns out, she knew the sumbitch. *'Byron B.,'* she says to me. *'Pinky, you can only be talkin' 'bout Byron Boudreaux.'* "

"You're kidding."

" 'Oh?' sez me," Pinky continues. " 'I think so,' she says. 'See, I grew up in Morgan City and right across the river they had this crazy kid name of Byron Boudreaux did some terrible stuff. I remember when they put that boy away because we all slept a little better. And it had to be round about 1983 or so because I was in high school at the time and I graduated in eighty-five. I think it's just gotta be him, Pink.' Sounds like it, I told her. So how 'bout that?"

I don't say a thing. *Byron Boudreaux.* Having a name for the man who abducted my sons has in some way given focus to my torment and for the moment, I'm so inundated with emotion, I can hardly see. Byron Boudreaux. I'm going to squeeze the life out of him.

"Alex? You there?"

“Yeah,” I manage. “Good work.”

“Blind fool luck is what,” Pinky says. “By the way, Miss Vicky went ahead and put in for that commitment order, which is good because there might be other information on there of use to us. But it’s gonna take a couple days to get our hands on it. You gonna get yourself over here?”

chapter 33

"Tell you what," Pinky says, once I'm settled into the Barcelona chair in his office. He's given me the case file. Clipped to it is a map of Louisiana, the route to Morgan City marked on it, and an index card listing the various telephone numbers of Miss Victoria Sims. "Why don't I come along?"

"Well, I —"

"Cajun folks is friendly but they can be a little twitchy toward outsiders. And truth be told, offshore rigs don't make for a particularly orderly populace, so Morgan City can be a kind of rough-and-tumble place. It's the second coming of shore leave when those boys come off shift."

"Well . . ."

"You thinking about the money, don't think no more. It's on the *château*, so to speak."

"Well, that's —"

"Hold the applause. I been thinking about those two little boys of yours. 'Bout time for the Pinkster to do a little pro bono *travail*." He gestures around the office. "Got nothin' pressing here. Nothin' can't wait."

Pinky's office and expensive clothing denote the value of his time. "I appreciate it."

"Oh, forget it," Pinky says. "I need to get out of the office, pleasant as it is. And I know some boys out that way might prove helpful."

We head out into the sunset in Pinky's car, a silver BMW X5 SUV so new that it still has that smell. "Albinos generally have bad eyesight," he tells me. "I'm the exception — I see pretty good, especially at night."

It's about a ninety-mile drive from New Orleans to Morgan City — where Pinky's secretary booked rooms for us at the Holiday Inn. Despite the darkness, the way the lights are strung along riverbanks, clustered on shores, absent in large black expanses, conveys the constant presence of water. Going through Houma ("HOME-uh," Pinky corrects me when I mispronounce it), we see faded remnants of patriotic support for the invasion of Iraq: tattered yellow ribbons and a big showing of the stars and stripes. When we swing around one corner, the BMW's lights illuminate a marquee above a defunct gas station:

SADDAM? NEAUX PROBLEM

Vicky Sims meets us for the buffet breakfast at the Holiday Inn. She's about thirty, with bad skin and a sweet, soft voice. "I located the case file at the courthouse in Franklin," she tells us, "after I talked to you, Pinky. It's in the public record, so there's no problem with getting it, although some of the medical opinion leading to commitment is likely to be under seal. I did my best to hurry 'em up over there, but it's going to take a couple days to retrieve and copy. Staff cutbacks, you know? Parish finances are just in terrible shape."

"Same everywhere," Pinky says. "Just pitiful. But why don't we just start with what you remember your own self about Mr. Byron Boudreaux. Then Alex and I plan to go talk to people mighta known the guy, what folk may still be around."

She dabs her lips. "Excuse me," she says. "I consider grits a platform for butter and salt. It can get messy."

"Obviously you don't indulge too often," Pinky says.

Vicky Sims smiles. "I don't know as I can help you all that much with Byron. He lived in Berwick — across the river — so I didn't really know him. Just knew about him — we all knew about him." She frowns. "Good-lookin' boy, and really smart, almost like a genius, or maybe *really* a genius. He had quite a following during his preaching days. He was the kind of kid could turn out to be a great man, or could turn out to be as crazy as a bedbug. Which was the way Byron went."

"He was a preacher?" I ask.

"Boy preacher, oh, yes."

"Really," Pinky says.

"Oh, yes, he could preach up a storm, that boy. He was like a little Billy Graham. People came from all over to see him. He was at the Primitive Baptist Church over to Berwick. As I recall, he took up preaching after his little brother drowned." She frowns. "I didn't live here when that happened. We were still in Baton Rouge then, but apparently there were rumors."

"Like what?" Pinky asks.

"Like it wasn't an accident. Like maybe Byron drowned his baby brother." She shakes her head. "But I don't know — Byron was just a kid himself when it happened. And I can't really remember whether people had suspicions at the time, or if it just came up later, after he killed his father."

"Is that what he did?" I ask. "He killed his father?"

"Now, this, I do remember very well. And it's what sent him away to the asylum. He murdered his crippled daddy."

"You're kidding," I say, although nothing this monster could have done would surprise me.

"I'm not. Byron was seventeen years old, and they were planning to try him as an adult. Then he was found incompetent. Which everybody figured was about right, because that boy was about as twisted as a corkscrew."

Pinky drains his coffee. "His father was crippled?"

Vicky Sims dabs at her lips with a napkin. "Claude, Byron's daddy — he worked out on the rigs for Anadarko. Had some kind of accident and surgery. He was on the mend, but he was still in a wheelchair at the time of the murder — which seemed to make it even more terrible."

"What'd he do — shoot his old man?" To me Pinky adds: "We tend to be kinda heavily armed down here."

"Oh, no, nothin' that normal," Vicky says. "Poisoned him in some sneaky way — through his *skin,* I think it was. Can that be right?"

"Transdermal," Pinky says. "Hell, yes! But *wow*. How'd he get caught?"

Vicky frowns. "I don't know as I ever knew that. It never did come to trial. But since it was *poison* — there was no question it was premeditated. So that's why they were going to try Byron as an adult."

"He pled insanity," I say.

"Right. The lawyers said he was crazy, that he heard voices, that his daddy abused him from when he was a little guy." She sprinkles some more salt on her grits. "Usual stuff. There'll be more about it in the court records. Or in the paper — *The New Iberian* might be your best bet there. Come to think of it, I know the editor — Max Maldonado. You want his telephone number?"

We call from my hotel room, with Pinky on the extension. I explain who I am and what I want, and Maldonado says he's on deadline but he was a reporter back in the day and of course he remembers the Boudreaux case. He'll call me in the afternoon. I'm agreeing to that when Pinky weighs in.

"Shame on you, Max. Start talking right this minute. Surely you can spare five minutes of your invaluable time for two missing *bambinos*. Come on now."

"Am I talking to the whitest private investigator in Louisiana?" Maldonado says. "Shit, Pink, why didn't you say it's you?"

"I'm testing your moral compass, Max." He lets out a rumble of laughter at the protesting hoot from Maldonado. "I am. I'm not kiddin'. All we want is a heads-up on this fellow. Like where did he live, where did he work, somethin' to go on. We don't want to twiddle our thumbs while we're waiting for them to find the damn court record."

"My moral compass, huh? Well, all right, I'll try to swing it around your way, Pink. Byron Boudreaux — why am I not surprised we didn't hear the last of him?" A sigh. "I can give you five minutes now, all the time you want later tonight."

"Great."

"Well, let's see. Byron's family lived over to Berwick in a trailer park called Meadowlands. Kind of a dog-assed place, although chez Boudreaux was neat as a pin. I know that because at the time of Claude's murder I was filling in for the photographer at the time and I took a bunch of pictures over there. Marie, Byron's mother — she was a fine woman, to all accounts. Claude — he was a good man, too, is what I hear, a hard worker. Worked for Anadarko out on the rigs. Imagine being poisoned by your own son! That boy was just plain *rotten* through and through. Most folks didn't believe that crap about Claude abusing the boy, that was a boatload of bullshit."

"Like the Menendez brothers."

"Just like that. Really — word was Claude was a stand-up guy. Let's see — if I was y'all, I'd head over to Meadowlands. Good chance there's still folk around knew the family. In the meantime, I'll set someone here to pulling up the old papers covering the case."

"Where do we find Meadowlands?" Pinky asks.

"Where are you?"

"Morgan City Holiday Inn."

"You get on across the bridge to Berwick, go along about . . . *hmmm* . . . maybe half a mile. Meadowlands, it's off . . . *hmmm* . . . Tupelo, maybe. Or Live Oak. One of the tree streets. You won't have any trouble finding it."

We hear a bunch of shouting in the background. Maldonado covers the receiver, but we hear him talking. Then he's back. "Okay."

"Does Boudreaux still have family there?" I ask. My voice sounds shaky. The emotion in it comes across so clearly that

Pinky raises his sunglasses and shoots me a look from across the room.

"I don't think so," Maldonado says. "No family left I know of. Daddy died from the poisoning, mom died a few years beforehand. And — hang on."

He's interrupted again.

"Sounds like you gotta go," Pinky says.

"I can meet you later tonight if you like — after we get this baby to bed."

"Buy you dinner," Pinky suggests.

"Deal," Maldonado says.

We cross the expanse of the Atchafalya River (*"'Chafalaya,"* Pinky tells me) on the Huey P. Long Bridge, and find Meadowlands within ten minutes. Despite the bucolic name, there's nothing resembling a meadow in sight. The complex consists of two dozen trailers, most of which have obviously been there for decades. Some are fenced in by stretches of chain link; most are patched together with slabs of plywood. A few stand out from the rest, with shutters and fresh siding, picket fencing, and plantings of flowers.

A sign shows a logo of children hand in hand and posts a speed limit of five miles per hour. The sign is bullet-pocked, with the concentration of hits within the silhouetted children. Brown plastic Dumpsters, most too full to allow their tops to close, sit out in front of many of the trailers. Ragged front yards hold plastic chairs, more seating in the form of inverted white buckets, kids' bicycles, toys of all sorts, plastic wading pools, boat trailers, discarded tires. Every trailer seems to have a vehicle or two parked in front — most of them pickups.

Pinky rolls down the road and pulls up in front of number 14, a siding-covered trailer with an awkward bay window clapped onto the front. The BMW gleams on the rutted dirt like an alien spaceship.

chapter 34

I rap on the door. A gray-haired woman with her hair in pink foam curlers (I've never seen this before, except on old TV shows) calls over from the porch of the trailer next door. "They ain't home. Help you with somethin'?"

"We're looking —," I start, but Pinky takes over.

"How're you doing today, ma'am?" he says.

"You selling something, sugar? 'Cause I don't have a dime; I might as well tell you that right off. I got time, though, so y'all can practice on me if you want."

"We're not selling anything," Pinky says. "We're —"

"Pardon me but are you a *albino?*"

I start to say something, offended on Pinky's behalf, but Pinky just laughs.

"Yes, I am," he says in a booming voice. "I'm a genetic oddity standing right here in your front yard, ma'am. I know it can throw people off their normal manners at first, just like someone with an unfortunate deformity. In a funny kind of way, I think it's a form of racism. Now, who would believe that here in Louisiana there'd be such a thing as being too white?" He smiles.

"Let me ask you something," the woman says. "You get sunburnt easy?"

"It's a big problem," Pinky admits.

"I'm really fair myself, plus I have the rosacea and I burn right up. Lord, I put sunscreen on with a spoon. Why don't you and your friend come on up here out of the sun, and tell me what brings you to Meadowlands."

Up here is a rickety deck made out of plywood and elevated by cinder block columns. Metal folding chairs and an ancient wicker coffee table comprise the deck furniture. On the table is an ashtray and a plastic caddy of manicure supplies. The woman has given herself a pedicure, her feet in some kind of device, her gleaming red toes separated from each other by nubs of foam.

"I'm Pinky Streiber," Pinky says. "And this is Alex Callahan." Pinky extends his hand.

"Sorry, honey," the woman says, holding her hands out, fingers splayed so we can see the fresh polish on them. "I'm not near dry yet. I'm Dora Garrity," she adds, then turns toward me. "I seen you on TV," she says, "right?" And then, the light really dawns. "Ohmygod, you the daddy of them two little tykes. Oh. My. Sweet. Jesus."

"We think Byron Boudreaux might be the one took those boys," Pinky says.

Dora's hand flies up and covers her mouth, the perfect red nails like blood against snow. "Oh, Lord." I'm familiar with the emotion that pinches her lips and seems to make her face shrink. It's fear. "That boy," she says, after lighting a cigarette, and exhaling a long stream of smoke. "That boy was born bad. Bad to the bone."

"Do you know where he is? Where any of his family is?"

She shakes her head. "Sorry, sugar. I can't help you there. I haven't seen that boy since they took him away. His folks're dead, of course. I didn't even know he was out of the asylum. When did that happen?"

"Ninety-six."

"Well, I'm right glad he didn't come home."

"What about the people who live there now? Are they related to Boudreaux?"

"No. Claude and Marie, they didn't own the home. It's a rental, you understand. So there's been a whole string of folk in there."

"I just had a thought," Pinky says to me. "There ought to be records. Claude must have left some kind of estate. We can check on that. Remind me."

"Way I heard it, everything went to Byron," Dora says. "Which royally pissed off Claude's brother, Lonnie. Not that there was much of anything left by the time Claude got buried and all. Course, Lonnie was in a real temper over Byron getting *anything*, but there wasn't nothin' for it. The way it came out, with the insanity plea and all, legally Byron didn't actually commit no crime."

"Lonnie live nearby?"

"Lonnie passed," Dora says.

"What about friends?" I ask. "Did Byron have friends here?"

"That boy had no friends. No friends at all. Time he killed Claude, he was spending most of his time over in niggertown, hangin' with some witch doctor."

"*Witch* doctor?"

"What I heard." She seems to bristle at my skepticism. "They got 'em, you know. Three hundred years here and they still ain't left the jungle."

I know I should keep my mouth shut, but it's hard. "You know, that's —"

Pinky interrupts: "You know this witch

doctor? Know his name?"

Dora looks offended. "Nossir, I do not. How would I know something like that?"

"But you did know Byron?" I manage.

"Honey, he lived right next door. Your home is a trailer, you spend a lot of time outdoors. I been living here for more than thirty years. And believe it or not, that's not even the record." A smoker's laugh, half cough. "Old Ralph Guidry been here even longer."

"Can you tell us about Byron?"

"Like what kind of stuff you want to know?"

"Everything," Pinky says. "Anything. We got no idea what might help us find him."

"Well . . ." She lights another cigarette, a Misty menthol. "Lemme see now. Byron was one of two children. At least, he was for a while. When Byron was ten and his brother, Joe, was about four, Byron saw — some say he *watched* — the younger boy drown in the municipal pool. It's gone now, but it wasn't but a mile from here. Real popular with the kids."

Pinky looks at me. "This is what Vicky was talking about. His brother drowned in front of him? That's terrible. Did he try to save him?"

"Well, that's the thing — why I'm telling

you this story. Everyone agreed it was a tragedy, but some people wondered if it wasn't something even worse. On account of it happened at night, when Byron and his kid brother snuck out of the house. Doesn't seem like that'd be little Joe's idea, does it? Anyway, they were marauding around the neighborhood. Byron had a bright idea and helped his little brother climb over the Cyclone fence around the pool, which was closed, of course. According to what Byron said, the two of them were horsing around when little Joe slipped and fell into the deep end. Since neither of the boys knew how to swim, that was it. Byron couldn't save his brother."

"They didn't know how to swim?" Pinky says. "Then why'd they sneak into the pool?"

"Well, you know, that was a funny thing. Marie — that's Byron's mama — used to take those boys to the pool. I'd see 'em settin' out with their towels and their float rings and all. But when Byron said he couldn't swim, Marie — she didn't say boo." Dora shrugs.

"So people thought — they actually thought Byron drowned his brother?"

"They were suspicious. See, there was

this aluminum pole with a net attached? — that they used to remove debris from the pool?"

I nod my encouragement.

"Well, when the police arrived, it was lying on the apron. Dry as a bone. Hadn't been touched. Byron was bone dry, too, and there was no water around the side of the pool. Now, Marie had read those boys a story and put them to bed just about an hour or so before Byron runs screaming down the street and nine-one-one is called. Yet when the Fire and Rescue guys got to the pool, everything was bone dry."

"Hunh." I don't see the point.

"Well, it stuck in this one paramedic's mind, see, bothered him, just didn't set right. Down here it takes a long time for water to evaporate. Mildew and mold's a big problem. Question was, it didn't look like Byron so much as went to the edge of the pool and stuck his hands in. Didn't look like he tried to reach out whatsoever. Why didn't he use the pole? It was right there. So it just didn't set right."

"I don't know," I say. "It's a big jump from that to think the kid murdered his brother. Maybe he just froze. It happens."

"That's what I thought, too," Dora says. "After all, the kid was only ten. And that's what Byron told the police: He didn't *see* any pole. He didn't *think* of reaching in. Then he cried and cried until they left him alone."

"You'd think at ten years old, you'd get the benefit of the doubt."

"Oh, even by then, that kid kinda scared people. And it wasn't just that. There was a witness, a waitress coming home from the Shrimp Shack. She walked past the pool that evening. She said she saw Byron sitting at the end of the diving board — you know, Indian style — looking down into the water. There wasn't anyone else around that she could see — and there certainly wasn't any 'horseplay.' The scene was as quiet as a photograph. So where was Little Joe?"

"Hmmm."

" 'In the bathroom,' is what Byron said. But that was a lie, 'cause the doors were locked. What we all thought was — that little boy's down in the water and Byron's just up there on the diving board looking down on him. Like to 'bout creep you out, you know? After that, Marie wouldn't let anybody near him. Said how they're cruel, Byron felt bad enough, he's cryin' his eyes out. It never did amount to nothing; nobody out and out accused him of anything.

I know the death was ruled an accident."

Dora delicately touches a finger to one of her gleaming nails. "Know what?" she says, rising to her feet with a soft grunt. "I got plenty more to tell you about Byron, but I b'lieve I'm dry." She rotates her hands in the air. "Why don't we go down the way 'n' see Ralph? Together we'll remember more. He knew the family real well. Worked with Claude — that's Byron's daddy. They were out on the rigs together. And they were fishing buddies, too."

She asks us to wait and comes back out, five minutes later, hair still in curlers but the pedicure sandals replaced by a gleaming pair of New Balance running shoes.

"Should we walk?" Pinky asks, looking at the shoes.

"Hell, no," Dora says. "I want a ride in that car."

Ralph insists on making iced tea. He distributes the glasses with elaborate care, then excuses himself to "fetch something." We wait in a miniature living room crammed with furniture, and Ralph comes back with a couple of dusty photo albums. "I had the camera bug in those days," he says, leafing through one of the albums until he finds the page he's looking for.

"Here," he says, and we lean in, looking at a three-by-five snapshot. "That's Claude," Ralph says, pointing to a handsome man with long sideburns, seated on a park bench. "And that's Marie." He indicates the demure-looking woman next to Claude. Her head is turned, and with a fond smile, she gazes at the handsome, well-scrubbed little boy next to her. The part in the boy's hair is as straight as a ruler.

"And that there is Byron," Dora says. "This was before little Joe came along. Oh, how she doted on that boy, Marie did. Isn't that right, Ralph?"

"Oh, my, yes. He couldn't do no wrong far as his mama was concerned."

"Wasn't nothin' that boy wants, she doesn't get for him," Dora says. "Every toy and game, every bicycle. Nintendo machine. Guitar. Trampoline. Go-Kart. Two-hundred-dollar sunglasses, if you can believe it. Clothes . . . nothing's too good."

"Claude, now," Ralph adds, "he loved that boy, too, but tried to give his son some discipline, you know, what kids need. Marie — she wouldn't let Claude touch the boy. Nor even speak harsh to him. And look what happened."

"I don't hold with blaming the parents," Dora tells us. "Marie was sweet as pie. And

Claude was a good man, too. I just think that boy was born twisted."

"Maybe so," Ralph allows. He finds another snapshot, taken a couple of years later. Byron is seven or so. Dressed in a suit, top hat, and what looks like a cape, he's got a curly mustache penciled onto his upper lip. Behind him, affixed to the double-wide is a handmade banner: BYRON THE GREAT.

I remember what Karl Kavanaugh said about magicians starting as kids. The photograph gives me chills.

"Oh, the magic shows!" Dora says. "I plain forgot about that. Byron would sell tickets for a quarter, and everybody was more'n glad to pay because Marie would fix lemonade and sandwiches and potato salad, so in the end it was quite a bargain."

"She made a mighty fine potato salad," Ralph says. "Although not," he adds diplomatically, "not as good as Dora's."

"Remember?" Dora asks. "We'd watch the show on folding chairs Byron set up outside the trailer."

"He got pretty good at it, too," Ralph says, "for such a little kid. I never did figure out how he did some of the shit he did, pardon my French. He had this one trick — he'd put a few feathers and scraps of grass in a pan, say some abracadabra stuff, and next time he opens the pan a bird flies out. I looked at the pan, too. No place to put a live bird in there."

A dove pan, I think, remembering Kavanaugh's description.

"Tell me about the father," Pinky says.

"Worked offshore, same as me. Hardworking guy, Claude. Marie, she worked, too, took in ironing."

But mostly, from what the two neighbors say, Claude was an absentee father. Working for Anadarko meant six-week stints on oil rigs in the Gulf, followed by three weeks at home. "When he was home, he wasn't really home that much. He was out fishing or shrimping." Ralph laughs. "Most of the time with me."

"Did Byron go along?"

"Nah. He got bored. He'd rather stay home with his mama."

"Did they go to church? I heard something about Byron being a boy preacher."

"My goodness, yes," Dora says. "They's churchgoers all along, mind you, but after little Joe died, Byron *really* got religion."

"A transformational experience," Ralph says.

"A what?" Dora asks. "Where'd you get that?"

Ralph blushes. "Bible study. That's what they call it — like Paul on the road to Damascus. When Joey drowned, the idea is, that must have set Byron to thinking about his mortal soul."

"I don't know about any transformation," Dora says, "but that boy did catch the preaching bug. Byron — he'd be preaching to anyone who'd listen, standing on the bridge, even thumping a Bible down by the wharves when the shrimp boats come in. Marie was havin' fits about it, the kind of men you got down there. Drunk and all, you know. But Byron — you couldn't stop him."

"He was even getting a reputation as a healer, right, Ralph?"

"Absolutely. Folks said he had a calling." Ralph pauses, then resumes. "It was bullshit, of course. But he had a following, no question about that. He was quite the little showman."

"What do you mean?" I ask. "What kind of 'showman'?"

"Oh, for instance, he give a sermon one time 'bout shirking responsibility. He's talking 'bout Pontius Pilate, and he's got this big clear bowl of water on the altar, and he's steamin' on about how Pilate washes his hands of the matter . . . 'Jesus

Christ is just not any of his business.' And little Byron, he lathers up with soap as he's preachin' and sticks his hands in that water and the water turns bloodred, and a big *oooooooh* goes up, you know — I mean damn! It's right dramatic. Byron, he raises his hands and they're dripping 'blood' and he's thundering on about how Pilate cannot wash away the blood on his hands."

"A trick."

"Some kind of gizmo soap is what Claude told me, but it gets your attention, know what I'm saying? He had all kinds of stuff like that. Snap his fingers, big puff of smoke comes up. And then that thing with the puppy happened, and —" He turns to Dora. "Didn't they bounce him out of the church?"

"What 'thing with the puppy'?" Pinky asks.

"This was later," Dora says, "when he was a teenager."

But I'm not listening. I'm thinking of the boy preacher with his hands dripping "blood." The boy preacher snapping his fingers to puffs of smoke. The boy preacher doing *magic tricks.*

The seven-year-old Byron the Great, honing his skills even then. Images of the

Gabler twins come into my mind. In their costumes. The police photo of Clara Gabler's lower half. I think about the Ramirez boys. One of them *dismembered.* The Sandling kids climbing ropes and doing "exercises." Why? To what purpose?

A real showman.

When I think about what this psycho has in mind for my sons . . .

"You all right?" Pinky asks.

"More iced tea?" Ralph suggests.

I shake my head. "I'm all right."

"What's this about a puppy?" Pinky asks.

Dora frowns. "You mind if I smoke, Ralph?"

"It's bad for you. But go on."

"That puppy," Dora says. "Oh, my Lord. That's when we knew the boy was really crazy."

"Put an end to his preachin' days, too," Ralph adds.

"What did he do?" Pinky asks. "Torture the poor critter?"

"Worse than that," Ralph says.

"What could be worse than that?"

Ralph lets out a sigh, rocks back in his chair. "It's Christmastime. And maybe this is hindsight, but what folks say now is that Byron was getting a little scary. No one can put their finger on it, but he put folk on edge. You just plain didn't want to be around the boy. He's still preaching a lot, but when he's not preaching, he disappears entirely for hours and hours. He's what?" He turns to Dora. "Fourteen?"

Dora nods.

"Marie — she's worried," Ralph continues, "says he's got some kind of secret place, she don't know where he goes or what he gets up to."

"And the boy next door," Dora says with a shudder, "gets a puppy for Christmas."

"Now, remember how Dora said Byron got *everything* he ever wanted?"

Pinky and I nod.

"But there's one exception," Ralph tells us. "Marie — she's got the asthma, bad, and she can't have no animals. Set her wheezin', send her to the hospital, you know? So Byron couldn't have no puppy or kitten, not even a hamster."

"What happened is this," Dora says. "Little Emory Boberg, the kid next door on the other side? He gets a puppy for Christmas, a little golden lab, cutest little thing. And he's out walking this little pup past Byron's trailer, and Byron asks can he play with it.

"Emory doesn't want to, but he's scared of Byron — so he hands him the leash.

Byron gave him some money, sent Emory down to the 7-Eleven to get Slurpees for the both of them. As soon as Emory's out of sight, Byron digs a hole in the yard and *buries* the puppy up to its neck. Now, if I'd been here, maybe I coulda stopped it, but I was off to Lafayette at my sister's."

"Byron tried to explain this later," Ralph says. "Some lame-ass story about how the pup keeps slippin' his collar and puttin' him in the ground is Byron's way of keeping him from runnin' off. While Byron does his chores. Like he couldn't wait ten minutes for Emory to come back. Like anyone believes Marie really told him to mow the lawn — it's *December*. Anyways, he gets the power mower from the shed and begins to cut the lawn."

"Oh," Dora says, putting her head in her hands as if she can't even stand the memory. "Lord."

"Little Emory comes back just in time to see Byron cut right over the puppy's head. I'm down here when Emory lets out this horrible scream. And me and whoever else is around, we come running. It's just a geyser of blood. You can't imagine."

"He mowed the dog's *head* off?"

"So, Emory's mother, she calls the police. And they come. And no one's buying it when Byron insists it was just an accident."

"He was charged with malicious mischief," Dora adds.

"And what happened to him?"

"Nothing. He got off with counseling. The Bobergs moved away as soon as they could."

"Word got out," Ralph says. "That Boudreaux boy ain't right. Got a screw loose, maybe more. Parents told their kids to stay away from him. The church wouldn't let him preach no more."

"A little while after that, Byron dropped out of school," Dora says. "And that's when he started hanging around down in Morgan City." She stubs out her cigarette. "Hooked up with that nigger witch doctor."

I'm so put off by the racism I want to leave. I stand up, but Pinky ignores me. "You got a name for this guy?"

"I already told you," Dora replies. "How would I know something like that?"

"I think I know who it is," Ralph says, "but I don't know his name. You go down around that area in Morgan City and you ask, and somebody will tell you where to find him. Hell, folk come all the way from N'Awlins to see him, get a number or who's gonna win the Final Four. He's world-famous, that fella."

"Just . . . uh . . . ask for 'the witch doctor'?" Pinky says. "That gonna do it?"

"Well," Ralph says. "They don't exactly call themselves witch doctors. They got some voodoo name for it what I don't remember. *Higgan? Hungin?*"

"Houngan," Pinky says.

"That's the one. And see, there's more than one o' these guys over there in the city. The guy Byron took up with after the puppy thing? Ask for the one with no upper lip."

"Get outta here," Pinky says.

"Swear to God," Ralph tells him. "I seen him. Maybe it's just some kind of voodoo jive — I don't know the actual cause of the injury." His face contorts into a look that's half smile, half grimace. "What *he* says is — a zombie got pissed at him and bit it off."

"Bit off his lip?" Dora gasps. She crosses herself in a surreptitious way, the motion so minimal as to be almost undetectable.

"Like this," Ralph says, and makes a lunging, biting motion toward Dora, "like a snapping turtle."

Dora lets out a yelp.

"One bite," Ralph says. "That's all it takes."

chapter 35

Pinky and I catch lunch at Katy's, a ramshackle place on the Bayou Boeuf that offers a bait shack and boat launch along with sandwiches and drinks.

"Now, that's a *good* po'boy," Pinky says, taking a big swig of Coke to wash down the last bite. "Good as the food is in N'Awlins, it's gettin' harder and harder to find a top-drawer po'boy. My personal theory is that you got to get out into the countryside, because the places in town go an' change the grease too often. What you think, Arthur?"

Arthur is the man behind the counter, apparently an old friend of Pinky's. ("No one ever forgets me," Pinky explained. "That's for damn sure.") Arthur's dark face opens in a sweet gap-toothed smile. He shakes his head. "This a genuine compliment or you sayin' my grease got whiskers?"

"No, I mean it," Pinky insists. "It's like aged beef. Young oil's got no bouquet. It's just neutral. Doesn't add anything."

"*Ça s'adonne. Comme çi ça se fait ici?* Not

just for Arthur's po'boys, no."

"My *ami* here," Pinky says, indicating me, with a slow doleful shake of head, "*tout mauvais*. Man stole his chirren."

"*No!*" He looks at me with a shocked expression, then looks back to Pinky. "*Vraiment?*"

The two go back and forth in a patois I can't understand, and then Pinky says, "Little boys, friend. Not but six years old. My friend breaking his head and heart tryin' to find them. Afraid they goin' come to harm, you know. Looking for the man who took them, the path brings him this way."

"To Katy's?" His eyes check over to me.

"No, not to Katy's, not direct. The path takes him to Berwick, where the man we lookin' for lived. Grew up in that place."

"You hunt this man?"

"That's right. *Boute à boute*."

"He a black man?"

"No, he's a white man" — a laugh — "although not as white as me. Crazy man, name of Byron Boudreaux. You know him?"

Arthur shakes his head. "Not me, no."

"Here's the thing. We hear this Byron took up with a *houngan* somewhere round Morgan City. This a while back, few years back."

Arthur's eyes widen. "You shittin' me?"

"That's what we hear. We're looking to find this *houngan,* see if he can tell us anything about where Byron might be now — because we think if we find Byron, we find those little boys. All we know about the *houngan:* he missin' his upper lip."

"Ain?" Arthur holds his upper lip between his thumb and two fingers. "No top lip?"

Pinky nods. "That's what I'm told."

"I *do* hear of this man," Arthur says. "They say zombie kiss him, take his lip. Man's famous."

"What's his name?" I ask.

"Diment. He the *houngan* without the lip. Doctor Aristide Diment. Big *bizango.*"

"What's a *bizango?*" I ask.

"A *houngan* — he's a voodoo priest, yes? And the *bizango,* that's kind of his congregation only they be real close, like a family," Arthur explains.

"More like a secret society," Pinky says.

"You got the sickness or problem in your life," Arthur says, "or you need advice, you go to the *houngan.* The *houngan* know how to please the *loa,* know how to make the mojo — keep your marriage strong, or find you a sweetheart, or get your business goin' on its way. Some of them know the dark ways, too. Some of them serve with both the hands." Arthur casts his eyes down, and I see him make a tiny sign of the cross. "Doctor Diment — he one of these."

" 'Serve with both hands'?"

Arthur continues to look down. He shakes his head.

"That means the priest is a sorcerer," Pinky says. "Got supernatural powers. Worship with one hand, do magic with the other."

I nod. "So Diment is a magician. Now I understand Boudreaux's interest."

"Yes, but it's not that simple," Pinky says. "Voodoo is a very, very complex thing. You could spend a long time with it and never begin to understand. I only know the little bit I do because I had a case once. Supposed to be this woman died of a curse, but her relatives didn't go for it. Came to me. Turned out she'd been murdered."

"She poison?" Arthur asks.

Pinky nods. To me, he explains: "There are herbs that heal and potions that sicken. The *houngans* and *manbos* — that's a female priest — study the remedies and poisons in the natural world. It's part of their training." He turns to Arthur. "Is that right?"

"That about right," Arthur says, once again displaying his warm smile. "You might be sayin' it's the doctor part of the witch doctor."

"Supposed to be," Pinky says, "they only cure you of what's got a supernatural origin." He nods toward Arthur. "This Byron Boudreaux, Arthur — he poisoned his own daddy, got sent away for that."

Arthur winces.

"Poison goes way back with voodoo," Pinky says, tapping his glass against the tabletop. "Down in the Indies on the plantations, some of the slaves used slow-acting poisons against their masters. That's what first got them worried down there about the religion of the slaves. Plus there were rumors of supernatural powers — to Christians, that was obviously the devil at work. Witchcraft. Between the poison and the magical powers — pretty soon the plantation owners running scared. You never knew where something bad might come from, who might put a curse on you or poison your food. That's when the authorities really started trying to repress the religion."

"Repress it?"

"Oh, they tried and they tried and they tried. Between the government and the church, they thought they could squeeze voodoo down. But what happened was repression just drove voodoo to hide itself. For the most part, it hid right in plain sight. See, the only way slaves could carry on their worship was to pretend they was Christian — which the masters encouraged. Eventually the voodoo got itself all mixed up with Christian practices. All the voodoo *loa,* the beings who rule the spirit world, have Christian figures or saints as counterparts. The *loa* Legba, for instance — he's St. Peter."

"I heard that once before." I remember Scott telling me about the figure on the dime: Mercury, St. Peter, and also Legba.

"You see the point, right? Slaves could pretend they're devout, worshiping St. Peter, and all the time it's Legba. And then after a while — it's *both.*" He turns to Arthur. "What's another one?"

"The Virgin Mary, she's Ezili. St. John the Baptist is Chango. St. Patrick, he's Dambala Wedo. It go like that right down the line."

I turn to Arthur. "What about Diment," I ask, "you know him?"

"Jamais," Arthur says. "Know of him, yes. He live near the cemetery in Morgan City. You go back on 182, get into Morgan

City. I think it's Myrtle street take you down toward the water. You cross over the railroad tracks, keep goin' little way. They's a place down there, Lasseigne's, little corner store. You ask the man in there, Felix. Tell him I sent you. He know where to find Maître Diment."

"Thanks, Arthur."

"Yes," I add, shaking the man's hand. "Thank you very much."

"Pas de quoi. Bonne chance." He nods. "I hope you find your chirren."

Felix is a small coffee-colored man. He and Pinky talk in an impenetrable Creole patois. Felix draws a crude map. And then we're back in the Bimmer, driving past a bank thermometer that reads one hundred one. For a second, I wonder if that's the temperature *and* the humidity.

"That thing about the lip," Pinky says. "If you don't happen to believe in zombies, they's another explanation. Seen it before. That kind of mutilation can happen when a fellow gets caught fooling around with somebody's daughter or wife. Father, husband — he mess up the man's face, make him ugly so women stay away."

"Well, at least that's straightforward."

At the Morgan City High School, someone is mowing the grass in the football stadium. A banner affixed to the fence advertises: OPENING GAME AUG 28. The man on the mower is bare-chested and gleaming with sweat. A bandana tied into a do-rag covers his head, and a little umbrella attached to the mower shades him as he rolls along. It's hard to believe anybody would want to play football in this heat, but the opening game is less than a month away. Just past the school, a bunch of kids in practice jerseys stand outside a snow-cone stand that advertises SNEAUX BALLS.

"Felix said we should take a present to Diment," Pinky says, turning a corner and pulling up in front of a liquor store. "Says the doctor has a fondness for rum."

And then we're on our way again until Pinky stops at a crossroads and consults the map. There's a little wooden shack on the right, nearly swallowed up by the surrounding vegetation. The place looks as if it's about to fall down — but there's a bright red pickup out front and a new satellite dish protruding from the roof.

"Let's see," Pinky says. "I think here's where we go to the right."

A few more turns and we're on a dirt road. After a mile or so, we pull up in front of a nondescript rectangular concrete building. The front yard is dirt, with a few patches of weeds and tire ruts full of standing water. One small window seems to have been added post-construction, crudely jammed into its space. The building would look like a storage shed, except for the "door," which consists of strings of plastic beads. I've seen doors like this before in Africa. The beads let the air in but keep the flies out. More or less.

"This is it," Pinky says, executing a little drumroll on the dash. "Chez Diment."

"Right."

We step out into the sledgehammer heat. Pinky hits a button on his key and the car lights flash.

There's no place to knock on a beaded door, so Pinky pushes the beads aside and sticks his head in. "Hello?"

"Come in then," a voice calls from some distance.

It's dark inside and even hotter than it was outside. Stifling. Airless. Behind the smell of dust and eucalyptus oil is the olfactory funk of human bodies, a whiff of excrement, urine, and sweat. In the moments it takes my eyes to adjust, I become aware of sounds in the room, labored breathing, snuffling, and coughing. Someone moans. Then the dozen or so humps on the floor resolve themselves into people — mostly children from the size of them.

"I heard about this," Pinky says. "It's a clinic. A voodoo hospital, like."

My immediate reaction — and I'm ashamed of it — is to breathe shallowly.

"This way," a robust voice calls from the back of the room. I can just make out an open door, and through it, the twinkle of colored lights, the kind you string on a Christmas tree. I follow Pinky through the corridor between the patients, whose hospital beds consist of straw mats on the floor.

"This way, this way," the voice says.

And then we pass through the open door into a separate room. It's about half the size of my room at the Omni and it's illuminated only by the string of lights and three or four votive candles. Facing me is a kind of altar, a stepped affair crowded with objects. My eyes skim over them: a baby's rattle, a black comb, statues draped in beads, bottles holding liquids, ropes tied in intricate knots, crosses, many bound up with layers of string, a painted skull, various bundles of cloth tied with string, flowers, tickets (also tied up with string), brightly colored jugs draped with beads, icons of the Virgin and Child with auras of gold, plastic icicles, Matchbox cars, a small soccer ball, plastic dolls, a photograph of JFK, a wooden carving of a madman in a tuxedo puffing on a cigar.

There are five folding chairs in the room and in one of them is Doctor Diment, himself. His teeth and eyes seem to glow in the dark. The missing lip is unnerving because all his upper teeth are visible, like the teeth of a skull. "Welcome," he says, in his rich voice. "The white man, and the not-so-white man." He chuckles.

"Pinky Streiber," Pinky says. "And this is Alex Callahan."

We shake. "Mr. Streiber," Diment says, "you so white, you almost a light source, you." A chuckle. "Sit down and tell me what Doctor Diment can do for you."

I hand him the bottle of Appleton rum, and he regards it and gives a little formal nod of his head. "Thank you. Appreciate it." Another warm chuckle. "The good stuff. You spoil me for my clairin."

"That's rum, too," Pinky explains to me. "Kind of white lightning."

"You know the local way," Diment says. "You translate for your friend. That's good, you help your friend. But which one of you need the doctor's help, you?"

I wipe my forehead. Sweat begins to trickle down my back. I nod. "I'm interested in Byron Boudreaux. They say he was a friend of yours. I'm trying to find him."

"By-ron," Diment says with a sigh. "Byron, he's not having any friends."

"We heard you knew him," Pinky says.

"Let's have a drink," Diment decides. He twists off the cap of the rum bottle and takes a long swig, then passes it to me. Even in the half light, I can see the spittle on his chin. The spittle, the missing lip, the coughs and moans from the back room — I don't really want to drink from the bottle. But somehow, I know I have to. I take a long slug. The rum burns, in a pleasant way, all the way down. Pinky declines and hands the bottle back to Diment.

I can see the doctor better now that my eyes have adjusted. What I see is a very thin man (AIDS?) wearing a dirty white tank undershirt and a pair of ripped khaki shorts. He wears an old pair of plastic flip-flops on his feet.

"What's your interest in Byron?" he asks. And then he holds up his hand, palm out. "No, don't tell me now. Let's look at the cards."

He pulls out a deck of cards and deals

onto a little table in front of him. There is some sequence involved, every fifth or sixth card being separated from the deck. Then he picks up the hand he's dealt himself. When he fans the cards out, they're so old and flexible that they fall over the back of his knuckles. I wonder if I'm hallucinating. The cards remind me of Salvador Dalí's limp and drooping clocks. Diment supports the cards with his left hand, forcing them upright, and regards them with a squint. "Okay," he says, pushing them back into a stack and placing them facedown on the table, "now you tell me your interest in Byron."

"I think he's kidnapped my sons, my two boys."

"Yes?"

"I think he plans to kill them."

"Hmmmmmmm." He fingers his mutilated lip.

"I need your help. . . ."

"I tell you this much," Diment says. "Byron, he comes to me after he killed that little dog. You hear about that?"

"Yeah."

"Well, wouldn't no one talk to him after that. The parents, they tell their children stay away. Byron's church — they turn their back on the boy. He finds me one night in the cemetery, making a *veve*. He's interested; I tell him a few things. Next day, he come after school to help me out here. He do the errands for me, clean the clinic, even wipe the shit off the poor ones in there." He nods toward the room. "In return he wants to learn what I know. The ways of the world."

Diment takes another hit of rum and holds the bottle out toward me. I have another slug.

"That business with the dog," Diment says, shaking his head. "We talk about that one, Byron and me. I tell him killing the dog is not so bad — not by itself. A dog is just a chicken with a tail."

"What do you mean?"

Diment ignores my reaction. "What was *bad* was killing the animal just to watch it bleed. I tell him, 'Byron, no one got anything out of that, least of all you.' So the dog's death was a waste. A waste of juju."

"Then what?"

"Then nothing," Diment announces.

"I don't get it."

He gestures toward the altar. "The answer you seek is right here. It's right in front of you."

I stare at the altar, but all I see is a panorama of weird tchotchkes.

"But I can't tell you any more," Diment says.

"But you haven't told me *anything.* Do you know where Byron is? How can I reach him?"

Diment looks sorry about it, but he shakes his head. "Something you don't understand, my friend. Byron is part of the *bizango.* We're a closed circle. I tell you more about him, I break the faith."

Pinky starts to list reasons why Diment should help us, including money. I plead with the doctor. But Diment is resolute. He'll say no more.

"My lip is sealed," he jokes.

"There's gotta be a way around this," Pinky suggests. "There's always a way."

"One way, maybe," Diment tells us. "If the man here wants to learn more, he'll have to become a part of the *bizango.* Then, we have no secrets from each other."

"Fine," I say. "Where do I sign up?"

Diment laughs. "It's not that easy. There's a ceremony. Initiation."

"Whatever it takes."

"Some people uncomfortable with it," Diment tells me. "Because you have to have faith — in me, the *bizango.* Then you'll be born again in *vaudoo.* And a part of us."

"I have to 'have faith'?"

"You don't have to believe any particular thing," Diment says. "It's like getting on the airplane. You put yourself in the hands of the pilot and those who built the plane. You put yourself in their trust. You fasten your seat belt. You roll down the runway. You don't understand what keeps the airplane up in the sky, you don't know the people driving the machine, but still you get on, buckle up, and trust that you goin' to end up where you want to go. It's like that. You put your faith in the *bizango*. You go through the initiation. You trust us." He stretches his hands out to his sides in a gesture of fairness and rationality.

"I don't know," Pinky says. "I've heard these things can be dangerous."

"Dangerous?" Diment says. "Sure. Crossing the street is dangerous. With the *loa*, we call them up, we know them, but we can't control them, no."

"Is this the only way you'll tell me more about Byron?"

"That is true," Diment says, nodding.

"Then let's go. Count me in."

"You're sure?" Diment asks me.

"Absolutely."

"Then come back at midnight."

"Tonight?"

Diment nods, and then he gets up and heads for the door. As we weave a path through the poor souls hunkered down in the heat and darkness, Diment asks a question that seems to come right out of left field. "What size you wear?"

"What *size?*"

"Yes!" He seems annoyed. "What size do you wear?"

"Forty-two regular," I tell him.

"Ahhhh," Diment says. "That's perfect." He pulls the beads aside. Pinky and I step through into the front yard, and the beads fall closed behind us with a kind of liquid rustle.

It's like leaving a matinee. I'm blinded. An image from Diment's altar seems to float before me in the sun haze: a painted icon showing two boys, each with a golden orb around his head, each holding a feather quill. *Twins.* I wonder what that means. I'll have to ask Diment. Pinky's car emits a little beep, and I hear the mechanical thunk as its door locks pop open.

"Whoa," Pinky says, once we're inside. "I'm not sure I'd be keeping any future appointments with Doctor D. there."

"I don't know. What was that question about my *size?*"

"I doubt he's gonna kill you for your

Gap khakis, but who knows?" Pinky says, turning the key and rolling down the windows. We lurch forward. "The guy looks like a death's head! Don't that *worry* you, pardner? And why's he want to know what size you wear? And that stuff about 'a puppy is just a chicken with a tail'? What's he mean by that, huh? I'm thinking he means that anything alive is nothin' but a life force, something that could be sacrificed. What if he's feelin' that way about you?"

"Yeah," I say. But the truth is, it's hard for me to work up any fear about Doctor Diment. Or worry about anything that might happen to me. I'm all played out on the fear front.

"You're not really going there?"

I shrug. "I'm thinking about it."

All the way back to the Holiday Inn, Pinky tries to talk me out of it. "It's crazy! You don't know this guy — or what crazy thing he might do. That *lip*, man. I can't believe you, drinkin' that rum! You see how skinny he was? Who knows what he's got? His eyeballs looked yellow to me. You're talking AIDS, hep C, who knows? And voodoo — it's nothin' you want to mess with. Not at all. It's all blood and drugs and bullshit. . . . I say let's see what

Maldonado says. Look, you can always go back to this guy if you have to."

"Yeah, we'll see," I tell Pinky.

Pinky has a service called OnStar, which he calls his "traveling concierge." He punches it on, secures Maldonado's number, and then instructs the machine to call the reporter.

"Hey!" Maldonado's voice booms from the dashboard. "Good news, Pink. I called up the doctor who admitted Claude when the ambulance brought him in. Sam Harami. If not for Sam, Byron would have got away with murder. The death probably would have gone down as 'natural causes.' "

"You saying what, Max?"

"I'm saying this is the guy really figured out old Claude had been poisoned. He's a friend of mine and he's ready to join us for dinner if you're buying."

"My pleasure," Pinky tells him.

While they go back and forth, figuring out where to meet for dinner, I'm thinking about how I'm going to get out to Chez Diment later tonight. Even though Pinky thinks it's a bad idea to go, maybe he'll lend me his car or give me a ride. If not, I guess I can take a taxi.

But I'm definitely going. I think of the

dimes, the bowls of water, mementos left to me by Boudreaux. Somehow I know that if I'm going to find him, the man with the death's head face will be the one to point the way.

chapter 36

We're supposed to meet Max Maldonado at Prideaux's Eat Place. It's an upscale restaurant in the countryside outside New Iberia, a pretty town a few miles from Morgan City. We're escorted to a table by the window, where a small gray-haired man bounces out of his seat at our approach. This is Maldonado, "seventy-five years young," as he later puts it. The compression of age, familiar to me from the ongoing shrinkage of my father, seems only to have concentrated this man's energy.

"Pinky!" he says, with an enthusiastic pump of the hand. "It's been way too long, baby."

Pinky introduces us.

"Pleased to meetcha, pleased to meetcha. And this quiet fella here" — he indicates a black-haired Asian man to his left — "this is Sam Harami." Harami raises his glass in acknowledgment.

"Would you like a drink?" the waitress asks.

"Absolutely," Pinky tells him. He orders

a Jack on the rocks. I ask for a draft beer.

"So . . . Byron Boudreaux," Maldonado says. "Remember when that son-of-a-bitch got out, Sam?"

Harami nods.

"We all took a deep breath when he got popped loose, I can tell you that. Checking our backs."

"That guy scared me," Harami says, his voice a strange combination of Deep South and Far East. A Japanese drawl. "And I don't scare easy."

"He did come right back to Morgan City, soon as he got out. That's had us worried," Maldonado says. "But he didn't stay long. Spent a week with that witch doctor, and that was it. Haven't heard a peep about him since."

We order dinner — a process that takes at least fifteen minutes because Maldonado has so many inquiries about ingredients and preparations.

"He drive me crazy," Sam Harami says. "Worse than a woman choose her wedding gown."

Finally, I get to ask what's on my mind. "What can you tell me about Boudreaux that might help me track him down?"

Sam Harami shrugs. "Not sure. What kind of thing you have in mind?"

"Just talk," Pinky says, throwing back his whiskey. "What'd you know about him? Not just the case with his daddy, although that, too. Anything. Everything. You never know what's going to help."

"Well, he never came across my watch," Maldonado says, "until that thing with the puppy. You know what I'm talking about?"

"Yeah," I say. "We heard from people at the trailer park."

"Most of what I heard was after Claude died," Maldonado says, "so you really can't trust it. I mean, you show someone a baby picture of Jeffrey Dahmer or Adolf Hitler and they're *bound* to nod and say, 'Yeah, there was always something *strange* about old Jeff.' . . . But that thing with the puppy — it about turned that boy into a pariah."

"I believe it," Pinky says.

"It put him on *my* map, I'll tell you that. People looked back at the way his brother drowned and it had to make you wonder. You remember, Sam?"

Harami raises his eyebrows, which are perfect crescents. "I wasn't here yet, Max. I get here only in eighty-six, right out of Tulane. What I know about Byron only goes back to when he killed his father."

"Ah, that's right," Maldonado says.

"Well, the next thing happened — after the dog — was Marie died. Got that ovarian cancer, that's a killer."

I nod. "I heard she died."

"Yeah. Byron was fifteen years old. A fine woman, Marie. Some people thought maybe that's what sent Byron over the edge — when she passed — because word was she doted on that boy. Anyway, a few months after she died, Claude gets hurt in an oil-rig accident. Messed up his back big-time. He's gonna be in a wheelchair for months. When he gets out of the hospital, Byron's the one who's goin' to 'take care' of him." The reporter makes quotation marks in the air.

"Joke," Harami explains.

"Let's just say he *took care* of him all right," Maldonado adds.

The waitress arrives with gumbo and oysters, and the food silences us for a while. Finally, Maldonado picks up the thread of the story. "So where was I?"

"Claude in a wheelchair, Byron taking care of him."

"Right! So anyway, here's old Claude, slowly making progress after this operation. Spinal fusion, I think it was." He looks at Harami.

"That's right."

"And then, for no apparent reason, he gets real sick one afternoon. He's in front of the tube, in his wheelchair, watching NASCAR with his friend Boots."

"At this time, I am admitting doctor at the ER in New Iberia," Harami says. "It's my residency, you know. My English not so good now, but then?" He shakes his head and makes a face. "Very bad. And Claude — the man can hardly talk by the time he gets to the hospital."

"Yeah," Maldonado jokes, "he can't talk and you can't talk." He smiles and shakes his head.

"But he has friend with him," Harami continues. "Boot. So Boot, he tell me what happens. They watch the race together, drinking beer. Plenty beer. All of a sudden Claude tell his friend the room is . . ." Harami makes a circular motion in the air above his head. He frowns. "Turning?"

"Spinning, Sam."

"Ah, right. *Spinning*. Claude, he feel light-headed. The friend make some joke about how he *is* light-headed, he not exactly mental heavyweight." Harami points to his head. "But then Claude start screaming. He telling Boot that his mouth numb, stomach hurt. Boot — he call nine-one-one."

"They come in record time!" Max says. "Had to be a record. Traffic's light and they get to the hospital pretty damn quick, too."

"This right," Harami says. "They get here very fast. Otherwise, Claude would be DOA and maybe I never figure out what happen to him. Anyway, they get here and I can't understand very much Claude saying, because by this time, he talks in a mumble. But okay — between Boot and the paramedics and the nurse, they sort of get what Claude is saying, and they tell me what happen. First, Claude dizzy and light-headed, then his lips and tongue numb. Boot say Claude very happy for short time, then gloomy. Boot, he say: 'Like a thundercloud sitting on his head. Really got the blues, Doc.' Then Claude vomits in ambulance. In ER, he tell me he feeling stiffer and stiffer by the minute, like he get arthritis all of a sudden."

The waitress arrives with our entrees and deals them off her left arm like a round of cards.

"Oh, boy," says Maldonado, "they know how to do crawfish étouffée here." He digs in.

Harami lets his Laotian catfish special sit for a minute. "I'm native of Japan," he tells us. "And I am" — he hits his forehead — "my mind blown away by my patient, Claude Boudreaux."

I can't imagine where he's going with this, why the fact that he's Japanese has any relevance to Claude Boudreaux. Pinky tosses me a look, equally perplexed.

"I have patient in front of me," Harami says, "and I tell myself: *'It can't be.'* I go over list of symptoms again." Harami counts them off on his fingers: *"Stomach pain. Paresthesia. Aphonia. Euphoria. Depression. Paralysis —"*

"Excuse me," I interrupt. "What's paresthesia?"

"And aphonia?" Pinky adds.

"Paresthesia is . . . creeping sensation on skin. Aphonia — you can't talk."

I nod. "So he has these symptoms?"

"Yes, and by now he finding it very hard to move, hard to breathe. He can no longer talk at all. I order him intubated. I order his stomach pumped; I start intravenous hydration. We administer activated charcoal."

"Doc knew he'd been poisoned," Maldonado says.

"It does not work," Harami continues, excited now. "Two more hour, Claude is dead."

"Here's the thing," Maldonado says. "On the death certificate, Doc writes: 'Respiratory arrest — fugu poisoning.' "

"Fugu poisoning?" Pinky sputters. "Isn't that what you get from eating some kind of fish?"

"In Japan," I add.

Harami nods, taking a bite of his dinner.

"That was a corker," Maldonado says with glee. "I wrote an article about it later. See, this is a death that normally befalls only Japanese gourmands. Crazy types, practicing what might be termed a form of culinary Russian roulette."

Harami nods. "This is true."

"These guys gotta feel risk is quite a flavor enhancer. So every year, fifty or so Japanese diners crash into their plates, struck down while indulging in the delicious taste of fugu sashimi. It's a puffer fish, fugu is, and it's a highly prized delicacy. The one serious drawback is that its skin, liver, and gonads are highly toxic."

"You rely on the chef skill," Harami says. "But sometimes . . ."

"All it takes is a little nick of one of these no-no regions by a sushi chef's knife to deliver a lethal dose of poison."

"Tetrodotoxin," Harami says.

"See, the thing is Claude comes into an

emergency room in *Louisiana,*" Maldonado says. "Most doctors would not have recognized the symptoms. But Sam, he's *sure.*"

Harami nods. "This man Claude Boudreaux? Classic symptoms. I *know* I'm right. I never doubt, even when autopsy shows deceased stomach contents not contain puffer fish. No seafood at all."

"All Claude ate was a couple of Slim Jims and some chips," Maldonado explains. "That and some beer. And that's all the autopsy shows in old Claude's tummy. The conclusion is that Sam was wrong."

"I know I'm not wrong," Harami says. "They want me change death certificate, but they can't tell me what make Claude stop breathing."

"So they do a test," Maldonado says, "just to shut Sam up. Gas chromatograph. And sure as shit, old Claude's bloodstream was *saturated* with tetrodotoxin."

"But none in his stomach," I say.

"The police were baffled," Maldonado says. "How can you get fugu poisoning without eating fish? Were there other sources of the toxin?"

"I don't know this answer," Harami says. "So the medical examiner refer the question to the Centers for Disease Control in Atlanta. Soon, answer comes back. California newt and Eastern salamander both sources of tetrodotoxin."

"But so what?" Maldonado says. "Right? Claude Boudreaux didn't eat any newts or salamanders. He ate a couple of Slim Jims. So how did the poison get into his bloodstream? By now, the M.E. is just as intrigued as Sam here. They get on it. Was it something he inhaled? Maybe so. Because we do find a source for the stuff. Turns out tetrodotoxin powder is a poison used in voodoo rituals. Zombie dust."

"So we think we got something now," Harami says. "M.E. pulls out deceased and does more tests. But no — Boudreaux's nasal passages and respiratory system show no trace of toxin. None." His hands fly up. "A real mystery. Finally we do another gas chromatography test. Focus on victim's bloodstream. This time" — Harami nods vigorously — "we get answer. In addition to tetrodotoxin, Boudreaux's blood contained traces of latex and dimethyl sulfoxide." He smiles. " 'Ahhhh,' we say."

Pinky and I look at each other.

"DMSO," Maldonado says. "It's a solvent. Byron mixed DMSO with tetrodotoxin and smeared it on the tires of his daddy's wheelchair. So old Claude, he rolls from room to room and this lethal cocktail of fugu poison and DMSO passes directly from the tires into his bloodstream."

"A transdermal delivery system," Harami says.

"Like the nicotine patch," Pinky says.

"From there, it didn't take long to figure out that Byron was the one who did it," Maldonado says. "Everybody knew he's hanging out with that voodoo witch doctor down by the cemetery. That's where he got the poison. And he ordered the DMSO mail order, through some weight-lifter catalog. Didn't even try to cover his tracks. But why would he? He was *sooo* unlucky. If the ambulance didn't make record time. If any other doctor in Louisiana had been on duty in the emergency room . . . If his interest in voodoo hadn't been so well known . . ." Maldonado throws up his hands.

"His goose cooked," Harami says, with a laugh. "I cook it. That's why I'm nervous when they release him. Why release this man? Someone like that — kill his father, so sneaky, so clever. Man like this — he not get better. And now we see." He looks at me with an expression of commiseration. "I am sorry. I hope you find your sons. How long they gone?"

"Since May thirty-first."

"I hope you find them," Harami repeats, then lowers his eyes from mine because — as I think he knows — he does not look hopeful.

chapter 37

On the drive back to Morgan City, Pinky's OnStar phone rings. The system is hands-free and broadcasts over the BMW's sound system.

"This is Pinky."

"Mr. Streiber?"

"Jez — is that you? The fair lady of Plaquemines?"

"C'est moi."

"I've got Alex Callahan in the car with me, so don't talk dirty."

"Hello, Mr. Callahan. Matter of fact, I'm calling about you."

"Hello, Jezebel. What's this about?"

"Mr. Streiber asked me to look and see if I could find the discharge order concerning Byron Boudreaux. 'Course, I couldn't. It went up in flames when the courthouse burned down. But I found the next best thing."

"What's that?"

"Who's that. A psychiatric nurse who worked out at the asylum. Worked there eight of the years Byron was there. Knew all about him."

"Jezebel, you are a wonder," Pinky says.

"Oh, yikes, it wasn't *hard*," Jezebel says. "I just asked my daddy and he asked his girlfriend and she asked her stylist. Anyway, like that. Finally I get to this person."

"So who is she? You got her number?"

"Well, that's the thing. She's a little bit afraid of Byron. So I'm not supposed to disclose her name. I promised."

"Jezebel —"

"I won't tell you, so you might as well save it. A good reporter can't disclose her sources. Place like this, nobody's ever gonna talk if you give 'em out."

"You're not a reporter, Jez."

"Well, I will be. I'm in training. Anyway, you interested in what I found out? Or not. Because I want to watch *Sex and the City*. It's on in ten minutes."

"We want to know," I say.

"You still have to pay me," she says, "even if the source remains anonymous. I spent three whole hours on this."

"That's fine," I tell her.

"Here's the deal. Wait a minute. Is this safe over the airwaves like this?"

"You said you weren't going to disclose the source."

"Right. So okay. Byron was a busy little bee while he was at Port Sulfur." Her voice changes and it's obvious that she's reading from notes. "First thing, he earned his G.E.D. at eighteen — because he never did graduate, right. He dropped out. Six years later, he earned a bachelor's degree in psychology — this is all by correspondence courses. Two years after that, he got his master's. His thesis subject was 'Prayer and the Placebo Effect.' He led a Bible study class at Port Sulfur. Byron also had a lot of hobbies; the therapists are real big on that. One was origami. That's folding up little critters and shapes out of paper, in case you're not familiar. And he learned to be a magician — although Miz Ma— uh, my source — she said he already knew how to do lots of card tricks and stuff when he came in. Apparently, he just spent hours and hours practicing his tricks. And he had classes for the other patients. And they let him give shows and all. And at these performances, the staff came; they even invited guests — that's how good he was. Professional level. My source told me everyone agreed that Byron was just about as good with a deck of cards as . . . let me see, I lost my place — oh, here we go . . . he was every bit as good as Ricky Jay." A pause. "Who's Ricky Jay? Never heard of him."

"He's a magician," I say. "Quite well known."

"Well, I guess that's not part of my cultural matrix," Jezebel replies. "Magicians, I mean. Anyway," she continues, "Byron had lots of hobbies and he also read like a demon. And on account of he was enrolled in these university courses by correspondence, he could get books from libraries through the City University of New Orleans. They'd send them. My source, she couldn't remember what all Byron read because it was *soooo* much, but he read lots about magic and history and religion. And psychology, of course, since that was his major."

"Right."

"He petitioned for release starting, like, the very first year he was in care, but he didn't get anywhere until ninety-four. That's the first time the release committee really considered his case, even though he was kind of a poster boy, getting those degrees and all. And according to my source, even though he did kill his own father, there were files and files and files about the abuse Byron's supposed to have suffered at the hands of his daddy when he was a kid. They didn't really believe that, but . . ."

"With the man dead, they couldn't entirely discount it, either," Pinky puts in.

"Right. So his case came up again the next year, ninety-five, but there was a holdout on the committee didn't want to let him go. That person moved or something, or retired — my source couldn't remember — so when it came up again in ninety-six, they decided Byron was sane, or sane enough anyway, and not a danger to himself or the community, that it was time to let him go."

"What changed their minds?"

"Time," Jezebel says. "More than anything else. It'd just been so long, for one thing. And there's all that supposed abuse he'd suffered at Claude's hands — this was still at a time when people were buying that as an explanation for all kinds of stuff. Plus he was a juvenile when he was committed, plus he'd done so well with his studies and all. They decided his act against his father was prompted by, let's see, uh . . . 'transitory conditions' — and that he was not likely to commit similar acts."

"Did Byron have any friends inside? Any special friends?" I ask.

"See, I knew you'd ask that," Jezebel says.

"And?"

"Charley Vermillion, right? You want to know if he was a special friend of Byron? And the answer is that Byron did spend time with Charley. Charley was in Byron's Bible study class, for one thing. And this was a real close group, according to my source. Byron was also some kind of nuthouse lawyer, mostly for the folks in his Bible group. Helped them file petitions and all. Helped them contact lawyers. I didn't think to ask who all was in the group. You want to know?"

"Yeah, I would," I tell her, "if you can find out."

"You're breaking up," Jezebel says. "Whereabouts are you, anyway?"

"Near Houma," Pinky says.

"I can't hear you. I'm going to my friend Felicia's now to watch TV. Call me tomorrow or something." She hangs up.

"Hmmmm," Pinky says. "That young lady is dynamite." He makes a right turn. There's no road noise with the BMW. I find this a little strange, as if we're gliding through space. "Between Max and his friend Sam, and Jez, we learned a lot today."

"Yeah."

"Maybe that list of Bible study people will give us a lead."

"Maybe."

"Why are you so quiet? You're not thinking of going out to that witch doctor's tonight, are you? Don't be foolish, pardner."

We roll past a gas station selling super-realistic framed artwork, paintings on glass so realistic they mimic photographs — except for the fact that every detail is in hyperfocus and the colors are unnaturally bright. Woodlands and birds and bright blue streams. The flag is a feature in many of them, along with the bald eagle. Each one has its own light source, and they glow brightly, attracting a mist of bugs. A couple of women contemplate one of the works while a man in shorts and a tank top sits on a folding chair, smoking a cigarette.

We roll on in companionable silence for some time. Pinky flips on the sound system. Half a minute of Beausoleil, and he flicks it off again. "I mean it's one thing to throw caution to the winds," he says, "and go all out looking for your boys. But it's another thing to head to a shack in the swamp to spend the night with some motherfucker ain't got no lip. And the only thing you really know about him is he was the only friend old Byron had, and — I might add — the likely source of the poison killed Claude."

I don't say anything.

"I'm going with you then."

"I think it's better if you don't. That way, if I don't come back, you can —"

"Call the po-lice? Jesus, Alex."

"I just have a feeling Diment might have some idea where Byron is."

"And he's gonna tell you?"

"Maybe. I don't know. But I got the feeling he might help me."

"I didn't get that feeling at all. Those folk coughin' away in that other room? All those things tied up with string. That spooked me out good. And you're supposed to go there at midnight? Put yourself in his *trust*. Whoa! Not this puppy. Explain to me why you would trust him? What about the man seems trustworthy, pardner? Huh?"

"I know what you're saying."

Pinky lets out a jet of air. "How you plannin' to get out there? You even remember how to go?"

"I was thinking . . . a cab. And maybe you could draw me a map."

"I'll draw you a map. But forget the cab. I'll give you my car."

"I can't take your car. What about you?"

"I'll be asleep. I'll have me some breakfast right at the Holiday Inn. Read the paper. You don't call or show up by noon or so, I'll sound the alarm. Anyway, call it an insurance policy."

"What do you mean?"

"First of all, it's easy to track the car. OnStar has this GPS system. Second thing is that the po-lice around here might not jump into action if some guy from Washington, D.C., gets hisself lost in the swamp." He glances over at me. "Some of our officers might not have the utmost respect for human life. But a sixty-thousand-dollar vehicle? Something like that goes missing, you see some action then, all right."

chapter 38

The car's xenon lights tunnel into the night, illuminating unmarked roads that seem indistinguishable to me. I get lost a couple of times, despite Pinky's painstakingly drawn map. I left plenty of spare time, though, and even with the wrong turns I arrive at Diment's place fifteen minutes before midnight.

I step out of the car into the warm night. A sibilant insect hum rises up around me, followed by some kind of animal or bird, some jungly cry of distress that makes the hair on my neck stand up. The BMW's lights stay on for a few moments, as if to light my way from my driveway to the door of my suburban manse. In reality, they illuminate with brutal clarity the concrete-block structure before me.

It looks like a great place to get killed. Only a dim, flickering light is visible through the one small window. A candle? I wonder for a moment if the structure has electricity, but then I remember the string of Christmas lights on the altar. I think about the weird collection of objects displayed. It is impossible to assign significance to them. What could the comb mean? A baby bottle?

On the scuffed ground in front of the door, a single tennis shoe rests on its side. It reminds me of Kevin's Nike, the one I spotted by the gate outside the jousting arena. That creepy resonance jumpstarts an intense wave of paranoia, and it's all I can do not to bolt.

The car gives a little click and the lights fade. I step forward a few steps and rap on the siding next to the door. No sooner have I touched the house than the beads are pulled open with a clatter. It's as if the two men were standing just inside, waiting. They smile at me.

"Welcome, welcome," one of them says. He's a skinny man, with a fuzz of graying hair. He's so thin he looks skeletal. He speaks in a high squeaky voice. "Come in."

"I'm here to see —"

"The *houngan* not here," the second man says. He's a big man and so dark skinned the light glints off the broad planes of his face. He's at least six-five, two-fifty, and while the skinny man scared me, I find this big man reassuring. "But first you have to get dressed," he says in his booming baritone.

"I *am* dressed," I tell them.

But, no. They tell me they have something special for me to wear. I follow the two of them, tiptoeing past the patients lying in a row against the wall. Someone moans. Another, off to the left, coughs — a terrible sound that concludes in a kind of gasping wheeze.

"In here," the big man says, opening a door. He pulls the string and I see what I'm being shown into: a john. "You change," he says. "We'll wait outside."

My new outfit is hanging on the back of the bathroom door: a white tuxedo with a red carnation in the lapel. Now I understand the reason for the question about my size. Still, it's not reassuring. A white tuxedo . . . ?

I'm drenched in sweat; it's coming off me in sheets. And suddenly, I have all kinds of questions:

Why do I have to change clothes?

Why the white tuxedo? Something Karl Kavanaugh said pops into my mind, something about white doves and blood.

Just what is "an initiation ceremony"? Skip the details, just give me the general idea.

And can you really just join a *bizango,* or was Diment putting me on?

And how can I join something if I don't know what I'm joining? Isn't there . . . a catechism, or something?

Diment said I had to enter into the evening with trust. How can I put my trust in Diment? I don't even know him.

And why midnight?

Some not helpful portion of my brain chimes in: *It's the witching hour.*

None of these questions makes it past my lips. What I say instead, hesitating at the threshold of the bathroom before I close the door is: "Uh, I'm not sure about this."

"You change in there," the skinny man says, as if I haven't spoken at all. He gives me a gentle push.

"I'm just —"

"We'll wait out here," the big man says, with a reassuring pat on the arm. And then he nudges me a little farther inside and closes the door.

It's a cramped, utilitarian room: a toilet, a sink, a paper-towel dispenser, a pump bottle of liquid soap. A sheet of reflective metal hangs over the sink instead of a mirror. The door shudders and creaks and

I realize the two men are leaning against it.

I fight off a reflex surge of claustrophobia and try to calm down. Maybe they're just leaning against it because . . . it's just a place to lean.

It's hard to calm down. I'm breathing too fast, and a voice inside my head is screeching: *What are you doing?*

The men outside the door mumble. The big man laughs, a hearty chuckle that seems absent of any note of malevolence. I take several deep breaths. *You came to him,* I tell myself. *You sought out Diment, not the other way around. You asked for his help.*

I put on the tuxedo, fastening the suspenders and the crimson cummerbund. Not surprisingly, it's a perfect fit. I put my clothes on the hangers and put my shoes back on. Then I step back and regard myself in the sheet of metal over the sink. There's something so goofy about the white tuxedo, a Liberace kind of excess, that for a moment I feel giddy.

I rap on the door.

It's pulled open. The skinny man cocks his head and contemplates me. "Aw*right*," he says, with a kind of cackle. "My man! You look good! Doesn't he look good?"

"Ummhmm," the big man says, and then reaches into his pocket and pulls out a bottle of Deep Woods Off. "Close your eyes," he says. Before I can protest, he's spraying me head to toe with a perfumed mist that stinks of deet.

Skinny turns off the light, and then we pick our way through the clinic again, single file, the big guy leading.

The BMW gleams in the moonlight, my getaway car. I finger the keys in my pocket, but I'm not seriously tempted to pop the lock and drive away from this. I've crossed some invisible barrier. Whatever I'm into here, I'm committed.

The big guy has a Maglite, but its batteries must be almost used up because the light it casts is a watery yellow disk that doesn't do much to illuminate our way. The moonlight barely penetrates the thick canopy. We're trudging along a narrow dirt path through a vine-tangled wood. The trees are spooky, shrouded with Spanish moss. The path is full of roots. The insect hum rises up around us, a rich vibrant tumult.

"The hills are alive," the skinny guy says, and then cackles with laughter.

The big guy chuckles.

"Where are we going?" I can hardly see the two men, but me? I practically glow in the dark.

"To the place," the big man says. "Don't worry, we'll be there soon."

I can't see much, but I can tell we're getting closer to water. The disk of light bounces off tangles of mangrove knees and occasionally I hear a frog splash. The air smells different, too, funky and dank.

After a few more minutes, I smell wood smoke, and hear the murmur of voices. And then finally, we emerge from the dark woods into a clearing. Diment and a dozen others, men and women, sit around a fire. A couple of bottles of what looks like rum are going around the circle, and in fact, I can smell alcohol. Out in the darkness, when the fire throws up a flame, I can see the gleam of water.

Seeing me, Diment gets to his feet. The rest of the *bizango* follows suit. Diment embraces me, then holds me at arm's length. "Damn, you look fine." He smiles, teeth gleaming. Everyone embraces me in turn, introducing themselves and offering a formal welcome. I feel at a remove from myself, as if I'm looking at this from above: a collection of happy people sitting around a fire, drinking, led by a man who lost his upper lip to a zombie. Then a man dressed in white comes out of the woods and joins them. It's a scene of visual extravagance, like something you might see in the Corcoran or the National Gallery, some nineteenth-century painting of an exotic crowd scene: *Initiation.*

My heart feels unsteady in my chest and over and over again, I hear that little voice saying: *What are you doing?*

After all the hugs and bows, my legs feel shaky. I'm more than happy to sit down next to Diment, as I'm invited to do. The skinny man and the big man join the circle. The rum goes around in both directions. This time I drink as much as I can when it's my turn, and my thirst meets with enthusiastic approval. I realize, after a few minutes, that most of the *bizango* is drunk.

Finally, Diment raises his hand, and everyone falls quiet. He turns to me and puts a hand on my arm. "Alex, are you ready?"

I nod. What I'm thinking is: *Let's get this over with.*

"*Bon!*" The big man distributes torches — these constructed of thick bamboo, with some kind of cloth wrapped many times around their ends. The members of the *bizango* dip the torches into the fire, and then we're on the move again, heading even deeper into the swamp. We have to duck under the limbs of trees and tread carefully over the rooty ground. The insects roar, and I'm grateful for the Off, which keeps them more or less at bay.

"Ho!" says a voice from the front of our file. And then, a minute later, I follow Diment around a big tree and into a clearing. A crude wooden cross stands waist-high, stuck into the ground at an angle. A few feet away is a freshly dug grave, and next to that, a pine casket.

It takes me a second to grasp what I'm seeing and when I do, I take a reflexive step backward. Everyone laughs.

Diment faces me. His bizarre smile is anything but reassuring. "Have faith, my friend."

It's a call-and-response thing, and the rest of the *bizango* chants its reply to Diment in unison.

"Have faith!"

"And trust in your brothers and sisters."

"Have trust!"

"Without faith, there's no resurrection."

"Without faith we are doomed."

"Without faith, we have nothing."

"Have faith!"

It goes on like that for a while and then everybody falls silent. Diment claps me on the back. "Don't worry, man! We dig you up quick!"

"Quick!" I say. "You mean, like, right away, or —"

Diment laughs, throwing his head back, exposing all of his teeth. "No," the doctor says, barely able to speak over his laughter. "See, you spend the night, restin' underground. We be up here, makin' music. Moving with the *loa*. When the sun comes up, your brothers and sisters here get you out."

"Amen!"

"Oh, yes!"

"Sweet sleep!"

"Lord on high!"

I take a deep breath. Jesus. Ever since the boys were taken, I keep venturing further and further away from what seems normal. I am so far out on the edge of anyplace I expected to be . . . I'm in the middle of a swamp in a white tuxedo. I stare at the coffin.

I take another deep breath. I think about the M.E. out in Vegas speculating that Clara Gabler had been in a pine box, maybe a coffin, but that she seems to have waited for her fate willingly, without struggle. "I don't think I can do this," I say.

The jolly look evaporates from Diment's face. Suddenly he looks grim with disappointment. "Then I can't help you," he says.

"Hell," I hear the skinny guy's voice say. "The last guy got buried just to get a number! Shit."

"I know," starts another voice, "this one jumpy, like that . . ."

Diment holds up a hand to silence them.

Standing in the moonlight, with my improbable tuxedo seeming almost to *absorb* the moonlight, I fumble for the words. "What I'm being asked to do," I start. My mouth is so dry, I can hardly speak. "What I'm being asked to do — will it be worth it?"

"That up to you," Diment says to me. His face is stone. His eyes glint in the torchlight. He looks tired and angry. Around us, the others murmur.

I feel like I'm at the top of a cliff, about to leap into space. "No," I tell him. "It's not up to me. It's up to you. Can you tell me how to find Boudreaux?"

Diment shakes his head. "You out of turn, son. That a question for *after;* you understand what I'm saying? First you got to prove your trust." But although the old man dodges the question, his rheumy eyes don't. They remain fastened on me. He stares intently, holding my eyes. There's no malevolence in his gaze. "If you trust me," he says, "I help you."

I don't know why, but I believe him.

A drumbeat starts up, a slow steady rhythm from somewhere to my left. Voices murmur. Someone chugs rum. The skinny guy cackles. A woman hums the tune of a lullaby.

I keep my eyes on my feet as I walk over to the casket. And then, before I can change my mind, I climb into the box. The whole crowd leans over me. I can see the big man, bending to lift the wooden cover. I close my eyes. *I'm crazy.*

"Alex!" Diment says, and my eyes snap open.

He's looking down at me. Behind him, the big man and a couple of others hold the lid of the casket. Diment drips some liquid onto my face from his fingers. It feels cold, but it seems to burn as it hits my skin. *Tetrodotoxin?* Are my lips beginning to feel numb?

"Wait!" I say, trying to sit up. Three men push me gently back down.

A clear soprano sings "Amazing Grace." Panic rolls through me. Isn't that for funerals? And then I think: This *is* a funeral. *They're burying me.*

"Trust me," Diment says, and then the

lid clatters into place atop the casket.

I keep my eyes shut tight. *Maybe I'm hypnotized or something. Because this is how people disappear.*

Suddenly, I can feel my breath against the wood, and my heart vaults into my throat. *Maybe they're going to let me out now,* I think for one glorious moment. *Maybe all I had to do was prove I'd do it, and then . . .*

But no. That hope evaporates and it's all that I can do to stop myself from panicking and hurling myself against the wood as they begin to nail the top of the casket into place. Why is *that* necessary? *If this is some kind of fake funeral, why real nails? Big nails, too. I saw them. And the coffin looks brand-new. Why wouldn't they use the same coffin over and over again if this is a regular thing? Because this coffin is going to stay here. The swamp is probably full of buried bodies.*

It's so loud, amazingly loud, each blow of the hammer a deafening concussion. There's also the impression — which makes me cringe down, away from the lid — that the nails might plunge right through the wood. The nailing starts at my head and goes down around to my feet and then back up toward my head. In the background, when the man driving the nails moves to a new site, I can hear the drumbeat, and singing.

The hammering starts again. It's so loud. I'd like to put my hands over my ears, but the coffin is too tight for that.

I count the nails as they're driven in, eleven so far. *Isn't that excessive?*

It's so loud.

And although I really can't stand it, somehow I endure the noise. When it stops, I find to my shock that I am praying. Praying in a mindless, stumbling way, repeating the Our Father over and over, a tumble of meaningless syllables. I'm not religious, and the rush of words in my head seems like a cheap trick. And a sort of collapse. I don't think I should be allowed to pray if it's not something I do regularly. It's like I'm borrowing something I'm not entitled to.

OurFatherwhoartinheavenhallowedbethyname.

Still, I can't stop.

Thykingdomcomethywillbedoneonearthasitis-inheavengiveusthisdayourdailybreadandforgive-usourdebtsasweforgiveourdebtors.

I have the impression that if only I can say it fast enough, perfectly enough, if only there are absolutely no silences between the words, nothing bad will happen to me.

Andleadusnotintotemptationbutdeliverusfrom-evilforthineisthekingdomandthepowerandthe-

gloryforeverandever.

Did I mess up? I think I did. I start over. *OurFatherwhoartinheaven . . .*

The casket shakes and there's a smell of plastic as a pipe, or something like a pipe, is fitted into a hole in the casket, just above my face. I never noticed the hole, which surprises me. You'd think I'd be all tuned in to anything like that. *See, your prayers are answered,* the voice in my head says.

I can't touch the hole, I can't see it, but I can tell it's there from the smell of plastic and the slightly cooler drift of air through it. With some effort, I can raise my head up and fasten my lips around the pipe and draw in air.

It's as if my entire body has been clenched like a fist while the coffin was nailed shut. Now, realizing there's a pipe for air, I begin to let go a little. I've been so clenched up, though, that relaxing my muscles makes me start to shake. I'm still caught in this spasm when I feel the casket sway as it's lifted into the air.

It seesaws back and forth, yawing right and left. I can hear voices, a shout, but I can't hear what they're saying. And then the coffin is lowered. It yaws gently as it descends, but then, with a couple of feet left, they let go. Newtonian forces prevail: I slam into the top of the coffin, my nose crashes into the breathing tube hard enough to make me cry out. I have a terrible fear that I've dislodged the tube. I squirm up, to see if my lips can reach it. *Yes*.

And then a shovelful of dirt crashes onto the wood. I wince, as if it might come through the wood and hit me.

Then another, and another.

Then . . . nothing. Just the darkness.

And the sound of my own breathing.

chapter 39

I'm not sure if I'm asleep or just in a kind of trance — or maybe oxygen deprived — when I first hear the sound. It comes from a long, long way off — like China. It's a muffled scraping noise, one that means nothing to me, that's happening independently, that seems to exist in a separate universe. I observe the sound with the detachment of a machine, one of those monitors in a museum, for instance, silently tracking humidity and temperature, keeping a record for future perusal by some sentient being.

The sound goes on and on, and gradually I adopt the idea that my new universe will contain this sound. I'm not sure how I feel about it because the sound is not actually pleasant, now that I contemplate it as a permanent condition. Now that it is omnipresent. Now that it occupies most of my consciousness. I cannot feel much — the wood against my fingers, the ragged surface of the breathing tube. I can see nothing. Smells are confined to the odor of my own body, the pine wood, the manufactured smell of the plastic pipe.

The only thing that changes is the sound, and so it comes to absorb all my attention. After a while it seems to me that the sound is actually inside my own head, that I've somehow invented it.

It's not until a shovel hits the wood that I'm jolted into the perspective of a true observer, that the sound represents an event in time. It's the sound of a metal implement striking the wooden object in which I am encased. The realization propels me out of my trance state.

I am buried alive and someone is digging me out.

Immediately, I'm inundated by a tsunami of fear and claustrophobia. *I'm buried alive!*

And I'm overcome with terror that whoever is digging me out will stop. Coming out of my trance, I don't at first remember how I got where I am or even where that is. An earthquake or an avalanche, a terrorist attack? What I do know is that I can't see, I can't breathe, that I'm trapped and panicked.

I try to shout — wanting to offer some sign that the effort is worth it, that whomever my rescuer might be, there's a person down here. I want to shout out: *I'm alive.*

I'm here. Don't give up.

What emerges from me is nothing like what I intend. It's not a shout, not even a scream. It's more like a moan or a growl, so low-pitched I doubt anyone could hear it. It's almost as if my voice lacks the velocity to break the sound barrier.

By the time the coffin is raised, and the cover pried off — a process that takes a long time — I remember how I came to be buried alive. I wonder, as they work on my exhumation, how long I was under. While I was buried, I lost my bearings in time and space. For a while, I even lost the idea of me, of Alex Callahan. Time seemed to expand infinitely. At first, I counted my breaths in cycles of one hundred, but eventually, I started losing track, and then I seemed to forget the proper sequence of numbers and then it seemed pointless. I went insane for a short time, screaming and writhing and trying to claw my way out, an effort that left my fingers raw and bleeding. I used the pain, for a while, to keep my spirits up. As long as it hurts, I told myself, I'm alive. A new Cartesian deduction. *Dolor ergo sum.* Or something like that.

I felt regret about it: disappearing. It would be tough on my parents and Liz. My main concern was for the boys, because I considered myself their last chance. Others might go through the motions, but everyone else had given them up for dead. That thought carried me for a while. By thinking of Sean and Kevin, by recounting every memory of them, by summoning up their faces and their voices, I was able to keep my head together for some time. And I had a vision of them, which I was persuaded was true, that I am still persuaded is true.

Somehow my mind slipped the temporal-spatial chains and delivered me to a room I'd never seen before. It was as if I were in the center of the ceiling, looking down. The boys were asleep in wooden bunk beds of the bulky, rough-hewn "western" sort. They slept under burgundy-colored fleece blankets, Sean on the lower bunk, Kevin on top.

Kevin stirred, under my gaze, and turned over from one side to the other. His mouth was open and I could see that his two new front teeth, which had just begun to emerge from his gums when the boys arrived from Maine, were almost fully in now. The edges had a vaguely scalloped appearance, ridges that must wear down over time, and the teeth looked too big for his face, as such teeth do. And then the vision vanished and I was back in the dark, trying to summon up anything, Christmas at the in-laws', Sean's face when he saw the bike under the tree.

Eventually, though, I suffered a collapse of the will. Diment had buried me alive. He was Boudreaux's friend. If I thought his kind look promised anything, it was wishful thinking. I wondered if Pinky would be able to track down my grave.

And then I passed beyond regret, into a new arena, where I was beyond any interest in myself. This is the way I think I survived. I gave up. I obliterated every thought because they all circled back on themselves: "What if I turn over?" always led to "*Can* I turn over?" And so on.

In a way, it was a relief to give up. To stop counting, to stop focusing on my pain, to stop thinking of Sean and Kev, to stop hoping. To stop thinking that Alex Callahan had any importance in the universe. To stop thinking at all.

As the nails are pried off, the screech is the loveliest music I've ever heard. When the lid comes off, I'm blinded by the light and my eyes reflexively slam shut. Hands grasp my arms and sit me up.

"Come on now, take it easy. Don't try to

open your eyes just yet. Just let the light filter in through your lids like."

Someone holds a paper cup of water to my lips and I gulp a few sips, a messy process. I try to lift a hand to my face to wipe my lips, but the hand shakes so badly I can't really do it; I just bat myself in the face.

"That's okay," says a voice I recognize as Diment's. "You be all right. Didn't I tell you, man? You jez have to trust. Body don't like bein' pinned down like that, that's all. But you be all right, same as I promise. Just take it easy. Let the world welcome you back, brother."

More water. It's delicious, an elixir. As is the damp air against my skin, which provides an exquisite rush of sensations. And the sunlight through my eyelids, flickering and patterned through something I can't see, is a revelation after the darkness.

"You a new man, now. You reborn. We gon' stand you up, come on."

Strong hands under my arms lift me to my feet.

"Open your eyes, Alex. Jest a little, tha's right, now a little more. Step out onto the earth."

The world is still bleached out, like an overexposed photograph, but I can see enough to step over the side of the coffin onto the dusty earth.

"Oh, yes!" a female voice calls.

"He one of us now!"

Their voices are sweet and wonderful, the most dulcet music. In fact, liberated from the coffin, I am drenched in sheer wonderment. The humid air against my skin, the sun, the trees rustling in the breeze, the dirt . . . I tremble with delight. I even start to cry, tears of joy and relief.

"Oh, yes! Now he see!"

On the ground to my right is an intricate design made out of a white powder. It's lacy and beautiful.

"That's a *veve*," Diment tells me, following my gaze. "That help bring the *loa* here." He leans down and, with his fingertips, stirs the design into the dust.

The members of the *bizango* are gathering flags and drums, and stuffing the bottles and plastic plates and cups into trash bags. Some of their faces are smeary with white powder. They look worn out, as if the night was a difficult one for them, too.

Once again, it's as if Diment can read my mind. "It not *restful* when the *loa* come into you. You shake and fall down and then you dance. We all tired now — you the only one get any rest." He laughs his alarming laugh.

I'm outside Diment's place, sitting on a disintegrating rattan chair in a little concrete patio hidden behind the structure. It's just a concrete slab, with a cable spool for a table and two sagging chairs. To the right are some animal pens or chicken coops of different sizes, handmade of bamboo and interlaced with vine. One of them holds a speckled hen, but the others are empty. The hen sits compact and motionless with the exception of her bright eyes.

I'm back in my own clothes and I put in a call to Pinky from the BMW's phone to let him know I'm all right. Now I wait for Diment to come out. Usually, I hate to wait, but for the moment I'm without impatience. The night underground propelled me into a new mindset. It would be overstating it to say that I feel "reborn," but I do feel refreshed and alive. And free of my normal impatience, my usual restless chafing against the constraints of any schedule not designed with me at its center. I take heart from that strange vision of the boys in their bunk beds, which reaffirmed my belief that they're alive.

* * *

"You know why I agree to help you?" Diment asks when he joins me, maybe half an hour later. The old man looks tired, his color bad, his rheumy eyes bagged and exhausted.

"No."

"Twins. You seek your boys and they are twins. It is for this. Otherwise, I am an old man who does not like to miss his sleep. Twins are very special in *vaudoo.* Above every other *loa* — which be the spirits in charge of the whole world, the living and the dead — above all of them, is the *Marassa.*" He nods.

"The Marassa?"

"Oh, yes, they the twins. They make the rain fall, they make the herbs that heal the sick. The two in one — they symbolize the harmony of the world as it should be, the balance of the earth and the sky, the fire and the water, the living and the dead."

"The twins."

"So it is," Diment says in his mellifluous voice. "So it is this way. The twins not entirely, what you say, *friendly,* oh, no. They get angry, sometime. They jealous. Things go out of balance. But in *vaudoo* — twin children in a family, this a thing of great importance. They are" — he searches for the word — "a reminder of the mystery. You must have ceremony for them — this you must do if you find your sons, yes? This you must promise me."

"Ceremony?"

"In their honor. Every year. You listen now. Every once a year. Christmas, this one possible day, but the celebration must be apart from the Christmas celebration, so that may be not the best choice. January fourth, that a second appropriate day."

"That's —"

But he holds up his hand to stop me.

"The third one is the Easter eve, the day before the Christian Easter. If you not have ceremony for the twins, it bring unhappy days."

"It's no problem," I tell him. "We always celebrate. Their birthday is January fourth."

This stuns him, almost scares him. "You are sent to me. So I may serve the Marassa." He closes his eyes, mumbles, crosses himself, lets his head fall to his chest. When he opens his eyes again, he looks so tired I ask him if he wants to rest for a while.

"Look, I need to get Pinky's car back to him," I tell him. "I can come back later."

"No, no, no, no." He draws his open hand down over his face. "I tell you now what I know about Byron. I might know one or two thing. We can hope —" He makes a gesture, his hands rising into the air. "We can hope it help you."

My mood sinks. It doesn't sound like he's got any hard information about Boudreaux's whereabouts.

We're interrupted when a woman arrives. She wears a long faded dress and has bare feet. She's nervous and very deferential to Diment. She holds a white rooster in her arms, confining it in such a way that it does not struggle. Diment makes a little bow in my direction and gets up to inspect the bird. He pulls its wings up and pushes its feathers apart here and there. The bird makes a clucking sound every once in a while and moves its head in little jerks, its red comb wobbling, its bright eyes staring. "It's good," Diment says, and instructs the woman to put the chicken into an empty pen. The bird goes inside in a flurry of squawks and feathers. The woman closes the pen by inserting a stick through a double loop of vine.

"She bring this for the sacrifice," Diment says, when the woman leaves. "She come back later. You are here first."

My mind vaults to the chicken blood on Kevin's shirt, the one the police found in my closet.

"You're going to *sacrifice* it?" Until Diment spoke of sacrifice, I'd been thinking the hen was there to lay eggs. And the rooster, was — I don't know — a pet.

Diment nods. "You don't like this."

I shake my head as if to dismiss his idea, but he's right, of course.

"That don't surprise me. You think it *primitive,* I'm right?"

"I guess."

"Sacrifice the core to all worship, go way back, all the way back, I'm thinking. The god or the gods create the entire world and give you life in it. To honor the god, you perform the ritual, you give him back one of his creature, you give the life of thing back to nourish him.

"Sometime, we have hard times. We have drought or the animals fall sick. Yet even then the animal for the sacrifice cannot have disease. Cannot have flaw. So to give the healthy animal back in hard times, that hard to do. But hard times when you need the *loa* most of all, yes?"

"I understand the idea, but —"

Diment makes a harsh and dismissive gesture, puts his hand on my arm. "Let me ask you one thing: You a Christian man?"

"Sort of."

"The Christian faith built on sacrifice, you understanding, yes? God ask Abraham sacrifice his son Isaac, then God relent. He take a lamb, instead. He take a *lamb* instead of Isaac. He take a life. No, he not require the son of *Abraham,* but God require this of *himself.* He *sacrifice* his only son, let him to die up on the cross in the hot sun, spill his own son's blood, take his own son's life. Not a chicken, not a bull, not a lamb — his only son. And Jesus, he know ahead of time. Don't he say at the Last Supper — 'This is my body, this is my blood.' The communion — this rite. It's about sacrifice, no? You drink Jesus blood, you eat his body."

"You're right," I tell him. "You're absolutely right. But —"

"You still think to kill the chicken — this somehow backward, yes? Let me ask you: How you respect life if you don't respect death? Let me tell you — you think I a bloodthirsty man, I like to spill the blood?"

"No. But —"

"You live in your head," Diment says, shaking his own head sadly. "Alex, you must also live in your body." He thumps his chest. "You must live in here. You must learn to live in here."

"I live in my body."

"No. Three hours out of the ground and already you back up here." He touches his head and sighs, a deep, fatigued sound.

"I'm sorry."

He shakes his head.

"I think maybe Byron still practices sacrifice," I tell him. "He left one of the boys' T-shirts at my house, soaked in blood. It made the police think I'd killed my sons . . . until they tested the blood."

"Byron — he like to kill things, yes?"

I don't know what to say.

He holds out a hand toward me in a gesture of . . . benediction. "No. Byron . . . like the owl or the panther." He shakes his head. "He hunts, he spill blood for his own self, to slake his own thirst. I try to teach him how to use that, but . . ." He shakes his head.

"What do you mean?"

"That dog," Diment says. "He come my way, about that time. I tell him that dog was a waste. I tell him, 'you piss away your power, boy, you got nothin' left.' And he ask, what power is that? So I tell him: the power you get when you put the hurt on things. The power you get when creatures be dyin'. The power of the sacrifice, yes?"

"And what did Byron say?"

Diment shrugs. "He asked me to teach him."

"About what?"

"Magic."

"Like card tricks?"

Diment shakes his head. "No, no, no. He already know that kind of thing. Byron — he could make you look the wrong way, every time. He wanted to know about the Mysteries. He wanted to know about the sacrifice, what we call the 'real magic.' "

"And you could teach him that?"

"Oh, yes. But I can't talk of this with you. You don't understand. You don't even understand your own faith about sacrifice. I tell you this: Something look like magic, this not always so." He taps his temple. "You can't see what happen, you can't see the true cause."

"But you could talk about it with Byron?"

He nods. "I could teach him. I did teach him."

"Like what? What did you teach him?"

"I teach him the *loa,* the signs and the meanings, the sacrifice, the dance, everything to bring the power of the other world into this world. How to help the spirit move on when somebody die. How every spirit have a place in this world, how to get the spirit come here without they hurt you. How to make the juju, the mojo, the *veve*. How to do every kind of thing I know how to do. Even how to get the spirit on your side to put the hurt on someone. I teach Byron everything I know. I teach him the herbs and leaves. And he use that to kill."

"His father."

"Yes." Diment nods slowly. "I teach him the ways. But he not really learn."

"What do you mean?"

But Diment just shakes his head. "He use everything only for Byron. That not the way. That the very first thing I try to teach him, with the little dog. He pretend to learn. But he stay the same way. The same Byron." I see tears in Diment's eyes. He shakes his head hard, as if to dispel them. "He come by here when he gets out, you know that?"

"From Port Sulfur?"

"Yes." He wags his head. "After those many year. He spend a few days with me. I hope . . . he's changed. So many years, he's a man now. But —" He shakes his head. "He the same Byron, only stronger. I am happy when he go away again." Abruptly, Diment stands up.

"You come."

I follow him inside, into the room with the altar. He steps forward, mumbles something, and plucks from the crowded array of objects what looks like a postcard. He hands it to me.

The light is bad — just a couple of candles and the Christmas tree lights. And what I'm looking at reminds me of the cards opticians use to test for color blindness.

"What is this?"

"You look," Diment says.

It still seems to be no more than a smear of colors. I have to stare at it for three or four minutes before it gives up its secret. Concealed within a field of bloodred blobs are a pair of clownlike faces, their eyes gazing implacably at the viewer.

"What is this?"

"Turn it over."

A printed note identifies the painting as

> *The Marassa* by Petit Jean,
> Port au Prince, Haiti, 1964.

"The twins," Diment replies. "You see?"

"Right."

"And you see it's addressed to me. And look what Byron say."

In the message box, across from the address, is a handwritten note:

> *Finished with the Castle.*
> *Doing real magic now.*

"What's 'real magic'? What does he mean?"

"The twins," Diment says. "They guard the gates to *les Mystères.* Without them, you can't do real magic."

"But what is real magic?"

But the old man ignores me. He taps the postmark with his forefinger:

> Aug. 10, 2000
> Point Arena, CA

"For *vaudoo* people, this a most important day. Sacred to the Marassa. This is why Byron sends the card that day. August tenth. You might say" — Diment smiles his terrifying smile — "this is our *vaudoo* Easter."

"You think Byron lives there? Point Arena?"

"I don't know. This is the last card I get from him."

Three years ago. I'm not exactly hot on his heels.

I look at the signature, which is a scrawl.

I squint, but there's no way it looks anything like *Byron*.

Diment looks over my shoulder. "The name?" he asks. "That's 'Maître Carrefour.' "

"Who's that?"

"It's the name Byron used when he worked as a magician. On the stage," Diment adds.

"*Worked*. But not anymore?"

Diment shakes his head.

"Why not?"

"You saw the postcard. He says he's doing real magic, now."

"But what does that mean?"

Diment inclines his head, frowns. "What it means is you make the world do your bidding, with the help of the spirit. You come to be one with them, they work with you, you make thing happen." He wags his head, a slow steady motion, like a metronome, his eyes closed. "That what it mean to me. With Byron, I don't know," he says.

"This thing about a castle . . ."

Diment shrugs. "I don't know what he means wi' that, either."

"And *Carrefour?*"

"Ah, yes. That I can tell you. Maître Carrefour is like . . . you would say a patron saint," the old man tells me.

"Of what?"

Diment looks at me, shakes his head. "Sorcery," he says.

chapter 40

I catch up with Pinky in the Holiday Inn's breakfast room. He's drinking coffee and looking at *USA Today*'s weather page. The map is bright orange, the whole country caught in a heat wave.

"Hell," he says, as I slide into the seat across from him. "You don't look half bad for someone got hisself buried alive. What was *that* like?"

"Dark."

Pinky lets out a peal of laughter that makes everyone in the room look our way. Somehow, *dark* strikes his funny bone and he ends up wheezing for breath. "I bet," he says finally. A sigh. "Well, I hope to God you found out something useful."

I shrug. "The bottom line is that Diment doesn't know where Byron is."

"Doesn't know? Or wouldn't tell?"

"I don't think he knows. There's something about twins and voodoo — I didn't quite get it, but twins are a big deal. I think he wants to help."

"But he can't?"

"He told me a couple of things. He told me that after Byron got out of the bin, he worked as a magician under the name Maître Carrefour. Made a living that way."

Pinky nods, and pulls out an index card from his pocket. "*Carrefour*, huh? We can put out an APB on that, so to speak. A magician. Got to be magicians' societies, professional associations, booking agents. Anything else?"

"Byron's retired — he's not performing anymore."

"So what *is* he doin'?"

"Diment didn't know. Last he heard, Byron said he was doing *real magic*." I bracket the phrase in the air with my index fingers.

"And what the hell is that? What's the difference between *magic* and *real magic?*"

"Diment couldn't really explain it, or maybe I couldn't understand. Byron went through the process of becoming a *houngan* — you know, a voodoo priest. And the faithful, including Diment, believe that the curtain between the natural and the supernatural, between the living and the dead, is porous. And that someone like Byron can more or less fuse with a *loa* and perform supernatural acts."

"Hunh. Thinka that. What else you got?"

"Byron sent postcards to Diment from time to time. The last one was from California."

"Whereabouts?"

"Point Arena."

"Doesn't sound like a big town. The witch doctor — he think Boudreaux lives there?"

I shrug. "Byron sent other postcards, but Diment threw them away when he got a new one. And he didn't pay attention to the postmarks. This was just the last one — and it came almost three years ago."

Pinky frowns, taps his pink fingers on the table. The fine white hair on the back of his hands catches the light. "So this is it?" he says. "Maître Carrefour. Real Magic. A postmark on a three-year-old card." Pinky shakes his head, looks at me. "For someone who spent the night in a coffin, you got fuck-all, buddy."

On the drive back to New Orleans, Pinky tries to soften his take on things. "We may get something out of the Carrefour thing. One thing you got going for you — at least far as we know — is that you know a lot about Byron, including his name, but he doesn't know he's even on your radar screen. Maybe he lives in this Point Arena. We can hop on that right away. Guy like that — he might just be arrogant enough to use his own name. Until we look, there's no way to know if he was just passing through or maybe he lived in this town for a while. Maybe long enough to leave tracks."

I'm so tired I can't stop yawning. "Maybe I should go to Point Arena."

"Maybe so," Pinky says.

Another huge yawn.

"Not restful, hunh?" Pinky said. "Sleeping in a coffin? I coulda told you that. You're probably all ripped up with cortisol."

"Cortisol?"

"Stress hormone." He taps the paper. "Read about it today. No good for you."

We roll along for a few more minutes.

"What'd it say on the postcard, anyway?" Pinky asks. "Besides this stuff about *real magic?*"

"It said: 'Finished with the castle. Doing real magic now.' "

"That's it? What castle?"

"I don't know. Diment didn't know, either."

"Hunh," Pinky says. "A castle. In California."

I'm semiconscious when it comes to me. It's like a bubble rising to the surface: Karl

Kavanaugh sitting across from me in a booth at the Peppermill in Vegas.

He's talking about the history of magic and how at one point, the center of magic relocated from Chicago to L.A. There was a club in L.A. The Magic Castle.

"Karl. It's Alex Callahan."

"Yeah, sure. How you doing? You back in town?"

"No. Actually, I'm in New Orleans. I'm just . . . following up on something."

"With the Gabler murders?"

"Right." For a moment I can't remember how much I told Kavanaugh. Did I tell him about the boys? I don't think so.

"How's that going?"

"I'm making progress," I tell him. "Reason I called — remember when you were telling me about the Magic Castle? Is that still in business?"

"Very much so. They have shows every weekend, different stages going simultaneously. Dinner and magic, that kind of thing. If you want to attend, I'd be happy to sponsor you."

"Is that necessary?"

"Well, it's a *club*. You can't just buy tickets. You have to be a member or the guest of a member. Or belong to the Society of American Magicians."

"I don't know about attending a show — but thanks for the offer. The thing is, the guy I'm looking for, the one who killed the Gabler twins — I think he might have worked there."

"*Really*. Got a name?"

"Maître Carrefour. His real name is Boudreaux."

"Carrefour. Boudreaux. Hmmmm." A pause. "No bells ringing, but that doesn't mean much. The L.A. scene is kind of its own thing, pretty insular. And I don't get over there much anymore."

"Do you know someone at the Castle I could talk to?"

"Sure. Let me think." A pause. "John DeLand, the curator, he'd be your best bet. Knows everything and everyone."

"Got a number?"

He gives it to me, then offers to call DeLand on my behalf. "Magicians can be a little . . . cliquish. There's a tendency to circle the wagons when someone starts asking questions about one of our own. If you'd like, I could grease the tracks . . . ?"

I'm in a borrowed cubicle in the back of Pinky's office in the French Quarter, checking my e-mail, when Kavanaugh gets back to me.

"John DeLand will be more than happy to talk to you. And yes, he remembers Carrefour — who worked at the Castle off and on for a couple of years."

"Great. Thanks! And DeLand — he's at this number you gave me?"

"Yes." A pause. "Although — if I could give you some advice . . . ?"

"Sure."

"Well, I don't know what your budget is, but if funds allow, it might be worth your while to go out to L.A."

"Oh?" Actually, I'd been thinking the same thing. If Boudreaux worked at the Castle on a regular basis, he must have lived somewhere. Must have had friends, a landlord, a life. Which meant footprints.

"Thing is," Kavanaugh says, "John's an awfully good source, but there'll be other magicians at the Castle who also knew Carrefour. John will be able to tell you who."

"Right."

"And then there's John himself."

"What do you mean?"

"Well . . ." A laugh. "John's simply never quite made it out of the nineteenth century. He's one of those older guys who shouts into the phone as if it's some kind of cups-and-wires contraption. You'd do much better to sit down with him. He's more . . . ah . . . forthcoming in person."

"Hunh."

"We magicians," Karl says, "we're at our best live and in person." A pause. "Now, isn't that a strange phrase, when you think about it?"

"I see what you mean," I tell Karl, although I'm not really paying attention. I'm tapping the keyboard to see what kind of flight I can get to L.A.

"Live! And in Person!" Karl intones in a hyped-up announcer's voice. "I mean, what's the alternative?"

chapter 41

The Magic Castle is a moldering Victorian mansion in the hills above Hollywood. And John DeLand looks right at home in it. His hair is white and wispy, his eyes pale blue and sharp. Half-glasses perch on his long nose. He's dressed in a shiny black suit with an old-fashioned cut and a vest with a watch fob. The word *waistcoat* comes to mind. The only anomalous note is the big blue digital watch with a velcro strap on his left wrist.

He meets me downstairs and takes me up a winding staircase to his office. "I've got just about an hour," he tells me, "although certainly we can talk more tomorrow. If I *can* talk, that is. I've got an appointment with the periodontist. He's promised to scour my gums into submission."

The door creaks open automatically when he speaks into a little brass grille: "Harry Houdini."

His office is straight out of Dickens: a cavernous space furnished with heavy Victorian antiques — lots of columns and curlicued wood and threadbare velvet. It's entirely cluttered, every surface covered: books, globes, crystal balls, cards, statues, skulls, plants, automata, crates, gadgets, papers, pamphlets, *objets* of every sort. Antique posters advertising various magic acts and magicians hang from every available patch of wall, with magic wands, jeweled scepters, and so on interspersed between them. Cats repose on the windowsills.

DeLand gestures toward a heavy carved wooden chair. "Not very comfy, but the felines don't like it, so you'll be spared the decorative dusting of cat hair."

He moves behind his huge black desk, which is two inches deep in paper, picking up a long-haired black cat from his chair before he sits down. He holds the cat in his arms and strokes her. "So you're here about Carrefour. And your interest, Karl tells me, is a murder case?"

"That's right. A series of murders."

"Oh, dear. And you think Carrefour is involved?"

"Yes."

He sits back in his chair and regards me with his pale blue eyes. "You don't say. And you're . . . what? A police detective? I only ask because we magicians are a kind of . . . oh . . . a brotherhood, I guess you'd say. If I'm to contribute to your effort to find Carrefour, I'd like to know to what end. And I'd like to know, as well, exactly how your inquiries brought you to the Magic Castle." He smiles his detached smile and strokes the cat, which purrs loudly.

"I'm not with the police," I start. "My interest is personal." As I tell him the compressed version of my story, DeLand's detached smile fades into a look of alarm.

"How terrible," he says, in a shaky voice. "I'm so very sorry. Of course I'll help you in any way I can." He picks up a black telephone. "Starting with a word to bookkeeping and the Society of Magicians. Obviously Carrefour was a member of SAM, as well as a member of the Castle. He'll have paid dues and literature will have been sent to him — we ought to have an address and telephone number."

When he's finished shouting instructions over the phone, he replaces the handset and strokes the cat. "Now, what can I tell you?"

"Why don't you just talk about Carrefour? Whatever you remember."

"I'm not certain how he came to perform here," DeLand starts. "Someone else might remember. Could be he came reputation in hand, already booked for a night or two. There's an equally good chance that he just . . . came to a show, and went on from there."

"What do you mean?"

"Magicians come to the Castle from everywhere — either as a destination, or just because they happen to be in town. The Castle is a kind of a pilgrimage site for magicians. We do have something like five thousand members."

"Really."

"Oh, yes. So, let's say a magician's in town and he comes to the Castle for an evening of magic. He wants to check out the competition, maybe pick up a new wrinkle for an effect, or maybe just show the wife or girlfriend a good time. Before the show — say, in the bar — or in the interval after dinner, or waiting in line for one of the performances — people take advantage of those times to perform. Show their stuff, you know. You'll see guys standing in the bar doing sleight of hand, or performing card or coin tricks while waiting in line. At times, someone will even pull off a rather elaborate illusion."

"So it's like an audition?"

"Well, it can be. It's one way to get your

foot in the door. And then . . . maybe a scheduled performer falls ill or has a conflict and a slot opens up in one of the rotations. The visiting magician might get a chance to fill in. After that, who knows?"

"So Carrefour ended up as a regular."

"Yes. And deservedly so. He's quite a gifted performer, brilliant stage presence. Really, everything he did was amazing. And, at first, very much in the tradition here."

"And what's that?"

"Well, obviously, we don't have the resources to stage the really big illusions — the sort of thing they do in Vegas. Most of those acts have specially built venues, just for the magician and his act. That allows for a good deal of technological gadgetry, elaborate trapdoors and substage tunnels and black lighting, not to mention wires and catwalks to enable levitation effects. Our stages are just . . . stages. There's a minimal use of lights and mirrors and gadgets and atmospheric distractions. Not only would our revenue not support it, we like to think of this as a virtue — that we present classical magic. Carrefour was no different from most of our performers, at least at first."

"And then?"

"Well, as time went on, he revamped his act. He reached back and began performing some of the tricks from earlier centuries, particularly from the Indian tradition. Amazing stuff, stunning effects . . . but . . ." He frowns, his hand lifting from the black cat and seesawing in the air.

"What?"

"Well, tastes have changed. His new act wasn't very popular."

"What do you mean? What tastes?"

"Tastes in what people want to see on the stage. They don't want to be terrified anymore. Amazed, baffled, delighted — but not horrified or scared out of their wits. And more to the point where Carrefour was concerned, people have lost their appetite for gore. His act, as it matured — was . . . well . . . it was quite *gory,* actually. Very much in the tradition, but . . ." The curator shrugs.

"You don't think people like gore? Hollywood would disagree."

The curator shrugs. "I concede the point. Spilled guts, gouts of blood, staggering body counts. *The Texas Chainsaw Massacre* kind of thing. And all of it terrifyingly realistic — but still . . ." He tilts his head to the side. "A movie is a movie. No matter how realistic, it's all been shot months ago and pieced together, and we all know that. It's been previewed and advertised, the stars have made their promo rounds. And *then* we see this product, and what we see is projected on a screen in two dimensions."

"Right. But even on the stage, you still know it's . . . *staged*."

"That's true, but it's quite another experience to see realistic violence in person, at close range, in real time. Even in the theater, there's a tendency to stylize violence. For one thing, it's very difficult to pull it off. Even a good fistfight — it's hard to make it look real. The truth is most people don't want to *see* violence that seems real. Good Lord, I was in Amsterdam once at some kind of arty theater and one of the actors dismembered a *plant*, ripped it to shreds on the stage — and I mean a potted *philodendron* — and some members of the audience were so shocked they walked out."

"Hunh."

"Spend a night at the Castle and go to the shows. You'll see that the performance venues are fairly small. Even the largest stage only seats a hundred or so. The magicians are right on top of the audience — as they need to be for close-up magic.

Some of Carrefour's illusions — good heavens — you were afraid of spatter. Like sitting ringside at a boxing match with a bleeder in the ring. Not the kind of thing popular with the ladies, no matter how carnivorous."

"But Carrefour was allowed to continue?"

"Well, before he revamped his act, he was very popular. His shows were jammed; he went straight onto our biggest stage. So even when he redid his act, there was some carryover. He was a tremendous performer. And although our public didn't much like his act as it evolved, there was a lot of support for what he was doing within the ranks of the Castle."

"Oh?"

"The effects he performed were famous within the history of magic, really storied illusions and, as I said, *brilliantly* done. Part of the Castle's *raison d'être,* if you will, is to preserve the history of magic as an art form. So it was nice to see some of these effects revived, if only as historical curiosities. It wasn't until one saw the performances that one realized how much tastes have changed. A century ago, the audience was quite bloodthirsty and no one would have batted an eye at any of what Carrefour did."

"That big a change."

"Lord, yes. Forget something as tame as a magic show which only *appeared* to shed blood. A century ago, bearbaiting and dog- and cock-fighting were hugely popular. Not to mention public executions. Lynchings. People simply *flocked.* Real blood? The more the better."

"But now it turns people off."

I nod, remembering Karl Kavanaugh commenting on this change in taste.

"Yes, even when they know it's an illusion. When this young magician David Blaine pulled his heart out of his chest on television — I mean, reached into his shirt and yanked out this bloody, dripping, grisly hunk of meat — the network wanted to cut the footage. And that was *televised.*"

"What kind of thing would Carrefour do?"

"Well, let's see. One of his standbys was the basket trick. An old, old trick, really ancient. Do you know it?"

I shake my head.

"Well, it's quite in the old tradition to put the magician's assistant in peril. You might see something stagy and antiseptic these days along that line: knives thrown around the pretty assistant, or a gadgety effect with the lady trapped or caged or sawn in half. No real sense of danger, though. This was not the case with the older tricks. The danger was emphasized. Everything possible was done to hype the peril to the assistant."

"I see."

"For tricks of the vintage Carrefour was working in, the magician would have had a child to assist him. Often, it was actually his son. We didn't get to the pretty girls until a bit later. Whether it's a pretty girl or a child, in both cases, the assistants are subservient to the magician and serve to reinforce his power. Really the advent of the female assistant represented a change in the dynamic. The magician and beautiful assistant are a kind of sexualized pair, really. With the young boy, you had instead a simulacrum of family life."

"Father-son."

"Exactly. The magician's power was that of a patriarch, although in some cases, it was more like a master-slave relationship or some would say god-human. One of the assistant's jobs, of course, is to serve as an agent of misdirection. You want to get the audience to look away from whatever you're doing, so the magician might toss a ball, say, to the assistant. The eyes will follow the ball — it's instinctive. As a source of misdirection, the scantily clad woman works well — it's also instinctive to look at such creatures — but she doesn't enlist empathy nearly as well as a child. She doesn't get the audience *on her side* the way a child does."

"I see what you mean."

"A child has other wonderful attributes as an assistant. He's small and can fit into smaller spaces. But mostly, he's far more vulnerable than a woman. Plus, he wears a mantle of innocence, so the audience never thinks of a child as in on it, so to speak, as part of the deception. You can't employ children now because of legal constraints, so Carrefour did the next best thing. He employed a young man — quite slight and youthful in appearance, but actually of legal age."

"Interesting. So, how did the act go?"

"The basket trick was only the finale of Carrefour's hour, mind you. There were many other effects and illusions. But in the basket trick itself, somewhere toward the end of the act, the boy blunders, does something clumsy with one of the props or acts defiantly.

"He's forced into the basket as a punishment by the master. Often the basket is placed on an openwork pedestal so the audience can see there's no trapdoor or anything of the sort, no way for the child to escape. So" — DeLand claps his hands together — "the boy's inside and the magician is carrying on with the rest of his act, but the boy won't shut up, just keeps whining and complaining. Finally, the magician loses his temper. He's in the midst of some effect requiring swords and he impulsively picks one up and thrusts it into the basket. The boy cries out — 'That really hurt! You really stabbed me!' — but this just enrages the magician further. With bloodcurdling screams emerging from the basket, the magician thrusts more swords into it, crisscrossing them in such a way that it seems no one inside could survive. He's in a fury, you see — interrupted in the midst of the ring trick or whatever. He returns to his act, greeting the screams of the boy with derision. 'Go ahead and scream, it won't help you. I'm not impressed. My Lord, what a baby.' The screams weaken, turn into moans, and then finally, there's silence.

"The audience is nervous. The magician heaves a sigh of relief and returns his full attention to his act — materializing rabbits, joining and separating rings, doing other tricks in his routine.

"The audience becomes concerned at the appearance of a pool of blood gathering beneath the basket. At their shouts — a plant is in the audience in case they don't do their job here — the magician stops what he's doing and crosses to the basket and sees the pool of blood. He yanks off the top of the basket and he's overcome with remorse. It takes a good actor to pull this off, mind you, but Carrefour *is* a good actor. He begins the process of removing the swords, a gingerly process with much hesitation and wincing and gritting of the teeth. Then the magician exhorts the audience to help him bring the assistant back to life."

The skin on my neck begins to crawl. I'm thinking of the detective from Big Sur, talking about the Ramirez twins. He was telling me that they'd put the pieces of the one kid back together, that the kid had been stabbed multiple times, *run through*.

And then I remember exactly what he said: *The kid was a pincushion.*

"You all right?" DeLand asks.

"Go ahead," I manage.

"Well, the thing about the basket trick — the swords are real, the thrusts hard. The trick works because the assistant has rehearsed how to squeeze his body here and there on cue and in sequence, so he's never touched. You can see why children are not permitted to perform such tricks nowadays. Like many of the old tricks, the basket trick *can* go wrong."

"Hunh."

"Some illusions are very dangerous. The basket trick relies on absolute adherence to a series of moves by two different individuals. There's no margin of error. Bullet catching is another risky one. It used to be a standard part of many acts, but it's quite dangerous. A famous magician died performing it in London in 1930 or so."

I'm only half listening as DeLand goes on. Boudreaux performed the sawing-the-lady-in-half illusion with the Gabler twins, the basket trick with the Ramirez twins. But what the Sandling boys told me didn't sound like preparation for either of these tricks.

"Penn and Teller," DeLand is saying, "do a simultaneous bullet catch — but Houdini, for instance, for all the different ways he put himself in harm's way, never caught bullets. His role model, Robert-Houdin, the very famous French magician of the mid-eighteenth century, performed the bullet catch quite famously in helping to quell an uprising in Algeria."

"Really?"

"Oh, yes. He was sent to Algeria by the French government because some Marabouts were fomenting an uprising, using simple bits of magic to stir up the locals. Robert-Houdin staged — in open air — a demonstration of his powers, and by extension the powers of the French — to show the locals, you know, whose magic was more powerful. The pièce de résistance of Robert-Houdin's demonstration occurred when he was challenged to a duel by one of the Marabouts. He caught the bullet fired at him in his teeth and then discharged his own still-loaded gun at the whitewashed wall of a building abutting the street where the duel took place. Upon the bullet's impact, the white wall was stained with a huge crimson splash of blood. That was the deal breaker for the Algerians. Robert-Houdin's French magic was more potent than the Marabouts' magic. The Algerians lost faith in the rabble-rousers and the resistance faded."

"The French government *hired* him?"

"Oh, there are more ancient and far more recent examples of governments hiring magicians. Our CIA, for instance, hired the magician John Mulholland to school spies in how to avoid detection. Mulholland did demonstrations, workshops, and he wrote a series of manuals for the Agency."

"Manuals?"

"On misdirection, sleight of hand, surprise."

"Really!"

"Think about it. What do spies do? It's all about illusion and deception. A spy appears to be something or someone he or she is not. A spy has to perform tasks in such a way as to remain undetected. What better skills to have for these tasks than sleight of hand and techniques of misdirection? If you can get the fellow to look the other way, or simply not to notice you . . ." He shrugs.

As interesting as this is, I want to return DeLand's attention to Carrefour. "So — the basket trick was dangerous."

"Yes. If the assistant didn't squirm about just in the perfect sequence — or the magician forgot the sequence, or had a muddy moment — the assistant could be killed." He stops, draws in a breath. "Good Lord, are you worried that your boys . . . ?"

"I think that Boudreaux might be using the boys in some kind of *act*."

"I do apologize for any . . . zeal . . . in

describing the effects. I wouldn't want my grandson to perform the basket trick."

I nod and DeLand continues. "Where was I?"

"The grief-stricken magician was pleading with the audience to bring the boy back to life."

"Right, yes. Then he does some chanting, something to concentrate his power. Finally, the magician is ready, he removes the top from the basket and *voilà!* — the boy climbs out, good as new."

"Hunh."

"It's a resurrection, you see, a person brought back from the dead. Really, this is the basis of an enormous number of tricks, a tradition that goes back as far as we can go in the history of magic. I suppose such tricks hearken back to the days when magicians were priests. Even Houdini's stunts, where he'd be lowered into the sea, manacled and in chains, would be classified as this type of effect. Or at least I'd argue that point."

"Really?"

"A symbolic, if not a real death. The lone figure, inviting death to take him, the crowd holding its breath in tandem with the submerged magician, waiting impossibly long minutes with no sight of him.

Would this be the time he went too far? Would this be the time death claimed him? And then, at last, the heroic resurfacing. That was received as a kind of miracle, a sort of resurrection."

"Resurrection or not, people didn't like Carrefour's basket trick?"

"No, they didn't. As I said, Carrefour is a gifted actor, and I'm afraid it was just too powerful. His rage, the blood, the screams — it was all too *real*. That was his entire problem. He scared people. Of course he did have his admirers."

"What admirers?"

DeLand frowns. "Hmmm. Let me think. I remember a little Thai fellow and a Russian woman. Olga something. There was a sheikh. A few Goth types — quite harmless really, but they do like blood." He sighs. "This was years ago and I don't remember names. Maybe somebody would. I could ask. Oh, except one: *Mertz*. I almost forgot Mertz — and he was Carrefour's biggest fan. A real devotee. I don't think he ever missed a night when Carrefour was on. And they usually left together, after the show. I only noticed because they were quite the odd couple."

"What do you mean?"

"Carrefour, you know, he's a tall fellow

and quite striking to look at. Mertz, on the other hand, is short and powerfully built, bald as an egg and almost as wide as he is tall. Rich as hell. Drove a Rolls. 'Course they were both Europeans, so that was a bond."

"What do you mean? Carrefour's real name is Byron Boudreaux, and he's not European. He's from Louisiana."

DeLand is shocked. "No. He's French."

I shake my head.

"You never knew *Carrefour* was a stage name?"

"Alain Carrefour — that was the only name I ever knew him by. Well, I'll be damned. I've been around the block a few times, even spent a couple of years in France. I never would have suspected. . . . I told you Carrefour was a gifted actor." He shakes his head. "Maybe Mertz is a gringo, too," he says, with a little laugh.

"Was Mertz a member of the Castle?"

The curator shakes his head. "I don't know. I can check. He didn't perform, but he may have been an associate member. Certainly, he was a regular. And he was quite serious about magic. And I don't think, by the way, that he was really an American unless he, too, was a brilliant actor. French or something. Maybe Belgian."

"How was he . . . serious about magic?"

"He collected rare books on the subject. Mostly about the old Indian rope trick. We talked about it a couple of times. He had some exceptional books in his collection. Things that were hard to find. And extremely expensive."

"The rope trick?"

"Ah, yes," DeLand says. "The legendary Indian rope trick. Marco Polo mentioned it in his journal — that's thirteenth century, but it's thought to be much older than that. Originated in China, probably, then brought to India on the Silk Road."

The watch on his wrist emits a series of sharp beeps, and he peers through his reading glasses to find the right button to turn it off. A sigh. "I have to go. My periodontist beckons."

DeLand stands. "Why don't you come back tonight?" he says. "You can take in the show if you like. I'll be back here in time to put together whatever info we have in the archives about Carrefour. Mertz, too, if we've got anything. I'll have it ready — you can pick it up."

DeLand's phone rings. It's his taxi. I follow him down the stairs. "And there's a fellow who knew Carrefour — he's on stage tonight: Kelly Mason. You might want to talk to him. He probably knew Mertz as well, because they had an interest in common."

"What was that?"

"The rope trick — Mason's written several articles about it and I believe Mertz allowed him access to his collection. So he might know where Mertz is, and then if you find Mertz . . ."

"Right," I tell him. "Look — Mr. DeLand . . ."

"Oh, please. *John.*"

"John. Look, I really, really appreciate your help. This information about Carrefour and Mertz and any addresses you might have — that would be just great. And I'd be very interested to talk to Kelly Mason."

"Happy to help," DeLand says. I've followed him down the steps and outside. His taxi waits in the oval drive. "I'll arrange a ticket for you," he says. "You can pick it up at the box office."

"What time?"

"Earliest show is at seven, but shall we say . . . eight? I'll meet you in the bar."

"Fine."

"I should warn you," DeLand says. "We

have a dress code. Suit and tie."

I lift my hand as the taxi rolls off, then watch the bright yellow car, now visible, now invisible, as it winds down the hill.

I'm thinking about Mertz as I get into my rental and head down the hill myself. I drive toward my hotel, which is way down Santa Monica near Venice, thinking about the whole idea of Boudreaux having *fans.*

And then it hits me. Boudreaux has fans, of course he has fans — and not just for performances at the Magic Castle.

I remember the medical examiner in Vegas telling me he thought Clara Gabler's body had been severed by a table saw, and how odd that had seemed to him because a chain saw would have done the job. Barry Chisworth — he sat across from me, mojito in hand, speculating about how hard it would have been to transport the table saw, a platform to hold it, and a power source to run it, all the way up to Conjure Canyon. The M.E. had been baffled. Why would anyone bother? Even when I puzzled it out — that the murderer went to all that trouble because the Gabler twins were killed in the course of a performance — I never gave a thought to a key element of any performance.

The audience.

Byron Boudreaux may have stopped performing magic in public. But he didn't stop performing. There would have been an audience on hand to see Clara Gabler sawn in half. A circle of spectators to witness the murders of Julio and Wilson Ramirez. Just as there will be an audience on hand to witness the spectacle when he murders my sons.

It must be that these hideous inversions of standard magic tricks are what Byron meant on his postcard to Diment, what he meant by the phrase *real magic*.

Do the members of this audience know that the illusions are not illusions? That lives are sacrificed in the course of the show? I think they do. I think they *must*. I think that's the point.

Mertz. *Mertz*. What had DeLand said about him? He was French or something and rich and he collected books about the rope trick.

The rope trick. What I know about the rope trick could be written on the back of a postage stamp: *It's something they used to do in India. They threw a rope into the air, and it hung there. Then they climbed it or something.*

And then I have a terrible sequence of thoughts. Mertz is Boudreaux's biggest fan. Mertz is obsessed with the rope trick. And what did the Sandling boys tell me about what they did in the "humongous house" before they escaped? They exercised. For hours, every day. They . . . climbed . . . ropes.

chapter 42

I drive to my hotel, a one-star joint down Santa Monica toward Venice. I check in, throw my stuff down, and take a look in the phone book under the heading *Magic*. I find two listings for bookstores specializing in books about magic and the occult.

The closest one is on Hollywood Boulevard, and it turns out to be the kind of place you have to ring a bell to enter. It's small, and crammed floor to ceiling with old books. That old-book smell, an amalgam of disintegrating paper and surface mold, pervades the air. The man who buzzed me in sits at a desk in the back, talking on the phone. He raises his hand to acknowledge my presence.

A central table holds bins of artwork and pamphlets, each poster or booklet protected by a plastic sleeve. I leaf through the pamphlets, most of them vintage booklets describing how to perform different illusions, while I wait for the man to finish his call.

A minute later, he joins me. He's young,

with long dark hair, wire-rimmed glasses, a gold hoop in one earlobe. "Help you with something?"

"I'm looking for a book about the rope trick."

"Are you a collector?"

"No, I just need something that describes it, talks a little about its history."

"Okay, I think I can find something." I follow him down a narrow aisle and watch him ascend a library ladder. He comes down with a battered paperback encased in a plastic sleeve. "This is a compilation of famous effects in the history of magic. The book itself is not in great shape, but it has a nice little chapter on the rope trick." He cocks his head, smiles. "Anything else?"

"One more thing. I'm looking for a guy. Used to live in L.A. Worked at the Magic Castle?"

"Okay."

"His stage name was Carrefour. Maître Carrefour."

"No." He shakes his head. "I don't think so."

"Or a guy named Mertz? European guy, maybe French. Collects books about the rope trick."

"Sorry." (Is it my imagination, or does he answer too quickly?) "But I'm just the hired help. It's my uncle's shop."

I know I'm being way too blunt. Normally I don't go head on like this. Normally I'd schmooze this guy, get him to like me, seduce him a little. That's how you get people to tell you things they shouldn't. I tell myself this, I give myself a little pep talk — but I can't summon the will to charm this guy. Maybe I'm all played out on the charm front.

"Could I get your uncle's telephone number? It's important. . . . Since this guy Mertz was a collector, and he lived here in L.A., this is exactly the kind of place he —"

"No," the kid says. He looks down at his hands, and once again I detect a slight hesitation before he answers me. "I'm sorry, but Uncle Frank's in Croatia." A pause. "Traveling. He doesn't have a phone."

"Hunh," I say. "When will he be back?"

"Couple of weeks."

"I guess just the book then," I tell him, sure from his body language that the kid is lying. He's heard of Mertz. I've done so many interviews I know the signs.

I follow him to the cash register, and he rings up the book ($9.25), then slides it into a paper bag. "Receipt in the bag?" he asks.

"That's fine. Let me ask you — you

know of any other bookstores or magic stores I might try? I really need to find this guy Carrefour."

This seems to relax him, the chance to pass the baton. "Sure — there's Magic Magic, over on Sunset. You might try there."

But Magic Magic turns out to be closed. The sign posts the weekday hours as ten until two. I'll have to return tomorrow.

I sit on the bed in my hotel room and read about the rope trick. The chapter is long and begins by describing how very old the trick is. The trick is mentioned in an offhanded way in the *Upanishads*. A bit later, chronologically, sacred Buddhist texts mention the rope trick as one of the entertainments performed in a (failed) attempt to raise a smile from the young prince who later became the Buddha — a boy who had never smiled in his entire life. The trick became so famous during the time of the British Raj that the wonder of it, and other such tricks, was considered a recruiting tool for enlistment in the British army. Indian officers were offered a year's pay as reward for finding a practitioner of the trick. In 1875, a magician's society in London offered a huge award to anyone who could perform the trick before an audience.

There's a long sequence about the trick's parallels with Hindu cosmogony, and also to the English folktale Jack and the Beanstalk and other stairway-to-heaven myths. There's even a Freudian take on the trick, focusing on the rope's unexpected rigidity.

And finally, I come to an excerpt from the 1898 edition of *The Lahore Civil and Military Gazette*:

> The conjuror took a large ball of rope, and after having attached one of the ends of the rope to his sack, which was lying on the ground, hurled the ball into the air with all his might. (In many versions, the ball repeatedly thumps back down to the ground before the conjuror succeeds.) Instead of falling back to the ground, the ball continued slowly to ascend, unrolling all the while until it disappeared high into the clouds. There was no house (or other structure) . . . where it might have fallen. . . . A large portion of its length remained rigid.
>
> The magician [then] ordered his son, who was his assistant, to climb the rope. Seizing the rope in his hands, the

little boy climbed . . . with the agility of a monkey. He grew smaller and smaller until he disappeared into the clouds as the ball had done. The conjuror then ceased to occupy himself with the rope and did several minor tricks. After a little while he told the audience that he required the services of his son and called up to him to climb down. The voice of the little boy replied from above that he did not want to come down. After having tried persuasion, the magician became angry and ordered his son to descend under penalty of death. Having again received a negative answer, the man, furious, took a large knife in his teeth and climbed up the rope and disappeared . . . in the clouds.

Suddenly a cry rang out and to the horror of the spectators, drops of blood began to fall from the place where the magician had disappeared into the sky. Then the little boy fell to earth, cut into pieces: first his legs, then his body, then his head. As soon as the boy's head touched the ground, the magician slid down the rope with his knife stuck in his belt. (In many accounts the magician is, at this point, inconsolably sad.

> "Oh what have I done," etc.)
>
> Without undue haste [the magician then] picked up the parts of the child's body and put them under a piece of cloth [atop a basket]. . . . He gathered together his magician's paraphernalia (often performing a ritual or muttering magic incantations), drew aside the cloth [from the basket] and (*mirabile dictu!*) the little boy [emerged] . . . perfectly intact.

A subsequent essay explains how the trick was thought to have been accomplished. It was always performed in rugged terrain, with a braided catgut cord or cable strung between two promontories. Platforms were thought to be erected on either side from which unseen assistants could pull on the cross support and thus hold the rope rigid. An acrobat or rope walker would wait above, in the mist and out of sight. When the rope was thrown, its weighted end would loop it around the cable. The assistant would walk out, and secure it. Then with the help of an assistant on the opposing platform, the rope would be pulled tight. The trick was always performed at dusk or dawn and in a location where fog was common, so as to obscure the area where the rope, and then the child, and later the magician, disappeared. If the nature didn't cooperate by producing fog or mist, smudge pots or braziers were employed.

As to the rest of it, opinions varied. Some thought the audience was subjected to mass hypnosis or that hashish and opium were aerosolized in the fires common at such performances — the hallucinatory air pushed out toward the audience by the vigorous salaaming of the magician. Some thought the performance venues were meticulously chosen so that at a particular point in the performance, the sunlight would blind the audience. Some thought the bloody parts of the child were actually pieces of a dismembered monkey, shaved of fur, the face smeared with blood and obscured by a turban. Some thought the pieces thrown down were parts of a wax effigy, ingeniously identical to the child assistant. In these cases, the child was thought to descend the rope hidden in the magician's loose robes.

One historian held forth on the origins of magic, in "the tabernacles of ancient religions." These were faiths in which sacrifice, even human sacrifice, were commonplace, part of the liturgy. "And what is sacrifice but a ritual in which the forces of destruction, those that cause death, are transformed into the forces of life and creation?"

According to this historian, the "magic" that we see on stage is a reenactment of these ancient religious rites. The defiance of natural laws embodied in the most famous effects (levitation, dematerialization, etc.) are restagings of ancient religious miracles — and so remain mysterious and powerful even after they have been rendered safe.

Gods, he went on to say, have supernormal abilities — it's one of the things that define them. The Buddha, while not exactly a god, often demonstrated his perfection by floating yards above the earth. The god of Abraham commanded nature. Not only was he capable of producing a voice in a whirlwind, or the spontaneous combustion of a bush, he could part the waters of a sea. Jesus of Nazareth demonstrated his power by multiplying loaves, by walking on water, by healing the sick and raising the dead.

As to the rope trick, in the course of its performance a boy dies and is later restored to life. Accordingly, it represents the most profound of these sacred reenactments.

And then the expert drily opined that the reason no one accepted Lord Northbrook's challenge — the offer of ten thousand pounds sterling (a fortune in 1875) to anyone who could perform the rope trick — was that the "key ingredient to the trick is a set of identical twins, and such are hard to come by. The secret is of course quite simple: one of the twins is sacrificed in the course of the proceedings."

I knew . . . of course I knew. I'd figured it out long ago, out in the Red Rock Canyon. Clara Gabler was killed on stage. Carla was produced, alive and whole and no doubt smiling wide to display her newly whitened teeth. And then, when the performance was over and the audience had dispersed, Carla was disposed of with one efficient shot. Ditto the Ramirez twins.

After these performances, the surviving twin became redundant, a nuisance and a danger. In the case of the Ramirez twins, Byron Boudreaux had planned it well. He'd undoubtedly helped Charley Vermillion petition his way out of Port Sulfur, and then set him up to take the fall for the murder of the Ramirez boys. I'm sure Boudreaux located the cabin near Big Sur, then provisioned it for Vermillion. After the performance in which the Ramirez boys were killed,

Boudreaux provided the cyanide capsule to Charley. Who knows what he told him it was. And then he tipped off the police.

I *knew*, yes, but I was guessing. To read an expert opinion, written in the detached, slightly dated prose of 1952 — before I was born — just about levels me.

I sit there for a minute, my heart thudding with dread. *I've got to find them.*

I plug *Mertz* into the Anywho website and come up with half a dozen listings in the L.A. area. But after checking them out, it's clear none of them is the man I'm looking for.

I call Mary McCafferty and ask for her advice. She found Emma Sandling; maybe she can locate Mertz. McCafferty's sorry, she's heading out for a wedding, but gives me the names and telephone numbers of two "information brokers" in L.A.

"And what do I tell them?"

"All you have is the last name? Mertz?"

"That. And that he's a foreigner."

"Tell them to find out if he has an unlisted telephone number. Also, they could try the court records. Maybe he owned a house or something."

I contact the broker. He promises to get back to me in the morning. And then there seems to be nothing left to do but hit the Yellow Pages, look up "magician," and start calling. It feels like the gerbil wheel again, but until it's time to go to the Magic Castle, I can't think of anything else to do.

I spend three hours on the phone. Mostly, I get answering machines. Of the few magicians I actually speak to, three remember Carrefour, all of them from seeing him perform at the Castle. None of them knew him personally, or can give me any information about where he lived, his friends, or whereabouts. They have never heard of "Byron Boudreaux" and knew him only as Carrefour, Maître Carrefour, sometimes Doctor Carrefour, a man who spoke English, but with an accent.

Time to go. I put on a clean shirt, and a tie, and head for the Castle, anxious to see DeLand and Kelly Mason, the magician who knew both Carrefour and Mertz.

The sky is full of clouds, and the Castle, a brooding structure worthy of a gothic novel, has a menacing look as I drive up the hill. But it's a sort of faux menace. Up close, the Castle has well-tended landscaping, well-dressed guests, and valet parking. I retrieve my ticket from the box office, where I'm given a schedule of performances, then pointed in the direction of an ornate door and told what to do. Which is to speak the words "open, sesame" to the red-eyed owl perched in the center of the door. The door swings open.

The whole place is like that — hokey and charming by turns, just the thing for a slightly offbeat date or an adventurous evening with one's mother. Contributing to the somewhat old-fashioned feel of the place is the fact that everyone's dressed up — an anomaly in this casual town. I make my way to the crowded bar, which reminds me of a nice English pub with its etched and stained glass, and fight through toward the bartender. The crowd is dense and convivial, with constant eruptions of laughter. I find a tiny table against the back wall. True to DeLand's promise, I see at least a half-dozen guys with cards in their hands, either doing tricks or in some cases explaining them. In the ten minutes before DeLand arrives, it becomes clear to me that at least half of the people around me are magicians.

DeLand has to speak to at least a dozen of them before he reaches me. Finally he sits down and slides a manilla envelope my way. "I don't know that this will be much help to you. There's an address and a telephone, some kind of tax ID number — although not a social security number. It's all probably useless, I realize. Remember, you're talking to a man who was persuaded the fellow was French. But I also checked on Mertz. He was an associate member of the Castle. Lived in Beverly Hills. The address is in there."

A woman dressed in pink satin delivers a drink. "Thanks, Sally," DeLand says, pressing a bill into her hand. "How'd you guess I wanted a drink?"

She chirps a warbly little birdsong, which no one but me seems to find remarkable, then retreats with a smile.

"Cheers," DeLand says, raising his glass. "I can't stay, actually. I'll take a look round and see if there's anyone you should especially talk to, and if so, I'll bring him your way. You'll want to catch Kelly's show at nine. He's performing in the Parlour. You can talk to him after." He gets to his feet and drains his glass. "If you're going to eat," he tells me, "the beef is quite good." He sets his glass down, and heads for the door.

Fifteen minutes later, he's only made it halfway there. I head for a quiet area to call in the addresses and telephone numbers in the packet to the information broker. Although I somehow doubt that Carrefour left a forwarding address.

"He scared me." I'm talking to Kelly Mason, in his tiny dressing room, after the show.

"Carrefour?"

"No. His act was a little gruesome, but he seemed a good enough guy. Luc Mertz — he's the one who scared me. He lived in this mansion —"

"You went there?"

"Yeah. He invited me. A Spanish-style place in Beverly Hills. But — I don't know. We had this interest in common, but . . ." Mason wears stage makeup and it exaggerates his expressions, so that now he seems the very picture of a man perplexed. "I couldn't talk to him. Maybe it was the language thing. Or maybe it was the obvious income disparity. He had stuff . . . I couldn't believe it. As a scholar, it was really a privilege to see some of the old posters and documents, and he was quite generous about letting me photograph them, even publish them. But the whole time I was there, I felt . . . uncomfortable. When he invited me back, I just bailed on it. As my hippie parents would put it, the vibes were bad."

* * *

I'm tired by the time I get back to my hotel, and when I get through the door, I find that someone's been there before me. The lamp and telephone are gone from the end table next to the bed, replaced by a display of Mercury dimes arranged in the shape of a cross. Above the top of the cross is something utterly unexpected — a sugary white marshmallow bird, an Eastertime confection. What do they call them?

Peeps.

A white Peep. And a cross.

I don't get it, at first. And then I do. Diment's ugly face flashes in front of me. He's pointing to the postmark on the card from Point Arena. *"For vaudoo people, this a most important day. Sacred to the Marassa. This is why Byron sends the card that day. August 10. You might say . . . vaudoo Easter."*

So now I know: who, what, when, why, and how. Byron Boudreaux is Who, and what he's going to do, what he wants to do, is to kill the boys — my boys, one with a knife, the other with a gun. It will happen four days from now in a performance of "real magic" that amounts to a kind of religious ceremony. I know all about it now. Who, what, when, why, and how.

I just don't know where.

chapter 43

There are dozens of ways Boudreaux could have learned I was on to him, but the fact that he knew where I was staying narrows the field of potential sources to people in L.A. Because no one else knows I'm here.

Maybe it was the kid at the bookstore, or one of the magicians I spoke to at the Castle. I left the hotel number when I placed all the calls to the Yellow Pages magicians, so that if they called back, they wouldn't have to make a long-distance call to my cell.

It doesn't matter. Byron found me and he let me know about it, got right in my face. It's Shoffler's smirk factor — big-time.

In some ways his intrusion is good news. It means that he's breaking cover. It means he wants to play. Maybe he'll slip up and I'll find him.

But I can't just sit around and wait for Byron and Mertz to come after me. *Four days.*

In the morning, I have an appointment

with the information broker. I park near his office in a down-at-heels neighborhood near Mann's Chinese Theatre. I make sure to lock the car, given the sketchy neighborhood. Tourists crouch on the various squares of concrete, fitting their hands into the imprints made by Arnold or Clint or Julia. Something about the way they pose and joke and smile for the camera depresses me. They're tourists, having fun. I guess it reminds me of the day the kids and I went to the Renaissance Faire.

"Got your phone call," the broker tells me. He shakes his head. "Carrefour was a complete dead-end. Sublet everything, leased his car. The tax ID was a fake, checked back to some retiree in Iowa. Your guy is a ghost. Had every document you need to survive in the information age, but none of it was legit. I checked the Boudreaux name, too. Got nothing. As for this guy Mertz, I did a little better."

"The house in Beverly Hills?"

"Barrymore Drive. A nice place. Mertz *was* renting it, but he left last year."

"Is there a forwarding address?"

"P.O. box. But he closed that six months ago."

I wasn't really expecting much, but even so, it's another dead end. And it's almost more than I can stand. I can't afford any more culs-de-sac; I can't spare a minute. A bead of sweat crawls down my spine. As I get to my feet, I reach for my wallet to settle up with the broker.

"Hold on," he says. "I did find something that might interest you."

"What?"

"Doing the courthouse search, I stumbled on something. They got it computerized now, you know? I was looking to see if the guy paid property taxes in Beverly Hills — which he didn't — but his name popped up in a court case."

"What kind of case?"

The broker leans toward me. "Customs. They seized some videos from Mertz and he sued to get them back."

"What kind of videos?"

The broker shrugs. "I don't know. But I copied the filing. Me — I can't get to it until tomorrow. But if you're in a hurry, you could just follow up on your own."

The name of the customs officer who testified in the Mertz case is Michael Aguilar. At the time he worked at LAX; and he still does.

I'm about a block from my car when he finally comes to the phone. He tells me he gets off his shift at noon. "So if you want to talk then, I'm down with that." He pauses. "Damn it. My daughter must have taken my cell phone. Tell you what — there's a bar in the concourse at TBI. We could meet there."

"TBI?"

"International terminal. *Tom Bradley* International Terminal."

"I'll be there. Say twelve-fifteen?"

"Perfect."

I want to check my messages at the hotel, maybe give Shoffler a call. See if he has any advice.

I unlock the car. There's a brochure on the driver's seat. At first I just pick it up and put it on the dash, but then it comes to me: *I locked the car.*

On the front of the brochure, a large infinity logo seems to float over the words HOLLYWOOD FOREVER. The front fold also displays a photo of an obelisk near a lake and four oval cameos of old movie stars. (I recognize Rudolph Valentino and Jayne Mansfield.)

I unfold the brochure and find that the interior is a map — street names and roads, lakes and trees — the map of a cemetery. Not far from the entrance, off to the left on Memorial Lane, two little stickers have been pasted: twin golden angels, side by side.

My hands are shaking and my head screams with unanswerable questions. A map of a *cemetery?* Does this mean my boys are dead?

I start the car and hang a u-turn, earning long bleats of displeasure from several drivers. I know about this cemetery. I know where it is — down Santa Monica in a gritty neighborhood near Plummer Park, the part of L.A. with a concentration of Russians.

We did a piece on Russian organized crime in the U.S. and shot some footage in this part of L.A. And sure enough, soon I'm passing storefronts with Cyrillic lettering. Stopped at a light, I roll down my window and call out to a pedestrian.

"Excuse me? Can you tell me where the cemetery is — you know, Hollywood Forever?"

The man turns to me, smiles. "Sure, buddy," he says, his voice thick with a Russian accent, "one hundred percent. Ten blocks down on your right. You'll see it."

One hundred percent. I remember the phrase from when we did the piece. It's what Russian émigrés say when they're sure of something.

Right now, I'm not sure . . . of anything. I was so certain that August 10 was it. . . .

But now . . . Hollywood Forever.

I'm terrified.

I remember seeing Diane or Barbara interview the young entrepreneur who bought the cemetery and rescued it from bankruptcy. The last resting place of many Hollywood greats — Cecil B. DeMille! Rudolph Valentino! Jayne Mansfield! Douglas Fairbanks (junior and senior) — had fallen on hard times. Then it was bought, renamed, and refurbished — for tourists as much as for the dead. As I recall, it's still a working cemetery — one of its specialties being filmed tributes, archived on site and available for viewing, so that after visiting the earthly remains, family and friends can also watch films starring the deceased.

I drive in through the gates. It's clear from the Russian and Latino graves that the changing demographics of the neighborhood are represented here. When I seem to be in the area marked by the angels, I park by the side of the road and get out of my car.

Nestled against a stone wall are the graves of children. Displays of toys, bronzed baby shoes, photographs, statuary of angels, heartbreaking testimonials of love and loss, crowd every tiny gravesite. I stumble past them, searching for I don't know what, until I reach the end of the row. And there — on a bare patch of earth, two plastic horses ridden by two plastic knights face each other, lances drawn. Looking on are two identical blond-haired Fisher-Price figures, their painted faces locked in perpetual grins.

For a moment, I'm paralyzed and then I'm running toward my car. It takes me a while, but eventually I persuade a woman who works at the cemetery administration building to accompany me back to the children's graves. We ride in her car, a somber black Mercedes. She is so used to talking to the distraught that my agitation doesn't seem to faze her. Periodically, she places a reassuring hand on my arm.

At the site where the plastic knights face off, she uses her cell phone to call the administrative center. Then — while fixing me with sympathetic eyes — she recites the number of the plot and its coordinates. "Call me back with the status on this, okay? I'd like to know the identity of the interred — date of interment, responsible party, whatever you've got. Great."

We stand there, waiting. "There's supposed to be a stone," she tells me. "But sometimes that takes a while."

I can't say a word. To her credit, she gives my arm a squeeze and lets it go at that. We wait. She seems to be studying the cloud patterns. I can't take my eyes off the plastic knights, the Fisher-Price figures, the raw earth.

Her phone rings, a discreet chirp. She turns away from me as she talks.

"No?" she says in a hushed voice. "You're kidding. Oh, God, people are something, huh?"

She puts the phone back in the holster on her hip and looks at me, a tiny frown marring her serene expression. "This is somebody's idea of a bad joke," she tells me, bending down to scoop up the toys from the dirt. "There's no one buried here. This is one of six plots that we've taken off the market. We're putting in a fountain here, for the little folks' area." She cocks her head, looks at me, puts her hand on my arm. "Look, it's a big place, it's easy to get confused. This isn't the only location where children are buried. If there's someone in particular you're looking for, you should go to the graves registration office. It's in administration, where you found me. Okay? I'll give you a ride."

She starts to walk off toward the car and I fall in step next to her. We both hear it at the same time: the crystalline notes of a flute. It's a haunting and beautiful sound.

"Isn't that pretty," she says as we turn in unison to look for the source of the music. "I didn't know there were any ceremonies this morning."

And then I see him — leaning casually against a gravestone not thirty feet from me. He's wearing khakis, a white shirt. He holds the flute to his lips.

"Hey!" the woman protests as I take off after him, but I'm gone, running between gravestones, crashing past startled cemetery visitors. I ran the four hundred in high school and although I'm out of shape, I'm still fast — and I'm gaining on him. He's heading toward a small lake, the grounds around it beautifully landscaped with trees and shrubs, interspersed with family mausoleums. The area provides so many places to hide that I lose him a couple of times — but each time he pipes a tune and then emerges from behind a tree or gravestone.

My lungs are burning, my quadriceps screaming by the time I see him run onto a little causeway that leads to an island in the middle of the lake. I accelerate: it's a dead end for him. I can practically feel it, his body under me when I launch myself and take him down.

We're running alongside the large mausoleum on the island and I'm so close that I can see what brand of shoe he's wearing — Nikes. He reaches the end of the structure and turns the corner. I'm seconds behind him, and yet when I turn . . . impossibly, he's not there. He's vanished.

chapter 44

I can't believe my eyes and yet . . . he's gone. I spend the next forty-five minutes searching — for him at first, and then for how he did it. Initially, I scan the landscape, thinking I'll catch sight of him again, that he's toying with me, like before. It doesn't happen. Then I explore the mausoleum and all the surroundings — the trees, the shrubs, the gravestones. I even stand at the lakeside and look into the water. I search for any place he could have hidden himself, even for a moment, trying to figure out how he could have pulled off his vanishing act. But I find nothing.

I approach other visitors to the island and its surroundings. Many of them saw The Piper, heard his flute, even saw me chasing him — but no one saw where he went. No one saw him disappear.

I don't believe that, of course. I know he didn't disappear. It was a trick, an illusion. He left the Hollywood Forever brochure in my car; he knew I'd be coming to the cemetery. He had plenty of time to make any kind of arrangements he wanted to in advance. He set up the display with the knights and the toys, waited for me to look at it, then led me on a chase. He knew where I'd go, because he was leading. But still — how did he do it? I can't find anything — *anything* — that would have enabled him to vanish like that. But he's a magician, after all.

Given a day or a week, maybe I could figure out how he did it, but I don't have time. I'm still shaking my head when I drive out of the cemetery and head for LAX.

Mike Aguilar is a laid-back Chicano who doesn't hold it against me that I'm fifteen minutes late.

"The traffic here, man?" He shakes his head. "You try to keep too locked on to a schedule, you make yourself crazy."

The bartender brings us a couple of Bohemias, chips, and salsa.

"So you're interested in this guy Mertz," Aguilar says. "Matter of fact, he's an innarestin' guy. I'm not surprised somebody wants to take a look at the man."

"I understand you confiscated some videos from him and he sued to get them back."

Aguilar shakes his head. "He sued all

right, but we didn't take them off him. We took the videos off an employee of his, a Japanese photographer who was coming to the U.S. from Croatia or some damn place. The videos are tucked into bogus slipcases, y'know? I think one of them was *The Lion King*. That's what made me take a look. I thought it was probably pornography, right? Because this guy didn't look like he was into kiddie stuff."

"So what happened?"

"We screened a couple of minutes of each video, and then we seized them."

"So it *was* pornography."

"No. It was worse than that. By community standards — and I don't care if we're talking about L.A. or Fargo — those videos should have been burned."

"But —"

"What it was . . . Mertz paid this guy to go around, making videos in places like Bosnia, Albania, Sierra Leone. So what you had were people being tortured and killed — on camera, real time! It was like a snuff flick, but without the sex. No politics, no context. Just ninety minutes of people dying in close-up. The impression I got: this guy went from detention camps to makeshift prisons, paying bribes and directing the action."

"And the judge let him keep that?"

Aguilar nods. "Yeah. Said it was art."

"And that was it? No investigation?"

The customs agent gives a hopeless shrug. "Nothing we could do. Mertz's lawyers were all over the case as soon as we grabbed the videos. We had the initial intake interview with the photographer, and that was it."

"Did he tell you anything?"

"Not much. The only thing I got out of it was that it wasn't just Mertz. It was like there was a club or something."

"What kind of club?" I ask.

The customs agent shakes his head. "I don't know. The photographer was going nuts when I grabbed the videos. So he started throwing out names, yelling — the people he works for are going to have my job. Mertz was one of the names he threw out. But there were others. A sheikh. Some Russian oil guy. People like that." He rubs his thumb and forefinger together. "Big bucks," he says. "Fingers in a lot of pies."

I press Aguilar for the names.

"Sorry, man, I just don't remember."

"What about that interview — you have a tape?"

He shakes his head. "Nah, we lost the case, right? Those tapes get purged."

"One more thing. What nationality is Mertz? French?"

Aguilar shakes his head. "Belgian."

I get an idea, stuck in traffic on Sepulveda. Maybe I can make Mertz come to me.

I catch John DeLand as he's leaving the Castle for lunch. "Just a quick question."

"Sure."

"This guy Mertz — he collects stuff about the rope trick. Is there a particular book he'd want?"

"Something he'd really covet as a collector? Let me think." He thinks for a minute, but then shakes his head. "You know, I really should ask Kelly. Let me see if I can get him."

DeLand puts the question to Kelly Mason, shouting into the phone. Then he's writing something down. "Can you spell that? Okay. Thanks, Kelly. Okay. Okay."

DeLand turns to me. "There is something, but Kelly says to warn you — he's never seen a copy."

"What's the book?"

DeLand looks at his note. "*The Autobiographical Memoirs of the Emperor Jahangueir.*"

"Could you spell that?"

Instead, he hands me his note.

"In case you can't decipher my hen scratch, the book was written in the seventeenth century," DeLand says, "but the edition Mertz is after is a translation by an Englishman, name of David Price. Published in 1829. According to Kelly, it contains one of the most complete descriptions of the rope trick that has ever been reported."

"How much would something like that go for?"

He thinks for a moment. "Rough guess? Hmmmmm. It's rare, but there's not that much market. Copperfield might bid for his museum, so that would drive it up a bit. Something of that vintage, that difficult to find? I should think Mertz might pay five thousand for it and be happy with that."

"I owe you a drink."

"I see where you're going, Alex," he says. "Be careful."

It takes me a few minutes to establish an e-mail account at Yahoo! under a name I pick out of the phone book, Daniel Helwig. I execute a quick Google search to come up with the shortlist of dealers who specialize in rare books about magic, then fire off an e-mail to the group.

Using the pseudonym, I offer a first edition of the *Jahangueir* for five thousand dollars, but note that the book will only be available for two days. After that, "Daniel" writes, he'll be leaving for an extended stay abroad — which is why he's selling the book. To make that stay even more extended.

With the e-mail on its way, there is nothing for me to do but bide my time — and in a burst of optimism, buy a gun.

Liz hates guns, hates the very idea of them — she never let the kids have toy guns, although her distaste obviously doesn't extend to swords. She grounded Sean one day when he playfully shot at her using a banana. Because the idea that I owned a gun was driving her crazy, I got rid of the old British Bulldog revolver my grandfather gave me. Gave it to one of my cousins. *His* wife belongs to the NRA.

Grandpa taught me to shoot and how to care for a gun. He didn't hunt, but he lived in the country, way up in northern Wisconsin, and despite opposition from my grandmother, he was of the opinion that everybody ought to know how to handle "a firearm," as he put it.

I stop by an ATM and then head for

Plummer Park. I went right by it on my way to the cemetery, so I find it without any trouble — a leafy green spot in the midst of the concrete city. It was a little more hard-edged two years ago, when we were here filming on the Russian mob, but I still think I can do business. Walking around, I see that the place remains a hangout for Russian émigrés, playing chess and schmoozing and arguing under the park's trees. From the whispered consultations and the occasional coat pulled open to display something, I can see that it's also still a marketplace of sorts, the right place to go if you want to buy a used Rolex, a hot Mercedes . . . or a gun.

I walk by the tennis courts where two Latino kids belt the ball back and forth with unbelievable power.

I sit down on a bench where half of the graffiti scratched into the green paint is in Cyrillic letters. Ten minutes later, a kid with big baggy pants slings himself down on the bench next to me. He wears a leather jacket, despite the heat, and he lights up a cigarette, then leans toward me: "You want something, man?"

"Maybe."

"Smack or crack?"

"I want a gun."

He shrugs. "Give me a minute." His hands are covered with tattoos, and I can see the tendrils of several extending above his collar as well. The tattoos are crude, the do-it-yourself kind you get in prison. He holds up a finger. "Cash money. Three hundred bucks."

I give him a noncommittal nod. "If it's right. I want a forty-five."

He comes back five minutes later carrying a Burger King bag. He looks a little nervous.

"Don't worry," I tell him, "I'm not a cop."

He laughs. "I don't give a shit about that," he says. "I'm flying back to Moscow end of the week anyway. I get busted? — all that happens, they deport me." He smirks. "Maybe I get a window seat."

I look inside the bag. It's a .38, not a .45, a fact I point out to the kid. I pull out the clip. "And it's only got three bullets."

He shrugs again. "You're welcome to shop around. This is what I got, one hundred percent. Take it or leave it."

I take it.

And now there's really nothing for me to do but check and recheck my e-mail and messages, waiting for a response. It's a long night. I finally get a bite at 9:22 in the morning.

A dealer in San Francisco has a client who is interested. Depending on the book's condition, cost is not an issue.

I reply with an e-mail of my own, seeking the client's name and address. *I can send the book for his examination. He could have it by tomorrow morning.*

But, no. The dealer is unwilling to give up the information, undoubtedly fearing that he'll lose his commission on the book. *If you'll send the book to me,* the dealer writes, *I can show it to my client in the afternoon. Naturally, I'll reimburse you for the cost of shipping and insurance.*

But it's impossible. There *is* no book. Nor, for that matter, is there any guarantee that the prospective buyer is Luc Mertz. Even so, it's the only lead — and the only plan — that I have.

I think about flying to San Francisco to meet with the dealer, but . . . it's not going to work. Without a book to look at, the dealer's not going to listen to anything I've got to say.

Which leaves the information broker. Because one thing is certain. The dealer — qjwynn@coastal.com — must have contacted his client after learning of the book's supposed availability. So they must have spoken to one another.

I call the broker, who confirms that he can find out who the dealer called the day before — but not until the end of the phone company's billing cycle. "Until they collate the data, I can't get at it," he explains.

Frustrated, I telephone a friend who knows a lot about databases. A friend from my college days, Chaz designs computer simulations — war games — for the Pentagon. But as it turns out, he doesn't have a clue as to how I can get a list of the bookdealer's phone calls. "And, anyway," he says, "how do you know he phoned him? Maybe he sent him an e-mail."

Good point. "So how do I get into his e-mail?"

Chaz thinks about it. "You know his user ID?"

"Yeah."

"Then all you need is his password."

"And how do I get that?"

"Depends. If he's got an e-mail program that lets him use unencrypted passwords, you could download an automated dictionary word list — and let it roll. But that could take you days, and you'd probably be caught."

"Why?"

"Because if they've got intruder detection on (and they probably would), you'd be beeping the system console every three seconds and time-stamping your IP address to the file server error log."

"Which is not good."

"You'd probably be arrested." Chaz pauses. "Of course," he says, "you could always try to guess it."

"Guess it?"

"The password," he says. "Nine out of ten people — almost everyone — uses the same passwords."

"Like what?" I ask him.

"*Password*. That's the most common. And *changeme* — that's big, too. So is *changethis*. And the names of pets. Does he have a dog?"

"I don't know," I tell him. "He might."

"Try *Brownie* and *Blackie*. *Jack*."

"Get outta here. I'm not gonna try *Brownie*."

"Then don't. So what's he do for a living? I'm telling you — guessing passwords is not rocket science."

"He's a bookseller. Mostly books about magic."

"Try *Houdini*. Like that."

And so I do. I try them all, including *Brownie*. When none of them works, I try the names of magicians mentioned in the books I've read about magic.

blackstone
kalang
thurston
kellar
copperfield
siegfriedandroy
siegfried&roy
siegfriedundroy
blaine
maskelyne
sorcar
lanceburton
penn&teller
pennandteller
johndeland
karlkavanaugh

Zilch. I try a different tack:

abracadabra
opensesame
sesame
hocuspocus
pocushocus

Immediately, the page opens.

Going to the dealer's inbox, I see a

dozen e-mails from the day before. Among them is one from *lxmertz@sequoia.net*.

> I'm interested, of course, but I'll have to see the book first. Are you sure the offer is genuine?

I read it, and I read it again. But that's it. There's nothing more to be gotten from it. Switching from the bookdealer's account to *sequoia.net*, I work for an hour, trying to crack Mertz's password — but it's no use. The Belgian is too clever to use anything someone could guess.

Then it occurs to me: *sequoia.net* is a business address of some kind. Using the Anywho search engine, I take a look, first for *Sequoia Net* and then for *Sequoia Networks*, and then for *Sequoia Enterprises* and so on, down the list of generic corporate names. I'm guessing the company is somewhere in California. (Otherwise, the dealer would probably not have promised to show the book to his client the next afternoon.)

And there it is:

> Sequoia Solutions, Ltd.
> 11224 Fish Rock Rd.
> Suite 210
> Anchor Bay, CA

I pop over to MapQuest and ask for driving directions and a map. I copy the directions on the hotel's pad, and take note from the map that Anchor Bay looks to be only a few miles from Point Arena — where Byron's postcard to Diment was mailed. Eureka — where the Sandling boys escaped at the shopping mall — isn't that far, either. I think it's possible that Byron and the Sandling boys were headed for Mertz's at the time.

It's possible the connections I'm making are hopeful and tenuous. Maybe Mertz simply has business concerns in northern California and doesn't live here at all. Maybe Mertz and Boudreaux parted ways long ago. Maybe Boudreaux is still here in L.A. Maybe it's all smoke, as Shoffler would say.

But I don't think so.

It's five hundred forty-five miles from L.A to Anchor Bay. A very long drive. If I can get a flight anytime in the next couple of hours, I should fly to San Francisco and drive from there.

I'm on the computer for twenty minutes, and ready to book a seat before I remember — the *gun*.

I consider driving, but it would cost me eight hours, at least. I think about tossing the gun, but now that I have it, I want to keep it.

I book the flight, then head out to Vons. I buy a box of Wheat Thins, two corkscrews, a pair of scissors, a kitchen drain stopper, stainless steel scouring pads, and a roll of aluminum foil. Cargo luggage is scanned, true, but mostly to detect explosive devices. I knew from a piece Fox ran not long ago that lots of criminals transport guns in checked luggage. It's easy to disguise a gun by putting it in a box along with other metal items and jamming the open spaces with wadded-up foil, then wrapping the entire box in several layers of foil. The scanner sees it as a metal shape with various densities.

I dump the crackers out and in five minutes, I'm packed and ready to go. An hour and a half later, I'm in seat 23A on United 1421, heading north.

chapter 45

By the time I cross the Golden Gate Bridge, after a slow crawl from the airport, it's almost five. The address I found online, with its suite number, is certainly an office and not where Mertz lives. I might have to make a trip to the Mendocino County courthouse in Ukiah, to look for properties belonging to Luc Mertz or Sequoia Solutions, but for now I head straight for Anchor Bay. It's not a metropolis. If Mertz lives nearby, maybe somebody will know it.

I'm getting close to Cloverdale when I put in a call to Shoffler. I'm thinking maybe he knows someone in the local constabulary, someone who can help me.

"So how was France?" I say when he answers.

"Great food. Unbelievable." A pause. "Who *is* this? Is that you, Alex? Where the hell are you? You sound like you're on the moon."

"I'm in California. I thought maybe you could help me with something."

"You know I will if I can."

"Know anybody in northern California? The coast above San Francisco?"

"Why? What you got?"

"I think my boys are here."

"Where?"

"Near Anchor Bay."

"Where's that?"

"About forty miles south of Mendocino."

"Hunh." He heaves a long sigh. "You better tell me about it. What makes you think your boys are there?"

I hesitate. "It's a long story, and there's no way I can get through it on this cell phone. Bottom line, I know who grabbed them."

"You *do?!*"

"His name is Byron Boudreaux, and if something happens to me, Ray, you've got to promise me you'll go after him. He's got a rich patron named Mertz. Luc Mertz." I spell it. "Mertz is a Belgian."

"Hunh." He heaves a sigh. "You know, for me to play backup, I really need to know the story, Alex."

"Look, do you know anybody out here or not?"

A sigh. "Not really. Used to know a guy in Healdsburg, but he got killed busting a ring of abalone poachers."

The telephone crackles and hums. "If something happens to me," I tell him, "get in touch with a P.I. named Pinky Streiber in New Orleans. He can tell you all about it."

"I don't like the sound of this, Alex. You're not gonna help your boys if you get whacked. Hold off a day or two. I know a couple of guys in San Francisco. Let me network a little."

As I make the turn to head for the coast, I realize I'm wasting my time. Law enforcement isn't going to help me. Everything is circumstantial. Paper rabbits and voodoo burials, postmarks and the rope trick. And the connection to Mertz is even dicier.

No judge is going to authorize a search warrant based on what I've got, certainly not for premises belonging to a litigious multimillionaire like Luc Mertz.

"Pinky Streiber," I tell Shoffler. "Decatur Street, New Orleans. You writing this down?"

"I'm telling you, Alex, hold off on this. I can —"

I press the button to cut him off, and drive on toward the coast.

I find the Sequoia Solutions address

with no problem. It's in a faux-Western wooden structure with dozens of small offices. It's almost ten, and everyone's long gone with the exception of the tired-looking man in Coastal Chiropractics.

He opens the door cautiously, lowers his reading glasses, and peers at me.

"Help you?"

"You know the guy in number two-ten, down the hall? Sequoia Solutions."

He wags his head. "No. I don't even think I've ever seen anybody in that office," he tells me.

"Guy named Mertz?"

He shakes his head again. "Lot of these offices, people aren't here on a daily basis, you know? I'm the exception. Sorry."

I ask him for the number of the rental agency, which he gives me. They'll have a lease, more information about Mertz. I'll get in touch with them tomorrow.

In the meantime, I need a room.

This turns out to be a problem. It's August, there are not that many places to stay, and they're all booked solid. I strike out in Anchor Bay. I head north toward Point Arena, and I strike out there, too. Everywhere I go, I ask about Mertz, and Sequoia Solutions. I strike out there, too. No one's heard of him.

The clerk at the Buena Vista Cottages in Point Arena takes pity on me and makes a few phone calls.

"Bingo," he says. "The Breakers Inn, in Gualala. They had a cancellation."

"Where's that?"

"Just go south on 101. It's the next town down from Anchor Bay."

"Thanks a lot. I appreciate it."

"Hey, my turn will come."

It's almost eleven by the time I pull into the Breakers Inn parking lot. Mine is a big room, with a balcony facing the sea, the kid at the desk tells me.

The motel's landscaping is heavy with flowers and rose-covered arches. Beyond a placid estuary, the surf crashes and ebbs. Everything about the place, including the happy couple behind me in line, suggests that it's popular for romantic getaways. Not exactly the way I'd describe my visit.

The clerk takes my card and runs it through his machine. I decide to get right to it. "You know a local guy named Mertz?" I ask him. "Short guy, bald, lots of money. But he's not really local. Has a place around here, but he's actually from Belgium."

"Sorry, man. I'm just here for the surf."

"You know anyone who might know?" I

ask, taking the key from him.

He thinks about it. "The little grocery store — right next door. That's open till midnight. Local people work there. You might try real estate agents — there's a flock of them. They stay pretty up on things. And there's a couple of restaurants in town that don't just cater to tourists. Try the Cliff House."

I thank him and look at the key, which has no number. "So where's my room?"

"You're in Canada," he tells me. "Down the walk, third on the left."

"Canada?"

"They're all named after places," he says. "Decorated that way, too. Thinking out of the box, you know. Someone thought numbers were boring. Too hierarchical."

"That is *sooo* California," the woman behind me says. "Don't you just love it?"

At the grocery store, I let an elderly lady in line behind me go ahead, and she does, with a little genuflection of thanks. She buys Salem Lights, a can of Pringles, and a half gallon of skim milk.

The woman working the register is young and huge, at least six-feet-two, two hundred fifty. With her round, cherubic face, she looks like a giant baby.

I put my bottle of Zephyrhills water on the conveyor belt. "I'm looking for somebody," I tell her. "Maybe you know him?"

She flips her wrist with a practiced motion and scans the water. "Dollar twelve," she says.

"Guy named Luc Mertz. He's —"

"— a fucking frog is what he is," the cashier snarls. "Tells me no, he ain't a frog, he's *Belgian*." She shakes her head. "Same difference. They hate our guts, too. Some kind of *allies,* huh?"

"So you *do* know him," I say.

Babyface doesn't miss the stupidity of this remark. "Duh," she says. "Yeah, I guess so."

I'm stunned. For a moment I feel the surprising and unfamiliar radiance of luck. I was prepared to grind it out.

"He live around here?"

"Hell, yes. I worked a party down there one time, bartending. Big place, down by Sea Ranch. Got some frogoid name." She concentrates like a toddler, her face contorted by concentration. "Mystère!" she says like a quiz-show contestant. "You know, it's like frog for *mystery*."

She puts my water in a plastic bag, places the receipt in it, hands it to me.

"Where's Sea Ranch?" I ask her.

"You don't know where *Sea Ranch* is?" Now I'm testing her patience. She rolls her eyes. "It's probably the biggest development between here and . . . *San Francisco* is all. You go south on 101. You could be legally *blind* and you couldn't miss the place. It's a million acres or something. You'll see these big old ram's horns — that's like the Sea Ranch" — she searches for the word on the ceiling — "*logo*. Got a rental office and all. Lodge, restaurant. Okay, maybe a few miles past the end of Sea Ranch, there's a little road on the right called Estate Road. You go down that and at the very end, you get to Mystère. Iron gates with a big old *M* in the middle. Guardhouse and all."

Before I head out, I throw my suitcase on the bed and dig the gun out of its foil cocoon. As long as I have the gun, I might as well take it along. I slide it under the passenger seat of the car.

I cross the county line, leaving Mendocino County and entering Sonoma County. So, a trip to the courthouse in Ukiah would have been useless.

Ten minutes later, I'm past the Sea Ranch, and I'm on Estate Road. It's almost dark now, and as I drive past Mertz's estate, all I can really see is the brightly lit cubicle of the guardhouse and the general lay of the land. A series of rolling hills fall away toward the sea, which is far enough away that I can't really hear the surf. And then I do — a dull and distant thud, like a faint heartbeat. The moon slides out from underneath a cloud and illuminates, for a few moments, a boulder-strewn patch of ocean. In the moonlight, the knobby pinnacles of rock look like a crowd of alien giants striding toward shore. The waves fracture against them, sending up spumes of white. And then the moon slips under the cloud again, and I can't see much but the rough contours of the land.

The estate — it's down there somewhere — is huge, its borders protected by the sea and by a towering iron fence whose vertical pikes end in sharp points. Every twenty yards or so, red diodes mark the location of surveillance cameras.

Somewhere down there is a house.

And somewhere in that house are my boys.

My heart seems to be outside my body.

What are they doing — Sean and Kevin? Is one of them rehearsing his lines for the performance? Is the other practicing his emergence at the end of the trick, with a big smile for the audience?

I can picture them together, Sean making fun of Kevin as he bursts out of the basket, arms thrust up in victory like a gymnast at the end of a winning routine. I can see them giggling, delighted by their part in the deception, the twin trick. What would Boudreaux tell the boy who'd been chosen to rise in triumphant life? How would he explain the bloody limbs and body parts tossed into the basket atop the one crouched there, waiting for the signal to come forth. It occurs to me that certainly the basket is specially built — like the dovepan described by Karl Kavanaugh — so that the waiting boy is spared contact with the hacked limbs and severed head of his brother.

I roll along at a crawl beside the iron fence, tempted to climb it right now, but deterred by the cameras. Then the road comes to an end in a gravel cul-de-sac on the edge of a cliff. I can see the property line clearly. The metal fence turns the corner and extends a hundred feet or so along the flat area at the top of the cliff. Then, as the land abruptly falls away into a rocky crevasse, the border of Mystère is demarcated by a multiple-strand fence of barbed wire that stretches as far as I can see, down into the sea. Its topmost run, at about nine feet in height, glitters in the moonlight: it's strung with razor wire. Even here, in terrain that would challenge a rock climber, surveillance cameras sit atop the metal stanchions supporting the barbed wire, every twenty yards or so as far as I can see down toward the ocean. It's eerie to see them whir and turn, robotic eyes restlessly scanning the misty night. I hope I've managed to stay beyond their reach.

I get back into the car, swing around, and head back toward the highway.

A half-dozen ideas on how I might get into the place flicker through my mind — disabling the guard, climbing the metal fence, renting a small boat and arriving by sea, cutting through the barbed wire, posing as a delivery person — but I reject each one after a few seconds of contemplation.

They share the same risk. What if I get caught? If the perimeter of Mystère is this well defended, I'm sure that there are interior defenses. And the house — with my kids isolated somewhere within it? The house will be a fortress.

If I go in now and I get caught, I don't think Boudreaux would hesitate to kill me.

He'd tuck me away somewhere until the performance was over, and then I'd be disposed of, along with the bodies of my sons. Somewhere far from here, would be my guess. Maybe just dumped at sea.

I've gone past the gates and guardhouse and I'm rounding a curve when a squad car comes into sight. I assume it's simply on patrol until suddenly it lights up like a Christmas tree, then swerves to block my way.

I wait, in my seat, a good citizen. I remind myself to take a deep breath. I used to get mouthy with cops who stopped me for speeding. But after a decade or so of going in and out of combat zones, I've learned to curb my issues with authority. Sometimes the baby soldiers at checkpoints are so nervous, stoned, or indifferent to the lives of others that almost anything could provoke a hail of gunfire.

I reach into my back pocket, extract my license, open the glove compartment, and take out the rental papers. It seems to take a long time for the cop to get out of his car. Then he taps on my window. I roll it down. I see he's young, early twenties. Bad skin and one of those trooper hats with the brim.

"What's this about?"

"License and registration," he says.

One of those. I sigh, hand them over. He scrutinizes the documents, then heads back to his patrol car. He's in there for a long time, maybe ten minutes, before he saunters back. He returns my documents. "What's your business here, sir?"

"I took a wrong turn."

"You 'took a wrong turn.' " He looks at me. "Hunh."

I try to keep myself from jabbering. Less is definitely more in a conversation like this. The kid has the gift of patience though, and I can't keep my mouth shut. "I was just trying to get a look at the ocean," I say. "I guess it's not the best time for sightseeing. Night. Where *is* the road to the public beach, anyway? Isn't it around here somewhere?"

He cocks his head. "You staying around here?"

"Breakers Inn," I tell him, happy to answer this question. It's an upscale place, the kind of spot an upright citizen stays in.

He nods. "You know why I stopped you?"

I shake my head.

"Down to Mystère [he pronounces it *Mister*], they called in a complaint. Car cruising by real slow. I'm thinking a poacher or maybe some guy casing the place for a burglary."

"No," I say, with a smile. "Just a tourist." I reach back for my seat belt, start to pull it across my chest.

"Step out of the car, sir," he says.

"What?"

"You can see the ocean just fine from the Breakers Inn."

"But you can't walk on the beach," I protest. "That's all I wanted to do. Come on, I —"

"Something's not right here," he says in a staccato voice. "Step out of the car."

I do. He tells me to put the palms of my hands on the hood. He frisks me. He tells me to maintain the position while he calls "backup."

Twenty minutes later, a second squad car arrives, lights blazing. There's a brief conversation — the upshot of which is that the two troopers concur they have probable cause to search my car. They snap plastic cuffs on me as "a precaution."

In the forty seconds between when they begin to search the rental car and the moment they find the gun, I fight the temptation to jump out of the squad car and run. I force myself to think of the boys. I can't help them if I get shot in the back, which is the likely outcome of jumping out of the squad car. How could I let this happen? I could shoot *myself* for driving around with the gun on me. What was I thinking? What do you get for illegal possession of a firearm? What are the gun laws like here in California?

Two and a half hours later, at 2:04 p.m., I've been processed. I'm in orange coveralls, in the temporary lockup in Santa Rosa, which is the county seat of Sonoma County. I've been read my rights. I will be charged with illegal possession of a firearm. The gun itself is the subject of a separate inquiry. I only hope it wasn't used to murder anyone.

I agonized over who to call, but eventually decided on my father. Even though I woke him up and he sounded terrified, I knew he'd find me a good lawyer.

"Dad?"

"What, Alex?"

"I'm in a hurry. There's not much time."

"What do you mean?" my father asks, his voice full of fear. But then he withdraws the question. "Never mind. What do you need?"

The night goes on and on and on. At first, all I can think about is how many ways things can go wrong, how the remaining time can drain away. I believe, from what I read about the rope trick, that the performance will occur in the early morning of August 10, before the fog burns off. It's August 9. When is court in session? Nine, I'd guess. When will my case be called? Who knows?

I pace. I can't sit still. When the audience is seated and ready for the performance of the legendary rope trick, when one of my boys joins Byron Boudreaux on stage as his assistant (the other already hidden until the moment of his triumphal emergence), will I still be here, pinned down in the Sonoma County jail?

And even if the lawyer does show and succeeds in springing me, how will I get into Mystère?

chapter 46

The lawyer shakes his head. "You picked the wrong county for this," he tells me. "This is Yupville with some hard edges, and we like to keep those elements under control. What I'm saying is that your north coast yuppies really frown on guns. It's gonna cost your dad a bundle to spring you."

"But you do think they'll set bail?"

"Oh, yeah. Unless Judge Upshaw had a *real* bad night. I mean, it's your first offense. Your friends came to bat for you — had to get 'em up in the middle of the night, but I rounded up some testimonials. And let's face it, your personal situation works for you. Someone abducted *my* kids? I'd probably be strapped, too. Question is — why didn't you do it legal?"

I just shake my head.

"The only loose cannon is that gun. You bought it in a park, from an illegal immigrant?" He narrows his eyes and winces. "Who knows?"

At ten-fifteen, I'm arraigned.

"Your Honor, I think that the state would be safe if Mr. Callahan were to be released on his own recognizance."

"Our notions of security differ, Mr. Doncaster. As Mr. Juarez" — he indicates the assistant district attorney — "has pointed out, Mr. Callahan has no ties to the community. No job, no local contacts. As such, there's an implicit risk of flight."

"But this would be a first offense. Otherwise, Mr. Callahan is an upstanding citizen. And Your Honor must take into account his recent suffering. *Counseling* about the proper channels for his understandable grief and anger might be an appropriate response —"

"Before you get carried away, Mr. Doncaster, I'm told your client's gun may be linked to a murder in San Diego County."

"What was the date of this alleged crime?"

The judge peers through his glasses. "Last Tuesday, August third."

Doncaster confers with me. "I was in . . . I think I was in Las Vegas. Maybe New Orleans."

"My client was not in San Diego County at that time, Your Honor."

"We'll take that up in court, Counselor.

Bail is set at one hundred thousand dollars."

"But, Your Honor —"

"Next case."

It's an hour and a half before the business with the bail bondsman is concluded, almost noon before my wallet and cell phone and pocket change are restored to me and I'm standing outside the Santa Rosa courthouse, more or less a free man. My rental car was towed to an impoundment lot in Guerneville, which is thirty miles south of Gualala. For a moment, I'm paralyzed with indecision. Should I take a taxi to the car? Rent a new car here in Santa Rosa?

First, although I don't want to, I call my parents to thank my dad, and let them know I'm okay. I'm relieved when I get the answering machine.

Instead of heading straight to the coast, I go to the information counter in the courthouse, where a friendly woman directs me to the county clerk's office. Ten minutes later, I'm sitting at a computer looking at a plat that covers the area of coastline I'm interested in. The property belonging to Sequoia Solutions comprises five hundred twenty-one acres, with almost a mile of coastal frontage. One big rhomboid and several smaller ones show the location of the house and its outbuildings. I note that they're set quite a ways back from the ocean.

The huge parcel belonging to the Sea Ranch lies directly to the north of Mertz's place. To its south sit several slivers of land extending from the highway to the sea, belonging to various individuals.

I ask the clerk if there's a store in town that sells outdoor equipment. She directs me to one in a mall on the outskirts of town and, when I ask her to, calls me a taxi.

I ask the driver to wait while I shop. Eight minutes later, I'm out of the store with hiking boots, socks, a backpack, a Patagonia fleece jacket, and a large Maglite flashlight. The big flashlight is heavy. But I don't have the gun anymore, and as a beat cop in D.C. once pointed out to me, there's a reason cops favor Maglites. They're better than billy clubs.

Then I ask the driver where I can rent a car. Twenty minutes later, I drive away from Santa Rosa Executive Rentals in a silver BMW.

It's only seventy miles from Santa Rosa to Gualala, but the road is full of twists and turns — and speed zones. It takes me more than two hours, even though I'm speeding the whole way. I planned to go back to the Breakers and get my suitcase, and especially my laptop, but I head straight for the Sea Ranch rental office.

The blonde at the desk doesn't seem to read my impatience. When I'm ready to take an available oceanfront condo on the southern fringe of the Sea Ranch property, she wants to show me all the other alternatives.

"No, really, the Housel Hut, that's perfect."

"It's three hundred twenty-nine dollars a night, minimum two-night stay. Actually," she says, tapping a few keys, "it's booked on Monday, so I could only really manage —"

"Two nights is all the time I have. That's perfect."

I put it on my Visa. She gives me maps of the compound, passes to various facilities, a tag for my car, a schedule of events, and finally, the keys.

It's five-twenty by the time I park behind the condo. I go inside only for a minute, long enough to grab the two bottles of water from the complimentary basket, along with the two wrapped biscotti. I put the water, the cookies, my wallet, the Maglite, my cell phone, and my fleece jacket in the backpack. At the last minute, I rummage through the kitchen drawers, and find a stash of Ziploc bags. I put the cell phone inside one, my wallet in another. I add a kitchen knife.

And then I head for the beach that abuts the land belonging to Luc Mertz. On my way, I pass a silver-haired couple, as fit-looking as nineteen-year-olds. The woman has a beautiful smile. They wave and stride on.

It's a wild landscape. For centuries, the surf has thrashed against the stone, leaving an archipelago of pinnacles, their shapes determined by the hardness of the varying striations of rock. They look like minarets or the cupolas of Russian churches, sculpted by the water. Standing among them is the occasional monolithic boulder and a scatter of rounded rocks, like giant bowling balls. The water thrashes wildly amidst all this. Near shore, mats of kelp strands roll in the surf. Which is thunderous. When the waves hit the rocks head-on, the impact is amazing, sending up geysers of spray fifty feet or more into the air.

The high-tide line is clear, marked by a dark irregular line of seaweed, driftwood, and other detritus abandoned by the receding water. Looking inland, beyond the tide mark and all the way to the bluffs, it's clear that the rocks closer to shore were not always beyond the reach of the water. The dramatic formations continue two hundred yards or more up into the hillside, where they end in a craggy cliff-face, above which glows the bright green of rolling meadowland.

And then I glimpse it, running straight down through the meadowland — the glint of razor wire that identifies the property line between Sea Ranch and Mystère. The tide is low and I'm careful as I approach to stay out of view of Mertz's surveillance cameras. As I suspected, the fence continues down into the rocky area, but stops a few feet short of the high-tide mark.

Like the residents of most states, Californians are constitutionally entitled to walk the beaches, the land between the high tide and low tide being deemed a public resource. The only problem is access. We did a piece about the public-private rift not long ago when activists organized a *beach-in* in Malibu. Advocates of greater public access transported hundreds of beachgoers by motorboat; the masses occupied the sand in front of the houses of the rich and famous for the few hours between the tides.

I have to admit that when I saw "beach" on the plat for Sea Ranch, I was thinking of sand, not rock. I'm wearing khaki pants and I picked out the fleece jacket for its beige color, wanting to minimize my visibility. Wrong choice. There's not much sand here. Just rock, and where the rock is wet, it's almost black.

There are two ways to go. One is to wait for night and try to creep into Mystère. But I'd have to do it here, through the rocks, and the landscape is so rugged that would be almost impossible. The moon might help if the sky clears, but right now, the cloud cover is thick and low.

The other choice is to go out into the water and try to climb from rock to rock until I'm far enough beyond the reach of the cameras. Such CCTV cameras normally don't have much depth of field. Then I'd traverse until it seemed safe to head in toward the shore. Of course, Mertz might have some kind of surveillance on the beachfront, but I doubt it. No one could possibly get a boat or even a kayak through these rocks without getting smashed by the surf. Almost certainly Mertz *would* have a security system protecting the house.

My watch reads six thirty-five. When does it get dark? Eight thirty? At best, I've got a couple of hours of light left.

I can't climb in the area close to shore because I'll be visible to the cameras. This means I have to get out past the surf break, which is wildly irregular, given all the rocks. The other problem is that the rock formations are not contiguous.

I see that almost inevitably, I'm going to get wet. The water is cold, very cold. I test it with my hand and try to guess. Fifty? Maybe fifty-five. Cold enough that after thirty seconds of immersion, my hand is numb. So cold that I should have a wet suit. Climbing shoes. Gloves. Picks and ropes.

I try to plan a route from rock to rock that will take me out beyond the surf. I pull the hood on, tighten the closure, shove my pants into my socks, put my head down, and go.

At first it's challenging, but not too bad. My boots are clumsy but the rocks are so craggy that I don't have any trouble finding footholds. At a certain point, I can't avoid the sea spray and I get a little wet. But then I come to a spot where there's no way to avoid going into the water without retracing my steps and losing maybe half an hour.

There's nothing for it. I don't have any choice: I go in up to my hips, holding the backpack to my chest. It's a clumsy process, thrashing through the cold water. The tug of the riptide means that I almost have to walk sideways, crabbing my way toward the rock.

By the time I'm on the rocks again, my legs are numb. The air temperature can't be more than sixty and there's a wind, so being out of the water doesn't provide much relief. I keep going, and the exertion helps me warm up.

As the sun goes down and the temperature drops, the cold is only going to get worse. I'm going to have to be very careful not to fall in.

I did a good bit of rock climbing, back before the boys were born. I liked the energy, precision, and focus it required. Most of all, I liked to test myself — to parcel out the risk in what amounted to controlled doses.

In a way, it was the opposite of what I

did at work. Working in a war zone, you do everything you can to minimize the risk, but it's not something that you can control. The danger comes at you from the outside and it doesn't come in doses.

Rock climbing is the opposite: *You* choose where to put your hand or foot. You alone know if you're strong enough or flexible enough to make a move. You might still get unlucky, get some bad rock, but for the most part you operate inside your own capability and fear. I liked that.

This is different. For one thing, I never climbed wet rock. For another I'm not really *climbing* to a summit. I'm climbing up and down only enough to traverse a lot of rugged terrain. And unlike recreational climbing, I'm in a hurry, with no option of bailing out because of cramp or fatigue. And instead of the velvety rubber of climbing shoes that can grab a tiny bump or crevice with conviction, I'm wearing hiking boots that require huge gouges or ridges as footholds. I'd take the boots off — and I may still have to do this — but my feet would be in shreds within minutes. And they're cold. I can't actually feel them anymore.

Still, I'm getting there. Before I left the Sea Ranch beach, I picked out the tallest pair of rock formations within the boundaries of Mystère. It's a little hard to be sure, but it seems to me — by sighting toward the two spires — that I've traversed far enough inside the fence line to turn back toward shore.

I stop for a moment on a rock that offers a good high perch and look ahead, trying to pick out a route through the surf line. The surf break is far from clean and linear, as it is on a beach. Because of the rock formations and the topography of the bottom, it's chaotic and broad. Where the surf really boils against the pillars and boulders, I can't go into the water. I'm going to need rock, contiguous rock.

I'm slowly making my way through the surf break when it happens: a little jump from one rock to the next — an easy jump. But the rock is wet and I land wrong and my ankle turns and the next thing I know, I'm in the water.

To say it takes my breath away doesn't begin to describe it. Not only does the cold water squeeze out the air from my lungs — the lungs themselves don't work at all. The moment I fell happened to be in the lull, just before the wave breaks and crashes. That was a piece of luck, and at first I think it's going to be all right, I'll be able to climb out.

And I start to, but before I make it to a good place to hang on, a wave crashes down on me. It seems to happen in slow motion, the way the surf tears me free, tumbles me over. The sound is deafening.

I try to grab onto a rock, scrabbling my fingernails for purchase, wedging my foot against the boulder's base. I've got it, until the water begins to recede. There's a tremendous sucking sound, a clatter and rush of gravel, and my grip on the rock is torn away. A second later, I'm slammed against rock.

Now, for the first time, things begin to feel seriously out of control. I still can't breathe, and I think I may have slashed my left calf. I felt something — not pain, exactly, because I'm too cold for that. A burning sensation in my leg.

I know that if I don't get out of the water now, right now, before another wave tags me, I'm not going to make it.

Something propels me. The thought of Sean and Kevin and what awaits them? Yes. The thought of my broken body in the surf? That, too. We're hardwired to produce an extra boost of energy to escape danger, so it must be a massive jolt of adrenaline that powers me out of the sea. Whatever it is, I climb the rock face like

Spiderman, high enough to reach an outcrop I can wrap my arms and legs around. The wave hits and it sucks at my legs, but I don't think a bomb could have dislodged me.

I'm in bad shape as I close in on the shoreline. The light is fading, it's getting colder, my ankle and my calf hurt, and I'm shivering uncontrollably. The backpack is heavy. I consider tossing the Maglite — I'm sure the salt water ruined the batteries — but I don't want to take the time. I move forward slowly, from behind one rock to the next, looking for the red eyes of surveillance cameras. Or any sign of motion. I see nothing. And then, at last, I'm back on dry land.

I find a sheltered spot and drink some of the water in my backpack. I take my boots off, dump the seawater out of them, squeeze out the wool socks. My ankle is the size of a small grapefruit. I put it all back on, lacing up the boot as tight as I can for support. I take a quick look at the gash on my calf. It gapes open like a mouth, the air against the pinkish flesh stings, but it doesn't look so bad. The salt water was probably good for it.

I take off my fleece, my sweater, my T-shirt. Wring them out, put them back on. I still can't stop shaking.

The kitchen knife is gone — it must have come out of the pack when I was in the water. The flashlight doesn't work, but I decide to keep it anyway, the only weapon I have now. I take a look at the cell phone, but no: there's water inside the Ziploc bag. It's toast too.

I feel like I need a forklift to get to my feet, but I manage to push myself up. It's twilight — the sun is already down. I have to find the site of the performance.

Amidst the rocks, and in the dusk, I can't get a sight line on the two rock spires I'd picked out before. I was sure that these would provide the setting for tomorrow's performance, but as I stumble around in the warren of rock formations — wasn't I just here? — doubt suffuses me. Maybe I should just go for the house, after all.

And then I find it.

I don't know what I was expecting, but the theater takes my breath away.

A flattened gravel stage is defined by huge concrete urns overflowing with flowers, greenery swagged between them. In this spectacular location, facing the stage and beyond it the sea, a tiny amphitheater has been fashioned. Set back from the stage only a few feet, three semicircles of polished granite are stepped back into the natural rise of the land.

The little theater is so beautiful as to make its terrible purpose even more chilling. To the right of the stage a latticed screen, draped with vines and flowers, conceals several padlocked chests — and, under a large canvas tarp, an enormous basket.

I'd like to look around some more. I'd like to reconnoiter — for the path that leads to the theater, for instance — but I've already abandoned the idea of waylaying the party on the way to prepare for the morning's entertainment. I know, from reading about the trick, that Boudreaux may well have an assistant, maybe two. I'd be outnumbered, and except for the Maglite, unarmed.

My only chance is isolation and surprise. And with the light almost gone, there's no time to do anything but ascend one of the spires before full dark. They are quite tall, more than sixty feet high, I'd guess. They're not identical — they're natural rock formations — but similar. The distance between them is a little more than a hundred yards. Thick at the base, the rock towers taper irregularly toward the tops, which even now are hidden in mist.

Ordinarily, the formation wouldn't present a challenge, even to a climber of modest ability, but I'm so tired that the climb proves very difficult. The darkness makes it more so. Above me, the moon scuds along beneath thick clouds, providing a watery and inconsistent light that's not much help.

Half a dozen times, one foot slips and my muscles are so fatigued that recovering is not easy. About halfway up, I come very close to my physical limit and almost . . . almost let go. That scares me and I halt my ascent for a few minutes, despite the encroaching darkness. I proceed slowly, resting every few feet. Finally, I find what I knew must be there: a wooden platform.

I pull myself onto it and collapse.

No more than four-feet square, the platform might as well be a palace as far as I'm concerned. It is such a relief not to have to maintain a grip and support my weight. After a few minutes of rest, I dig my remaining water bottle out of the backpack and drink half of its contents.

There's really not much light, but my eyes long ago adjusted to the darkness. I can see that two cables cross to the opposite spire. But there is no platform on the opposite side — at least I can't see one in the dark. I practically weep with thanks that I picked the right tower to climb. I never would have made it down this one and up the other.

One cable extends from beneath my platform, the other some four feet above me. The one beneath me is attached by a kind of flywheel-and-winch contraption. The one above has several levers and gears and some kind of bulky power source bolted into the rock.

Dangling several feet down from the cable beneath my platform, hanging into the chasm between the spires, are several dark loops. Suspended from the cable above me is a contraption that seems to have a wide "mouth" consisting of triangular metal teeth, like a giant version of the constricting jaw into which you insert drill bits.

It takes me a few minutes to figure out how it all must work. The magician throws the rope (letting it fall back down the first few times, just for effect) until it catches one of the dangling loops — which must be covered with Velcro or something like it. At that point, a hidden assistant up here — or maybe the mechanism works through radio signals — brings the device on the second cable into play, guiding it into position and lowering it until it bites the loose end of the rope. The mechanism is then withdrawn vertically and winched tight until the rope is held taut.

At first I think — with horror at the risk of it — that Sean or Kevin, whichever has the job of climbing the rope, must walk on the cable to the safety of the platform. But no. A loop of rope, like a rappeling loop, waits hooked to a brass fitting on the cable above me. Anyone climbing the vertical rope can slip a leg into the loop and pull himself over to the platform.

I sit down on the platform. There's no way to know if the mechanism requires an assistant — or simply works by remote control. I'll just have to wait.

I'm still wet and the effect of evaporation makes me even colder. I concentrate on conserving warmth. It seems impossible that I might fall asleep, but just in case, I set the alarm on my watch for five a.m. I hunch my knees to my chest, tighten my hood, lock my arms across my chest, jam my hands under my arms, and settle down to wait.

chapter 47

A family outing. Harper's Ferry. The Potomac River. Liz and I and the boys float along on rented black inner tubes, drifting in the current toward the pickup point. The sky above the leafy branches, ballpoint blue. The water is warm and just deep enough that we don't scrape on the rocks. The boys paddle to try to make themselves go faster, but strapped into their life jackets, in the huge inner tubes, they can hardly reach the water.

"What if there are fish?" Sean asks.

"Yeah, what if one bites my butt?" Kevin concurs.

"I don't think there are any carnivorous fish in the Potomac River," Liz says.

"What's 'carnivous'?"

"Carni*voro*us. It means *meat-eating*."

"I'm not *meat*," Sean protests. "Ewww. That's gross."

"I'm not so sure about the fish here," I tell Liz. "I heard they lost a man down by the pickup point."

"Daaaaaad!"

We're not alone. A couple floats just

ahead of us. A pod of teenagers cruises behind. They keep pushing each other out of the tubes, screaming and hooting. This doesn't bother me — they're just having fun — but when I hear the peremptory beep of someone's cell phone, I'm irritated.

"Can you believe that?" I ask Liz. "There's no sanctuary from the things."

"They'll be making them waterproof next," Liz says, adjusting her sunglasses.

The sound keeps up and I'm about to shout to the teenagers that at least they could answer the damn thing, when —

It's my watch.

I wake up, all at once and with a gasp. It's still dark, and so foggy I can't see any farther than a few feet. I drink the last of my water, fumbling at the cap with frozen fingers. I feel as if I'm a hundred years old; every part of my body hurts. I wait for my eyes to adjust. I try to stretch out.

Half an hour later, the sky begins to brighten. Behind the platform, on the opposite side of the rock, is a small ledge, almost a niche. It's eighteen inches deep, I'd guess, but the rock face hangs over it. The only way I could fit into the space would be to crouch. I reject it.

I climb the spire, looking for a place to hide. I find one without too much trouble, fifteen feet above the platform, a spot I can wedge into, where I don't have to balance or support my own weight. I can see the platform and the cables, the center of the chasm. But no one can see me.

I look at my watch every few minutes. After an hour passes, I'm worried. The cold is getting to me. I bite down on the fleece to keep my teeth from chattering.

And then, at last, I hear them, although thanks to the continuous thud of surf, not until they're almost in the theater. I hear the scrape and click of shoes on rock. I hear the voices of two men — no, *three* — one speaking in an odd cadence that suggests a foreign language. And then — tears crash into my eyes — interspersed between the low voices of the men, I hear the high, sweet voices of children.

Sean laughs — his characteristic high-pitched chuckle, a laugh totally unlike Kevin's raucous guffaw. My heart lifts, floating in my chest. I can hardly breathe.

I hear their voices, but I can't understand what they're saying. There is the sound of padlocked chests being opened, the moving and dragging of heavy objects.

Obviously, they are making preparations for the performance, setting the props and furniture in place. Someone begins to whistle.

I work to keep within myself. Ordinarily, I'm good at waiting. It's something that comes with spending a lot of time in airports.

But now, the immobility is almost too much. I consider making my way down the rock, taking them on. But no. My chances on the ground — three of them and one of me — are terrible. I'm only going to get one shot and it's got to be up here.

One of them starts climbing. He's not a stealthy climber. He bulls his way up the rock. I'm grateful for that because it makes it easy to track his progress.

Maybe it took me half an hour to climb the rock last night. It takes him about ten minutes. I see him, moments before he reaches the platform, emerging from the mist. His head is shaved. He hoists himself onto the platform easily. He's a big, strong-looking guy, with a Maori-style tattoo curling up from the neck of his Windbreaker. He opens the metal cover of the box bolted below the upper cable and throws a switch. He pulls a walkie-talkie out of his pocket. "Okay," he says. "Let's go."

I realize what this is: a test run.

A rope is tossed up and catches on one of the loops. The mechanism suspended from the upper cable moves, obviously on a signal from a remote-control device below. There must be some kind of homing mechanism attached to the end of the rope, because the pipelike device, which has a kind of articulated neck, descends, locates the rope, and tightens over the rope's end. Winches and pulleys spring into action on either side of the chasm, pulling the cable — and with it the rope — taut as a drum. The machinery is amazingly silent, all this occurring with no more than a faint whir.

"Got it," the big man whispers into his walkie-talkie. "Coming back your way."

He flicks a switch on the gray box and the mechanism reverses, cables slacking, jaws holding the rope end opening to release it. The rope slaps back down to the ground.

To my relief, the big man also descends.

Twenty minutes later, I hear music from down below. Drums and a sitar. Not long afterward, the guests arrive. They make an enormous amount of noise as they enter the area of the stage.

I try not to think about the "guests" as the clink of glasses and the murmur of conversation float up to me.

At one point, I get a tickle in my throat and work hard to suppress the urge to cough, my eyes streaming tears. I'm stiff as a rock and beginning to worry that when the time comes for me to move, I'll be unable to do so.

And then the show begins. I can hear Boudreaux's banter as he performs different effects, and very occasionally, Kevin's voice — or is it Sean's? — in counterpoint. From the audience: crescendos of laughter, bursts of hearty applause and exclamations of astonishment.

The Piper, performing his tricks.

And then it happens. The Piper heaves the rope up. "Get up there!" he commands. The rope plops to the ground. "I don't know what's wrong," he says. "The heavens are defying me."

A sprinkle of laughter.

"I'll have to really *concentrate*."

Again, the rope slaps back down onto the gravel.

Again the Piper complains, urging the

audience to help him *will* the rope to "catch in the sky."

The child's voice says something I can't hear, but it earns an appreciative burst of laughter.

Another try. And then the end of the rope comes into view, ascending through the mist. How far does he have to throw it? It's quite a feat.

And then he gets it — the rope catches. The audience cheers.

The mechanism moves into action, catches the rope in its jaws. Instantly, the pulleys and winches begin to do their job, tightening the rope from both directions until it's taut.

"Let's just see if it's really up there," the Piper says. The rope shakes — he's testing it to make sure it won't fall out of the sky.

"Why don't you climb it? See what's up there?" the Piper suggests to my son.

"I don't know," Kevin replies. "It's *high*."

"You'll do as you're told," the Piper tells him.

"Oh, all right."

A big round of applause as the boy starts up the rope.

The Piper continues to talk, but I'm not listening. The rope twitches back and forth.

I watch the rhythm of the rope and then I see it — Kevin's blond hair shining as he comes up out of the fog.

He's dressed in a loincloth, with a sash across his chest. He's concentrating so intently that he doesn't look toward the platform until he's very nearly to the top. When he sees me — tears in my eyes, finger to my lips, head moving side to side in warning — there is complete and total astonishment in his eyes. I'm afraid, for one terrible moment, that the shock will loosen his grip and he'll fall.

He fits himself into the sling with practiced ease, and then pulls himself toward me.

Then he's on the platform. I have my arms open to embrace him, but he's wearing a lavalier mike, alligator-clipped to his sash. I hold my finger to my lips, unclip it, fold it into the hem of my fleece jacket, squeeze it into my fist.

"Dad," Kevin says in a whisper, his face a mix of delight and perplexity, "what are you doing here?"

I don't know what to say.

He continues in a furious whisper. "He said we wouldn't see you till Christmas. He said that they came to get you at the joust, the station did, that you had to go on 'signment, that he would take us home until Mommy got there. He bought us pretzels. And he *did* take us home, but only for a little while. And we tried to call you — he said you were on your way to the airport. *I* tried to call you, and you said hello, but we got cutted off. And then he told us you got in a car accident and you were very *very* hurt, that Mommy had to take care of you and she couldn't take care of us, that —" His voice trails away. His face begins to collapse.

He must have known that there was something *wrong*. On some level, he must have understood that he was a captive. But he's held himself together all these weeks, fitting in with what he's been told, accepting the strange life he and his brother have been leading, trying to frame it as somehow okay, as some kind of normal existence. But underneath, he must have worried about the holes in The Piper's story. He must have wondered why his grandparents didn't step in. He must have wondered a million things.

Now he's my little boy again and he starts to cry.

At last he comes into my arms and I hold him.

It's not possible, really, to describe how

this moment feels, the ineffable sweetness of reunion as I hold my son in my arms.

But it doesn't last. I push him away, hold him at arm's length. "*Kevin,* listen to me. What are you supposed to do now?" I gesture down toward the stage. "You've got to do everything just the way you're supposed to."

He shakes his head. He looks terrified. "Nothing. Oh. I have to slide this back." He flicks his wrist and sends the sling back to the middle. "Then I just wait."

"How long?"

He shrugs.

"Until he calls up to me."

"Look, Kev." I put a hand on his shoulder. "You have to understand that —"

"I thought I made you crash," he tells me, his voice thin and full of tears. "Mommy says cell phones are *dangerous.*"

"Kevin — I wasn't in an accident. Mr. Boudreaux lied to you."

"Who?"

"Mr. Carrefour?"

"*Doctor* Carrefour," he corrects me. "*Doc.*"

"Okay. Well, whoever he is — he *kidnapped* you. I wasn't hurt or sick. Mom and I have been out of our minds searching for you. Do you think your mother would really not be with you boys, no matter what?"

"But he *said* we were helping, he said we . . ." His voice is querulous now, unsure. He starts to cry again.

"Kevin." I pause, shut my eyes. "He's planning to kill you — it's part of his magic. It's a part of his show. And then he'll kill Sean, too."

"But *why?*"

I shake my head. "You have to help me now."

"Dad? Is it going to be okay?"

"Absolutely. But you have to listen to me. You have to do exactly what you're supposed to do. And then, when he comes up the rope — I want you to hide." I take his hand, pull him around, show him the tiny niche behind the platform.

"What if I fall? Dad — I might fall."

"You won't fall. You have great balance. Remember the Jacob's ladder? You were the only kid who did it."

The Piper's amplified voice rises up to us. "What do you see up there, boy?"

"Dad," Kevin whispers, "the Jacob's ladder — that was *Sean*."

Stupid as it is — this stops me for a moment and I can't think of what to say. It's a cardinal sin for the parents of twins, mixing them up.

"*Kev* — you can do it. There's plenty of room. You have to. Look, I'm going to give you my backpack. I need you to keep it safe." I do give him the backpack, more to give him a task than anything else — although I take the Maglite first, and stick it in my waistband.

The Piper's amplified voice again. "You asleep, boy?"

Kevin looks frozen.

"I *said,* what do you see up there, boy?"

I open my fist, unfurl the mike from the fleece, pin it to Kevin's sash. "Tell him," I whisper.

"Sky," Kevin says, his voice trembling.

A laugh from below.

"What else?"

"Clouds." He still sounds as if he's about to cry.

Another laugh.

"I need you back down here now." The voice is matter-of-fact.

"But I like it up here. I don't feel like coming down."

They go back and forth, The Piper growing more irritated as the boy grows more defiant.

* * *

I have to leave Kevin, climb up the rock.

"If you don't get down here this minute," The Piper says, his voice stern now, "I'm going to have to come up and get you."

"Go ahead," Kevin says. "Try it, old man. I bet you can't even climb the rope."

I'm now wedged into my old perch above the platform. Kevin looks up at me. I motion for him — time to hide.

The rope begins to twitch back and forth as The Piper ascends.

The audience cheers.

And then I see him, his brown glossy hair coming up through the mist. Like Kevin, he's dressed as a fakir, and like Kevin, he's intent on the climb. In his case, the climb is made more difficult by the fact that — pirate style — he holds a knife with a curved blade between his teeth.

Very slowly and cautiously, I begin to make my way down toward him.

Once he's reached the sling and put an arm through it, he looks toward the platform. And frowns. I can read his mind: *Where's Kevin?*

He pulls himself onto the platform, and removes the knife from his mouth. "Where are you, lad?" he calls out, still in character. "Come on now, I've had it with you. I'm serious!"

Laughter wells up from below.

The magician gets to his feet and begins to turn.

I'm not a fighter. It's not that I run away from confrontation. Physical fights — it just never came up much. Where I grew up, nobody got into fights; we were all too busy with scheduled activities. It wasn't hip, it wasn't something you did. Once I decked a kid who took my legs out in a soccer match, but the fact that I actually hit him was a piece of luck. I got kicked out of the game, benched for the next two, and had to sit through a lot of crap about the importance of self-control.

I never took karate or boxing lessons.

In other words, nothing about my background has prepared me for what I'm about to do.

And yet I come down off that rock like a raptor.

Before the man even knows I'm there, before he can turn, I've hit him so hard with the Maglite that I can hear the bone splinter in the back of his head. Suddenly, there's blood everywhere — on me, on the rocks, in the air, *on him.*

He's staggered, but to my amazement, he doesn't go down. He makes a wretched, wounded sound that's picked up by the mike, and then he turns, eyes alight, sword in hand. I could swear he's smiling. Then he slashes at me with a sidearm motion, that misses the first time, then catches me on the way back, laying open the sleeve of my jacket and the arm beneath.

A gasp flies from my mouth as Boudreaux takes a swipe at my throat. Incredibly, the world has gone silent — or almost silent. In the adrenalized slo-mo of what seems likely to be my murder, I can hear the surf crashing and the hushed expectancy — or maybe it's the puzzlement — of our audience beneath the fog.

I take another swing with the flashlight, and miss, then block another swipe of the knife. The edge of the blade skitters along the Maglite's shaft, slices into my fingers, and sends a spray of blood into my eyes.

Boudreaux takes a step backward, and gathers himself. For a moment, he stands there, panting and swaying, the knife hanging down at his side. It's almost as if he's about to collapse. Heartened, I take a step toward him, then stagger back, as he lunges toward me with a roar. Like an orchestra conductor gone amok, he slashes wildly at the air, snarling, feral and insane. The madness comes off him like heat from a furnace.

From behind me, I hear a gasp from Kevin, half-whimper, half-scream. The sound electrifies me. At once frantic and enraged, terrified and furious, I throw myself at the magician, and we go down on the platform in a tangle of blood, growls, and groans.

Incredibly, I'm on top, with my forearm across his throat, and my right hand pinning his wrist to the ground. He makes a feeble effort to hit me with his other hand, but he hasn't any strength left. After a moment, his muscles relax, and his eyes soften.

"Now what?" he asks.

With my heart slamming against my chest, it takes more than a moment to get my breath. When I'm able to stand, I do and, reaching down, grab Boudreaux by the hair, and pull him to his feet.

He's leering. "And how do you think you're going to get me down?"

I speak in a low voice, almost a growl. "That's the easy part, you wiggy fuck," I tell him. And with that, I grab him by the scruff of the neck, spin him around, and, with a shove, send him off the edge of the spire, tumbling with a scream toward his fan club sixty feet below.

It's chaos down in the amphitheater, everybody screaming and shouting. Kevin crawls out from the little niche toward me, terrified and sobbing. I'm cut, bleeding all over the platform. Still on my feet, I'm shaky and there's a lot of blood, but I'm okay.

I know we have to act quickly. Right now, the people below may be thinking simply that Boudreaux's fall was an accident. Then again, maybe not.

I don't know what makes me think that the boys who were to be the centerpiece of the show have, for the moment, been forgotten. Sean himself might easily have wondered what was going on and emerged from his hiding place to find out. But I don't think so. I think he's in the basket, waiting for his cue.

"Kevin," I say, "we have to get Sean."

He doesn't argue, although his eyes are huge. "Dad, you're really bleeding."

"It's okay."

Kevin's a natural. Together, we scramble easily down the rock face. Halfway down, we come out of the mist and I tell him to stop for a moment. "We have to be careful now. Stay to the side near the ocean, so they don't see us."

"Okay."

Kevin climbs down, surefooted and agile as a monkey. He actually has to wait for me from time to time. I'm the one having trouble. The arm that Boudreaux cut is weak. My hand is a mess. The blood is slippery.

Even so, we're on the ground in less than five minutes.

I have to rest, lean against the rock. From the amphitheater come the sounds of disagreement. Not too many voices. Obviously, some of the guests have decided to leave. They're quarreling about what to do.

"*What* a disappointment," a female voice says.

"A different *dénouement* is all," says a British man. "Equally dramatic in its way."

"We're not going to call nine-one-one," an accented voice says. "I won't have them crawling all over the place."

"There's a back way," Kevin tells me. "I can sneak in. I can talk to Sean. He'll hear me through the basket."

I follow my son as we creep along toward the back of the stage. The sound of the sea helps because I'm so weak I'm clumsy, and more than once I stumble.

From our vantage point, I can see the little gathering of guests, I can just see Boudreaux's leg, crumpled oddly at the knee, at an angle impossible in life.

The basket is at center stage, terribly exposed.

Before I can stop Kevin, he's gone. I see him approach the basket, I see the basket quiver slightly. I can't believe Sean can get out of it without being seen.

It comes to me: *misdirection*. Just as I see the top of the basket tremble, I pull the Maglite from the pack and hurl it to the right, throwing it as far as I can. It cartwheels through the air, end over end, and lands, with a huge percussive clang against the rocks.

All heads turn toward the sound as Sean scrambles out. I see the little group in the theater begin to move slowly toward the0. point of impact, as the boys dash toward me.

It couldn't be more than a half-mile walk from the amphitheater to the Sea Ranch beach. We don't have to go out into the water. It's a simple walk along the hardened sand, amid the rocks. I know that sooner or later, someone will come after us and I do my best to hurry. It seems to take forever before I see that string of razor wire demarcating the property line between Mystère and the Sea Ranch.

Another silver-haired couple — the same ones? — walk the rocky beach. I turn toward them, one boy on each arm. They're tugging me along now, I'm moving so slowly. And then I just can't manage another step.

"It's okay," I tell the boys, trying to get my feet moving. "It's going to be okay." I stumble and fall.

Kevin takes off like a shot, and I see the three figures, the elegant couple bending slightly to catch my son's words. Kevin points — they look our way.

Sean holds my hand in a ferocious grip.

Kevin and the couple are running now, and I see that the man has a cell phone to his ear.

My eyes close.

"Dad," Kevin says.

"Sea Ranch," the man is saying into the phone. Down on the beach. "Meg, I'm going to get the Jeep."

"Oh, my *God,*" the woman says. She wraps something around my injured hand. "You boys, you press down on this," she says. "Just like this, okay?"

"Yes."

"Stan! Your coat." She wraps my injured arm and compresses the wound. "Keep up the pressure, boys, that's great."

"Is he going to be all right?" Kevin asks, his voice trembling.

"Yes," the woman says in a confident voice. "Everything's going to be just fine."

And somehow, although I suspect she's said this just to calm the boys, I know she's right.

acknowledgments

Thanks very much to Detective Kevin Manning of the Las Vegas Police Department and to Leo Behnke, magician, for valuable help in guiding the author through unknown terrain. Thanks are due as well to Sam and Elisabeth Johnson for their unflagging support. A tip of the hat to Sara Murray for useful comments upon reading the manuscript. And cheers, as always, to Elaine Markson, to Joe Blades, and to everyone at Ballantine who helped bring the book into print.

When acknowledging assistance, it would not be right to omit mention of the following books, which provided valuable information about the book's subject matter: *Voodoo: Search for the Spirit* by Laennec Hurbon, *Panorama of Magic* by Milbourne Christopher, *The Art of Deception* by Chuck Romano, *Mysterious Stranger: A Book of Magic* by David Blaine, and the fascinating *Net of Magic* by Lee Siegel.